Alley Ciz

TAP OUT

BTU Alumni Series Book #2

ALLEY CIZ

HOUSE OF CRAZY
PUBLISHING

Also by Alley Ciz

BTU Alumni Series

Power Play (Jake and Jordan)

Musical Mayhem (Sammy and Jamie) BTU Novella

Tap Out (Gage and Rocky)

Sweet Victory (Vince and Holly)

Puck Performance (Jase and Melody)

Writing Dirty (Maddey and Dex)

Scoring Beauty- BTU6 Preorder, Releasing September 2021

#UofJ Series

Cut Above The Rest (Prequel)- Freebie

Looking To Score

Game Changer

Playing For Keeps

Off The Bench- #UofJ4 Preorder, Releasing December 2021

The Royalty Crew (A #UofJ Spin-Off)

Savage Queen- Preorder, Releasing April 2021

Ruthless Noble- Preorder, Releasing June 2021

What would you do if you came face-to-face with your celebrity crush?

Rocky Steele is surrounded by professional athletes.
It's her job.
As a physical therapist in a world renowned gym, she works with the best of the best, from hockey players to MMA fighters. Celebrity status does not impress her. Nor do big, strong men in peak physical condition.
Nope.
When it comes to her job, she's one hundred percent professional.

Enter Gage James.
Her celebrity crush.
And the newest fighter to train in her gym.
Where it will be her job to put her hands on every inch of the six foot seven two hundred and sixty pounds of utter Alpha male perfection.
She's got this....*Maybe.*

Gage 'The Kraken' James is the reigning MMA Heavyweight Champion.
When he walks into The Steele Maker for the first time, it's like he's hit with a one-two punch to the chest in the form of a certain raven haired firecracker.
His coach's daughter.
His physical therapist.
His every waking thought.

He's in for the fight of his life.
The stakes are higher... *outside* the octagon.
Time to release The Kraken.
GAME ON.

TAP OUT is the second book in the BTU Alumni Series and can be read as a stand-alone. All your favorites return as a new cast of characters joins in on the fun. Prepare for major #squadgoals as you get your first peek inside The Coven. This book features a hella sexy UFC champ, feisty besties, the most awesome coffee house ever, and a heroine who can fight her own battles thank you very much. Time to touch gloves, HEA guaranteed.

Tap Out (BTU Alumni, Book 2)

Alley Ciz

Digital ISBN: 978-1-950884-02-5

Print ISBN: 978-1-950884-03-2

Cover Designer: Julia Cabrera at Jersey Girl Designs

Editing: Jessica Snyder Edits

Proofreading: Gem's Precise Proofreads; Dawn Black

❧ Created with Vellum

For Gemma, my OG fangirl.
Gage James is yours—you licked him first.

Contents

Text Handles xv

Chapter 1 1
Chapter 2 12
Chapter 3 20
Chapter 4 34
Chapter 5 45
Chapter 6 52
Chapter 7 59
Chapter 8 76
Chapter 9 83
Chapter 10 95
Chapter 11 101
Chapter 12 104
Chapter 13 108
Chapter 14 113
Chapter 15 120
Chapter 16 133
Chapter 17 151
Chapter 18 160
Chapter 19 164
Chapter 20 173
Chapter 21 182
Chapter 22 191
Chapter 23 197
Chapter 24 205
Chapter 25 214
Chapter 26 229
Chapter 27 237
Chapter 28 244
Chapter 29 252
Chapter 30 259
Chapter 31 267
Chapter 32 277

Chapter 33	284
Chapter 34	293
Chapter 35	300
Chapter 36	307
Chapter 37	314
Chapter 38	320
Chapter 39	323
Chapter 40	333
Chapter 41	339
Epilogue	346
Thank you!	353
Playlist	354
Randomness For My Readers	355
For A Good Time Call	357
Sneak Peek at Sweet Victory	359
Acknowledgments	361
Also by Alley Ciz	363
About the Author	365

Text Handles

The Coven
>**Rocky:** ALPHABET SOUP
>**Jordan:** MOTHER OF DRAGONS
>**Skye:** MAKES BOYS CRY
>**Maddey:** QUEEN OF SMUT
>**Becky:** YOU KNOW YOU WANNA
>**Gemma:** PROTEIN PRINCESS
>**Beth:** THE OG PITA

The Boys
>**Jase:** THE BIG HAMMER

IG Handles
>**Gage:** TheKrakenUFC
>**Rocky:** RockyToughAsSteele

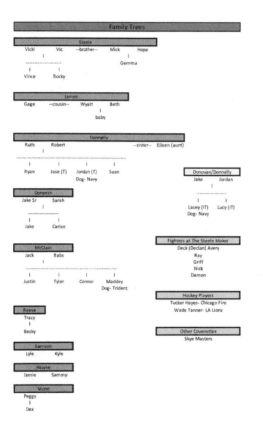

Family Trees

Steele
Vicki | Vic | --brother-- | Mick | Hope
Gemma
Vince | Rocky

James
Gage | --cousin-- | Wyatt | Beth
baby

Donnelly
Ruth | Robert | --sister-- | Eileen (aunt)
Ryan | Jase (T) | Jordan (T) Dog- Navy | Sean

Donovan
Jake Sr | Sarah
Jake | Carlee

McClain
Jack | Babs
Justin | Tyler | Connor | Maddey Dog- Trident

Reese
Tracy
Becky

Samson
Lyle | Kyle

Hayke
Jamie | Sammy

Stone
Peggy
Dex

Donovan/Donnelly
Jake | Jordan
Lacey (IT) Dog- Navy | Lucy (IT)

Fighters at The Steele Maker
Deck (Declan) Avery
Ray
Griff
Nick
Damon

Hockey Players
Tucker Hayes- Chicago Fire
Wade Tanner- LA Lions

Other Covenettes
Skye Masters

Chapter One

G age James thought the local sports bar, The Ring, showed major potential as he looked around for his cousin. It had the standard oak bar, beer taps and giant TVs, but what he really loved was the two-story ceiling. As a UFC Heavyweight Champion standing six-seven and tipping the scale at two-sixty, he was not a small guy and often felt claustrophobic in dark, tightly-packed bars.

He eyed the two dozen beer taps that ran the length of the bar, longing for the bliss a good IPA provided as he felt the phantom twinge in his hip from a past injury. Unfortunately, he needed to abstain from alcohol for the evening—his meeting in the morning was too important.

Running a hand over his short-cropped hair, he looked around for his cousin, Wyatt, and found him playing darts with a few guys in the next room.

Without any siblings of their own, they were closer than typical cousins growing up. But after high school, Wyatt moved east with his high school sweetheart, and now wife Beth, while Gage stayed in California to train.

"Can't believe they let your ugly mug in this place," he joked as he clapped his cousin on the back.

"I'm ugly?" Wyatt retorted, smiling broadly. Their looks were as close as their relationship, with dark brown hair and bright blue eyes from the James genes. "Have you seen your face? Looks like someone has taken one too many shots in the octagon."

Gage laughed along with him, but they both knew how rare it was that he actually took a hit to the face. In fact, it was legendary throughout the UFC. He attributed some of it to his height, but mostly the honor went to the fighting skills he spent countless hours honing.

"Don't be jealous, cuz. Not all of us could be so lucky to look as good as me." He flexed his biceps, making the black ink on his arm dance.

"Yeah, yeah, yeah, whatever you say, cuz," Wyatt countered and turned to introduce him to the other guys from the firehouse he was playing darts with.

"Honor to meet you."

"Hell of a last fight you had."

Once their initial statements about his career were over, he was relieved when the guys reverted back to treating him like they would any other normal person. He wasn't a huge celebrity—outside of the fighting community, he could go most days without being recognized, unless he was actively promoting a fight. And he preferred to fly under the radar. But with social media making it easier for fans to engage with athletes, celebrity was a small price to pay to be able to support himself doing something he loved.

At twenty-seven, he was already working on the back half of his career, having held on to his title for two hard years. Luckily none of his fights since had been as grueling as when he first took the belt.

His hip twinged again at the thought of the five punishing rounds he'd endured to beat Curtis "The Cutter" Cutler. The ex-Heavyweight Champ was a beast of a man, as well as a terrible human being. The guy had earned his fighting moniker by intentionally drawing as much blood from his opponents as possible.

Gage rolled his shoulders, hoping to rid himself of all thoughts of The Cutter. He didn't need that kind of negativity in his life. The guy was already like a gnat buzzing around his head with the way he trolled him on social media, he didn't deserve to have him actively thinking of him.

Besides, he had his own shit to focus on if he wanted to avoid the dreaded "R" word for as many years as possible.

A server came by their table to see if anyone needed a refill. She took orders for another round of beer for the fire-fighters with a smile and turned in his direction.

Her gaze traveled up and down his body, blatantly checking him out, and he couldn't repress a smile. As if scripted, her smile widened and her hip cocked out to the side. "What can I get you, hon?" clearly offering more than what was on the bar menu.

She was a cute girl, college-aged probably, with dark blond hair and brown eyes. He returned her smile, making sure to keep his friendly instead of come-hither like hers. He wasn't here to pick anyone up. No, tonight was for hanging out with his best friend and getting his head on straight for his big meeting tomorrow.

"I'll take a club soda, thanks." He didn't like to drink while training. There were no fights scheduled at the moment, but since he was meeting with potential new coaches and trainers in the morning, he didn't want anything to slow down his instincts.

"You got it." She gave him another flirty smile and made her way to the bar to fill their orders.

"I still can't believe you're moving here," Wyatt said.

"Well, I want to be around to see my godchild grow up, and Beth is getting ready to pop soon. So it seemed like a good idea to me."

From the moment he got the phone call telling him he was

going to be godfather to the next generation of James children, he knew it was time to be closer to those who were most important to him, aside from his own parents.

Tony Malone was one of the top MMA coaches on the west coast. He'd trained some of the best fighters throughout his career of forty-plus years. He had already been nearing retirement when he started training Gage in high school, then continued on for another dozen years when he saw the potential in him. But Tony was finally ready to retire.

Gage was happy for his mentor—Tony deserved to take it easy after decades of building champions. And though moving across the country was his idea, changing gyms and forging a relationship with a new coach added to the long list of complications that could pop up for him. He didn't need someone new digging into his history.

"What are you going to do about your training though? Don't you MMA guys have a gym you usually work out of and a coach or something?" one of Wyatt's coworkers asked.

"When Wyatt and Beth found out they were expecting, it was right before my last fight. My coach had been hinting for a while now he felt it was getting time to retire, but I think he was hanging on for me. So when I told him about the baby, he started helping me find gyms and coaches in the area that I could meet to be closer to them and then he wouldn't feel guilty about retiring. I'm starting with the Steele Maker tomorrow."

The past six months had been spent researching and interviewing potential candidates. Tony was even pickier than him when it came to selecting the new "home" of his prized fighter. There was a *very* short list to work from. Like the stars aligning, the top pick also happened to be near his cousin.

The Steele Maker had made a name for itself with a handful of boxing and judo champions, then emerging as one of the top MMA gyms in the last decade. Gage was so impressed by the owner, Vic Steele, during their video chat, he decided to become one of his fighters without even seeing the place in person.

"You must be meeting with Vic, right?"

He nodded his head. "How'd you know?"

"He's pretty well known around here. He was an Olympic champion at judo, and his brother, Mick, was a world champion boxer. Vic's son is projected to be the next UFC Light Heavyweight Champ."

Gage was impressed a layman knew that—it spoke highly of the gym and its reputation. More proof his gut was right, even with his other reservations.

"It's good to know it's such common knowledge outside the fighting world." He paused to take a sip of his club soda. "From everything Tony has told me, Vic's who he was looking at if I wanted someone to take over my training before I even mentioned moving here."

"Vic's a good guy. A bunch of the guys from the firehouse work out at his gym so we've gotten to know him through the years."

Wyatt had been all too willing to provide additional intel on the Steele Maker.

They played darts for the next hour, and he enjoyed getting to know some of the guys his cousin worked with. He was happy Wyatt had such solid people as his firehouse family. Tony had been like a second father, but he never really had that closeness with the other fighters who trained in his gym. If he was being honest with himself, it was something he was a little bit jealous of.

He checked his watch and noticed it was getting close to ten. He was ready to call it a night when a commotion from the next room caught their attention.

• • •

ROCKY LOOKED ACROSS the pool table and lined up her shot, ignoring Becky's attempts at distraction. She smiled as she sunk the eight ball in the corner pocket.

"Damn. I thought I had you that game," Becky said on a laugh.

Rocky stood and grabbed her beer off the pub table they'd commandeered, then took a long swallow before responding. "It was close that time. I only beat you by a ball."

Once a week, she and her friends would frequent The Ring, a hybrid restaurant/sports bar establishment about twenty minutes from where most of them lived. Most nights it was a low-key establishment, a place they could go to unwind or grab a bite to eat while watching live sports on the many televisions throughout the place.

"Yeah, I know, but I was hoping to sweep you tonight," Becky said, leaning against her pool stick. "It's okay, I still have one more game to kick your ass again."

She laughed. Her bestie was as fiery as her red bob haircut. They grew up next door to each other, and there wasn't a time in her life when she could remember not being friends with Becky Reese. Nowadays, Becky managed Rocky's family's gym, The Steele Maker, running it with military precision.

Becky's emerald eyes sparkled with mischief as she racked the balls for their last game. She was bent over to put away the racking triangle when a drunk asshole started heckling her.

"Oh yeah, baby, look at that ass. Why don't you give us a little shake, darling?" he called and laughed with his friends as if he was the cleverest man ever.

"How about not," Becky retorted as she moved to the other end of the pool table to join Rocky.

"You know, it's times like these I miss the rest of The Coven."

Rocky had to agree. The Coven, as the guys liked to call her and her best friends, was made up of six of the fiercest chicks around, and when they were together, no one messed with them. To be fair, their group consisted of a physical therapist to a group of professional MMA fighters, their nutritionist, and the woman who kept their gym in line, plus a best-selling author, and two women who ran a sports public relations empire. They were no shrinking violets.

Plus, when they were out in a group, they were less likely to be approached by idiots like these.

Since Rocky had won their last game, she made her way to the end of the table to break. The girls traded shots back and forth for a few minutes, doing their best to ignore the drunk idiots nearby. Unfortunately, a few plays later, she had to go to the other side of the table to be able to line up her next shot. Her eyes narrowed as she took in the group across the way. With the cocky leans and popped collars, they just screamed frat boys. She sighed as she trudged down the table.

Once she was stretched out to take the shot, a hand grazed her bare thigh, trying to make its way up to the hem of her jean cutoffs. She shot straight up and turned to glare at the asshole who thought he had the right to touch her.

"Touch me again, and I promise you *won't* like what happens," she practically growled at the guy.

She was met with a chorus of *ooooooh*s.

"Whatever you say, babe." The guy leered at her.

"I am so *not* your *babe*."

Rocky may not have chosen to step into the ring herself, but she made for one hell of a sparring partner. A bunch of drunk assholes—especially those who felt entitled to put their hands on women—should watch themselves.

Shrugging it off, she bent to retake her shot. Right after she made contact with the cue ball, a hand made contact with her ass. Reacting purely on instinct, she dropped the pool stick, spun around, grabbed the wrist of the offending hand, pulled back, and twisted the arm up and back while shoving his face down on the table by the back of his neck. She put pressure on his elbow, making him let out a startled squeak.

"Now you see…" She kept her voice calm. "I know my ass is nice because I work out and train with my brother. Who, I guess I should mention, is a fighter in the UFC. And this right here"—she pulled back on his arm more—"is a variation on one of my favorite moves of his, an armbar."

She took a moment to check on the douchebag's friends, but they all stood around in a drunken stupor.

"Usually, you use your legs to help pull the arm back and keep pulling until the elbow hyperextends and breaks." She paused to give the statement a chance to sink in. "That is if the person doesn't tap out first," she added. He didn't take her hint though.

Using the space between her thumb and forefinger, she pushed at the top of his elbow joint.

"This move isn't ideal in a standing position, but my brother wanted to make sure I knew how to defend myself properly from assholes like *you*, so he showed me how to put the right amount of pressure on the joint to do it while standing. So you see…" She pushed harder on the joint. "All it takes is a little more pressure and *snap*"—she popped the p—"goes your elbow."

His jaw clenched as he bit back a retort, her threat finally clicking inside his alcohol-addled brain. She smiled a little.

"You see, you have two choices. Door number one, you apologize to both me and my friend, or door number two, you keep being an asshat, and I push until I hear that *satisfying* snap."

She gave another push for emphasis.

"What's it gonna be?"

It didn't take long for the guy to make what was probably his first good decision in a good long while.

"I'm sorry, I'm sorry." His words came out so fast they were tripping over themselves to get out.

Once she released his arm, some of his bravado came back. She prepared to defend herself against his next move. She knew the type—if a guy had no qualms about sexually harassing a woman, they usually fell on the wrong side of the moral line when it came to putting their hands on them in other ways.

Before things had the chance to escalate, a deep voice cut through the tension.

"Is everything alright over here?"

She turned toward the sound. And looked up, and up, and up at a curious stranger. At five-ten, she wasn't used to most guys being significantly taller than she was, but this one managed to tower over her.

His voice was sexy enough, and the rest of him was equally delicious, given the way his black t-shirt clung to his muscular torso and strained against his bulging biceps. Her gaze continued its path up his body to his face, with its strong jaw clenched in anger and full lips she wouldn't mind feeling pressed against hers.

Damn, he's tall. Her neck canted back at an angle she generally didn't experience.

As if the rest of the package wasn't distracting enough, his eyes were a magnificent electric blue, like a crayon, framed by thick dark lashes and striking against his dark olive complexion.

Then it hit her. There was something familiar about him. *Very* familiar.

Gage James.

Her mind screamed as it made the connection. Any person with even the most basic knowledge of mixed martial arts would recognize Gage James, and as the staff physical thera-pist at a professional MMA gym, she certainly was anything but basic.

Worse than that though, was the fact that Gage James was *her* celebrity crush. Some of her closest friends were the biggest names in the NHL, but no, true to her upbringing, her celebrity crush was a fighter—even if she had a personal motto *not* to date one.

"Oh, shit! You're Gage James." Clearly, her brain/mouth filter was not working, and her cheeks heated in embarrassment. She felt a little better when she saw his eyes crinkle in amusement and a smile start to play at his lips. She had imagined what those lips would feel like on her body more times than she could count through the years.

"Yes, I am. And you are?"

"Raquel." *Crap! Why the hell did I say my legal name? Get your shit together, Rock.* She cleared her throat to get rid of the squeak. "But my friends call me Rocky." *There much better. See? You do remember how to flirt.*

"It's very nice to meet you, Rocky."

Oh, he called me Rocky. That had to be a good thing. Right?

She also liked the way her name sounded rolling off his tongue.

"You've got some moves."

Oh my god. Is he flirting with me?

She swallowed, her face heating as she realized this professional fighter witnessed her using a submission move in public. Sure, her brother taught her well, but this was Gage-Freaking-James. The man had won five of his fights with the move alone.

"Umm…thanks."

Who the hell is this timid person? Where the hell are your balls, Rock?

It was *never* good when she started talking to herself in the third person.

A quick glance at Becky revealed she was thinking along the same lines.

"So, Rocky, where does a girl learn to—" The rest of his sentence was cut off when Cindy, their server, cut in.

"Hey, Rocky, Jimmy wanted me to let you know that your tab for tonight is taken care of," she said.

"Why would he do that?" Her brow furrowed.

"He said he should have had security keep a closer eye on those guys and it's his fault things escalated," she explained as two bouncers escorted the drunks away.

"No. Absolutely not." Rocky shook her head. "Where is he?"

Cindy pointed toward the bar in the front room. "Behind the bar like usual."

She followed the direction of Cindy's finger and narrowed her eyes when she spotted Jimmy. She leaned in to give the server a quick hug goodbye. "Don't worry about it, Cin, I'll clear this up with him. Thanks for everything tonight. We'll see you next week."

With a nod at Becky, she gestured for them to make their way to the bar. Regret coursed through her at not being able to talk to Gage longer. She turned to look up at him again.

"You have *no idea* how awesome it was for me to meet you." She tried really hard not to gush. "But we have to go deal with this drama. But seriously so *awesome*." Her words strung together in a rush.

She would love to spend more time with her crush, but in the end, she knew it was probably best to avoid temptation. The last thing she needed was to do something she couldn't take back with the only fighter able to make her break her own rule.

Using what had transpired as an excuse, she beat a hasty retreat.

Chapter Two

T he last thing Gage expected when he met up with his cousin the night before was to come across one of the most intriguing women he ever had the pleasure to meet.

Rocky.

God, even her name was perfect.

What fighter wouldn't appreciate that? As a lover of all things Balboa—with the exception of *Rocky V*, because seriously, he could have done without that one—he was drawn to the raven-haired bombshell.

However, it wasn't her beauty or her name that made every cell in his body stand at attention. No, it was the easy way she pinned that asshole to the pub table, all while calmly explaining what she intended to do to him if he didn't apologize for his dickish ways. In his world, submission takedowns were highly respected and hers had been admirably executed.

She was taller than most women—a fact he could appreciate given his own massive height—topping out somewhere around five-nine, five-ten if he had to guess. Her killer legs had been displayed in all their muscular glory in a pair of cutoff shorts, ending in a pair of badass army boots.

A fan of the Dark Knight himself, he could respect her choice to rock the long-sleeved Batman shirt. It also helped that the tight v-neck hugged her curves and displayed a generous amount of cleavage.

Visions of the way her long, blue-black hair fell in waves to her waist played through his memory as he pulled into the large parking lot on the side of The Steele Maker gym.

He also may have had dreams of a certain pair of exotic steel gray eyes, peeking from her hair like storm clouds rolling through a copse of trees. He woke up harder that morning than he could remember being in months from imagining what that blood red, cupid's bow mouth of hers would look like wrapped around his favorite part of his anatomy.

It really was unfortunate he didn't get her number before she left to deal with the fallout from her confrontation with Tweedledumb and his merry band of morons.

Having been on the way out himself, he didn't get the chance to ask if Wyatt knew anything about the chick with the badass submission moves. His career came first—he needed to focus on making a good impression with his new coach and not on what his dick wanted.

That didn't mean he wasn't hoping the opportunity would present itself to ask about her when he went to Wyatt's for dinner that evening.

Lost in thoughts of the night before, he was nearly late for his meeting with Vic Steele. *Focus, man. Is a girl really worth the cost of your career?*

He pushed open the door to his Escalade, banishing all thoughts of sexy-as-fuck beauties to the back of his mind where they belonged.

Following Vic's instructions, he jogged across the street to the local coffee shop. They'd decided it would be best to meet outside of Vic's gym first, so as not to be distracted by probing eyes and invasive questions. A gym known for training MMA fighters was an entirely different ballgame compared to being out with the general public. He knew how famous he was in their world—it wasn't his ego talking, it was fact.

He noted the café's sign and grinned. The Espresso Patronum boasted its name in old-school Broadway marquee bulb lights, with a lighted cartoon to-go cup brandishing a wand and adorned with the trademark Harry Potter glasses and lightning bolt scar.

Cute.

He liked to listen to the books on audio—it helped break up mundane conditioning and was a good way to block outside distractions on fight days. He appreciated his fellow Potterheads at this place.

A bell chimed as he stepped through the glass door to the shop and was hit with an explosion of color.

With the same skill he used inside the cage, he took in the rest of the space in a glance. The floor was a diamond pattern of black and white tiles that contrasted the eclectic furniture.

As he'd noticed on The Steele Maker, the entire front wall of the shop was made of glass. A long, mosaic-tiled counter ran along half of it with crazy barstools for seats. As the sounds of The Fugees' "Killing Me Softly" played through the speakers, he stepped up to the counter to order a large dark roast coffee.

"Well, *hello,* handsome. Aren't you a tall drink of water?" The barista—as colorful as the shop—greeted him with a flirtatious smirk. The guy's sandy brown hair was spiked all around his head, the tips of the spikes dyed hot pink and neon green. There were straw sized gages in each ear, and both his arms were fully sleeved with impressive artwork.

"That's what my driver's license says at least," Gage replied with a grin. "Can I get a large coffee?"

His response caused the barista to laugh.

"You must be one of Vic's new guys," he commented as he prepared the drink.

"Why would you say that?" How'd the guy peg him so quickly?

"Oh, honey." He waved him off like he was being silly. "Why do you think I opened this place across from a gym that trains guys like you?" His fingers waved up and down the length of Gage's body. "I can pick a fighter out a mile away."

"You own the place?" He indicated with a circling finger.

The barista nodded, holding out his black coffee. "According to the mortgage, I do."

He accepted the paper to-go cup that advertised the same Harry Potter-style logo as outside and stretched a hand across the counter to shake the guy's hand. "I'm Gage. Nice to meet you."

"Lyle." His handshake was firmer than expected after that flirtatious banter. "I'm sure I'll see you around. My place is a favorite of all you gym rats. Vic's in the back corner talking to our resident author." He pointed to a section by the window.

Even seated, Vic Steele was an easy man to spot at six-five. He was currently leaning over, talking to a very pretty woman who looked a few years younger than Gage's own twenty-seven.

Vic made his excuses as Gage approached.

With a smile that bespoke their closeness, the blonde slipped a pair of Beats headphones decorated with Mickey Mouse over her ears, refocusing her attention on the pinkish Mac in front of her.

"Gage." Vic rose to stand, stretching out his hand in greeting. "Nice to finally meet you in person."

"Same here." He returned the friendly smile, then had to shake his head to clear it when he met Vic's grey eyes. They reminded him so much of Rocky's that it was clear she hadn't been banished far enough from his thoughts.

As he settled into an armchair with—*owls?* Yup, those were definitely little Hedwigs on the chair—Lyle delivered an over-sized mug topped with whipped cream to the blonde author.

Lyle tapped her on one of her Mickey earphones and nodded toward Gage. "Fresh smut inspiration, Madz." His whisper-shout could be heard by their entire section and Gage couldn't stifle his laughter.

The girl glanced at him with icy blue eyes then turned back to Lyle.

"You're the worst, Ly. What does your *husband* have to say about you ogling Vic's guys?"

Lyle's eyes watched him unabashedly as he spoke to her. "Oh, *honey.* You know he doesn't care where I get my appetite, as long as I eat at home."

She facepalmed as she giggled. "I can't even with you." She looked back at Gage. "Don't mind him. We told Kyle not to let him out of his cage, but he's a sucker."

"Kyle and Lyle?" he asked.

She held up a hand as if to stop him. "Don't even get him started"—she hooked a thumb at Lyle—"or your coffee will be cold before you and Vic even get around to talking." She repositioned her headphones again, looking back to the troublemaking barista. "Thank you for my refill. Now go away"— she shooed him with her hands—"I'm on a deadline."

With a wink at him, Lyle returned to his place at the front counter.

He may not have gotten a formal introduction but his morning was turning out to be way more entertaining than he thought it would be when his alarm went off.

"So...Tony sings your praises," he mentioned to get his conversation with Vic started.

Vic nodded and sipped his own coffee. "Yeah, Tony and I go back to my judo days. I can't believe he is actually retiring. Never thought I'd see the day."

He laughed. Vic wasn't the only one. "Yeah, I have a feeling if I wasn't looking to move, he would have kept on going until I was ready to retire myself." A day he was afraid might be closing in on him faster than he would like.

"That sounds like the Tony I know." Vic paused for a moment. "So what made you decide to move to Jersey? Pretty big change from California."

He appreciated the man's directness, not shying away from asking the important questions.

"My cousin and his wife are expecting their first baby in a few weeks and I wanted to be able to see her grow up. They asked me to be the godfather so it only reinforced the drive to be closer." He set his coffee cup on the table, spinning the paper cup between his scarred hands.

"Good reason. One I can really respect." Vic maintained eye contact as he spoke. "Family is important to the Steeles. It's a family-run business at The Steele Maker."

"So I've heard. I know your brother is also a trainer and you coach your son."

Vic nodded. "He's got a pretty impressive record already. Lots of buzz about him being the next Light Heavyweight Champ."

If memory served, Vic Steele's son, Vince, was the same age Gage was when he won his first belt. "It really speaks to your team's talent."

Vic beamed with pride. "Thanks. Kid's got drive like no one I've ever seen and from what I've heard from Tony, you are the same. My daughter and niece also work with the team."

He was curious to learn more about the team that would be responsible for keeping him healthy. When he and Tony were going over the specifics for picking Gage's new gym, they focused more on the credentials and specialties of those employed at the gym, not necessarily the personnel.

From what he'd learned last night, there was a tight-knit,

core group of fighters who all trained together at The Steele Maker. It was a concept he had a hard time wrapping his head around. In California, aside from his family and coaches, he hadn't been really close to anyone else.

"What do they do?" he asked.

"My daughter is our physical therapist. And my niece— Mick's daughter—is the team's nutritionist and a personal chef."

"That's gotta be helpful when your guys need to cut weight." As a heavyweight, he was one of the lucky few that didn't really have to cut weight for a fight. As long as he maintained a reasonably healthy diet, he didn't have to make many changes in the weeks leading up to a fight.

"It is. For the most part, I try to keep my guys from needing to drop too much weight before a fight. Helps keep their strength up. To be honest, both girls are major assets to the success of my guys. My daughter might even be more brilliant about fighting than my son. Great instincts and eye on that one, that's for sure. Too bad she doesn't want to be a fighter," he said with a shake of his head.

He chuckled. It's wasn't every day you met a dad who was disappointed his daughter *didn't* want to fight. "What, couldn't convince her to step in the cage?"

Vic snickered. "Oh no, *that's* not the problem. She gets in the cage all the time, loves to spar... No, she'd rather heal than hurt. Gets it from her mama, that one." The smile stretching across his face reflected the obvious love and pride he had for both women in his life.

"It's obvious now why Tony wanted you to take over my training." For as crotchety as his old coach could be at times, he was a family man at heart. It looked like Vic Steele was cut from a similar cloth.

"Have you made any decisions on when you'd want your next fight to be?" Vic asked, getting down to the business of his career. "I know The Cutter has been making a lot of noise about a rematch between the two of you."

He frowned at the mention of his *least* favorite fighter—hell, person—on Earth. Even now, the mere mention of the guy brought a throb to his hip. But he wasn't the only one to walk away a little worse for wear after their fight. After over twenty minutes of beating on each other, The Cutter had not only lost the title belt but sported a smashed nose and a few broken ribs as a souvenir.

"Yeah, never going to happen," Gage said adamantly.

Even as he spoke, his phone vibrated in his pocket, and he knew when he checked, there would be at least one notification of The Cutter's attempts to goad him into a rematch.

Ignoring his phone, Gage continued to talk business and life with Vic a little longer. The trainer knew his stuff and they got along seamlessly so far. He was looking forward to seeing the gym that would be his new home.

"What do you say about heading over to The Steel Maker? Everyone should be in the middle of training so you can get a good feel for the place right away."

"Sounds good to me. I parked in the lot behind the gym before so I'll grab my bag when we get there."

Chapter Three

Rocky had more letters designating all her specialties as The Steele Maker's physical therapist than were in the alphabet—that's how she felt at least. As the daughter of a nurse and an MMA trainer, she knew early in life what she wanted to be when she grew up. Her father and uncle's genes gave her the talent and skill to make a go of it on the women's circuit, but like her mother, she was drawn to fixing people instead of breaking them.

By the time she finished high school, she was already a licensed massage therapist (LMT), a certified yoga instructor (CYI), and a certified personal trainer (CPT).

She earned her Doctorate of Physical Therapy two years sooner than most, using her nerd powers and high school AP classes to enter college as a sophomore, and maxing out her course load while attending BTU.

It was how she ended up with more letters after her name than could fit on a business card—if she had business cards that is. But when your boss referred to you as Pumpkin, that formality usually isn't needed.

She may technically be Raquel Anne Steele DPT and a whole bunch of other things—but to the guys of the gym, she was just Rocky, or Alphabet Soup when they thought they were funny.

Sports were her life, athletes were her specialty, and though she had once hoped to work with one of the professional teams that courted her during school, she ended up succumbing to familial obligations and stayed at her father's gym. Every certification she acquired helped prove she'd *earned* her position instead of having it handed to her because she happened to be born a Steele.

It wasn't all bad though. As much as the guys liked to joke, she was respected and they followed her PT instructions like gospel.

Such as right now, for example.

She flipped one of her long pigtail braids over her shoulder and reached out for her brother's hand. His right wrist and hand had presented some tightness lately, and she wanted to ensure it hadn't been aggravated from his morning workout.

Gripping the edge of the athletic tape, she began to unwrap it, followed by the soft gauze cloth underneath. She could wrap and unwrap hands in her sleep, the muscle memory from doing it countless times as natural as breathing.

Once she had everything off and rolled in a ball to throw away, she reached for his hand again to evaluate it.

She bent his wrist back and forth.

Left then right.

Finally, she gently moved it around in a circle, completing the move both in a clockwise and counterclockwise motion.

Satisfied his wrist was fine, she grabbed his massive paw between her much smaller hands, running both her thumbs along the center of his palm from the base of the wrist up to the pads of his fingers, then out along the pads to stretch his fingers.

Nothing felt out of place to her. The swelling she'd felt in the tendons earlier in the week was gone. Treating fighters might not have been her first preference, but no one put them back together like she did.

"How's all that feel?" she asked, watching his face for any ticks of pain while she manipulated his hand.

"Great, actually."

Good, things were right on track. A big part of keeping the guys in fighting shape was reining them in when they needed to take it easy for a few days. It was much easier to prevent an injury than to rehab one, especially if it was an avoidable one.

Of course, keeping a group of competitive athletes in line was not easy. Thank god they all feared her and the rest of The Coven more than they worried about their fragile male egos.

She smiled and bent to get the new gauze needed to rewrap his hand and wrist. "You're never going to guess who I met last night. You'll be crazy jealous."

"Who?"

She continued to wrap and refused to answer because messing with your big brother was fun.

"Rock." He was getting impatient.

With her smile stretching as far as it could, she finally said, "Gage James."

Her brother's eyes grew comically wide, the whites around his rain-cloud grey irises forming perfect circles.

"No. Shit!" he said in disbelief.

She only smiled bigger in response, knowing it would drive him crazy.

"Where did you meet him? And why didn't you call me so I could come meet you wherever you were?"

She laughed. "Beck and I ran into him at The Ring last night."

"Damn. I knew I should have gone with you guys last night." He made a fist with his rewrapped hand and hit it against the palm of his other, testing to make sure he was good to go. He would be—she was pro, after all.

"Well, we do *always* invite you to come." She laughed at his scowl. Even though most of the weekly visits to The Ring turned into a Coven night out, the guys were always welcomed to join them.

"I would have called you, but I *literally* realized he was standing in front of me and had to leave. So it wasn't anything to write home about."

Her brother gave her an incredulous look. Everyone, and she meant *everyone*, knew about her crush on the current Heavyweight Champion. Passing him on the street would warrant a gushing retelling of the story worthy of the biggest fangirl. She wasn't sure where she found the ability to be so blasé over her encounter with the Greek God of perfection, maybe it stemmed from knowing she would never date a fighter, maybe not, but her current performance was definitely worthy of an Oscar.

Vince waited while she finished putting away the gauze and tape. "But still...Gage James."

"Yeah, I know." A dreamy sigh broke free. "And he's even hotter in person than on TV." Okay, so that was a little gushy. Whatever, she was due.

He scrunched his nose in disgust, nudging her in the side with his elbow. "*Sooo* didn't need to know that part."

She chuckled. "Sorry."

He shook his head. He knew it was her duty as the little sister to torture her big brother when the opportunity presented itself.

They left her treatment room and headed back to the main gym area, Vince tugging on her braids every once in a while. Like most of the Steeles, Vince was tall, topping out around six-four, but being only a few inches shy of six feet herself, she never really felt like a delicate flower amongst fighters.

Unlike last night as she stood near Gage James. She knew his personal stats by heart—fangirl, remember—so she knew he stood at an impressive six foot seven inches and two hundred and fifty-five pounds of rock hard, mouth-watering, panty-melting muscle. It really was a shame she didn't date fighters.

While she'd made a conscious effort to act like a normal human being the night before, instead of the gob smacked fangirl she really was, she couldn't stop herself from wondering how it would feel to be lifted in those strong arms of his.

The daydreams were once again trying to take over. She needed to keep her head on straight—she was at work, for god's sake. When she was alone later, she could let herself imagine all the things she was sure he could do to her, but not now. *Time and place, Rock, time and place.*

Vince pulled her hair again.

"What?"

"Have you seen Dad at all this morning?" he asked.

She glanced around the gym. Had she? Most mornings, they got together to discuss the fighters and any concerns either of them had, but it wasn't one of those days. "You know what, now that you ask, I don't remember seeing him when I got in this morning. I mean, I saw his car in the lot but not him."

The sparkle in Vince's eyes spelled trouble. "I know he isn't a super fan of you being in the cage without his permission." He chuckled at the understatement of the century. Their father had trained her how to fight, but his precious pumpkin wasn't supposed to spar unless he was around. "But want to spar?"

She gave a devilish smile. There were a few things she'd been meaning to address with Vince, and she knew just the way to needle him. "You're getting predictable in some of your takedown moves." She tossed out the comment as if it wasn't an insult.

"*Predictable?*" His jaw dropped.

"Well…predictable might not be the right word." She

drew out the silence between them as they headed toward the cage. "But you're giving away your moves a split second before you actually make them. I can tell you exactly which move you are thinking of before it happens."

"Lies." He gave her a look of disbelief.

They entered the cage in the middle of the main training area. Everything at The Steele Maker was top of the line, from the regulation octagon they climbed into down to the padded floor mats throughout the building. It may not have been her dream to stay in the family business, but she couldn't complain about the work environment.

Normally she would wear protective gear when sparring, but she was confident enough in her ability to read the tells he'd recently developed to forgo it.

"Come on, I'll prove it." She dropped into her fighting stance.

They took position across from each other, and as predicted, she was able to sidestep his move, calling it out without being touched. "Single leg takedown."

Vince's back shot straight up, the look on his face absolute shock. "*How* the *hell* did you know that?"

She grinned at him. "I told you, you give it away." She graciously left the "duh" implied.

He shook his head. "Okay, let's go again."

Again they assumed their positions and like before, she read her brother's every move. "Leg trip."

He motioned for them to reset their positions.

"Double leg takedown."

Another reset.

"Duck under."

"*Shit!* Man, I can't believe it." He ran his hands through his hair in frustration.

"Don't worry it's an easy fi—"

"RAQUEL ANNE, WHAT THE HELL DO YOU THINK YOU ARE DOING IN THE CAGE WITHOUT ME HERE?"

Rocky and Vince turned in the direction of their father's roar. "Shit," they said in unison.

GAGE MADE HIS way into The Steele Maker with Vic. He was immensely pleased with how nice it was. He'd seen pictures of the place and was given a virtual tour, but neither did it justice. The building stood two-stories tall and took up more than half the block. The outside was all reflective glass, and aside from the glass door Vic held open for him to walk through, you couldn't see inside from the street.

"One-way glass," Vic explained when he caught him glancing back over his shoulder.

To the right was a mirror-walled room he assumed was used for classes.

To the left was standard gym equipment: treadmills, ellipticals, rowing machines, free weights, along with the more hardcore stations of battle ropes, plate drags, and tire flipping.

His old gym was nice, but The Steele Maker was in a class by itself.

As they walked farther inside, he spotted a large half-circle reception desk with the gym's logo displayed behind it. Manning that desk was a very familiar redhead.

Elation shot through him. His attention may have been locked in on Rocky the night before, but the bright red of her friend's hair was hard to miss. Now all he needed to do was convince her to give him Rocky's number.

He may have been telling himself he didn't need the distraction Rocky would certainly be, but hell if he wasn't going to pursue the opening.

After Vic was done giving him a tour of The Steele Maker, he'd circle back to her, confident he could charm her into giving him her friend's information. She represented the first kernel of hope for tracking down the girl who hadn't been far from his mind for the last twelve hours.

She was on the phone while doing something on a large computer monitor as they made their way past the desk, acknowledging Vic with a wave, all while keeping her eyes on the screen in front of her.

His brain happily clicked back into work mode as they moved deeper into the gym. While the front was impressive, it paled in comparison to the main fight training area.

Like the front, the walls were the same one-way glass. The floor under his sneakers was covered with high-quality black and gray mats that boasted the gym's logo. Along the window to the right were rows of floor-to-ceiling anchored punching bags, as well as a row of speed bags.

In the back, beyond the guys grappling on the mats, were a state of the art, black- roped boxing ring to the left and a training octagon to the right.

Vic pointed out the other coaches and fighters. "Working with my guys on the mats are my Muay Thai coach and Brazilian jiu-jitsu coach."

Gage took a moment to observe the practices, sizing up each of the fighters' strengths at a glance. The way the four fighters laughed and joked with each other between sets intrigued him. He'd never had that kind of close camaraderie with his training partners.

The two coaches acknowledged them with a tilt of the chin, but their fighters remained focused on the skills they were practicing.

While Vic continued with the tour, Gage admired the tasteful black and white portraits hanging around the gym and the magnificent wall mural that combined the American flag and Olympic rings.

"In the ring is Deck working with my brother Mick, our boxing coach. And in the cage is..." Vic's words trailed off as he took in the fighters in the cage. *"Sonofabitch,"* he said to himself before roaring, "RAQUEL ANNE, WHAT THE HELL DO YOU THINK YOU ARE DOING IN THE CAGE WITHOUT ME HERE?"

The two fighters immediately stopped grappling and spun toward him, then the female came forward and hooked her fingers through the PVC-lined links.

"Hi, Daddy," she answered innocently.

There she was—temptation herself. Fuck if she didn't look as good in athletic wear as she did in those tiny shorts last night.

"Don't you *hi Daddy* me."

Jesus, Rocky was Vic's daughter. That suddenly complicated things.

The doors to the cage pushed open, and Gage recognized Vince Steele as he exited. He held the door open for his sister, both seemingly unconcerned over their father's ire and too absorbed in whatever they were laughing about to notice him standing by Vic's side.

"Rock, seriously, what were you doing in the cage? You know I don't like you being in there when I'm not around."

Her toned body was shown off in a black sports bra with leopard print edging and straps, the restrictive top plumping her breasts in a way that had him imagining all the ways he wanted his mouth on them. Black leggings with leopard print details inside cutouts encased her long legs from hip to ankle. Even her Nikes had the animal print in the signature swoosh.

His life was complicated enough at the moment, the *last* thing he needed was to add a girl to the mix. Yet...

Getting involved with a girl was bad enough. His new coach's daughter—worst idea ever.

But Gage James lived for a challenge and he had never tapped out of a fight.

He mentally touched gloves.

Let's get ready to rumble.

"I was just trying to prove a point to Vince," Rocky said,

pointing to her brother. Vince looked mildly uncomfortable, whereas his sister seemed completely unfazed by the displeasure pulsing off their father.

"And that would be?" Vic crossed his arms over his broad chest. Even decades retired, the man still maintained a fighter's intimidating build.

"He's been giving away his takedown moves before he makes them."

"You had your brother practice takedowns on you?" Vic's tone was incredulous as he shot an accusing glare at Vince. "Are you *out* of your *mind*?"

If Vince looked uncomfortable before, now he was turning positively green.

"Dad, you know I wouldn't do that." Vince defended himself. "Besides...even if I wanted to, I never got the chance." He explained as he nodded to his sister. "She was able to call out all the moves as I made them, stepping out of the way *before* I could touch her." He ran a hand through his hair in obvious frustration. "*Apparently* I have a tell."

"Well, I'll be damned." Vic looked at his daughter with pride.

During their meeting, he had mentioned how knowledgeable his daughter was on the sport. Now knowing his daughter and the chick with the submission self-defense moves were the same person, Gage had to believe the statement.

"I don't think it's *that* obvious." One of her hands went to her hip and he saw that her nails were painted purple. Why was he noticing all these small details? "I've just watched him fight all his life, so it's easier for me to spot than most." She placed a comforting hand on her brother's shoulder. "I think it's easy enough to fix, we just need to take some game tape to review."

Vic wasn't kidding when he said her instincts were spot

on. Most fighters watched footage of their opponents, but not many reviewed their own. It was a smart idea.

He knew the instant Rocky realized he was standing next to her father. Her silvery gaze ran over his body like a physical caress.

"What are you doing here?" she asked, her voice squeaking a little at the end. Good. He was happy to note she was as unsettled by him as he was by her.

"Raquel, manners," Vic chided.

He offered what felt like his first genuine smile since stumbling across her using a submission move on a drunk. "No, it's okay, Vic." He was quick to reassure his new coach— he didn't need any unnecessary wedges between him and any of those responsible for his training. "I actually had the honor of meeting Rocky yesterday, but I was unaware she was your daughter." His eyes tracked back to hers. "Though I gotta say…I'm not surprised by the revelation after witnessing her moves last night."

Rocky's teeth bit into the lush pillow of her bottom lip. He wanted to be the one to do the biting.

Bro, what is wrong with you? Get your head in the game.

"Moves?" Vic inquired.

"Oh, yeah." His smile widened. "When I met her, she had some asshole's face pinned to a table while threatening to snap his elbow."

"*Raquel?*" Vic looked flabbergasted and sent his son an accusing look. "I'm guessing this is your influence?"

Rocky put her head back and sighed. Probably being called Raquel three times in as many minutes was not a good thing.

"No, Dad, it's not like that. There was this drunk guy at The Ring last night who was harassing Beck and me. After a while, he decided my ass just *had* to be introduced to his hand. So I showed him the error of his ways." She shrugged.

He'd admired how she dealt with the situation last night

and was equally fascinated with how well she handled herself in front of her father. As each piece of new information about her fell into place like a game of Tetris, he started to understand his magnetic draw.

Vic took a moment to digest the information, then turned to shout toward the front of the gym. "REBECCA DANIELLE, GET YOUR ASS BACK HERE!"

The redhead came out from her perch behind the reception desk. "Yeah, Papa Steele?" She approached their group with caution.

Vic relayed the story in an attempt to piece together all the facts.

"Absolutely," she quickly confirmed. "First the asshat was harassing me and didn't stop. She even let him slide after he felt her up the first time. But the second time he put his hands on her, she put a stop to it. Honestly...I'm surprised she let him go with as many warnings as she did."

Vic sighed heavily, using his thumb and the knuckle of his index finger to rub along the ridge of his brow. Gage didn't envy the guy at all. Aside from his mother, the only female in his life he had to worry about was Beth, and Wyatt really had that handled. "What did Jimmy have to say about your little display?" Vic asked his daughter.

"He comped our bill," Rocky said.

"He wouldn't even change his mind when we tried arguing with him about it either," Becky added.

"I swear, you kids stress me out more than watching my guys fight." Vic shook his head and the girls laughed at his dramatic flare.

"Anyway." He turned to Gage. "Even though you've already met, this is my daughter, Rocky. Like I explained earlier, she's the team physical therapist. She's pretty much certified in anything related to treating athletes."

"Overachiever," Vince announced through a fake cough, earning him a backhand to the gut from his sister.

Vic ignored their antics, placing a hand on the redhead's shoulder with fatherly affection. "And this here is her best friend—and my unofficial daughter—Becky. She manages the gym for me."

"Nice to *officially* meet you."

"Yeah, it was a little crazy last night." Becky chuckled.

"And this here is my son, Vince." Vic gestured to his son.

"It's an honor to meet you." Vince reached out a hand for him to shake.

"I think *honor* might be too strong of a word," Gage said with a self-deprecating laugh. "Plus, I honestly think you'll be at my level very shortly."

"How's the wrist and hand feel?" Vic asked his son, getting back to business.

Vince opened and closed his fist a few times. "Feels great, actually. Rock did her thing to check"—he looked down at his sister—"*whatever* it is she checks, and deemed it good."

Vic looked to Rocky for confirmation. "Really, Dad, everything looks great. I'll check it again at the end of training today, but I think he's finished healing."

"Exactly what I want to hear." Turning to Gage, he cautioned, "Fair warning, if anything doesn't feel right, she'll find it and bench you even without you needing to say a thing. So I don't suggest trying to hide any tweaks or pains."

He nodded his understanding even as his hip spasmed, as if to jump up and yell *you are screwed*. No way was he going to be filling Rocky in on his hip injury. If what Vic said was true, she *definitely* would bench him from training, and he'd worked too hard keeping it to himself to risk that happening.

Layer by layer, stress just continued to pile up. Cutler, his hip, the need to hold on to his title, the move, his growing concern over assimilating into a family-like group of fighters, his unwanted attraction to his new physical therapist. The pressure from it all was starting to make him feel like one of those hoarders that Wyatt told him they had to rescue after getting trapped by the twenty years of newspapers they refused to get rid of. He needed to get back to training and rid himself of all the extra bullshit, focus on his body, his goals.

"Come on." Vic clapped him on the back. "Let me introduce you to the rest of the motley crew."

Yet, as his eyes landed on Rocky laughing with her brother, he couldn't bring himself to throw out what he felt toward her.

Chapter Four

After meeting her favorite fighter randomly the night before, Rocky couldn't comprehend how he was standing in front of her again. And from the sounds of things, her dad was his new trainer.

Umm, is this real life?

How was it she'd had no idea he was not only shopping around for a new coach, but that her own father was in the running for the job?

The move to The Steele Maker was going to be a major story. She made a mental note to bring Jordan and Skye in on this latest development since they handled all the publicity for the gym and its fighters.

Becky went back to the front desk while her father took Gage around to make introductions. Immediately, she felt her phone vibrate from the side pocket of her leggings.

YOU KNOW YOU WANNA (Becky): OMG is this real life or are we in one of your dreams right now?

. . .

ALPHABET SOUP (Rocky): IDK but if this is a dream DO NOT WAKE ME UP!

ALPHABET SOUP: *GIF of smashing an alarm clock*

YOU KNOW YOU WANNA: In the immortal words of Michelle Tanner. You got it Dude!

YOU KNOW YOU WANNA: *GIF of Michelle Tanner giving a thumbs up*

ALPHABET SOUP: This is why I love you so!! *kissy face emoji*

YOU KNOW YOU WANNA: Seriously though. You HAVE to go for it…how many people get their celebrity crush put in front of them for the taking?

ALPHABET SOUP: Maybe I will *winky face emoji*

YOU KNOW YOU WANNA: NOT GOOD ENOUGH. Looping in the rest of The Coven.

The rest of the girls would definitely have opinions. She may have said in the past that she would make a move on Gage if she ever had the chance, but in her heart of hearts, she knew she wouldn't. Besides, she'd thought she had a billion in one chance of ever meeting the guy. He was a fighter, so he would never be more than a celebrity crush. Unavailable crushes were safer than dudes in real life.

YOU KNOW YOU WANNA: You guys are NEVER going to believe who the newest fighter to join The Steele Maker is

QUEEN OF SMUT (Maddey): Enough with the cliffhanger. I'm on deadline here Beck

PROTEIN PRINCESS (Gemma): Seriously. You are the WORST with this sometimes

MAKES BOYS CRY (Skye): Don't make me come down there

MOTHER OF DRAGONS (Jordan): Seriously, spit it out before the twins wake up from their current milk comas

MOTHER OF DRAGONS: And Skye, you're on the West Coast, don't make idle threats

PROTEIN PRINCESS: Rock, you're with her. Make her tell us ALREADY

ALPHABET SOUP: *GIF of Mariah Carey dramatically putting on sunglasses saying "No Comment"*

· · ·

YOU KNOW YOU WANNA: Pff… It's about her…she's not going to say anything. But fine I'll put you guys out of your misery…

QUEEN OF SMUT: I swear to god Beck, I will sick my editor on you when I miss my deadline because I left my writing chair at Espresso Patronum to strangle you

YOU KNOW YOU WANNA: Such a flare for dramatics. It's obvious you live in a world of fiction. Anyway…

YOU KNOW YOU WANNA: The newest fighter to be trained here at The Steele Maker…

YOU KNOW YOU WANNA: Is…

PROTEIN PRINCESS: BECKY!!!!!

QUEEN OF SMUT: BECKY

MAKES BOYS CRY: BECKY

MOTHER OF DRAGONS: REBECCA!!!

QUEEN OF SMUT: Also…am I the only one who's noticed Rock has been suspiciously quiet through all this

• • •

MOTHER OF DRAGONS: Hurry up before I have to parent again…

YOU KNOW YOU WANNA: Ok ok ok

YOU KNOW YOU WANNA: GAGE JAMES!!!!!!!!!!!!!!!!!!!!!!!!!!!

There was a long pause while everyone processed that, followed by a barrage of text messages tripping over each other to be the first to ping through.

PROTEIN PRINCESS: WHAT?!

MOTHER OF DRAGONS: Like the current UFC Heavyweight title holder Gage James?

MAKES BOYS CRY: You mean like this fine hunk of man meat?

MAKES BOYS CRY: *GIF of Gage flexing in only his tiny fighting shorts*

QUEEN OF SMUT: OMG total hero inspiration

QUEEN OF SMUT: Oh shit. I think I saw him at EP with Papa Steele this morning

• • •

YOU KNOW YOU WANNA: Look I know he's hot. Like melt your panties, take me back to your lair and do whatever you want to me hot. But that is not the most important thing here people

PROTEIN PRINCESS: Because we all know we'll be here until tomorrow if we wait for Beck to FINALLY get to the point, I'll make it for her

PROTEIN PRINCESS: Rocky has a huge lady boner for him.

Knowing her cousin Gemma's revelation would only lead to another torrent of messages from her friends, she switched her phone to silent and got back to work.

She made her rounds amongst the other fighters there for mid-morning sessions, evaluating how they moved, checking to make sure they weren't trying to work through any unnecessary pain or restrictions. These guys were the core group and most serious of the fighters that trained at The Steele Maker. She loved them like family, but sometimes they let their machismo get in the way of their common sense.

Knowing this, she did frequent check-ins, reducing the chance of them risking further injury when they were too bullheaded to admit pain. Fighters were the worst—she much preferred the hockey and football players she worked with during college.

Fifteen minutes later, she finally felt like she had herself back under control. No more thoughts of a certain too-sexy-for-his-own-good fighter invading her brain.

Then Gage came out of the locker room in his workout gear.

Discreetly checking her chin for drool, she admired the

way the loose basketball shorts hung from his narrow hips. Her nipples pebbled against the thin material of her sports bra—dammit, she shouldn't have left her zip up in her office earlier—while her eyes traced the obsidian lines of ink of the octopus tattoo that curled over his entire left shoulder, up his neck, across parts of his back and chest before wrapping down his arm. She couldn't wait to get her hands on him.

In a professional sense, of course.

Keep telling yourself that, Rock.

A couple of deep inhalations got her hormones under control enough for her to make her way over to where he stood with her father. Part of her job included evaluating each of the fighters, cataloging any past injuries, and making notes in her records of any areas that were cause for concern. Which meant she needed to take Gage back to the treatment room connected to her office for his intake eval.

Her very private office in the back.

Away from prying eyes.

Where she would need him to strip down to his underwear.

Was he a boxers or briefs type of guy? *Dammit, Rock, not the point.*

Where she would have to put her hands on him.

Alone.

With him.

Half-naked.

Without jumping his bones.

Fuck my life.

It didn't help that her phone hadn't stopped buzzing against her leg since Becky informed their friends of this latest development. Even now, Becky was waggling her eyebrows at her from the front desk. Rocky turned away and covertly flipped her off behind her back. She would do her damnedest to ignore the human equivalent of the devil on her shoulder. Becky was personally responsible for them getting into trouble more times than she could count while they were growing up, earning herself the text handle still used today.

"Hey, Dad," she said when there was a break in their conversation. "I was thinking of doing Gage's eval today before I have to head out. This way you'll only have one day where I'm cutting into training hours."

"Good idea. Well." He clapped Gage on one of the shoulders she wanted to sink her teeth into. "I'll leave you in Rock's capable hands."

Why the hell did that sound so suggestive?

She sucked in a breath when Gage trained his baby blues on her. Those bad boys were ridiculously bright, seriously something straight out of the Crayola factory.

Gage held a hand out for her to lead the way. She would never admit that she put a little extra sway in her hips as she did so.

All the offices and locker rooms were located opposite the main training area. Both her office and treatment room had doorway access to the hallway, so she pointed to the one leading into the treatment room for Gage, while she entered her office. She needed to grab a shirt to help hide her hard-enough-to-cut-glass nipples.

Her ass brushed against Gage's groin as she bent over to reach for the yoga jacket that matched her leggings. She heard him suck in a harsh breath at the accidental contact. He must have followed behind her instead of heading to the treatment room like she indicated.

Her own respiration sped up as her mind reminded her of every dirty, fucked on a desk scene she had ever read. Every guy she treated at the gym was attractive, but never once had she had any trouble marshaling her thoughts like she did with Gage.

She was also aware that bent over the way she was, her

ass looked spectacular, thank you very much. She didn't do squats for nothing.

Her body demanded that she rub against him like a cat in heat, but her brain somehow managed to overrule the impulse. Hell, she worked on her ex-boyfriend without an issue, and they'd seen each other naked.

She chalked it up to the fantasies she'd woven around *UFC Champion Gage James* over the years. The Gage James standing in her office right now was a fighter and her client and therefore off-limits. Because she *did not* date fighters. Her entire life had been spent coming in second place to them—she didn't need to actually feel like she wasn't the priority to one of them.

She inhaled a deep breath to help clear the lust from her system, only it had the opposite effect thanks to the way it caused her ass to brush against his—*is it getting hard?*—dick.

You CANNOT fuck him in your office, Rock. Don't be a cliché.

Luckily, he stepped back, mumbling an apology before she could do anything stupid.

"You sure have a lot of accreditations." He pointed to the wall of her framed certificates, his statement finally breaking in enough for her to focus on what was important—her job, not his dick.

She was damned proud of her accomplishments. She'd worked her ass off for each one, spending countless hours studying and logging every clinical hour she was offered. Sure, working at The Steele Maker might not have been her dream, but that didn't mean she wasn't going to be the best damn physical therapist because of it.

She turned around to face him as she shrugged into the yoga jacket, only this position wasn't much better. His towering body had her boxed in against her desk, the scent of fresh soap and raw maleness invading her senses.

Her eyes lifted to meet his and she was startled to recognize the heaviness of attraction there. Gage James was attracted to her. Her, Rocky Steele, the girl with the hugest celebrity crush on him. The girl who didn't date fighters. Maybe she really was still asleep.

"What can I say... I'm a bit of an overachiever." Her eyes tracked over the corded muscles of his forearm stretched out alongside her. She swallowed—hard—at the arm porn perfection now inches from her face.

Jacket zipped to the base of her sports bra, she steeled herself against temptation, pulling up every one of her professional reserves. She could do this. She'd treated some of the hottest athletes throughout her short career and tenure at college. He was no different. Or at least that's what she tried to tell herself as she led him into the treatment room and asked him to strip down to his underwear.

It worked too.

Until she turned around.

And sweet mother of all things Calvin Klein underwear model. He was Michelangelo perfection in his white boxer briefs. Mark Wahlberg had *nothing* on Gage James. Sure, she wasn't even born yet when the super-hot actor posed for the campaign, but thank you, internet, for immortalizing that underwear model paragon.

"You can sit up here," she said, patting the treatment table.

Without a word, he did as she asked.

Stepping into the space between his spread knees, she was afforded her first up-close look of his tempting tattoo.

The head of the octopus took over half his pectoral muscle, stretching up and over his shoulder with its sleepy eye looking at her from the front of his shoulder. The body covered his bulging biceps, with six of its tentacles wrapping around his forearm down to his wrist and two reaching along his back and up his neck.

The tribal design of the body was gorgeous on his tanned

skin. Her hands itched to trace the diamond shapes and swirls.

Then she remembered that was exactly what she was about to do. It was her professional duty, after all.

Some days she really loved her job.

Chapter Five

Gage settled himself on the padded table, willing his dick to stay down as Rocky entered his personal space, the sweet scent of blueberries coming with her. He had barely gotten himself back under control after his accidental brush against her ass. Her firm, heart-shaped, bent-over ass.

How he'd had the self-control to not reach out and grab her hips was beyond him. Especially with the million different possibilities of what he wanted to do to her running through his head.

As disappointed as he was when she covered herself with a jacket, it was probably a good thing if he was going to get through her evaluation without embarrassing himself or him acting on his baser urges.

The goosebumps breaking out on his skin had nothing to do with being practically naked and everything to do with the thought of her hands on his body.

Running down my chest, her nails scratching along the way.

Slipping under the hem of my boxers.

Wrapped around my co—

Nope.

He cut off that train of thought before it had a chance to finish off the last of his control like a roundhouse kick to the head.

He felt something vibrate against his thigh.

"Do you need to get that?" He gestured toward her leg with his chin.

"No. Ignore it," she said, picking up the iPad from where she'd placed it next to him on the table. "It's what I've been doing for the last fifteen minutes since Beck stirred the pot." The smile tugging the corners of her lips revealed she wasn't upset with her friend.

She stood close enough that he was able to appreciate the perfect cupid's bow shape of her lips. All night, he had imagined what those lips would look and feel like on his body. Again, he felt a stirring below the belt, so focusing on *anything* but her anatomy was what he needed to do. Not more fantasizing over if she could handle his entire length or if she liked to swallow.

No, he needed to think of fighting his way out of the armbar she seemed so partial to and punch combinations.

"I take it you guys are close?" Beyond the obvious physical attraction, he had a drive to learn as much about this woman as he could. Plus, focusing the questions on her took his mind off how good her hands actually felt on him as she inspected the scars scattered across his hands. They were par for the course for any fighter.

"Yup." She made a popping sound with the p. "She's my sista from another mista. My blood from another stud. The trilogy to me and Vince."

He laughed at her description of their friendship. "I get that. My cousin, Wyatt, is my brotha from another motha," he said with a grin that she returned.

She asked him questions regarding his medical history and if he had any problem areas she would need to watch. His pulse beat in his hip as he denied any issues. Sweat beaded on the back of his neck. Keeping his injury a secret was going to be a constant challenge, but it didn't truly bother him that often, so he wasn't going to allow it to bench him.

Her experience in the sport was evident in the way she questioned if he had any injuries not made public. Not even Tony knew about his hip—that information stayed between him and the doctor bound by his Hippocratic oath to keep it.

She demonstrated complete confidence in everything she did, making it obvious that she'd earned each of those certificates he saw in her office earlier.

She tested the range of motion for each of his joints. He barely bit back a groan of discomfort when he had to swing his leg around. His hip had better range when he was warmed up. Vic's warning about trying to hide an injury from her echoed in the back of his mind.

He needed a distraction. "So did you start working for your dad recently? You can't be out of school long." He was the worst at guessing ages, but he knew from her brother's profile he was twenty-five, so he assumed she was around his age given how close they had seemed earlier.

A frown tugged at her face, giving him the impression she wasn't all that happy about being a part of her father's empire. "It feels like I've worked here all my life." She motioned for him to step on the medical-grade scale in the corner. "I've taught yoga, been a personal trainer, and served as the physical therapist as I worked my way through my degrees to my doctorate this past May." She paused to record his weight in his chart.

"You're older than your brother?" That was surprising.

"No. Vince has me by thirteen months. BTU—where I went to college—offers an accelerated program that I qualified for."

He liked that she was smart. He liked it a lot.

She leaned against the table close to where he resumed sitting and he watched her input more information about him in the iPad. He breathed a sigh of relief when she didn't make any mention of his hip.

She looked to him when there was a knock on the door. Not sure if she was asking permission to answer or not, he gave her a nod anyway. It wasn't like he was shy about being in front of people in his underwear. He did his weigh-ins—broadcasted on TV—in his trusty Calvins, so he was used to it.

"Come in," she called out.

A russet colored head popped through the doorway, dark eyes bouncing around the room. "Alphabet Soup," the guy he said when he spotted Rocky.

"What's up, Deck?"

"Do you have any Kinesio tape?"

"Shoulder?" she asked, already walking to one of the cabinets on the far wall.

"Yeah."

Deck, the fighter he recognized who sparred with Mick earlier, stepped inside the room with them, automatically turning to the side so Rocky could tape up his shoulder with the therapy tape meant to stimulate healing. She created a U-shape around the ball of his shoulder with blue tape, switched to black for a strip from the side of his neck down to the middle of his biceps, then finished by running a strip of blue from the bump of his collarbone to the middle of his shoulder blade.

A little crinkle formed between her black brows as she concentrated on the precise placement of the tape.

"Good?" she asked and Deck rolled his shoulder a few times before nodding his approval.

"Hey, can you give Vin a ride home later?" she asked. "Beck and I are leaving for Jordan's in a few and he came in with me this morning."

Gage studied their interaction, trying to gauge the relationship between them. With the added dynamic of her being his new coach's daughter, he wasn't sure if he should come right out and ask her if she had a boyfriend—not that he *should* anyway.

"I thought last night was your Coven meeting?"

"No, it was just Beck and me last night." She turned to Gage. "Don't ask," she said, probably reading the confusion on his face. "Deck and the guys just have jokes when it comes to me and my friends."

"And 'alphabet soup'?" he asked.

Her laughter made him smile. This easy-going girl was a direct contrast to the serious clinician she was during her evaluation just moments before.

"It's my nickname because of the letters of my certifications." She lifted a hand in the direction of her office. "Even abbreviated, my full title is a mouthful."

"That's what she said," Deck quipped.

"What are you, five?" she scolded him with a laugh.

The guy shrugged, unfazed. "You know you love me, Rock."

"That's debatable."

"One date." Deck waggled a finger in front of her face. "That's all I'd need to have you fall in love with me for real."

"*Pff.*" Her lips quirked into a playful smile. "Maybe you need to sit the rest of the day out, because *clearly* you've taken one too many hits to the head with a comment like that."

His eyes followed her as she moved about the room, putting things away and resetting it back to order.

"Besides, Deck, you know I don't date fighters. So forgetting the fact I think of you as a brother, you've got that going against you too."

Whoa. What the hell? What did she have against fighters?

"You know I joke, Rock. I like my balls attached to my body, and Vince would take much too much joy in trying to remove them if he thought I was hitting on you for real. Don't even get me started on how Papa Steele would react."

"Truth," she agreed with a sardonic smile.

The longer he listened to their conversation, the more he thought the universe was warning him to keep his distance. Too bad he felt like there was an invisible string between them, drawing him to her.

"What are you going to Jordan's for?" Deck asked.

"Tomorrow is the first regular season game, so I'm going to make sure Jake is good to go. I'm sure Ryan will be there too and it'll save me a trip to his place to do his."

"Umm...I'm *pretty sure* the Blizzards employ their own PTs to do that," Deck said.

She was treating members of New Jersey's hockey team too? Gage was becoming more fascinated by the minute.

"Yes, they do. Which I remind them of. But you boys are all babies when it comes to your superstitions. Now get out of here." She shooed Deck toward the door. "Ice the shoulder when you get home and put heat on it before bed. I'll check on it again in the morning."

Deck snapped his heels together in attention and saluted Rocky before striding from the room, leaving them alone once again.

"I have so many questions right now," Gage deadpanned.

He was a little intimidated by how many people she seemed to be friends with. He wasn't a total introvert, but he definitely fell more on the loner side of the spectrum.

"Yeah, Deck has that effect on people. Don't worry." She patted his shoulder, electricity sparking through his body at the casual touch. "You get used to it after a while."

Done with his physical, she motioned for him to get dressed as she went into her office to grab her bag.

"Try not to let the guys run you off before tomorrow. They're an acquired taste. But there's no place else like The Steele Maker. Glad we were able to *officially* meet this time."

And with a wave and a short "Bye, Gage," she breezed out the door, leaving him alone in her treatment room. The night before he was hit by her beauty. Today, he got firsthand experience of her professionalism. Both were like a one-two punch, telling his gut there was no way he could let her wiggle herself away from him like an opponent trying to get out of a rear naked choke.

In the last twelve hours, he'd told himself multiple times he couldn't afford any distractions if he was going to defend his belt.

Yet as he learned more about her and his physical reaction to her strengthened, all the reasons he *shouldn't* faded away.

The fact that she said she didn't date fighters barely even registered as a blip on his radar. He'd find out the reason for her aversion and then change her mind.

Looked like it was time for him to step into the cage again.

Game on.

Chapter Six

R ocky punched in the code for the gate surrounding the property of the Donovan estate. Thanks to a generous signing bonus when becoming the Blizzards goalie, a multi-million-dollar salary, and a handful of lucrative endorsement deals via his PR guru of a wife, Jake Donovan had purchased a six-bedroom home and the few acres of land it sat on. For as large as the house was, it wasn't ostentatious and fit its owners perfectly.

Jordan texted her earlier that the girls were awake, so she didn't have to worry about Navy, Jordan's large black Labrador, waking up any babies as she and Becky let themselves in through the front door.

Five months ago, while the Blizzards were battling it out in the playoffs for the Stanley Cup, Jordan gave birth to identical twin girls—Lucy and Lacey, the two most perfect babies in existence. Luckily for Jake, his wife happened to go into labor on a break between two home games.

Jordan had grown up in the hockey world just like Rocky was raised with fighters—the difference was Jordan loved it and used it to follow her passion in public relations, whereas Rocky was pigeonholed into her dad's gym.

Navy met Becky and her at the entrance and led the way to where all his humans were hanging out in the open kitchen and family room at the back of the house.

"Drink?" Jordan greeted them, wine bottle in one hand, cooing baby in the other.

Her friend was hella sleep deprived thanks to her newborn twins and still managed to look like the fierce matriarch of their group in black leggings, one of her husband's old college hockey t-shirts, and a messy bun. But then again, Rocky learned early on never to underestimate Jordan Donnelly—now Donovan. She wanted to be as together as Jordan when she grew up, it didn't matter they were the same age.

"Now *that's* my type of greeting," Becky said dropping a kiss to Lucy's—or Lacey's?—head, relieving Jordan of the bottle to pour three generous glasses.

"You can drink when breastfeeding?" Rocky was never one to turn down a nice Moscato and accepted the glass held out in offering, clinking it against the rims of her besties'.

"Yeah. It's only one glass and I just finished feeding for what I swear was like the tenth time today already." Jordan led them from the kitchen into the family room, where her husband, Jake, was swaying with the other twin on his shoulder.

"Hey, Rock. Hey, Beck." He walked over to drop a kiss on each of their cheeks.

"Hey, Jake," they returned.

Rocky reached her arms out, wiggling her fingers. "Now one of you give me a baby. I need to love up on my nieces while I'm here."

Though technically not related, these babies were going to grow up with more aunts and uncles than they could count.

"Where's Captain America?" Becky asked, looking around for Ryan, Jordan's brother.

After three years with the team, he had been named the

new captain after their Cup win in June and Rocky knew there was no one better suited for the role.

"I'm right here." Ryan stepped through the doors from the backyard, pausing to pull Becky into a hug, and stopping Jake from handing over the baby in his arms. "No, take Lay." He nodded toward the baby snuggled in her mom's arms. "I want my goddaughter."

"I'm impressed you can tell them apart so easily," Rocky said, handing him Lucy before taking Lacey from Jordan.

"I helped dress them after an *epic* poop explosion. I remember who was in what," he said with a wink.

"Okay, okay." Jordan waved her hands in the air to bring the conversation back around. "As *glamorous* as the facts of mom life are, can we please focus on what's important here?"

Her gut clenched, knowing *exactly* where her friend was about to take them.

"Why is it when we're with you girls I always feel like I'm stepping into a conversation already in progress?" Ryan asked as he settled onto the couch.

"Because with their Coven conversations we pretty much always are," Jake confirmed. But he dropped an arm around his wife's shoulders and kissed her temple.

"Please don't distract me, mommy brain is real." Jordan placed one hand against her husband's stomach, then looked straight at Rocky. "So what are you going to do?"

"About what?" Playing dumb was a great tactic.

"Don't even try it. I may have put my phone in the fridge earlier when we were texting, but I *didn't* forget what we were talking about."

"Really, babe?" Jake asked.

"Yes, *really*. Don't judge. Now put those things away before I lose my train of thought again." Jordan pushed her finger into one of his dimples. "What are you going to do about this whole Gage situation?"

"There is no *situation*." It took everything not to roll her eyes.

"Bullshit," Becky declared. "There's a situation, all right. Specifically, in that boy's pants when he looks at you. Because *hot* damn." She shook out her hand like she'd touched something hot.

"Anything you guys want to share with the class, maybe?" Ryan asked.

"We have a new fighter at the gym." Rocky was almost reluctant to part with the information.

Becky snorted in the most unladylike way, reading her like a book. "Yeah a *fighter*," she sing-songed the last word. "Nice try downplaying the information." She rolled her eyes as if to say *pathetic*. "What she means is *Gage James* is now the newest member of Papa Steele's prized fighters."

And that, *that* right there was why nothing would ever come of her attraction, her crush, on Gage James. He would forever be one of her father's fighters, and *god forbid* she do something to jeopardize that.

"Really?" Ryan questioned, turning blue eyes her way, which only had her comparing them to Gage's bright cerulean ones. It didn't matter how much she told herself fighters—especially Papa Steele's—were a no-go, she hadn't been able to snuff out the flame of attraction.

"Oh, man." Jake attempted to smother his laugh in Jordan's neck. "I wish Tuck was here right now."

"Bro." Ryan failed to hold back his laughter too. "He would totally be starting a pool on how long it took the two of them to bang."

"Oh, I'm texting M-Dubs right now." Becky's eyes lit with her usual devilish gleam as she pulled her phone out.

"You leave the man whore *out* of this." Rocky pointed an aggressive finger at her *so-called* best friend. The last thing she needed was for the biggest playboy of their group and troublemaker—which was saying something given Becky's own penchant for mischief—to add his two cents.

"What?" Becky held her hands up in innocence. "I'm just saying. He's your celebrity crush. He's been put in front of you. The math totally adds up."

"What math?" she asked, already regretting the decision.

"That you should bang."

There was never a wall around when you needed to slam your head against it.

"Don't you give me that look," Becky cautioned. "All I'm saying is P plus V equals O. *As in orgasm*," she whispered the last. "See…math."

"Okay," Jordan said to preempt any bloodshed. "While this has been fun and all, since you guys have my spawn under control, I'm going to go shower. I can't remember the last time I did."

"It's been two days, babe," Jake supplied helpfully.

The look of shock on Jordan's face made the rest of them laugh. "*Shit.* Really?" He nodded in confirmation. "Damn. I lose all concept of time when I work from home instead of going into the office."

"Come on, babe," Jake said, putting an arm around his petite wife. "I'll help you wash your back."

It always fascinated Rocky how her barely over five-foot friend so effortlessly commanded athletes well over a foot taller than her, but she did so every day. Along with her take no prisoners best friend and business partner, Skye, the two rarely had one of the athletes on their client roster step out of line.

"Gross. I don't need to be hearing about you having sex with my sister, Donovan," Ryan grumbled.

"*Hey.* How else do you think you got that perfect little bundle in your arms right now, huh?" Jordan teased.

"Don't listen to your crazy mommy, Lu." Ryan nuzzled his nose against Lucy's much smaller one. "The stork dropped you both off here and my little sister *does not* have S-E-X." He spelled the word like the five-month-old had any clue what he was talking about.

"That's about as true as me never getting a peek behind the curtain into your sex life with one of my best friends. Oh, wait." Jordan snapped her fingers. "I've read *every one* of Maddey's books. She may write fiction, but you *can't* tell me you didn't inspire some of those scenes when you guys dated."

Ryan blushed but smartly stayed quiet.

Rocky wanted to help him, but knew if she did the focus would fall back on her. It was an actual miracle the whole Gage revelation hadn't been talked about more. She had no idea how to begin to process her feelings on being faced with her celebrity crush in real life. So for now, mum's the word.

"Now come on, sexy husband of mine. Let's go have some hot shower sex while other people take care of our children for us. I gotta stock up now, since I have to catch the red-eye to Chicago tomorrow after your game." Jordan made sure she spoke loud enough for her brother to hear just to torture him as she and Jake walked away.

"Chicago?" Becky asked Ryan.

"I thought Skye was doing all the travel lately to give Jor more time home with the girls?" Rocky added.

"She is. But Tuck has an interview and photoshoot with some magazine. You know she wouldn't miss anything important involving her BB3." Jake's best friend had declared himself Jordan's "third big brother" back in college and the nickname had stuck.

"Plus," Ryan continued, "there's also the issue of Tuck trying to get Skye back in bed anytime he sees her since she slipped and slept with him after the wedding."

Becky sputtered her sip of wine.

"Your sister's wedding? The one that was more than a year ago? That wedding?" Becky asked incredulously.

"That would be the one."

Wow.

Tucker and Skye had had an on-again-off-again friends with benefits situation during their junior year of college, but as far as any of them knew, Tuck hadn't been successful in talking his way back into Skye's panties since. Guess her friend had been holding out on them.

As if reading her mind, Ryan said, "To be fair, she only recently confided in Jordan when she asked her if she could handle anything to do with their Fire clients. I'm sure it would have come up at your next Coven meeting."

"You guys always make us sound so official. Maybe we should get business cards made," Becky quipped.

"You guys do have matching tattoos." He pointed to the small black witch's hat all the girls had tattooed on their right wrists.

"All right." Rocky passed off the sleeping baby to Becky. "Let's get you checked out. I still have to go into the city for your brother. You guys are so high maintenance."

"You love us."

And she did. Other things in her life may not be settled, but as long as she had her friends, everything else would work itself out in the end. Even if her friends were *just* this side of crazy.

Chapter Seven

G age was a goal-oriented person and he had never been more torn in his life.

Make a living as a professional fighter? Start training with Tony.

Be the best in his weight class? Train and work himself up the ranks until he took the belt.

Remain the champ? Avoid all distractions and work through any lingering pain from a past injury.

He had the second part of the equation down to a science, it was the first part giving him issues.

Rocky—AKA the ultimate distraction.

As badly as he wanted to get to know her, the next couple of weeks were spent with him getting his affairs in order from his cross-country move. Besides a handful of times their paths crossed when he stopped by The Steele Maker for mainte-nance workouts, they didn't get to spend much time together.

When they'd first met, he thought it would be his libido that would be the problem since his attraction for her was off the charts, but instead it was the overwhelming curiosity he had about her—her favorite movie, how she took her coffee, even the random things, like if she put her socks on left to right.

It was a problem. A big, *big* problem.

He'd been staying in his cousin's guest room, helping Wyatt and Beth get the nursery in order for when the baby was born. The day before his first meeting with Vic Steele, the broker he'd hired had closed on a three-bedroom condo for him. He'd been so caught up in the other aspects of his life that he hadn't even seen the place aside from pictures and a video tour. He hadn't been interested in spending time furnishing the place, so he hired a firm and called it a day.

He'd opted to sell his place in California furnished instead of dealing with shipping everything across the country. Without even a bed to his name, he had to wait for the decorators to finish doing their thing to be able to move in.

Today was that day.

First though, he had to survive his initial training session with Vic. He was pretty sure he was going to get his ass kicked by his new coach, but at least he'd get to spend the entire day around Rocky. That was a win, even if he knew better.

Becky was leaning against the reception desk, drinking a coffee from an Espresso Patronum to-go cup and talking to Lyle when he walked inside The Steele Maker.

"Hey there, handsome." Lyle greeted him with a full-body scan. He had grown accustomed to the coffee shop owner's flirtatious banter. He'd had the honor of meeting his husband, Kyle, the other day, and *entertaining* seemed too tame of a word to describe the encounter.

"I didn't realize you made deliveries," he said.

"He doesn't," Rocky said, coming from the back of the gym. The sight of her made his body hum. "He only does it so he has an excuse to watch you guys work out."

Damn, the girl did amazing things for athletic wear. She wore snow white leggings, with mesh sections giving a peek at the skin beneath and tempting him with thoughts of how easy it would be to rip through a particular spot on her upper thigh.

He could see the straps of a matching white sports bra in the wide collar of the loose, black, long-sleeved crop top. He laughed when he read the white writing on her shirt—"Run like you're late for Platform 9 3/4." It was clear Lyle wasn't the only Harry Potter fan in the bunch. It also served as a reminder of yet another thing they had in common.

Her long hair was restrained in a high ponytail and when she smiled up at him while accepting the coffee offering from Lyle, he swore his heart skipped a beat.

What is she doing to me?

He cast a look around the gym. Aside from the handful of paying customers in the regular workout area, he didn't see any of the other guys he knew trained full-time.

"Lyle's visit is a little premature today. When he found out you would be sparring later, he may have gotten a *tad* excited." Becky held her thumb and index finger less than an inch apart.

"Can you blame me?" Lyle said with a sigh, making both girls laugh.

"Behave, Lyle, but thanks for the coffee." Rocky held up the paper cup in her hand. "Don't mess with my guys. Just sit there with Beck and keep the catcalling to a minimum." She nodded for Gage to follow. "Come on, Gage. Let's get your stuff settled in the locker room."

He liked being considered one of her guys, regardless of his warnings to himself, but he still hadn't worked out his feelings on where he stood on the rest of the people he would train with.

He hadn't been around on a consistent schedule the last couple of weeks, mostly doing his maintenance workouts by himself. Working out here sporadically had afforded him the opportunity to observe the six other full-time guys and he still wasn't sure how he would fit in to such a close-knit group. Something like that was completely out of his wheelhouse.

After ditching his bag and hoodie in the locker room, he met Rocky in the hallway and they headed back to the main area.

"Do you want me to wrap your hands for you?" She nodded toward the black Mexican-style wraps he held.

"Sure." He'd take any opportunity to have her hands on him, clearly a glutton for punishment.

They stopped at the empty boxing ring. He tossed one of the wraps down inside it while handing her the other before resting back on the edge of the ring. He braced his feet hip-width apart, allowing her enough space to step inside while she worked, her proximity bringing the blueberry scent he was growing familiar with.

When his leg brushed against the outside of hers, she surprised him by leaning into the contact. It wasn't as if she avoided him when he'd stopped by lately, but she wasn't as *warm* with him as she was with the others. He chalked it up to her having history with them, but again, he had no idea how the group dynamics worked.

She took one of his hands in both of hers, slipping the thumb loop on his finger before wrapping down his wrist and up his hand, the ease with which she worked speaking to years of experience.

"You nervous about today?" There was a mischievous glint in her gray eyes.

"I thought I wasn't, but something makes me think maybe I should be."

Her head dropped as she giggled, the sound way more adorable than he would have expected. Adorable? Really? Puppies were adorable, babies even. *The word you're looking for is sexy. You're losing it, man.* At least he wasn't saying it out loud.

"You'll be *fine*." The way she said the word fine didn't boost his confidence. "Just be prepared to really be put through the paces."

She finished wrapping his hand, her thumb smoothing across the long section of Velcro to secure it. Before she could release him completely, he reversed the position, running his thumb along the sensitive skin on the inside of her wrist and over the ink he spotted there.

"What's it mean?" he asked, continuing to trace the miniature witch's hat, her arm trembling slightly in his hold.

"It-It's kind of like a friendship bracelet, except, you know, permanent."

"The Coven?" He recalled the nickname he'd heard used to describe her friends.

Her mouth, her tempting as hell mouth that he wanted to kiss, tipped into a smile. "Yeah. The guys thought they were funny calling us that, instead, we ran with it. There's six of us that have it now. Though we're not actual witches, like Wiccan. Just a group of girlfriends."

He couldn't say how long they stood like that, her hand in his, before the sound of the front door opening and the voices of the other guys rang out.

The spell broken, she reached for the other wrap and his unwrapped hand and set to work repeating the process. Not wanting to lose *all* the intimacy they'd started to build, he placed his wrapped hand on the curve of her hip and her eyes widened at the action.

It wasn't inappropriate contact, anyone looking would think it was a comfortable place to rest it while she finished on the other.

It was what they *couldn't* see that would raise a few questions. His thumb stroked across the silky skin of her toned stomach, hidden by the edge of her cropped top. He took immense pleasure in the way her breathing hitched and her pupils dilated at his touch.

It was nice to know the feelings were reciprocated, even if things would be far less complicated for him if they weren't.

HE WAS TOUCHING her.

Gage was touching her.

And she liked it.

Rocky forced herself to concentrate on the pattern of weaving the hand wrap between Gage's large fingers and over his knuckles and not on the flash of heat she felt from his thumb exploring her stomach.

She reminded herself he was a fighter and she *did not* date fighters. Even if the rough calluses on his fingers did feel delicious. She needed to find herself a new celebrity crush *immediately*. It was the only way she could relegate him into the same category as the other guys she worked with.

She'd never been more grateful to hear Nick and Damon —the gym's two Boston-born fighters—arguing about how the Bruisers were the superior team in the NHL. Fan loyalties ran deep, regardless of having friends who played for other teams.

Talking. Talking would be good. It would give her something to focus on besides how badly she wanted to know what it would feel like to be carried off by Gage. His large stature was giving her all sorts of ideas about what it would finally feel like to be dainty.

"You know…" A thought came to her as she finished off the last layers of his wrap. "I don't think I ever asked where you've been staying since you made the move out here. Are you staying in a hotel? Renting something?"

Those almost fake-looking bright blue eyes locked onto her with an intensity she hadn't had much experience with. She shivered beneath his gaze.

"I've been staying with my cousin, but I'm actually moving into my place after I finish here today. It'll be the first time I'm even seeing the place in person but it's not too far from here."

"Oh, yeah? Where?" She finished securing the wrap and stepped back, needing to put some distance between them.

"It's a condo in a building called The Hightower."

Her eyebrows flew up. *No fucking way.* "You're shitting me, right?"

He chuckled at her shocked response, his own brows creating a harsh slash on his forehead in confusion. "Umm...*no*?"

"I live in The Hightower." She pointed to her chest. He looked at it. She should stop encouraging him to look at her boobs. But she kinda didn't want to.

"You do?"

"Yeah." She nodded. "Actually, most of us do. I share a place with Beck and Gem. Vince, Ray, and Deck live across the hall from us."

It was his turned to look stunned.

She missed the weight of his hand when it lifted from her hip to grab the back of his neck. She had no complaints, however, on the way the move made his biceps pop.

She would have thought learning he would be around people he knew—albeit not that well yet—would be a good thing, but the longer she studied him, the more it seemed the opposite was the case. His fingers continued to knead the back of his neck and his jaw was clenched so tight she could practically hear his molars grinding.

"What are the odds?" she said more to herself as a memory worked its way to the surface. There was a third apartment on the floor where they all lived, and over the last few weeks, she recalled seeing various pieces of furniture delivered.

"I guess pretty good since it's close by."

"Good point," she agreed, picking up her coffee. "Your place doesn't happen to be on the twelfth floor, is it?"

"I think so...I bought 12C."

"No shit." Her responses were stuck on repeat. *God, why do you hate me?* It was bad enough she would have to work with him five days a week, now she'd be seeing him in the elevator and hallway at home too. She was only human. How much temptation was she supposed to endure?

"Why do you look like your favorite contestant just got eliminated from *Dancing with the Stars*?" her brother asked, his tatted arm draping around her shoulders as he joined them.

"Looks like we can officially rename the twelfth floor The Steele Maker floor." She hooked a thumb at Gage. "Turns out Gage was the one to buy 12C."

"Ahh...no wonder they were so tight-lipped about who bought it," Vince observed. "You done here?" He nodded his head toward Gage.

"Yup," she answered, automatically reaching for the Spider-Man hand wraps her man-child of a brother chose for the day.

"Good." She went through the same dance with Vince as she had with Gage, except her brother didn't give her butter-flies like Gage did—which was good, because that would be illegal.

"I think you need to 'work' with Griff today," Vince said with air quotes. "He's kind of a mess over tonight."

Their group had plans to see the girl Griff had been dating spin at a club in New Brunswick. The relationship was rela-tively new and Griff was kind of a basket case over it.

"Of course." She dropped his hand. "What would you boys do without me?" Sure, the gym wasn't her first choice of employment, but there were moments that more than made up for the compromise she made.

"We'd be *lost* without you, that's for sure." Sarcasm dripped from her brother's words and she rolled her eyes.

"Yeah, yeah, yeah. Whatever you say, bro." She took him

by the shoulders and pointed him to the front of the gym. "Now you two go warm up on the treadmills and let me do my job."

She glanced at Gage one more time, unable to read the expression on his face as he watched her and Vince interact. It wouldn't be the first time a person couldn't figure them out. Though talkative earlier, he hadn't said a word since her larger-than-life brother joined them.

He seemed to hesitate, rolling back his shoulders, shaking out his now wrapped hands, before he followed her directive and headed for the treadmills with her brother.

⚜

Training with the Steele brothers was no joke. Gage used a towel to wipe the sweat from his face, sucking down water like a camel in the desert. He wondered what he did in the past to piss Tony off enough to be subjected to this torture. He'd thought Tony pushed him to his limits training, but his old trainer had nothing on the force these two were.

"Come on, Kraken, get your ass back in the ring and show me what you got. Lord knows your boxing skills could use some work." Mick used the fighting moniker Gage had earned by being one of the best grapplers in the sport. Almost all of his fights ended in a submission of his opponent. One of the perks of the long limbs his height afforded him.

Dropping the empty water bottle to the light purple mat inside the boxing ring, he retook his position across from where Mick held up the mitts used as targets for his punches.

"One," Mick called out the command for a jab.

Gage, a southpaw, struck out fast with his left hand, hitting the mitt with a loud *swack*.

"One-two," Mick called for the double hit of a jab then a cross.

Again, out with his left hand first, then crossing his right across his body, he hit the same target back-to-back.

"One-two-three." The call for the jab-cross-hook combo came without delay.

This time when he swung his left arm out and around for the hook, instead of letting the punch hit the mitt, Mick ducked down to avoid the punch like he would in a fight.

"Good." Mick held the mitts back in position. "One-two-three-four."

Lightning fast, he completed the punch combination with an uppercut hitting so hard that Mick raised up on his toes to help absorb the blow.

"Much better. We'll make a boxer out of you yet," Mick praised him before running him through the paces for another fifteen minutes.

"One."

Jab.

"Three."

Hook.

"Two-three."

Cross-hook.

"One. One-two."

Jab. Jab-cross.

"Two-four."

Cross-uppercut.

"One-two-three-four."

Jab-cross-hook-uppercut.

Over and over, Mick called out different variations of the punches for him to complete.

By the time he stopped calling combinations, Gage's arms felt like overcooked spaghetti. The one advantage to boxing was it gave his hip a small reprieve. The pivoting worked it but was nowhere near the strain on his recovering joint the way Brazilian jiu-jitsu and Muay Thai were.

He was uncapping a new bottle of water when he heard

Vic call out to Rocky. His eyes tracked across the gym to find her working with Griff.

He wasn't sure yet how he was supposed to integrate with such an established group, but the guy must be nice since Rocky hadn't stopped smiling the entire day. And yes, he'd noticed. He noticed way more about her than he should.

Your focus is shit, man. Your title is all that matters. Not a girl.

He should probably be concerned with how often he had been scolding himself in third person.

Yet he still couldn't take his eyes off her.

From around the gym, a chorus of laughter rang out as the guys watched Griff jump to his feet after being taken down by a leg sweep from Rocky. The bear of a man bowed like the whole thing was planned.

"What's up, Dad?" Rocky joined her father next to the boxing ring. He didn't miss the heated look in her eye as she watched him finish off another bottle of water. Those looks from her made it impossible for him to curb his attraction.

"I know you brought it up at the beginning of Vince's camp, but are you really able to tell all his moves before he makes them?" Vic asked.

Once again, he was happy to note it took her a few seconds *too* long to focus on her father's question instead of him.

"Not *all* of his moves," she said with a shake of her head. "Only his takedowns. His punches and kicks are fine, which is probably why we haven't discussed this the last few weeks. *But* when he goes into one of his takedown moves, I've noticed a tell."

"Okay." Vic was silent for a long while before he spoke. "Get in the ring with your brother so we can get it on tape. I need you guys elevated to get a better read on things myself," he instructed.

A beautiful smile stretched across her face, as she was clearly excited for what she was about to do. "Hey, Beck," she called out to her friend at the front of the gym. "Can you get me Peter Parker and Jimmy Olsen, please?"

Using the ropes, she hoisted herself onto the ring, and he certainly did not stare at her ass as she bent between the upper and middle rope to enter the ring. *Lies.*

When he saw Becky setting up a camera on a tripod, then walking over to hand a GoPro to Rocky, he understood the references to the popular comic book photographers. He may not have spent a ton of time at this gym yet, but he'd already learned how much their group loved nicknames and super-heroes. Hell, earlier he was admiring Vince's sleeve of Marvel- and DC-inspired ink.

He watched, enthralled, as Rocky removed her loose top, leaving her clad in her matching snowy leggings and sports bra. The outfit highlighted the way her waist nipped in. She hung the shirt over the ropes and walked out to take position across from her brother.

The white of her outfit contrasted against her olive complexion and the vibrantly colored tattoo that ran along the left side of her body. He needed to get a closer look at the artwork, but even from a distance, it was striking. Almost as lovely as the canvas it was inked on.

He probably should move from the corner he was standing in, but he couldn't bring himself to as he watched her clip the GoPro camera to the edge of her sports bra so it sat on the swell of her right breast.

"Beck, let me know when you can see all of Vin on the feed," Rocky said, adjusting the camera on her bra, causing the mouth-watering, motorboat-inspiring cleavage to jiggle.

He bit back a groan as he imagined sliding his dick between the plump curves. *Fuck! Now is not the time to be thinking with your dick. You're at work, man.*

Becky called out directions to both Steele siblings as she watched the camera feed on the iPad in her hands. Once the GoPro camera angle was set, she set up the tripod cam. By shooting this way, they were able to capture both the outside and opponent views of Vince's tells.

"You're going down this time, sis," Vince taunted, prowling around his side of the ring.

"Whatever helps you sleep at night, *bro*. I can read you like one of Maddey's books." She buffed her nails on her chest.

The two circled each other, Vince bouncing on his feet like he would in a fight, but time after time, Rocky was able to call out the move while stepping out of reach before he could make contact.

The longer they worked, the more creative Vince's mumbled curses became. When they were finally done, the siblings were laughing, with Vince pulling Rocky in for a noogie.

"Damn good eye, kid. Damn good," Vic praised Rocky as she jumped down from the ring. A proud smile she'd sure as hell earned lit her face.

THROUGHOUT THE DAY, Rocky constantly found herself drifting off as she watched Gage train with her father and uncle. Even now, while working on the weakest of his specialties—if you could say the prizefighter had a weakness—it was obvious why he'd been the reigning title holder for two years running. His movements were surprisingly graceful for a man of his size—it was almost like watching a dancer as opposed to a fighter.

She laughed as she read the text message dancing across the face of her smart watch.

YOU KNOW YOU WANNA: Take a picture. It'll last longer.

. . .

YOU KNOW YOU WANNA: *GIF of a Polaroid camera spitting out a picture*

Ignoring Becky, she went back to covertly—or maybe not so covertly—watching Gage while she worked with Griff. She told herself she was watching him in a professional capacity, but she couldn't even lie to herself about her motivations.

"We're all set for later tonight. I got everyone on the list so we don't have to wait on any lines. We have a booth in VIP and we even have comped bottle service." Griff's sentences ran together as he spoke.

"Griff. Dude. Chill." She placed a comforting hand on his biceps. "We all agreed to tonight. We got your back. So, *please*, for the love of god, relax."

She couldn't remember ever seeing her friend this out of sorts. His nervousness over their plans to see the DJ he'd been dating was a true testament to how much he liked her.

Griff was a dark, muscled bear of a man. At first glance, he looked menacing as hell, with his size and black ink covering both arms and his chest, but underneath he was more teddy than grizzly. Secretly, she loved that he was the biggest softie of the bunch.

He had been training at The Steele Maker since high school. Growing up a few towns over, it made sense for his boxing career to study under her Uncle Mick. He was now the gym's top contender for the WBC belt.

"I know. But you guys prefer to hang out at Rookies—especially when the Blizzards play—so I worry you guys will want to back out of going to a club."

He wasn't necessarily wrong. Their group spent the majority of their nights out at Rookies, a sports bar located near the BTU campus, or The Ring, where she'd first met Gage. Jordan's aunt owned Rookies, so they were able to relax in the separate, second-story bar area away from rabid fans who wanted to get too close to hockey players. That was the draw of the place, not a dislike like for a more traditional club.

"Dude, seriously. It's no big deal. Beck and I can't wait to dance. I'm hoping Gem will get done in time to come too. Make sure she's on the list just in case."

Using her distraction as they chatted, Griff attempted to pull her into a headlock. Accustomed to their group's ongoing challenge of who could get who to concede first, she went limp then struck out with her leg, taking her bear of a friend down to the mat, flat on his back.

She clucked her tongue as she looked down at her friend. "Wow. You must be more nervous about tonight than I thought. I've taken you down *twice* today."

She laughed as she offered a hand to pull him up, then turned to see if anyone else had watched her takedown.

Of course, her eyes instantly locked on Gage while he talked with Vince. *God. Why is he so sexy?*

The guy was a true test to her self-control. It didn't help that the rest of the girls had been asking for daily updates, with the two redheaded devils—the hair color more than appropriate, if you asked her—listing all the places the two of them could fool around in the gym.

And the list was long.

And *very* detailed.

Par for the course with a romance writer in the group.

They completely ignored the fact that she *didn't* date fighters. Also hooking up in the gym—a gym owned by her father—not necessarily the best of ideas.

Actually, they were the worst ones of the bunch. Relationships between members of the staff and the fighters were *strictly forbidden*. According to employment policy, she or Gage could have their contracts terminated if they were caught in a romantic relationship.

Regardless, as she caught the heated look in his cerulean

eyes as she stared at him, those butterflies that had taken up residence in her belly from his earlier touches now attacked her like the flying keys did Harry in the first *Harry Potter* movie.

She shot a furtive glance at her father, making sure he wasn't picking up on any of the tension pulsing between her and Gage. She sighed with relief when she saw his back was to them as he discussed something with her uncle.

Rocky shook her hands out to release some stress and headed toward the front desk. Maybe Becky would have some paperwork for her to work on or a new client record to review.

Luckily, her dad called for the end of training for the day. "Ready?" Becky asked, making her way over.

"Yup," she answered but turned to find her brother. "You coming to yoga today?"

Vince bent down to pick up his workout duffel. "Nah. The guys and I are gonna try and keep Griff from completely losing it before tonight."

That was probably for the best. Griff had been off all day. Being with the guys instead of going back to his own place should keep him from completely spiraling.

"All right. I guess I'll see you at home later." She turned to face Gage. "I guess you too, neighbor."

He smiled down at her with one of his panty-melting grins, his earlier unease now gone. *Damn, that thing is lethal.* "It would seem so."

She watched him exit the gym, Becky snickering next to her when she caught her checking out his ass. She may be adamant on her stance on not dating a fighter, but it didn't mean she couldn't objectify his buns of steel.

Yoga had always been one of her favorite ways to work out. It kept her limber and toned and helped her muscles recover from the tougher sessions she put her body through.

She also figured it was good to practice what she preached to the guys.

For the next hour, she pushed all thoughts of tempting fighters from her mind and focused on finding her Zen while bending her body like a pretzel.

Chapter Eight

Rocky loved living with her cousin and best friend. Having her brother right across the hall was another perk she'd come to cherish over the years.

After living at home his freshman year at BTU, Vince had convinced all the parents to invest in the two apartments, covering the mortgage as they would have room and board. They had taken over the mortgage payments now that they all had real jobs, but even those weren't that bad thanks to the generous down payment the parents had made combined with splitting the cost between multiple roommates.

Though the rest of their gym crew didn't live in the building, they did spend a lot of time there. Even now Griff, Nick and Damon were over at the guys' place while they waited for her and Becky to finish getting ready.

She bumped up the volume to Alexandra Stan's "Mr. Saxobeat" as she made her way into the open concept living room, getting into the proper mindset with one of her older favorite Jersey club songs.

Bopping along to the music, she joined Becky where she worked on mixing up a batch of margaritas at the kitchen island, the two of them lost in their own private dance party.

"Hey, Rock, can you go over to the guys' place and see if they have tequila? We're out."

Her head snapped up. "*You and I* are out of tequila?"

Blasphemy.

Tequila was a major food group, along with pizza and mac and cheese—those usually reserved for Coven nights, since most of the guys in their lives needed to follow a strict diet to maintain peak athletic performance.

"It would seem so."

"Wow, that's like a crime against nature."

Becky laughed but couldn't deny the fact.

"Sure, be right back."

She let herself into Vince's apartment. The doors to both apartments were rarely locked when they were home— maybe too many *Friends* reruns?—and everyone came and went as they pleased. She wondered how Gage would feel about it now that he would be living down the hall from all their crazy. She'd been picking up a vibe that he was not about this life. She smiled a little, knowing how little choice he would have in the matter.

Boundaries was not a word in their group's vocabulary.

"Hey, losers, we need tequila."

Ray looked up from where he was playing Mario Kart with Nick on the couch. "You two are out of tequila? Isn't that a crime against nature or something?"

She laughed and offered him a fist bump. "That's *exactly* what I said." She loved Ray. When he first started coming around the gym with Vince during their freshman year at BTU, she instantly took a liking to the Chicago native.

"There should be some Patrón Silver in the bar in the living room," Deck said as he came out of his bedroom. He was putting his shirt on but paused when he caught sight of her. "Not really sure the pajama look is dress code appropriate, even if they are Ninja Turtles."

"Ha ha." She flipped him off on her way to the bar.

"Do you guys need much longer to get ready?" Vince asked from the kitchen.

"Nope, just need to change."

"Okay, great," Griff said from where he sat in the living room, playing with his phone. "I'm going to order the Ubers in about an hour."

Tequila bottle in hand, she gave Griff a thumbs-up and caught Deck staring at her butt as she rose. "Get your eyes off my ass, Deck."

The guys laughed and Vince smacked his childhood friend upside the head. "Dude. She's practically your sister. Gross."

"Anyway…" She held up the tequila bottle. "Margaritas will be ready in five. Whoever wants to partake, you know where to find them." She headed out their front door.

As she stepped into the hallway, she heard the chime of the elevator. Her heart rate doubled.

Gage.

WITH THE MAJORITY of work taken care of by his decorator, Gage didn't have much to move into his new place. Wyatt and two of his buddies from the firehouse helped so it only took them about an hour to finish moving the few boxes he'd kept with him, then he'd treated them to dinner at a local burger joint as a thank you.

The guys from the gym had invited him out with them for the night, but he'd declined because Wyatt was about to start another twenty-four hour shift at the firehouse and he wanted the move complete so he could unpack over the weekend. And yet he still hadn't managed to shake the overwhelming sense of disappointment from missing out on an opportunity to spend time with Rocky outside of work. A fact he shouldn't even be focused on, but he couldn't help himself. She settled something inside him he wasn't even aware was unsettled.

Sometimes adulting sucked major donkey balls.

He must have been thinking about Rocky more than he realized because he swore he heard her voice. Shaking himself out of his daydream, he turned toward the door of his new place.

"Howdy, neighbor." She gave a playful wave from down the hall.

And there it was again, that comforting feeling like being swaddled in a warm blanket. How the hell did she manage it without doing anything? Maybe there was something to be said about the whole dating thing, after all.

As his head and heart warred with each other, he took a moment to take in what she was wearing. Were those Ninja Turtles on her pants?

"Did you finish moving all your stuff?" she asked.

"I did," he said with a nod. "Then I took the guys out for burgers."

"Go anywhere good?"

Conversations were easy with her, like they had been friends forever. He was used to people acting like they knew him because of his celebrity status, but she came across as if she couldn't care less he was the Heavyweight Champ. That made sense since she was friends with a number of professional athletes.

"They took me to a place called Jonah's. It was a bit of a drive but it was the best damn burger I've had in my life." It was probably a good thing she stood down the hall from him. The caramelized onions on his burger were delicious but he doubted they did anything for his breath.

Her eyes flashed silver as she smiled. "Oh, yeah, Jonah's is amazeballs. Anytime we played the U of J we would go there to eat after." She paused for a moment before asking, "Do you want to come out with us tonight?"

The guys had made it sound like they were going clubbing when they extended the invite to him earlier. Even if he hadn't legitimately had plans, he wasn't sure he would have accepted the invitation. He would never admit it out loud, but he was a little intimidated by the sheer number of people in their squad. Who needed that many friends anyway?

He took in her appearance. Her long dark hair hung around her shoulders and down her back in loose waves. Her makeup was done up in that smoky way girls did to make their eyes pop and her lips were blood red. She was fucking breathtaking.

But the artfully done makeup didn't match what she had going on below the neck.

"And where exactly are you going that pajamas are an acceptable choice of wardrobe?"

She giggled, the sound like a flashlight, lighting up the darkest parts of him. "You boys are all so literal. I still have to change, I was only wearing this while I got ready. *Anyway…* we're going to one of the local clubs. Griff is dating one of the DJs and we're going to hear her spin. He said he's gonna book the Ubers in about an hour, so if you want to come, you should have enough time to get ready."

He couldn't deny the opportunity to hang out with her tonight a second time. Plus, it would give him the chance to get to know his teammates in a social setting, hopefully eliminating some of the pressure he felt on being welcomed. The fighters of The Steele Maker were like a family and he was a little surprised to find himself wanting to be included.

"Sure, I just need a few to shower and change. Whose door should I knock on when I'm ready?"

"You don't have to knock, the doors will be open. It's easier when we are floating back and forth between places constantly."

"All right, sounds like a plan." He turned to his condo to prepare himself—in more ways than one—for the night out.

Once inside, he headed straight for the shower in his master bath. It was one of his favorite features about the place

—it was huge and, like the Jacuzzi tub next to it, could easily fit four people. He was a big guy and liked anything that didn't make him feel claustrophobic.

He turned on the water and almost immediately, the room started to fill with steam. He stripped his workout clothes off and stepped under the huge rain shower faucet. The wall jets massaged his back for a few minutes while the tension from the day drained away.

Remarkably, his hip wasn't giving him any issues, but he would pop a few Advil before heading out for the night. Vic's warning played a constant loop in his mind.

As he washed, the realization that Rocky was down the hall hit home. He had been drawn to her from the first moment he saw her at The Ring. She was like the light to his dark with her bubbly personality sparkling over his own reserve. At the core though, he recognized their similarities—she approached her job with the same determination he did his, striving to be the best.

She was the daughter of his new coach. Not the *smartest* choice for the first girl he had more than a passing interest in.

His hands ran over his abs as the image of her exotic gray eyes looking up at him in pleasure filled his mind. He could imagine how her cupid's bow mouth—painted blood red like earlier—would spread into a smile as she kissed her way down his body. She would continue her assault until she was on her knees in front of him. He groaned out loud and his hand wrapped around his hardening cock to relieve some of the building pressure.

The only way he was going to make it through dancing with her at a club, feeling her body pressed against him, moving in time with his, would be if he got rid of the tension he was feeling now.

He let the fantasy play out in his mind, stroking himself from root to tip and back again.

He watched her open her mouth as wide as it would go to

accept his girth. His head slipped past her lips and she let out her own moan of pleasure. She braced herself with one hand on his thigh, the other around the base of his cock, as she took as much of him down her throat as she could handle. He let her play for as long as he could stand, then threaded his fingers through her long, blue-black locks to maneuver her how he needed.

His soapy hand continued to move up and down his cock in sync with the image of her sliding it in and out of her mouth. He reached his peak, spraying his seed against the shower's tiles at the same time he spilled down her throat in his fantasy, her name echoing in the acoustics of the space as he came.

He stroked himself until he was completely spent. Grabbing the body wash off the shelf for the second time, he turned the water to cold and finished his shower.

Chapter Nine

H oly shit.
Holy shit.
Holy shit.

Did I really just initiate hanging out with Gage outside of work?

Rocky's mind was spinning as she went back into her apartment. Making a beeline for the kitchen island and not waiting for the margaritas, she took a shot of tequila straight from the bottle.

She was going to need a moment to wrap her brain around what she had just done.

She was going to need reinforcements.

ALPHABET SOUP: HELP!!!

ALPHABET SOUP: *GIF of Harry Potter saying "Help Me."*

• • •

MOTHER OF DRAGONS: What do you need girl?

PROTEIN PRINCESS: Please tell me this has to do with our newest neighbor?

YOU KNOW YOU WANNA: O

YOU KNOW YOU WANNA: M

YOU KNOW YOU WANNA: G

YOU KNOW YOU WANNA: Did you guys just have a quickie?

ALPHABET SOUP: What? No. Geez

YOU KNOW YOU WANNA: Well that's disappointing

YOU KNOW YOU WANNA: You should have

YOU KNOW YOU WANNA: It would have been good

YOU KNOW YOU WANNA: I can tell these things

· · ·

MOTHER OF DRAGONS: Duuuuude!!!!! I have 5 month old twins. You REALLY need to learn how to get to the point in a SINGLE text. You're killing me Beck *facepalm emoji* *water gun emoji*

ALPHABET SOUP: *GIF of girl saying "Same"*

ALPHABET SOUP: God *facepalm emoji* it's so much worse being able to see you while you text a million times

PROTEIN PRINCESS: Wait up! Gage is there with you guys?

YOU KNOW YOU WANNA: OMG OMG OMG

YOU KNOW YOU WANNA: Madz it's like perfect plot point for your next book

YOU KNOW YOU WANNA: It's like one of those accidental roommates books

YOU KNOW YOU WANNA: *GIF of Beyonce pointing to her temple*

PROTEIN PRINCESS: *GIF from the *Sandlot* saying "You're killing me Smalls"*

• • •

YOU KNOW YOU WANNA: Ok ok. Geez guys

ALPHABET SOUP: And no, Gage is not here right now but I did a thing

YOU KNOW YOU WANNA: You kissed him?

YOU KNOW YOU WANNA: He kissed you?

YOU KNOW YOU WANNA: He shoved you against a wall to kiss you?

YOU KNOW YOU WANNA: You touched his penis?

MAKES BOYS CRY: Madz when you are done with your edits and you turn your phone back on, you for reals NEED to teach this girl how to stick to one storyline

PROTEIN PRINCESS: Beck will you shut up for a minute so Rock can tell us what she did

MAKES BOYS CRY: *GIF of guy pointing up saying "This, all this."*

ALPHABET SOUP: I invited Gage to come out with us tonight

• • •

MOTHER OF DRAGONS: *GIF of Barney Stinson saying WHHAAAAATT?!*

MAKES BOYS CRY: *GIF of Minion saying WHHAAAAATT?!*

MOTHER OF DRAGONS: ^^And this is why we're best friends

PROTEIN PRINCESS: *GIF of Joey Tribbiani looking shocked*

MAKES BOYS CRY: Rock, guuurrrrllll, you finally better be doing something about this. I mean look at all this.

MAKES BOYS CRY: *GIF of Gage flexing in his fighting briefs*

PROTEIN PRINCESS: Damn now I'm so mad I can't make it out tonight *angry face emoji*

MOTHER OF DRAGONS: This almost makes me want to call Maddey's landline and fill her in... ALMOST... Rocky what are you going to do about it?

YOU KNOW YOU WANNA: What I really want to know is does this mean you're finally going to forget about your 'no dating a fighter' policy and do something?

MAKES BOYS CRY: Yeah Rocky... Tell us

• • •

PROTEIN PRINCESS: Cuz, where you at?

ALPHABET SOUP: I need new friends. You guys are ridiculous

MOTHER OF DRAGONS: No you don't. You love us

MAKES BOYS CRY: Plus we have matching tats, so we're yours for life

MOTHER OF DRAGONS: True story

YOU KNOW YOU WANNA: Plus we've been friends since like birth so you've been stuck with me for 24 years already, so that's not changing anytime soon

ALPHABET SOUP: Dude why are you texting me. You're standing like 5 feet away from me

YOU KNOW YOU WANNA: You're doing it too

YOU KNOW YOU WANNA: Plus I know they will all support me saying you should go for it with Gage

• • •

MOTHER OF DRAGONS: Hell yeah. You should go for it. Remember… I didn't date hockey players anymore and yet I'm married to one

MAKES BOYS CRY: Well, as much as I love Jake and all, you don't have to marry the guy Rock. But I do think you should take that Stallion for a ride

PROTEIN PRINCESS: Seriously, cuz. Who else gets their celebrity crush put in front of them? You should go for it

YOU KNOW YOU WANNA: See???

YOU KNOW YOU WANNA: They agree with me.

YOU KNOW YOU WANNA: Bang that boy like a screen door in a hurricane

ALPHABET SOUP: OMG I'm not doing this. See you all tomorrow for yoga.

Putting her phone away, she grabbed a margarita and went to her room to get dressed.

As usual, she was the first one ready. Going next door to corral the guys, she found a few of them locked in a fierce Mario Kart battle.

"I'll be out in the hall when you guys *finally* stop playing with your toys," she said with an eye roll.

She was double checking her clutch to make sure she had everything she needed for the night out when she heard Gage's door open then close.

She stared at him while the rest of their group came into the hallway. She would think that after seeing him in his workout gear at the gym, nothing would look better. But the way the dark jeans hugged his muscular thighs and the rolled-up sleeves of his black shirt displayed the black tattoo on his powerful forearm, she'd clearly underestimated things in that department.

He was sex on legs, ridiculously tall, long, muscular legs.

And, yup.

Now she was wet.

Damn her friends for putting ideas in her head.

Crazy ideas.

Dirty ideas.

Ideas she longed to fulfill.

She was so screwed.

GAGE STEPPED FROM his apartment, locking the door behind him as the rest of the people from the gym filtered out of their respective doors, talking about their plans for the evening. The first person he saw was Rocky and the sight of her damn near knocked him on his ass.

Gone were her cute pajamas. In their place was a body-hugging, black, strapless mini dress and grayish-brown, over-the-knee cowboy-heeled boots that had buckles running up from the ankle. A lickable width of toned thigh was exposed between the top of her boots and the hem of her dress.

Shaking his head to expel some of the insta-lust coursing through his body, he used the same deep breathing techniques he did before a fight to regain his composure before he was caught staring like an idiot.

His training kicked in, and not a moment too soon because she turned and saw him standing in the hall.

"Hey there, neighbor," she said with a smile bright enough to light up a room.

"Hey yourself." He couldn't help but smile in return. "You look fantastic by the way."

An endearing blush spread across her face. "Thanks. You clean up pretty good yourself." She motioned to his clothes.

"I aim to please." He winked.

"I bet you do." Her storm cloud eyes stayed locked on his as she spoke.

Is she flirting with me? The thought pleased him more than he would have thought possible.

Clearly oblivious to the sexual tension filling the air, Griff strode over to the elevator to press the call button. "The Ubers are here. Let's head out." He was bouncing on his toes with excitement.

"Relax, lover boy, we'll be there soon enough." Nick clapped him on the shoulder.

Already feeling the first twinges below the belt, Gage was grateful for the interruption. If Rocky affected him this much just standing in a noisy hallway with her, he was in for one hell of a long night.

Dancing with her.

Feeling her lush curves under his hands.

The roundness of her ass brushing against him as they moved together might just kill him.

With a *ding*, the elevator arrived and everyone piled in. He was pretty sure this many people should have taken two trips. He moved to a back corner and Rocky followed, planting herself right in front of him as the others continued to squish in and harass Griff.

His arm snaked around her middle in an effort to adjust in the tight space. Her belly tensed as she sucked in a breath. He loved how responsive she was to a simple touch. Anytime she had to touch him for work, his body lit up like a Christmas tree, so it was only fair that it wasn't one-sided.

"*Mmm*...blueberries," he whispered against her hair as he tugged her closer, the familiar scent invading his senses.

Her whole body shuddered and she leaned back against him slightly. Even as he took her weight, he had to mentally calculate the fastest way to a takedown to keep from anything popping up without his permission.

After the longest elevator ride of his life, the doors opened and they went outside to the waiting SUVs. They split up, five in one vehicle and four in the other. Since the girls were smaller, they went with the bigger group and he made sure to join them. Becky and Rocky sat in the back row, he and Vince took the captain's chairs, and Griff rode shotgun.

Not once had they ceased in their teasing of Griff.

"Where are we going anyway?" he asked, not like he would know the place, but curious all the same.

"This club in New Brunswick called The Lounge. Simone spins there on the reg," Griff answered.

"Simone?"

"Griff's love of his life...at least for the moment," Becky said with a chuckle.

"What can I say? Deep down, I'm a hopeless romantic." Griff placed a hand over his heart.

The whole car burst out laughing and spent more time razzing on Griff.

The whole thing reminded him of how he and Wyatt were with each other. If he could keep that in mind, focusing on the individuals instead of the group as a whole, he just might be able to navigate his way around their dynamics.

"It's a nice place. Not a complete college scene. More like fifty-fifty," Vince said, shifting to face him.

"It's not our typical scene, but we do like to branch out," Becky added.

"And what would be a *typical* night out for you guys?" He

was curious about them. And not just because of his attraction to Rocky. Between home and work, it didn't seem like he was going to be spending much time away from these people.

"Well, if we want something laid back, with some good food and maybe a round of pool, we'll go to The Ring, where we first met you." And where had likely changed the trajectory of his life forever. "But if we wanna go *out* out, we go to Rookies. It's a sports bar our friends' aunt owns."

"There's a separate bar area there, so it's easy enough for us to chill," Vince said.

"Plus, it's got a little of everything—whatever sports event is currently going on playing on the TVs, alcohol, and a dance floor for when I feel like getting down with my bad self." Becky threw her arms in the air, dancing in her seat.

"I can't take you anywhere, Beck," Rocky said with a laugh.

"Fact. It's a *huge* risk taking her out without the rest of The Coven, that's for sure," Vince quipped.

"You guys talk about 'The Coven'"—he put air quotes around the name—"all the time. When do I get to meet the rest of them?"

"Bro. No," Vince warned with a smile. "You want to avoid a gathering for *as long* as humanly possible. Enjoy your freedom while it lasts, because the six of them are going to *rule* your life."

"Don't be melodramatic, Vin," Rocky scolded.

"You trying to tell me Jordan doesn't run a tight ship?"

"No. But you act like we control *everything* in your life. It's only professionally you have to listen to us."

"Yet you guys are like puppet masters, pulling the strings behind the scene."

Rocky shrugged, neither confirming nor denying the accusation.

"Besides, Vin," Becky cut in. "Has she not helped you

make an *insane* amount of money in endorsements *before* you even have a belt?"

"No, you're right. I bow down to the master." Vince mock-bowed in his seat. "Maybe having Gage joining the gym will help tip the scales in our favor."

Hearing how easily they accepted him into the fold both thrilled and terrified him.

Chapter Ten

A few minutes later, their Uber driver was pulling up to a curb, letting them out to meet up with the guys from the other car. The line outside the nondescript black building was half a block deep waiting to get in. They bypassed the line and within moments a hostess greeted them and quickly showed them to a private table section in the back.

Keeping the two girls between them, they made their way through the already crowded dance floor without much issue.

Everyone settled into the couches in the seating area of their roped off section and gave their drink orders to their server for the night. Gage watched Griff smile when Rocky pointed out that they were right next to Simone's DJ booth, waving when he caught her eye.

This club wasn't bad, even if he normally preferred a low-key bar like they talked about earlier.

The Lounge had a simple setup—a bar on either side of the large dance floor, with private seating areas like theirs scattered along the edges. The place was packed and the dance floor bumping. Griff's DJ knew how to get the crowd going. He was sure his ears would be ringing when they left, but at least he wasn't stuck listening to bad house music. He considered it a win.

Like in the car and at the gym, conversation and jokes flowed easily amongst the group. He attempted to weave in occasionally but was content on the outskirts.

Shortly after the server brought their next round of drinks, he noticed a couple big guys pointing at them then heading in their direction.

"Yo, Rock," one of them called.

She looked over when she heard her name called and smiled. "Dude!" she called out and much to his chagrin, she walked down to where the two men stood and hugged them.

Becky joined them by the ropes and after a brief conversation, the girls stepped down from their roped off section, the guys looped their arms around their shoulders, and all of them walked over to where they were pointing earlier.

Wasn't that interesting?

He ground a layer off his molars watching some stranger put his hands on Rocky. It didn't matter how unreasonable the reaction was. He interrupted whatever conversation Vince and Deck were having next to him. "Boyfriends?" he asked with a nod toward the foursome walking across the dance floor.

"Them?" Vince asked.

"Nah," Deck said. "They know the girls from when Rock worked with the hockey team before she graduated."

"Yeah, Rock is like the mayor of the world. Anyone who gets to know her loves her. I think before her season with the team was over, more than half the guys were ready to propose," Vince chuckled.

Gage did not feel like laughing. No, he wanted to hit something, preferable any male who made eyes at his girl.

Whoa. Hold on there, cowboy. Back up. Rocky is not your girl. Just because you're open to the possibility doesn't it make it true. So chill with the caveman urges until you have the right.

His inner monologue didn't help quell his irrational urges though. He was supremely grateful for the beer in his hand at the moment. Taking a long pull from the bottle, he tuned back into what the guys were saying.

"—even with them dating she got hit on *all* the time." Shit. He'd missed the first half of what Nick was saying.

"Yeah, but Cap kept everyone in line. He knew her instincts were too important to the team to let them be a bunch of puck heads and risk scaring her off," Damon added.

"Nah, we all know Rock can handle herself." Vince paused to take a drink of his club soda. Since he was in the middle of a training camp for a fight, he didn't mess around with alcohol or anything that might disrupt his nutrition goals. "Honestly, I'm just grateful she chose to work at the gym and didn't accept the offer she had from the Blizzards."

Gage frowned at that. It was a gut feeling, but the few times it had come up in conversation with Rocky, he had gotten the impression it wasn't what she would have chosen for herself.

Try as he might, he couldn't keep his attention from being drawn back to her. His free hand balled into a fist when he noticed she and Beck were now on the dance floor with some of the guys. He had no claim on her but he was determined to change that—as soon as possible.

He was trying to come up with a reason for joining the girls on the dance floor and interrupting their current partnerships without being too obvious, when Nick said, "Let's get out there."

Rocky and Becky greeted them with cheers. A few other girls had gravitated toward the group and he made his move behind Rocky.

His hand went to the dip of her waist and she turned around sharply when she felt his presence. Her face eased into another one of those breathtaking smiles when she realized it was him. "Hey."

"Hey." He took the chance to pull her closer to his body.

She responded by draping her arms over his shoulders, never missing a step. "Wasn't sure if you would dance."

"Why do you say that?"

"Not all guys like to dance." She shrugged. "Or really know how to move once out here, anyway."

Her luscious body brushing against his made him envision them doing the same in a more private setting, without any of these pesky clothes in the way. He knew the instant she noticed the effect she was having on his body by the widening of her eyes. Instead of pulling away, the little brat invaded his space even more and continued dancing.

He gave her a wolfish smile then proceeded to demonstrate *exactly* how skillfully he did move.

🐙

Between the alcohol and Gage's dance moves—and praise all things Channing Tatum, the guy could move—Rocky lost count of the number of songs she spent on the dance floor with him.

Her burning cheeks had nothing to do with exertion and *everything* to do with grinding herself against the apparent wreck bag he kept in his pants.

She wanted nothing more than to straddle one of his legs and grind herself on what she knew firsthand was a rock hard thigh, and she knew that was a terrible idea, so she spun away from him and let her ass do the grinding instead.

He held her with a hand on her stomach, his fingers so long they brushed the underwire band of her bra.

She loved that even with the short heel she had on, he still had more than half a foot on her. Sure, her last boyfriend was tall enough that she could wear heels around him, but it was nice to feel what most girls got to experience with guys.

Finally needing a break, everyone—along with some of

the others the guys picked up dancing—headed back to their private seating area.

Her head spun a bit—*thank you, tequila*—as she dropped to the couch next to Gage with a less than graceful plop. It was a tight squeeze of people in their little sitting area now, so she draped her legs over one of his tree trunks in a move she would have never been bold enough to make without the aid of alcohol lowering her reservations. His hand landed on her bare thigh, hot, heavy and possessive.

"Any marriage proposals tonight, Rock?" Declan ribbed.

She let out a bark of laughter and stretched out to smack him on the arm. "Shut up. You *do* know none of them actually proposed, asshole." She gave him a *get serious* look. "Besides, there is no way any of them would dare say anything like that to me with all you guys here." She circled a finger, indicating their group.

"Why? Scared of these guns?" Ray said as he flexed one of his impressive arms, straining the seams of his shirt. The guys guffawed like he was the cleverest man in the universe.

"Idiots, I swear. All of you." Her smile took all the heat out of her words.

"You guys act like you're so tough," Becky teased.

Gage was the only one not really joining in on the joking, but she couldn't expend too much brain power on the thought, too busy luxuriating in the feel of his touch.

His large hand was still cupped around her leg, his thumb stroking the skin exposed between the hem of her dress and the top of her boots. She was thankful for the padded bra she had on—otherwise the whole club would be able to see the effect he had on her.

It didn't matter how many times she reminded herself she didn't date fighters. Anytime he turned those vibrant eyes in her direction, the breath hitched in her chest at the heat banked within those blue depths.

She was so screwed.

And that wasn't even taking into account that he was technically forbidden. Gym rules.

🐙

Gage spent the night soaking up every bit of information he heard like a sponge. He even thought he did a decent job assimilating into the different discussions the group bounced between.

When they finally called it a night, Griff stayed behind to wait for Simone, Nick and Damon cabbed it home, and everyone who lived at The Hightower piled into an Uber together.

Deck rode up front with the driver, Ray and Vince took the captain's chairs, and he squeezed in the back row with the girls. It was a tight fit but he wasn't going to complain about having Rocky's body pressed tight against his for the ride home.

He'd made a decision tonight. Before they reached their destination, he leaned over to nuzzle her ear. He couldn't stop his grin when he felt her body shudder. He relished that visceral reaction from the simple brush of his lips on her skin. It settled something primal inside him.

Taking another deep inhalation of the blueberry scent he now associated with her, he whispered, "Just so you know...I have every intention of making you mine."

Chapter Eleven

Rocky shut the door to her bedroom and leaned against it. Her knees were still weak from Gage's declaration in the car. Part of her wanted to immediately reject the idea that he was serious, but instinctively she knew it was the truth.

Gage James, her celebrity crush, was one thing. She'd followed his career since he started fighting in the UFC as one of the undercard fighters.

Gage James, the man, was a whole other ball game—she didn't stand a chance.

Making her way over to her bed, she sat down to pull off her boots and socks. Pushing her bare feet into the floor to stretch them out after being propped in the short heel all night, she let out a groan of relief at the simple pleasure. There was nothing better than taking off a pair of heels after dancing most of the night away.

Standing to peel her tight dress down her body, she felt another tremor run down her spine as she replayed his growled words for the millionth time. The memory of them whispered in that gravelly, sexy voice of his gave her delicious shivers.

Reaching behind her back, she unclasped her bra and let out a shuddering breath at the memory. His. He said he was going to make her his.

She was in trouble. Big, big, six feet seven inches of panty-ruining hotness trouble.

She climbed into bed in her underwear and lay on her stomach. Her body melted into the memory foam mattress beneath her as she pulled the plush comforter up around her shoulders.

She had a feeling she was about to break the *only* rule she set for herself—no fighters.

Snapshots of the last couple of weeks flashed through her mind.

Looking up and seeing Gage at The Ring.

The way his muscles flexed and shone while sparring at the gym.

The hungry look in his eyes when he saw her dressed up for the club.

How he moved against her dancing. *God,* it was hot.

There was an almost easy possession in the way he touched her. Holding her waist, his fingers skimming up her back as they swayed, his palm pressing flat against it to eliminate the last of the space between them.

And finally, there was the vibrant fire she saw blazing in the bright blue depths of his eyes when he made his declaration in the car.

Her body heated under the covers and it had nothing to do with the down filling and everything to do with Gage. Her nipples puckered and she pulsed between her legs. Pressing her thighs together to alleviate the ache was no help. There was no way she would get any sleep without relieving the pressure.

She was so worked up from their foreplay on the dance floor, the feel of his hands on her body, stroking the bare skin of her leg while they all talked at the club, she knew it wouldn't take much to push her over the edge.

Pulling an arm from under the pillow, she worked it down her body and under the edge of her panties. She wasn't surprised to find herself already wet and swollen.

Getting right to the point, she pressed her finger to her clit. The weight of her body trapped her hand and created extra pressure for her ministrations.

She imagined Gage pinning her to the mattress. His large frame always made her feel petite.

He would keep her body tight to his, the same way he did while they danced. His hips would move back and forth, riding the curve of her ass as he worked her with his fingers.

Her own fingers mimicked the relentless pace she had a feeling he would set, her index and middle fingers pulsing one after the other in a quick rhythm.

Index-middle.

Index-middle.

Gage growling in her ear.

Index-middle.

She felt the first tremors of orgasm ripple in her belly. A few more strokes and off she went.

She continued to caress herself lightly as she came down from her high. After she was completely spent, she pulled her hand from between her thighs and wiped the moisture off on her underwear then relaxed back into the mattress.

Visions of cerulean blue eyes followed her into her dreams where the word *mine* echoed as she drifted off to sleep.

Chapter Twelve

Normally after a late night out, Gage would take it easy the next day, but he had to do something to help release the tension coursing through his body.

What did he do?

He got up and ran ten miles.

Did it help?

No, not really.

No matter what he did, he couldn't force the memories of Rocky from his mind. The way she looked in her body-hugging dress that was clearly designed to make men stupid. Or how well they moved together dancing. He could only imagine how it would feel horizontal. Hell, they didn't have to be horizontal, he had absolutely nothing against taking her pressed against the wall or bent over a table. The possibilities were endless.

Pulling the hem of his t-shirt up to wipe the sweat from his brow, he stepped onto the elevator. When the doors were closing, he heard someone call out, "Hey, hold the elevator." Instinctively, he reached out his hand.

"Thanks," the woman said with a cursory look at him

before giving him a double take. "Hi, Gage. I heard you moved in. I'm Gemma."

He looked into the familiar gray eyes. Unlike her tall cousins, Gemma Steele was average height and had shoulder-length brown hair instead of the dark blue-black. She didn't spend the same amount of time at the gym as Rocky or Becky, but he'd seen her around.

"Hey, Gemma." He hadn't met a member of the Steele family he didn't like. It was one of the things helping him ease into this new environment.

The short ride to the twelfth floor didn't allot much time for conversation. When the doors opened, he put his arm in the opening, allowing her to exit before him.

"Guess I'll be seeing you around," he said and stepped toward his apartment down the hall.

"It's practically guaranteed," she said nodding at her own place behind her. "Welcome to our house of crazy," she said before disappearing inside her apartment.

He couldn't help but laugh at how apt the name was to describe his new home.

Rocky and Becky were lounging around the apartment in their pajamas before they had to get ready for yoga class when Gemma came home.

"Hey, Gem," she called out to her cousin.

"How was last night?" Gemma asked, dropping her duffle by the door and joining them at the breakfast bar.

"Awesome."

"Pretty sure Griff is in *loooove*," Becky sing-songed.

"Still crushing on Simone?" Gemma asked.

"Oh, yeah. And let me tell you, the boy has taste. The girl looks like freaking Tyra Banks. He's got it bad," she answered.

"Well, hopefully she appreciates him for more than his body. That boy needs substance in his life," Gemma said ruefully.

It was true. He was a big teddy bear. Unfortunately for him, most women saw his killer body and didn't usually look beyond that.

"Agreed. The one plus is he told me they've talked almost non-stop for the past month," Becky said as she passed a glass of juice across the island to Gemma.

After taking a big sip from the glass, Gemma sat up straighter. She must have big news. "So...I ran into Gage on my way up just now."

"Oh, yeah?" Rocky feigned disinterest. She may have decided to break her self-imposed rule about fighters—at least for a one-time physical release—but she wasn't quite ready to share that information with the class.

"I was in the elevator with him." Gemma nodded. "God, he really is a hottie. After being around him in person, I totally get why you crushed on him for so long. Even looking like he just got back from a run, the man was *fine*."

"I still can't believe he bought 12C. Like seriously, what are the odds?" Becky pondered.

"Did you say he just got back from a run when you were coming home?" Rocky asked.

"That's what it looked like to me."

"Perfect." Going with her gut, she set her juice glass down on the counter and headed for the front door. His declaration the night before had led to one hell of a restless night's sleep. In the early morning light, before she finally drifted off, she decided that if the opportunity presented itself, she would take her friends' advice and make a move.

He was home and awake, so there was no time like the present.

Before she could lose her nerve—or remind herself of how

it felt to always come second to a bout—she raised her hand and knocked on his door.

When he opened it, she was happy to note the shock on his face quickly morphed into pleasure the longer he stared at her.

She grabbed him by the front of his sweaty blue t-shirt and pulled him down for the hottest kiss of her life. He was never going to forget her.

Chapter Thirteen

G age had just turned on the shower when he heard a knock on the front door. It had to be one of his neighbors, so he jogged back out to answer it while the water heated.

Plus, it could always be Rocky.

They were only a few weeks from Halloween, but maybe Santa had decided to bring him an early gift. He had been a *very* good boy this year.

Still, it took a few seconds for his brain to register it really *was* Rocky at his door and not a physical manifestation of his fantasies.

He took in her familiar Ninja Turtle pajama pants and green tank top and smiled. She was too damn cute for words.

Before he had a chance to say anything, she yanked him down by the collar of his shirt.

At the first crash of Rocky's pillowy lips against his, electricity sparked down his spine.

When he didn't pull away, she rose on tiptoe, threw one arm around his neck, and closed the last bit of space between them. He growled when her fingers scratched through the buzzed hair on the back of his head.

He wasn't sure if this was real or if he was still standing in his bathroom stuck in his daydream about Rocky, but he was going to go with it regardless. The feel of her soft breasts pressed against his chest was amazing, and when her nipples pebbled against him, he looped an arm around her back and dragged her inside his apartment and kicked the door shut.

He didn't speak or stop to question what was happening, too afraid to break the spell. Threading his other hand in her damp hair, he pulled slightly on the long locks, angling her better for his own assault on her mouth. He traced the seam of her lips with his tongue and was delighted when she responded by opening her mouth.

While their tongues dueled, he backed her up against the wall next to his front door. He absolutely loved how she wasn't shy in her approach and kissed him back with fervor.

After what felt like forever, yet too quick at the same time, they broke from their lip lock. Resting his forehead against hers, he tried to catch his breath, his body still pulsing from the pure lust coursing through it.

He wanted to see where things could go between them, but this was so much more than even he suspected.

Trouble. He was in big, *big* trouble.

"Damn," he whispered against her forehead.

"What's wrong?" She looked up at him, her pupils completely blown out by desire, the gray only visible in the small ring around them.

"Absolutely nothing, babe." The endearment slipped out.

He ran a hand over his head, buzzed spikes of his hair tickling his palm. "That was just better than *anything* I've been imagining it would be like since I first saw you."

More. The word continued to echo in his brain.

And that smile? It made his heart skip a beat.

"You thought about what it would be like to kiss me?"

"Only from the moment I saw you pinning that douchebag to the table at The Ring."

"Wow." She seemed to take a moment to process. "So why'd you stop?"

He ran his nose and mouth along her jaw, down her neck, pressing little kisses along the way. He enjoyed the tremors coursing through her body. He placed a kiss in the soft spot behind her ear, breathing in deep and catching the faintest scent of blueberries. He didn't move as he answered her.

"Because I can tell you are clean by how delicious you smell and the fact that your hair is still damp. I'm also hyper-aware of how gross and sweaty I am from running ten miles this morning."

"Ten miles." She squeaked as he bit down on her earlobe.

"Yup. I did it to work off some of this tension I was feeling about a certain sexy gray-eyed girl I know." He continued his sensual assault on her. "But smelling your fresh scent made me all too aware of how badly I need to take a shower myself. So to answer your question, I stopped before I made you all gross or dragged you into the shower with me."

"I wouldn't object to the latter."

He growled against her throat.

She grinned as she recaptured his mouth.

The press of her lips against his snapped the last of his control. He reached under her butt and lifted her up his body, nudging her to wrap her mile-long legs around his waist for leverage. Turning, he stalked to the bathroom.

He wasn't sure if taking a shower with her was too fast, but his inner animal was dictating the scenario for now.

ROCKY'S HEAD SPUN as Gage carried her through his apartment toward the sound of running water. He must have been planning to take the shower he claimed to need before she showed up unexpectedly at his door, if the amount of m already gathering in the bathroom was any indication.

e inside, she slid down his body, making sure to

slowly rub against each bump and ridge of muscle she felt along the way. God, he was glorious and she was about to get all up close and personal with each of them. And this time, it had *nothing* to do with professional responsibilities.

No, this time she was allowed to act on every single wicked thought she'd had during her evaluation of his Adonis body that first day at The Steele Maker. Things were about to get so dirty, even Maddey, their resident Queen of Smut, would blush when she heard about them. That was, before she decided to use it as part of her next bestseller.

She was fully on board with taking one for the team. What else were friends for?

Gage may complain about being sweaty from his run, but the way his damp t-shirt clung to his body, outlining *all* of his muscles, was so damn sexy it was probably illegal in some states.

She had just slipped her fingers under the hem of the shirt when there was a flurry of knocks on his front door.

"Sonofabitch," Rocky cursed.

There was only one person it could be.

She was about to be clam-jammed so hard. Damn adult-ing, it *seriously* knew how to ruin a good time.

"Ignore it," he said, going in for a kiss before pulling back instead. "Unless this is too fast for you."

She shook her head, touched by the concern she saw lurking in his eyes. "No, it's not that at all." She was seriously considering killing her best friend at the moment. She had four others, she wouldn't miss her—much. "But Becky isn't going to go away. We're supposed to be going to yoga."

"Can't you skip it?" He brushed the pads of his thumbs across the exposed skin between her top and the band of her pants.

Tingles spread out from his touch. Finding words was hard in the wake of that heat, as seemed to always be the case. The struggle was real. "Normally, yeah, I wouldn't even think twice about it." She sucked in a breath as his large hand spread out, taking up half her back. Trying to get her mind back on track, she continued before she completely lost her train of thought. "B-But Becky needs my help in hiring a new instructor for the gym. This class is like the interview for the girl."

More brain cells scattered as he sucked on her collarbone.

"I see." He continued to run his fingers along the bumps of her hip bones. "When do you have to leave?"

"For the class? In ten minutes," she answered with a pout. "To keep Becky from getting embarrassing? Now."

"How about this." He placed a finger under her chin and raised her gaze to his. "You go back to your place and change. I'll jump in for the quickest, *coldest* shower on record, and meet you at your place before you leave."

"You want to come?"

"Sure...I like yoga. I'm nowhere near as bendy as you are, but it still feels good to stretch the muscles. Unless it would be weird for me to go?" Doubt flashed across his features and she shook her head.

"No, the guys are coming too."

"See you in ten." He dropped a quick kiss on her lips and nodded toward his shower with a smirk. "We can pick this up another time."

Never one to back down from a challenge, she called over her shoulder as she left, "I'm gonna hold you to that." She was out the door before he could formulate a response.

Chapter Fourteen

Less than ten minutes later, Gage was locking the door to his apartment and turning to join the boisterous crew heading to the elevators. His gaze found Rocky's, drawn like a magnet, and they shared a knowing smile.

Damn, he'd been close to having her earlier.

Now that he'd gotten a taste of her, there was absolutely nothing that could keep her from him.

Even though he was currently suffering from the worst case of blue balls of his life, he was actually grateful things stopped before he was able to get her into his shower. Since he'd made the conscious decision to pursue this, he wanted more from her than a quick fuck to scratch an itch.

Having confirmation she reciprocated his feelings, it was time for him to turn up the heat without crossing the line. He trained to go multiple rounds in the cage, he had the stamina to go the distance.

Yes, he was going to fuck Rocky. But he wouldn't do it until he had her *begging* for it.

She lifted a yoga mat off her shoulder and held it out to him as they reached the elevator. "Wasn't sure if you had one, or if it was unpacked if you did. It's one of our extras. Sorry that it's pink."

He took the mat and slid the strap over his shoulder. "No worries, real men wear pink."

"Careful, man," Vince cautioned with a laugh. "Becky will get you pink wraps for training if you're not careful."

"Ain't that the truth," Deck confirmed.

"How'd you get roped into coming to this thing?" Ray asked him before turning to address Becky. "What? Not even going to give it time to break him in before he has to submit to your dictatorish ways?"

She laughed and swatted at his arm. "Please, you guys love me, and the gym would be a disaster without me."

"Yeah, stop giving her shit," Gemma said from her perch on Ray's back.

They entered the elevator and Rocky stood next to him, laughing with her cousin. For a group of rough, tough, alpha males, he'd heard plenty of times how the women were the ones to run the show.

"Whoa!" Gemma exclaimed as Ray feigned dropping her.

Ray only laughed as he adjusted his grip on her legs.

"You'd think you'd be better at this by now," she quipped, causing everyone to laugh.

"Yeah, you've already been her chauffeur for two weeks, dude," Deck teased.

"Just keeping her in line, bro."

"Please." Gemma rolled her eyes.

Just when he was starting to feel like he was getting a foothold on the group's dynamics, they came at him with a whole new level of crazy.

"I'm afraid to even ask with you guys," he said.

"Ray lost a bet with Gemma," Vince explained. "Now, anytime she wants, he has to give her a piggyback ride."

"It's been an entertaining month," Deck said.

"For you," Ray grumbled.

"I feel like I should be questioning my decision to train with you guys."

✤

Like normal, the girls took one car while the guys piled into another. The drive to The Steele Maker wasn't long and Gemma didn't waste a second of it.

"So…you want to tell us what that was all about earlier?"

"I don't know what you mean." Rocky feigned innocence.

"Don't play dumb with us, Raquel Anne," Becky scolded.

It was never good to be called by her legal name, let alone when her middle name got tacked on after it.

Still, she couldn't stop chuckling at how she could never get anything by them. Becky could sniff out anything remotely scandalous, so of course she hadn't missed her kiss-swollen lips or the almost-sex hair she sported from Gage tunneling his fingers in it when she'd exited his apartment. She needed a moment to bask in how hot *that* particular move was. What girl didn't like that?

There was no use fighting it, so she quickly described her encounter with Gage. A nice sense of satisfaction enveloped her at being able to stun them into silence.

"What the hell are you doing going to yoga?" Becky took her eyes off the road to send her a baffled look.

"That wouldn't exactly be how I would want the guys to find out I'm sleeping with Gage. I could see it now." She made a sweeping gesture, like seeing the declaration in lights.

"True," Becky conceded as she pulled into the parking lot.

They hurried inside. Arriving only moments before the class was due to start, introductions would have to wait. Mats were spread out on the floor and everyone jumped right into the warm-up sun salutation.

"Jesus." She heard Gage breathe out as she folded over to move through to downward dog.

Once pressed back into position, she dropped her chin to her chest and looked through her legs where he was bent behind her, head lifted out of alignment to stare at her ass. "What's wrong, already too much for you, big guy?"

He huffed out a laugh. "No. I just shouldn't have set up behind you."

Everyone lifted their left leg in the air and swung it through to move into crescent pose. "And why's that?"

"Because now I have a prime ass viewing position."

She broke pose and turned to face him, her mouth agape. "*What*?"

He only shrugged those deliciously broad shoulders.

"You *can't* be serious?" Sure, he made his intentions known to her, but *never* had she expected him to say anything in a room full of people.

People who trained at the gym.

The gym she *worked* at. Where it was against the rules for her to get involved with any of the fighters who trained there.

"Of course I am. It's hard enough to keep my eyes off it in general, but you bending over in front of me, it's like waving a red flag in front of a bull."

"Stop it," she hissed.

"Why? You have a great ass," he said it as if they were alone and her brother wasn't five feet away.

The other guys laughed and agreed. Jerks.

"Come on, guys, that's my sister you're talking about," Vince groaned.

YOGA WAS USUALLY a relaxing activity with the added bonus of aiding in muscle recovery and helping with the range of motion in Gage's hip. This last hour—not so much.

He had positioned himself behind Rocky, figuring it would give him real estate for ass viewing. Instead, it was turning out to be a grave error in judgment.

Watching her bend and contort herself like a pretzel had him concentrating on not growing an erection in his shorts rather than focusing on his breath like he should have.

When the instructor finally called an end to the torture— er, class—he was tenser than when it started. Between the almost shower sex and now this, his balls were 0-2 for the day, and it was barely noon.

He hung back from the group as they started to talk, bending down to pick up his borrowed yoga mat to roll up. Not getting the memo, Vince came over while he did the same.

"So, ladies." Vince spoke to a pretty redhead and her equally stunning blonde friend Gage had never met. "Let me do the honors of introducing you to your newest victim—I mean—newest member of The Steele Maker, Gage James." Vince reached out to put a hand on his shoulder. "Gage, this fireball to my left is Skye, and to my right is Jordan, or JD, whichever you prefer. She'll answer to both."

"She's also known as Khaleesi," Deck added as he popped into their little circle.

"No one calls me that, Deck," Jordan said with an eye roll.

"Sure they do."

"No, they don't."

"Are you, or are you not, the leader of The Coven?" Deck held up her right hand, pointing to the small tattoo on the underside of her wrist. Gage recognized it as the same mini witch's hat that Rocky sported.

"I still can't believe you guys call us that," Jordan said with a shake of her head.

"I blame our brothers," Rocky said as the circle expanded to include her. A sly smile teased her lips as she peeked up at him.

"Don't we always?" Jordan chuckled.

"*And…*" Deck continued as if no one had spoken. "Is your text handle to us not 'mother of dragons?'"

Jordan let out a frustrated sound that had all the guys laughing.

"*Anyway.*" Jordan turned her back on Deck and faced him. "It's nice to meet you."

"Likewise."

"JD and Skye handle all the PR for the gym and its fighters," Deck said.

"Yup." Vince put an arm around each of the girls. "These two are the best in the biz. They own and operate All Things Sports."

"Really?" Impressive. He'd heard of the quickly growing public relations powerhouse but hadn't realized it was run by two people so young. "I've heard of you guys. Didn't you kind of corner the market on most of the top hockey players in the NHL?"

"We did," Jordan said humbly. "To be fair, a lot of them came from familial connections and BTU being such a dynasty in college hockey."

"Yeah and Rick Schelios is her *godfather.*" Deck whispered the last word like it was a secret. He guessed it wasn't every day you met someone with a personal connection to one of the greatest goalies to ever play in the NHL.

"Yeah, because it wouldn't matter that her husband is Jake Donovan or anything," Skye said sarcastically.

"The goalie for the Blizzards?" The people connected to The Steele Maker fascinated him. Donovan's skills between the pipes were impressive as hell. Not only did he help lead the US team to their first gold in the Olympics since the Miracle team, he was also one of the biggest reasons the Blizzards stole the Stanley Cup from Gage's hometown team last year.

Jordan nodded, the smile on her face displaying how much she loved her husband.

"Wow. I don't know if I should ask you to introduce us or not."

"Why's that?"

"I'm not sure if I would ask him for his autograph or curse him for robbing my Lions of the Cup."

"You're an LA fan?" Skye jumped in to ask.

"All my life," he said with pride.

"Wade Tanner is one of our guys," Skye said.

"The starting winger?" he asked.

"Yeah, another BTU alum," Jordan explained.

"Wow." These ladies were legit.

As the conversation topic changed to Vince's training camp, his attention went back to Rocky standing next to him. Her long legs looked amazing in her white and maroon marble-print leggings.

While he checked out the Steele that captured his attention, Jordan and Skye ticked off all the things Vince needed to do for his fight happening in a few months. It was a long list.

"You *sure* you want to join our gym?" Rocky tapped him on the leg with her rolled mat, nodding at her friends. "It's only been a few weeks, you can still back out before it's too late."

He reached out to brush a lock of hair that had escaped her ponytail behind her ear and her eyes flared at his touch.

"Never been more sure of anything in my life." He meant so much more than just about settling on where to train.

Chapter Fifteen

Gage had barely been in his new apartment a week and he was already learning *just* how much the full-time fighters and staff from The Steele Maker were like family. Even though they were together over six hours a day training at the gym, they all spent most of their nights in either 12A or 12B.

It was an adjustment for him.

On Sunday, the guys invaded his place to watch football while he unpacked the last of his boxes. Monday, he was dragged to Rocky's to watch *Dancing with the Stars*. Tuesday night was a Mario Kart tournament while the girls went out with the rest of The Coven.

And now tonight, Wednesday, he was once again headed to the guys' apartment to watch the Chicago Fire take on the New York Storm. He learned real fast hockey ruled supreme. Given their alma mater and their connection to Jordan Donovan, it made sense.

All three apartments had the same layout, but each had a very different feel. Whereas the girls had created a homey, colorful vibe, Vince lived in a pure bachelor pad—tastefully decorated, but one hundred percent bachelor. He couldn't fault them for it. If he hadn't hired an interior designer, he was sure his home would have one recliner, a sixty-five inch TV, and a futon…and that was it. At least the black leather couches and recliners they had in the living room were stupid comfortable.

This squad made it impossible for him to stick to his typical introverted ways. In an effort to keep from getting overwhelmed by the sheer number of people always in attendance, he tried to find his own small bubble amongst the crowd.

Rocky wasn't the only Steele he felt a kinship with. Her comic-loving brother was quickly becoming one of his favorite people, both in and out of the gym.

He was in the middle of a game of pool with Vince when the apartment door opened and a flurry of female voices sounded. Automatically, his gaze found Rocky and he couldn't help but smile at how good she looked in her purple marble leggings, Hawkeye t-shirt and purple Nikes. The girl had a pair of sneakers to match every outfit. Carrying a bunch of groceries, she was in workout gear, with no makeup and a messy bun, and she was breathtaking.

As if she felt the pull of his stare, she met his gaze and he was happy to note the banked heat swirling in hers.

Much to his disappointment, there had been no repeat performances since their hot-as-Hades kiss a few days ago. Instead, they had been circling their attraction like a pair of sharks.

He hoped to change that soon.

ROCKY WAS GLAD to see Gage already at Vince's, saving her from having to track him down. Though he had been hanging out with them outside of the gym, she occasionally sensed some hesitation on his part. He always seemed to hold himself separate from the group, as if he was on the outside looking in.

She and Vince seemed to be the exceptions to this. Gage smiled more when they were together, and if she were being honest, so did she. All the guys treated her with respect at work, but there was something different about the way Gage was with her. He had a way of making her feel valued as an individual, outside of anything having to do with her family name.

Since their almost shower sex four days prior, they hadn't had much opportunity to pick up where they'd left off. It was *almost* like he was purposely dragging things out.

When she first made the decision to sleep with him, she figured it would be a one-time thing, like a hall pass on her anti-fighter rule. But with each day they spent together, that scenario seemed less and less likely.

She liked him.

She. Liked. A. Fighter.

She still didn't believe it herself. The thought both terrified and thrilled her.

Though she doubted she had to worry, she had made a point of seeking out each of the guys to make sure they wouldn't say anything about her and Gage around the gym. Granted, there was nothing to tell for now, but there *would* be.

She needn't worry about the girls. Her lips quirked just remembering their reactions last night.

"I've been *begging* you to make a move since the day he showed up," was all Becky had said on the subject.

"I'm with Beck." Gemma toasted her with beer. "I fully support this."

"Go for it. Forbidden romances are hot," Maddey agreed.

"Our group does have a good track record with them," Jordan pointed out. "We are batting a thousand."

"A baseball reference?" Skye feigned offense. "Shouldn't you be using a hockey one?"

"This one works better."

Even as she unloaded the last of the weeks' meals Gemma had prepared for Vince, she couldn't help but bask in the unwavering support of her friends.

Heat sizzled along her nape and she glanced up to find Gage staring at her. Her heart skipped a beat at the fire she saw blazing in his eyes.

"Man, most people hate having to follow a meal plan while training but, Gem, your food is the tits." Deck's declaration finally broke her out of Gage's laser beam.

Gemma chuckled. "Thanks, dude."

"Oh, man, is that your mom's venison chili?" he asked, holding up a huge bowl.

"You know it."

Deck turned, bowl of chili in hand, and tried to make a break for it.

"Declan Michael Avery, where the hell do you think you are going with that chili?" Gemma scolded.

"*Ooooh*, she used your full name," Ray called out from the living room.

"I'd listen if I were you," Griff added.

Gemma reached out and took the bowl from him. "Besides, I made extra for the house. So *please* lay off Vince's food."

Deck hooked his arm around Gemma's neck and pulled her in to kiss her forehead. "Marry me."

She swatted his chest. "Deck, I've lost count of how many times you've proposed to me. If you ever did it without my cooking involved, I might *actually* take you seriously."

"You wound me, woman."

"Please…I don't believe that for a second."

Rocky laughed at her friends as she finished unloading her bag of stuff into the fridge, before settling on one of the stools around the island.

Done with his game, Gage slid in next to her, his body

brushing against hers as he leaned back on his elbows to watch Becky take on Vince in the next round of pool.

Her breath hitched at his nearness. This close, she caught the clean smell of his soap and the tempting scent of his deodorant. She had a feeling he was teasing her on purpose, and when he leaned down, skimming his nose along the soft spot behind her ear, she stopped breathing altogether.

"I like when you wear your hair up." He whispered the words as his lips trailed down the curve of her neck, setting off shivers in their wake. "It gives me easy access to do this." His teeth bit down on the tendon of her neck, marking her like an alpha would his mate. If she wasn't already sitting, her knees surely would've given out and her ass would have been on the floor, melted into a puddle of desire.

"*Gage,*" she whisper-hissed. She scanned the room to see if anyone was watching, but no one was paying them any attention. Sure, she laid the groundwork with her friends, but she would like to make it to the main event before having to hear shit about it.

She felt his lips spread into a smile against her skin before he straightened back into his original position.

The jerk. He knew *exactly* what he did to her.

She sent up a quick prayer of thanks when Nick informed them the hockey game was starting. With friends on four different professional teams, hockey was almost always on September through June. Everyone found spots to sit around the living room and kitchen island to watch the game.

During the first intermission, they broke apart to eat before settling back in for the second period after a scoreless first. With so many people in the apartment, Gage and a few others made themselves comfortable on the floor in the living room. He rested his back on the couch in front of where she sat.

Turnabout was fair play and she was going to give him a taste of his own medicine. Placing her hands on his broad shoulders, she used her thumbs to dig into the hard muscles. Following the edge of the muscles, her fingers traced from the top of his spine down the curve of his shoulder blades, loosening any knots she felt along the way.

When his head dropped forward on a groan, she thanked all the hours she'd had to log to finish her DPT program.

Her fingers stretched out, toying with his ears, then her nails scratched along the short hair on his head. The soft, prickly sensation invited her to run the flat of her palm against it and he pressed his head into her outstretched hand.

The game continued to play out on the flat screen, but she barely noticed the action, only looking up when everyone cheered to see the Storm player who scored was their friend Jase Donnelly. Then she was immediately drawn back to the black ink peeking from the collar of Gage's shirt.

She loved his tattoo. It was a true work of art with intricate details woven throughout the octopus design. He'd told her that the massive piece had taken five sessions spread over six months to complete.

She'd come to terms with her attraction—accepted it even. It was how much she was starting to *like* him that scared her most.

Who knew one of the best pound-for-pound fighters to come out of the UFC was also a Harry Potter buff? Not her. He'd proudly declared himself a Weasley when he saw her sorting hat shirt the day before with the words *Another Weasley* under it and she almost didn't believe him.

She made him promise to let her be there when he told Lyle, because where she was a Potterhead, it was her friend's *superpower*.

He let out a deep, masculine groan as her knuckle worked out a particularly tight knot in his latissimus dorsi, the sound having a direct effect on her clit.

Her plan had been to torture him with her touch, but that was clearly backfiring as the ache between her legs grew.

She was grateful for the distraction the collective *oooh* of the room provided from the only man tempting enough to have her breaking every rule she had ever set for herself.

On the TV, the broadcast replayed the hard check their friend Tucker, who played for the Fire, laid on Storm defenseman Jase. She watched Jase skate back to the Storm bench, her professional eye noticing that one of his knees was giving him trouble. Whether she wanted it to or not, her brain was always watching, always assessing those she cared about for injury.

"Oh, man. M-Dubs is in trouble with The Coven now for that hit," Vince said. Her brother and Jase were the two who referred to them as The Coven the most because they were supremely proud of the fact they came up with the name in the first place.

She wanted to say he was being overdramatic but his assumption wasn't wrong. Her phone was already lighting up with texts on the armrest next to her. She gave Gage's shoulders one more sweep of her hands before she sat back to pick up her phone.

MOTHER OF DRAGONS: I know he's my husband's best friend, but is it wrong for me to want to smack Tuck for that hit on Jase?

MAKES BOYS CRY: Oh I love when you get all pissed at M-Dubs

QUEEN OF SMUT: Rock are you watching? Did Jase look like he was skating funny after? You're the expert

• • •

ALPHABET SOUP: He was. I'll text him to let me know if he needs anything. Lord knows he'll be too stubborn to admit anything to his own trainers **insert eye roll here**

MOTHER OF DRAGONS: I know it's all a part of hockey, but it still makes me want to fly out to Chicago and give my BB3 a piece of my mind

PROTEIN PRINCESS: Nah. I bet before the game is over Jase will pay him back in kind

YOU KNOW YOU WANNA: And if not, you know he'll say something to him along the lines about you being pissed, and that'll be enough to torture Tuck with all the what ifs

She looked at Becky sitting in one of the recliners across the room. "Dude, you are so right."

"Just the *mention* of how she will react will be enough to put the fear of god in M-Dubs," Gemma agreed.

She loved her crazy friends.

🐙

Gage's plans of teasing Rocky more with his close proximity by sitting in front of her backfired in spectacular, cock-hardening, fashion. The feel of her hands on him, rubbing the tired and sore muscles of his neck and shoulders, had him instantly pitching a tent in his joggers large enough for Boy Scouts to camp in.

As if working out the kinks in his back wasn't pleasurable enough, she started to scratch her blunt nails through his hair.

The action had him seconds away from throwing her over his shoulder and carrying her back to his place to finish what they started over the weekend.

Thank god for the distraction the hockey game provided.

When the second intermission rolled around, he figured it was a good opportunity to turn the tables back around.

"Wanna play some pool?"

"Are you sure you want to do that?" she asked, rising from the couch.

"Why wouldn't I?"

"Well, you lost to Vince. Are you sure you can handle losing to a girl?" she taunted.

"Sooo confident." He stepped into her personal space as he passed her a pool cue. Once again, he was happy to note the quick indrawn breath she took whenever their bodies brushed.

"All right, Champ," she taunted. He already knew her well enough to know she was never one to back down from a fight, and sure enough, she maintained eye contact with him as she chalked the stick. "Let's see what you got."

He was momentarily distracted by watching her lips purse to blow the excess chalk from the tip. He'd been fantasizing about those lips since the night he first laid eyes on them. The way her lower lip plumped out more. The perfect cupid's bow dip of the upper lip. And now that he'd experienced the feel of them pressed against his own, anytime his eyes locked onto them, all he could do was try and calculate the fastest way to get them back on his body.

She offered to let him break and he sunk both a striped and solid.

The first shot she lined up to take was close to the edge of the table and she didn't bend over much to make it. Using her standing position to his advantage, he came up behind her, placed a hand on either side of her hips on the mahogany wood, bracketing her body with his arms, and pushed against her so her back was flush with his front.

"*Gage*," she hissed.

"*Rocky*," he mocked.

"I'm trying to shoot." Her eyes flashed silver as she tilted her chin over her shoulder to glare daggers at him.

"No one's stopping you, Blue."

He was pretty sure she let out a small growl as she resettled the cue between her fingers, then muttered a curse as the ball she was aiming for hit wide of the pocket.

He hit his next two shots in quick succession before missing, turning it over to her once again.

Hip to his ways, she made fast work of her next shot, not allowing him time to get to her before taking it.

Everything inside the apartment faded away as they played.

"I think we're better matched than you think." He was starting to believe that was true for much more than just a billiards game.

"I wouldn't be so sure about that, Champ."

"Oh, yeah?" He leaned against his pool cue. "If you're so confident, how about we make things a little more interesting."

"What did you have in mind?"

"How about a little wager?" She arched a brow but stayed silent. "For every ball we sink, the other has to answer a question."

She seemed skeptical but agreed.

He smiled as he lined up his shot, the ball rolling into the corner pocket he aimed for.

"What's your guilty pleasure?" he asked.

She *hmm*ed while she considered her answer and he wondered if she made that sound in bed. *Focus, man.*

"I guess watching reality TV, the worse and more dramatic the better."

That was not at all what he expected. "Which ones are your favorites?"

"Now you're trying to cheat." She tsked. "But I'll answer anyway. I'm a sucker for *The Bachelor* and *The Bachelorette*, but my favorites have always been the Jersey-based ones. I love yelling at the TV during *The Real Housewives of New Jersey* or *Jersey Shore* for how inaccurate they are."

His next shot went wide but hers was right on the money.

"My turn." She tapped her chin while she thought. "Okay, got it. What's your favorite color?"

He huffed out a laugh. "*That's* what you want to know?"

"Hey!" Her hands went to her hips. "Don't judge. You're the one who came up with this game."

He moved to join her on her side of the table. "Well…if you asked me a few weeks ago, I would have told you it was green." He was full of crap, he didn't have a favorite color, but he could spin this to work in his favor.

"Wh-What changed?" Her words stuttered as he moved deeper into her personal space.

"Well, you see." He fingered a fine piece of hair curling by her ear. "Suddenly I find myself being partial to a particular shade of blue." Even now, the light caught the strands and gave them a blue tint.

She gasped, her lips forming that enticing O shape, and blinked up at him a few times. He was shocked he'd managed to stun the girl who always had a comeback.

When she finally broke eye contact and moved to take her next shot, she missed it by millimeters.

With a smirk, he made quick work of sinking his next ball in the side pocket, chuckling at the scrunched up face Rocky made as he straightened up.

"Alright, Champ. This time try to come up with something better than what's my guilty pleasure."

"I'm pretty sure you're the one who had the lame *what's your favorite color* question."

"Whatever." She waved him off. "Ask your question and take your next shot already."

There was one thing he was dying to know but hadn't had the opening to ask. Now was his chance.

Not wanting her to feel pressured by what he had a feeling would be a heavy question, he stayed on his side of the pool table.

"Okay…there has been something I've been curious about."

"Oh, really?" She arched one of her black brows. "*Do* tell."

He swallowed. "Why don't you date fighters?"

He held his breath, anticipation bubbling under the surface as he waited for her answer. Instead, she only blinked, not uttering a word.

As the silence grew awkward, he lined up his next shot for something to do, but she spoke before he could take it.

"You know what?"

He lifted his eyes to hers.

"I'm *not* going to answer that one, because *technically* I answered two for you earlier."

He let her have the out—for now—and missed the pocket he'd aimed for. After his failed shot, the position of the cue ball on the table had Rocky bending over to stretch her upper body fully across the felt.

Under the completely bullshit guise of helping her with her shot, because she was clearly skilled, and to create a delicious distraction, he once again molded his body to hers.

The way she was bent over put her ass in the perfect position for him to thrust against her. If they were alone, he would have stripped her leggings from her body and been inside her faster than delivering a knockout punch. Instead, he settled for lining up his erection with the crease of her ass, delivering a subtle thrust of his hips, knowing she couldn't miss the dumbbell currently residing in his pants.

His left hand rested on the table beneath her arm holding

the pool stick, his knuckles grazing the nipple straining against the shirt and sports bra she had on. The thin material did nothing to hide how beautifully her body reacted to him.

Caging her between himself and the table, his right arm stretched along hers, he was pleased to see the goosebumps trailing in the wake of his touch as he lay dominant over her. One day soon, they would be repeating this position.

Naked.

He scratched the slight stubble he was currently sporting along the sensitive skin of her neck and moved to speak in her ear. "Do you *feel* what seeing you bent over like this does to me?" Another slow rock of his hips.

Her forehead dropped to rest against the felt of the table. He knew she was biting back a moan, but with their bodies pressed this tightly together, he could feel the rumble of her chest.

"I may have to get a pool table for my place. Because I can think of about a dozen ways to have you on it."

"*Gage.*" His name was a broken plea on her lips.

"Come on, baby. Take your shot."

The tip of the stick skidded across the felt as she scratched, costing her the game.

They straightened from their positions, her mercurial eyes blazing.

"You play dirty," she accused.

"You have no idea how dirty."

Chapter Sixteen

As Gage went to work rewrapping his hands to spar with Vince, he swore he could feel a fresh callous forming, one that had nothing to do with fighting and everything to do with having to relieve his own sexual frustration from teasing Rocky to the brink. He'd rubbed one out so many times in the last six days he felt like he was a teenager again.

In order to avoid walking around with a perpetual woody while training at the gym—damn Rocky and those sexy leggings and sports bra combinations—he'd taken to adding a jerk-off session to his morning showers.

Even as he grappled with Vince, he couldn't help but admire the way her long legs looked in a pair of Marauder's Map-printed leggings and a tight v-neck proudly boasting she solemnly swore she was up to no good. No one made geeking out look as good as she did.

"Looking a little slow today, Champ," she teased as Vince slipped out of his hold, her eyes sparkling as she watched them.

He might be a weight class above the older Steele sibling,

but it was barely a factor with the top- notch grappling skills Vince possessed thanks to his years wrestling in high school.

"The hell I am," he huffed out, scrambling around on the mat, jockeying for position behind Vince.

"I wouldn't be so sure of that. You're supposed to be a submission specialist...not really seeing it right now."

It was true. He'd only won two of his past fights by knockout—all the rest were won by his opponent tapping out. But hearing the word submission spoken in that husky voice of hers had his mind going in a completely different direction.

Lately, they had been working on eliminating any tells Vince was giving away before going into a takedown move. Though he'd studied the guy, Gage hadn't been able to spot them himself.

Of course, since Rocky was the only one who could read her brother that closely, she usually trained with them. And Gage was not complaining. Even when she was busting his balls—and not in the way he would prefer.

He finally got Vince in a rear naked choke, a hold that had his left arm around Vince's neck, the middle of his throat in the crook of his elbow, while locking that hand on his own bicep of his opposite arm. His right arm hooked around the back of Vince's head, applying enough pressure to make him pass out or tap out.

Neither was the goal for this training session though. Instead, they were working on Vince's ability to break the hold and eventually turn the tide against his opponent, should he be faced with a similar situation in his upcoming fight.

The training program the staff at The Steele Maker put them through was no joke. Gage could only imagine the intensity of it once he booked a fight and entered an official camp like Vince was in at the moment. Being an integral part of another fighter's training was another first for him. Each day that passed, he grew more comfortable with the team aspect of his new gym.

His back bowed against the mat as he stretched back with Vince on top of him. His hip pulled and an arrow of pain shot down his leg as he tried and failed to hold the position.

"What's wrong? What happened?" Rocky's words were rushed.

He was warned, multiple times, not to keep an injury from her, but damn if he was admitting to anything. He'd been managing fine—okay, fine-ish—since his last fight. He wasn't about to disclose anything that could potentially sideline him now.

"Nothing. I'm fine." He released Vince and rolled to his side. With a deep breath, he made a conscious effort not to wince as he pushed himself from the padded floor.

"You made a face." Her eyes narrowed as she scanned his body, and not in the way he enjoyed. Gone was the flirtatious girl he'd been getting glimpses of all week and in her place was the formidable physical therapist he'd been warned about.

She was cataloging each inch of his body like she had X-ray vision and could pinpoint his trouble areas with only a look. Hell if he wasn't turned on by this side of her as much as the other. Her brain was as sexy as her body.

"Of course I made a face. I had a two-hundred-pound man on top of me." He moved closer and lowered his voice "I bet you'll make a face when I'm on top of you."

"Don't do that." She held up a hand to stop any further comment from him. "Don't try and act all macho. You may be a big, badass MMA fighter, but you're still human. If you're hurt, tell me. I can't fix you if you don't."

It would be so easy to do as she asked. In the short amount of time he'd spent training at the gym, he had witnessed her do exactly that for several athletes. Still, he held himself back.

"You know as well as I do, Blue, I'll take *any* opportunity I can get to have your hands on me." The prettiest blush stained her cheeks. "But I don't need any fixing at the moment."

Before she could respond, harsh electronic screeches blared through the speakers of the gym, causing a few people to cover their ears and wince.

"Damon, what the *hell* did we say about trying to add Skrillex to your playlist?" Becky shouted before the music abruptly cut off.

The Steele Maker didn't pipe in the standard generic radio station. Instead, they rotated between daily playlists picked by the staff and main fighters of the gym. It sure kept things *eclectic.*

"You know what that means?" Rocky threatened with a smile.

Every male in the place let out a single collective groan.

"Boy Band Bonanza," she and Becky cheered together, throwing their hands in the air.

The guys put up a fuss, but when *NSYNC's "I Want You Back" picked up where Skrillex left off, more than a few of them were singing along with Justin Timberlake and the boys.

And when Vince, Griff and Deck joined the ladies in the choreography from the band's "Bye Bye Bye" music video, he knew it was all posturing.

"Oh, man. I feel like I should be taking video. JD and Skye would *flip* if they saw their badass fighters getting down with their boy band selves," an unfamiliar male voice cut through the laughter.

He caught the surprised smile on Rocky's face before she ran toward the newcomer.

"Jase!" she cried as she jumped, wrapping her body around him in an excited hug.

Who the fuck was this guy? His vision went hazy as the

dude buried his face in Rocky's neck and returned her embrace just as tightly.

After what felt like hours of staring at Rocky's legs locked around his waist, Gage finally took a breath when the guy lowered her back to her feet. "Missed you too, Balboa."

He nearly cracked a tooth at the casual use of a nickname.

"I *want* to say I'm surprised to see you. But I saw the way you were skating after the hit."

Rocky's words registered through the scream of jealousy in his head and he realized the man standing there in a Storm hoodie was Jase Donnelly, one of the leading defensemen for both the Storm and the National Hockey League.

"Well, you do know you're the only one who's ever been able to fix me." Donnelly gave her a smarmy smile that made Gage want to knock his teeth out. One by one.

"Bullshit," she said with an eye roll that marginally soothed Gage's ire. "You *do* know the Storm employs numerous *qualified* professionals to make sure you're in top shape, right?"

"Yeah, but you know you have magic hands, Balboa."

He was going to kill him. Those *magic hands* were his.

"No way. You just don't want them to know you sprained it playing paintball this summer."

"Yo, Jase. What's goin' on, bro?" Vince said, sharing a complicated handshake with the guy, only serving to ramp up Gage's frustration. It'd been difficult enough learning to navigate a whole new set of friends and expectations. Now this asshole was going to throw off that dynamic he'd been settling into.

"Vin, my man." Donnelly turned to greet the rest of the people who were making their way over. "Heard you all are coming to the game tonight. At least I know I'll have one of you cheering me on," he said with a nod to Griff.

"You know it," Griff stated proudly.

"Sure I can't convince you to wear one of my jerseys tonight?" he said to Rocky, pulling her in with an arm over her shoulders.

"Sooo not happening. You know I'm a Blizzards girl all the way."

She didn't have a boyfriend—Gage had point-blank asked—and she wouldn't have kissed him the way she did if she was committed to someone else, but something about the way the two interacted bespoke a closeness deeper than friendship. Were they a friends with benefits situation whenever he was in town? Donnelly played for the New York City Storm, so it wasn't like he was that far away. Only a quick train ride and Rocky could be in the city.

His thoughts were spiraling. He needed more information stat. But how was he going to ask the questions without coming off like the jealous ass he was?

"Come on. Let's get you checked out so we can have you back in time for your pregame nap." Rocky took Jase's hand to lead him to her treatment room.

"Yeah, you pussies need a nap before a game," Deck said with a laugh.

"Umm, I'm pretty sure you guys nap the day of a fight, so don't even try it, Deck," Donnelly tossed back, walking backward to face them. "Plus, you know it's the dream to have a job that has built-in nap time. I'm living the dream, man." He shouted out the last line with pride.

As Gage watched Rocky disappear from sight with a professional hockey player in tow, he had to physically force himself to stay rooted in his spot and not go charging after them to stake his claim like a caveman.

With a deep breath to center himself, he figured now was as good a time as any to learn what he could.

"I take it the two of them know each other from when you all were at BTU?"

"Yeah. The hockey team was Rock's main assignment while working on her degrees," Vince explained.

"They also dated for a few years before Jase was drafted," Griff added.

Fuck. Seriously? The two *did* have history. A long one too.

"Why'd they break up?" They clearly remained close, so it couldn't have been a bad breakup.

The guys all looked at each other, most of them shrugging like they didn't have the answer.

"You know, I don't really know. It was almost like one day they were together and the next they weren't," Vince finally said.

What the hell did that mean? If it wasn't an emotional separation, did they still want each other, even casually?

"They're still pretty tight." Vince's voice broke in echoing his own thoughts.

"Do you think they want to get back together?" And there was his biggest fear. He'd been laying the groundwork to date her, once he had come to terms with his own reservations. There was too much at stake to rush into the sex he *knew* they both wanted. He wasn't prepared to lose before the round even began.

"I don't *think* so. Aside from Skye and Tuck, the rest of our group has maintained pretty close friendships with their exes."

"Yup, that's true," Griff agreed. "Ryan and Maddey are *like besties,*" he said in his best Valley girl accent.

"Yeah and Ry proposed," Vince added. "It's just the way they're wired, I guess."

He should have been reassured by this information, but until it was blatantly obvious Rocky was *his*, he wouldn't be satisfied.

❀

"All right. Lose the pants, Donnelly, and get your ass up on my table." Rocky gave Jase the *don't fuck around* voice.

"You know I love when you take charge in the bedroom, Balboa," he said with a playful smirk.

She rolled her eyes at him. "You keep trying to talk dirty to me and I'll tell your sister," she threatened.

"Low blow, Rock. *Real* low blow." He shot her a scowl.

"Relax," she said, taking his left leg in her hands to inspect his knee. "You know I'm a member of The Coven—as you love to point out—I can handle you all on my own."

"Yeah ya can." He waggled his eyebrows suggestively.

She pinched her fingers around his joint, causing him to let out a squeak of pain.

"Behave. Keep making lewd comments and I'll start to worry you took one too many pucks to the head."

"You know I only mean it as a joke," he said.

She knew he did. If she really thought he was serious, they wouldn't have been able to remain comfortable with each other after they'd been together romantically. It helped that they'd been friends before dating.

Looking back, she couldn't pinpoint the precise moment when things transitioned from a romantic relationship back to a platonic one because it happened so naturally.

In all honesty, Jase was the *last* person she wanted flirting with her, even if it was in jest.

Gage was the one she wanted. The sexual frustration he instilled in her with every brushing touch and whispered dirty word in her ear was *driving* her insane.

She wanted him so badly it was a miracle she hadn't locked him in her treatment room and demand he relieve the blue clit he'd been leaving her with for the past six days.

"So...Gage James, huh?" Jase asked as she continued to manipulate his leg.

"What are the odds, right?" she said offhandedly, as if her crush on Gage wasn't common knowledge in their squad.

Jase knew her too well to fall for her nonchalance.

"I take it you guys banged already?"

Her head snapped up and she dropped his leg.

"Really?" Her eyebrows flew up. "You want to talk about my sex life? Does that mean you want to tell me about the current bunny warming *your* bed?"

His knee was fine. As she suspected from watching the end of his game against the Fire, it was only a minor tweak from the angle he hit the boards. She'd wrap it with some Kinesio tape for the game later that evening, but other than that, he was good to go.

"Look," he said as she grabbed the tape from the cabinet. "I know we don't have the most conventional friendship but I'm only asking because, based on the way he was looking at me out there"—he gestured to the door with his head—"he thought I was trying to encroach on his territory."

"We will get back to the whole *his territory* thing in a minute." She ripped a piece of hot pink tape from the roll. "But first"—she secured the tape in a semicircle around the left side of his knee, then looked him in the eye—"how *exactly* was he looking at you?"

She exchanged the pink tape for a neon green one to encase the other side of his knee.

"Like he wanted to use me as his personal punching bag."

She snorted.

"He was not," she protested. A strip of black tape went underneath his kneecap, a strip of purple above and he was all set to tear up the ice later tonight.

"He was," Jase countered. "I know I'm a big bad enforcer, but this guy fights—*professionally.*"

He did make a formidable opponent on the ice. Standing somewhere around six-four with shoulders wide enough to fill a doorway, he was as physically intimidating off the ice as he was on. Add in the fact he was one of the toughest enforcers in the league, and most people wouldn't dare step to him.

Gage James, however, was *not* most people. Jase knew how to throw a punch, but Gage had built a very profitable career around fighting.

She cleared her throat. "I am *not* banging Gage." Yet.

"Really?" It was his turn to arch a brow.

"Really," she said with a shrug. "Besides...I don't date fighters."

"Okay, my turn to call bullshit."

Ignoring him, she gathered up the tapes and returned them to their cabinet.

"Rock." Jase waited for her to look at him before he continued. "Look." He ran a hand through his blond hair. "I get it. I *know* why you have this *thing* about fighters—hell, it worked to my advantage in college—but I also saw the way *you* looked at him out there."

"Oh, yeah? How's that?" The question came out with more snark than she intended but her defenses were at an all-time high.

"Like JD looks at Jake."

Shit. Was that true?

If it was, she was *so* screwed. She did not need feelings getting tangled up in this attraction.

Fuck my life.

❦

Gage was so distracted by the thought of Donnelly with Rocky, in her office, behind closed doors, that Vince was able to break out of every one of the holds they worked on. It didn't help that no matter how much he tried to ignore it, his hip was giving him issues.

He hadn't had a performance this bad since he first started training with Tony back in high school.

"Oh, man, Champ." Vince smirked at him. "Guess it's a good thing Rock isn't out here right now, because I'm schooling you."

"Shut it, Steele," he said, going for Vince's legs for a double leg takedown.

He managed to take him to the mat, but yet again, Vince quickly took the upper hand and reversed them so he was the one in control.

"Dude," Vince laughed as he reached a hand out to help him up.

"Whatever, man. I'm having an off day."

"What I wouldn't *pay* to see Rock get you in the ring right now. She would school your ass more than she did mine. Though…" His words trailed off as he looked across the gym. "Not sure if he would allow *that* to happen."

He followed Vince's gaze until he spotted Vic Steele working with Deck. "Your dad mentioned she spars all the time."

"Yes and no. He'll let her step into the cage with us, but he keeps a pretty tight leash on who he lets her spar with. No one can hurt his pumpkin."

Before they could continue their conversation, Rocky and Donnelly came up from the back hall, laughing and nudging each other as they walked.

What was it about this hockey player that set him off? He'd witnessed Rocky's interaction with several men at the gym over the past weeks and the way she teased and played around never bothered him. But the obviously deep connection between these two had him utterly losing his shit.

"You get our boy all hooked up so he can help block all of his brother's shots tonight?" Griff asked Rocky.

"Yeah, he's all set. But I'm not sure even I can help him block Ryan. They're seven games into the season and he already has eleven points. He's looking to break his rookie season." She smiled as she turned to Gage. "Sorry, I totally spaced on intros earlier. Gage this is Jase. Jase this is Gage."

When Donnelly reached out a hand for him to shake, he wanted to be a dick, he *really* did, but his mother would beat his ass—professional MMA fighter be damned— if she heard he refused to shake someone's hand all because he was acting like a jealous baby.

"I hear you had the honor of meeting my other half," Donnelly said with the smile that'd launched many an endorsement deal. Gage wondered what it would look like if it resembled a jack-o-lantern, missing teeth and all.

"Who?" Choking back his anger made him sound like he'd swallowed a box of nails. *Is this jockhole really rubbing his relationship with Rocky in my face?*

"My sister told me you got suckered into taking yoga with the Covenettes last weekend," Donnelly said as if it explained everything.

"Your sister?" Now he was really confused.

"Yeah. JD—Jordan. She was a Donnelly before my puck-head of a best friend put a ring on it and she decided to take his name."

Oh.

He'd thought Jordan was connected in the hockey world between her husband and godfather, but with both her brothers as top players in the league as well, it was no wonder ATS was so entrenched in the NHL. And that was *before* you considered the BTU connections.

"You call your sister your other half?" He might not have any siblings of his own, but that was a little strange, right?

"Yeah." Donnelly's smile never lost any of its wattage. "We're twins—we shared a womb and all, so ya know." He ended his statement with a shrug of his shoulders.

Now that the haze of envy was starting to clear, he was able to see the resemblance to the tiny, force of nature blonde he'd met. Her hair was a lighter shade, and his features had a masculine roughness, but their eyes were a dead match.

"Speaking of my wombmate…" Donnelly clapped his hands in front of him. "I better get to her house now if I'm gonna have a chance to love up on my nieces and get a nap in before the game."

"Kiss those babies for me," Rocky said, giving him a hug that had Gage fighting back the urge to yank her out of his arms.

"I will," he agreed. "See you guys at Rookies after?"

"Will someone end up in the sin bin tonight?"

"Storm Blizzards?" Donnelly pretended to give it some thought. "Fuck yeah."

"Well, there ya go. Besides…who else is going to protect you from the bunnies?" The smile she gave him was full of hidden meaning.

"You are the best BFBB," he said with a matching smile.

"Careful," Becky called from where she helped a guest at the front desk. "Don't let Madz hear you say that. Them be fighting words."

"No worries. I'll proudly share the title with my girl," Rocky readily agreed.

"You guys are so corny with your nicknames," Vince complained.

"Says the guy who fights as 'Man of Steel,'" Donnelly tossed back.

"And don't you forget it, *bruh*," Vince said, flexing so the Superman emblem danced on his shoulder. "You might hold your own in a fight on the ice, but we both know who would win if you were to drop the gloves with me."

"You know…" Donnelly turned back to face Rocky. "It's probably a good thing we broke up after college. Because if we stayed together, I could have ended up with this asshole" —he hooked a thumb at Vince—"as a brother-in-law."

"Yeah," Rocky scoffed. "Like you and Ry are a walk in the park for Jake."

"That hurts, babe." Donnelly rubbed a hand over his heart.

First, it was the nickname and the full-body hug when he got to the gym, then it was whatever inside joke they shared with BFBB, and now the endearment. Gage was one pet name away from raging like The Hulk.

"Now, I say this with total love. Play good tonight, but I hope you lose."

After a round of goodbyes that wasn't quick enough for his liking, Donnelly left the gym and Gage was taking Rocky by the hand, stalking toward her office.

ROCKY DIDN'T PUT up a fight as Gage practically dragged her to the back. The way her hand felt engulfed by his much larger one felt too damn good.

She only wished he didn't have hand wraps on. She longed to feel the toughness and callouses earned from years of hard work to be the best of his weight class running along her skin, preferably bare skin, if she had her say.

The concern her father would see and suspect something was going on between them pricked at her mind but she brushed it off.

Not a word was exchanged as he led her down the hall. Or when he shut the door just shy of slamming.

A tiny squeak escaped her as she felt his hands hook beneath her armpits and plop her unceremoniously on the massage table. Gage, however, was still silent as a mime.

His eyes though. They were screaming. Those cerulean depths churned like the ocean in the midst of a category five hurricane.

His hands came up to cradle her head between them, then he was crashing his lips to hers.

This kiss was nothing like their kiss from almost a week ago. That one was driven by lust.

But this kiss.

This. *Kiss.*

It was raw emotion.

A primal declaration.

An alpha claiming his mate.

Holy shit.

His tongue licked inside her mouth, not waiting for permission. No, this time he took her mouth like it was his mission in life to erase from her memory any mouth that came before his.

His teeth nipped at her bottom lip before sucking it into his mouth. She moaned, then moaned again when he ground his hard-as-steel erection against her center. The way her knees were spread to accommodate his hips left her open for whatever he would give her.

If he kept kissing her the way he was, like he would *die* if he stopped, she was more than willing to be a puppet for his pleasure.

Her own hands got in on the action—scratching against the prickly fuzz of his buzzed scalp, curling themselves around the curve of his skull since there wasn't anything long enough to hold on to.

"Fuck, baby." His words were spoken with a guttural intensity.

Since her brain cells had hung up a sign saying *out to lust, check back later,* all she managed was a hum in response.

Anchoring herself with her hands locked around the back of his head, she shamelessly closed the last remaining centimeters that separated them and rubbed her body against his.

A crack went through the room, but it went unheeded as they tried to fuck each other through their clothes.

One of her hands left its perch on his head to fist his workout tank, lifting it to expose the bottom ridge of his abs.

When his mouth left hers to trail nipping kisses down the side of her neck, her head canted to the side and she caught a glimpse of those v cuts that made girls go stupid, as well as his *very* happy trail, if the head of his glistening cock peeking above the band of his shorts was any indication.

The gleam of pre-cum had her licking her lips as a yearning to taste him flooded her.

Before she got to quench her desire to have his dick in her mouth, another crack—this one much louder than the first—sounded, and a second later she was no longer in his arms. She was falling, dropping like a *rock* to the hard floor.

Gage let out a surprised, "Oh, shit," as he dropped down in front of her. "Are you okay, Blue?" he asked, tilting her face up to his.

She nodded, stunned silent for a moment, her hand going to her now sore ass…and not for the reason she would *want* it to be sore either.

"What the hell just happened?" he asked.

Breaking from her stupor, she shifted around to face her new archenemy, the massage table. When she spotted the u-shaped pillow where a person's face was meant to rest when they were lying on their stomach, she knew exactly what happened. In his haste to mark her, he had placed her on the one section of the massage table *not* meant to bear the full weight of a person. Eventually, the piece lost the good fight and dumped her on her ass—literally.

"You should've used the treatment table."

"I didn't want to be anywhere you were with *him*." His vehemence confirmed her suspicions this was about him figuratively peeing on her to mark her as his own.

Damn alpha men.

Why the hell did she find it so hot?

Not moving from her new home on the floor, she reached

out to cup his cheek, her thumb moving along it in a soothing manner. "You *do* know there's *nothing* between Jase and me but friendship anymore, right?"

"So I heard." His tone said he was anything but convinced.

"You"—she gave his ear a gentle tug—"are the *only* person I want to sleep with. And if my friends and I weren't so damn codependent, it would have happened almost a week ago."

His deep laughter warmed a place deep inside her.

"That's *one* way to put it."

"Another would be that you were too busy being a damn tease to finish what we started in your bathroom."

His eyes flashed at her.

"I didn't want to rush it and have you thinking it was going to a one and done for me." It was his turn to cup her cheek. "Because, baby...once I get you in my bed...I might not ever let you out of it."

Holy shitballs.

If she wasn't already wet from dry humping him like a teenager minutes ago, that declaration would have done it.

He talked a big game, but there was still this part of her, the deeply insecure part, that wondered if he meant it. Because if things progressing between them was really important to him, wouldn't he have made it a priority? Or were they stalled because he was too focused on his training?

She hated every one of those thoughts, the deep-seated unworthiness she'd always felt bubbling inside her.

Her gut had told her Gage was different. That he'd be the exception. The *first* person to put her before fighting.

But what if I'm wrong?

"Come on." He offered her a hand to help her stand, breaking her from her inner turmoil. "Let's get you an icepack for your ass."

She snorted out a laugh, pointing him to the cabinet where the squeeze-to-activate cold packs were located.

As they made their way back to the training area, Gage leaned in to whisper his parting shot. "Now…the next time it hurts for you to sit down, it won't have *anything* to do with faulty furniture."

Oh, my.

Her heart might not be fully on board, but her body sure as hell was.

Chapter Seventeen

Rocky had been to The Ice Box—the arena of the New Jersey Blizzards—hundreds of times in her life. First as a fan growing up, then to support her friends after they were drafted.

Jordan owned a row of seats next to the team bench in front of the boards since her parents had switched to a luxury suite after their granddaughters were born.

During hockey season, if the Blizzards were home, the girls spent their nights out at The Ice Box. If she couldn't work with the team like she wanted, the next best thing was being able to cheer them on as loudly as possible.

The Donnelly suite was *packed* when they walked in. She introduced Gage to Jordan's parents and then Jake's as they worked their way through the room. When she spotted Simone, now officially Griff's girlfriend, talking to Sammy and Jamie Hawke, she dragged Gage across the room to say hello and make more introductions.

Sammy planted a smacking kiss on her lips as she wrapped her free arm around him in a tight hug. She caught Gage's dark look and how his hand tightened around hers as

Sammy kissed her, more attuned to his jealous streak since earlier with Jase.

"Hey, Jamie," she called her friend's husband. "Control your man before he gets his ass kicked by a professional fighter."

A deep chuckle cut through the mounting tension as Jamie Hawke—rock star extraordinaire, front man for the multi-platinum selling, seven-time Grammy-winning band Birds of Prey, and Sammy's spouse—came to retrieve Sammy before his pretty face could be damaged.

"Spins," Jamie scolded his husband, "I thought we discussed this. You need to have *permission before* you go around kissing people."

"You're right, Jam." Sammy shrugged. "You know I get excited when I see my girls."

"I know, babe." The look Jamie gave him bled with affection, even if the two didn't show it physically.

The rock star had shocked the world, breaking millions of female, and even a few male, hearts when he came out of the closet and married Sammy a few months ago in a private ceremony.

"Gage, I want you to meet my friends. Sammy grew up with Maddey, and Jamie—"

"Holy shit! You're Jamie Hawke. My entrance song is by Birds of Prey." She laughed at the starstruck expression on Gage's face. She was used to seeing people react similarly when meeting her friends, but it was even more amusing to watch him since he was a celebrity in his own right.

"I am. And you're Gage James."

"You know who I am?" Gage sounded two seconds away from fanboying over being recognized by the singer.

"Oh, yeah. Spins and I were at your last title fight."

Gage's wide eyes met hers and she giggled again at his slack-jawed expression.

"Sammy is a DJ also, and he's the one who introduced

Griff and Simone," she explained.

"You know…" Gage dropped an arm around her shoulders. "I was impressed by how cool you were when we first met. But now I get it." He shook his head. "Do you hang out with anyone *not* famous?"

"To be fair…all the pro athletes I know—with the exception of you—were my friends before they went pro. Jamie is the only celebrity who wasn't part of our original crew."

He leaned down to whisper in her ear, "Would I totally lose my street cred if I asked for a selfie?"

"No." She snorted. "But using the word *totally* might have cost you a few points."

She let him get his photo, then took him by the hand. "Come on, there's still a bunch of people you need to meet."

GAGE FOLLOWED ROCKY through the crowded suite. There had to be close to two dozen people scattered throughout the room. He spotted the other Covenettes, all dressed in variations of navy and white Blizzards gear.

Rocky in a white Blizzards away jersey, another pair of curve-hugging leggings, and those army boots he remembered from the first night they met damn near had him swallowing his tongue. He wouldn't think being covered by the large hockey sweater would be a ball-tightening outfit, but the way the material formed to her curves when she moved, hinting at what lay beneath, made him want to rip the shirt from her body to discover the hidden treasures.

But that was for later because she was introducing him to even more people. Jordan's adorable babies were dressed in matching mini Blizzards jerseys rocking their daddy's number but instead of reading DONOVAN across the shoulders theirs said DADDY. He also got a kick out of the noise canceling headphones the girls wore, proudly sporting the Blizzards Yeti mascot.

Not once had Rocky let go of his hand. It was as if she was able to tell he wasn't used to being a part of a large group—and her squad was *huge*.

Through the years, there was always a part of him that was a little bit jealous when Wyatt would regale him with stories from the firehouse, his cousin finding his own tribe of people outside the two of them.

Though Tony was like a second father to him, he'd never developed a kinship with the others he trained with. His old gym was *nothing* like The Steele Maker and he was learning to feel more at ease around Rocky and the girls quicker than he was with the guys.

He felt a squeeze on his hand as he looked around at all the people in the main area of the suite.

"You okay?" Rocky asked, her eyes assessing when he glanced down at her. There she went again, reading him like a book.

"Yeah." They settled into the seats overlooking the empty ice below. "Still not used to *how* many of you there are."

She shifted in her seat, eyes taking in the room full of people. "It is a lot to handle." She smiled as she focused on him once again. "But I have complete faith you'll be a full-fledged member of our squad soon enough."

His heart gave a kick at the idea. He relaxed back, choosing to enjoy the moment instead of over-analyzing it.

"Jor, can we hold the babies now?" a young voice asked.

He turned to see a small boy who looked to be around eight with light brown hair and blue eyes wearing a Ryan Donnelly jersey and a pretty dark-haired girl about the same age with bright green eyes in a Jake Donovan jersey.

"Of course, honey. Why don't you and Carlee take a seat and you can each hold them for a while," Jordan said sweetly.

"Sean," Vince called out excitedly, dropping into a seat. "My man, pots and pans, what's up, little dude?"

The boy reached out a hand to do the similar funky handshake Gage had seen Donnelly do with Vince earlier that day. "Is your sister here too?" Sean asked. "Or is she in her usual seat?"

"Yeah. She's right over there." Vince laughed at the brush-off and pointed across the aisle to where he and Rocky sat.

"Rock. Put it on me," the kid said, puckering his lips at her. He had hella game for a second grader.

Rocky giggled a tinkling laugh as she released his hand to take Sean's face in both of hers, laying a smacking kiss on his cheek. Sean smiled proudly to himself as she pulled away. "Dude. What, are two wives not enough for you? You trying to collect another?"

"To be fair, I called dibs on Madz before Ryan. And we all know you were only with Jase while you waited for me to be legal. Ten more years, Rock." He held both hands up, illustrating the number with his fingers.

Gage bit the inside of his cheek to hold back a laugh. He didn't have much experience around kids, but Sean was hysterical. His game was smoother than most guys he knew around his own age, let alone someone who wasn't even in the double digits.

"Dude," Rocky said with a shake of her head. "Where the hell do you come up with this stuff? You're eight."

The kid looked like a mini version of Ryan Donnelly and Gage assumed he was another Donnelly sibling.

"Oh, shit. You're Gage James," Sean said, his blue eyes going wide when he spotted him in the seat next to Rocky.

"Sean," Jordan chastised. "Don't let Mom hear you curse. Not unless you want her to ban you from hanging out at my house when the guys are over."

"Sorry, Jor," Sean said before focusing on him once again. "But, whoa. Like seriously, this is so cool." He looked over his shoulder at someone. "Oh my god. *Jamie*. Did you *seeeeeee, Gage James*"—he whisper-shouted his name—"is here. He knows *our* friends. How flipping cool is this?"

"I know, buddy." Jamie Hawke, *fucking Jamie Hawke*, agreed.

He couldn't believe that the rock star he was fanboying over a few minutes ago was doing the same with an eight-year-old about him.

"You had Velasquez tapping out in fourteen seconds to keep the belt in your last fight," Sean continued to gush.

For the next few minutes, he listened to Sean recap his entire career, only breaking to introduce his best friend, Jake Donovan's younger sister, Carlee. The kid was also well versed on the stats of all the other fighters from The Steele Maker.

But when their mom called them to come eat, they ran off like normal youngsters on the hunt for food.

"Vin. Oh my god. Thank god you're here." A pretty blonde, the one with the ice blue eyes he recognized from his first trip to Espresso Patronum, dropped herself across Vince's lap.

"Hey, Madz. What's up?" Vince hooked an arm around her waist, letting her legs hang over the armrest of the seat they now shared.

"I need a favor."

"What kind of favor?" he asked skeptically.

"The kind you're *perfect* for."

"Use your words, Madz. You're an author, it shouldn't be too hard for you."

Looked like this was the last member of the infamous Coven that he hadn't met yet.

"Exactly *how* hard would it be to convince you to be the cover model for the book I *just* finished?"

"*Ohhhhh*. You're so right. He'd be perfect," Skye said and the other girls chimed in to agree.

"How would you guys know?" Vince asked.

"We're her beta readers for everything she writes," Gemma explained.

"Duh," Becky added helpfully.

"So, will you do it?" Maddey asked again.

"What, run out of hockey players?"

Maddey rolled her eyes, undeterred by Vince's lackluster response. "I need someone...grittier. And you have that Theo James *Divergent* feel about you. But if you're not up to doing it, I think at least one of my brothers should be home soon and I can ask them to do it."

"I didn't say I wasn't interested," Vince hedged. "Is it going to be one of those ones where I have to stand around shirtless by myself so you girls can ogle me?"

"Vin, don't play dumb. You know I always do couple shots for my covers. I have the perfect girl to be your partner, just say yes already. You know you want to."

"Of course I'll do it, Madz."

"Love you, Vin." She gave him a beaming smile, then turned on Gage. "Now you."

He wasn't a small guy, being on the top half of the six-foot measurement mark, but some of these ladies were *intimidating* in their intensity.

"Do you have any idea how hard it was to meet my deadline when *all* Lyle wanted to do was wax on in *very* specific detail about the newest fighter at The Steele Maker?"

He had the overwhelming urge to apologize, and Rocky buried her face against his side, laughing as he did so. Over the last few days, she had been less hesitant with the physical touches. He liked it.

"No worries." Maddey brushed off his apology. "You'll make it up to me when you don't fight me when I need my next model."

Every warning he'd ever heard about how charming Maddey was flashed through his mind, and he was confident she would end up being right.

The babies were passed around, getting love from everyone until a representative from the Blizzards entered the suite to walk the women down to their seats for the first period.

Vince, a baby cradled in his arms, moved into the seat next to Gage.

"You doing all right?" The speculative look in those familiar gray eyes made him think Rocky wasn't the only member of the Steele family able to read him.

He shook his head. "But I will be."

🐙

Rocky loved watching the game so close to the ice. It reminded her of her time working as one of the PT students assigned to the Titans during college.

Down here, it was like being in the middle of the action. When the players checked each other into the boards, you could feel the vibrations of the hit in your bones.

At the start of every Blizzards game, Jordan put her fist to the boards to share a knuckle bump with Ryan through the glass and pressed her lips to it—regardless of how gross it might be—to give her husband a good luck kiss before he took his position between the pipes.

"So what's going on with you and Gage?" Jordan asked the moment she settled into her seat.

"*Yes,*" Skye cried. "*Please* tell me you climbed that boy like the tree he is."

"Would it be wrong if I took notes?" Maddey asked with a playful smirk.

She'd known she would have to face the inquisition at some point. She wasn't at all surprised they jumped right into it as soon as they were alone.

"Unfortunately, no." She scrunched her nose in disgust.

"Still holding out on you?" Jordan's words were laced with sympathy.

"Oh, yeah. Every day he does something to tease me.

Taunt me. I swear he takes some sort of evil pleasure in getting me all worked up, only to leave me with major blue clit."

"Yup, that's totally going in a book," Maddey commented.

"If I didn't *feel* how much he did, I would start to question if actually wanted me," she confessed, that familiar insecurity burning like acid. But there was no denying the hard press of his trouser snake against her body when he would brush his body against hers.

"Oh, he wants you," Becky confirmed. "I swear he looked like he wanted to bash Jase's pretty face in when he stopped by the gym earlier."

She spent the bulk of the first period filling them in on everything that had transpired during and after Jase's visit to The Steele Maker. She knew better than to leave out a single detail.

"You are *so* getting laid before the weekend is over," Gemma declared when she finished telling them about getting clam-jammed by the massage table.

"Why do you say that?" She failed to keep the hope from her voice.

"He's this close"—Gem held her thumb and pointer finger centimeters apart—"to breaking."

"I agree with Gem," Jordan said. "If he almost fucked you in your office over *thinking* you and Jase had something going on, just think of how he'll feel after spending the night out at Rookies with him and a bunch of both my brothers' teammates."

She didn't want to play games to capture his affection. She wanted to be picked because she was *enough*, not due to some misguided jealousy. Still, she knew her friends might have a point.

"Besides," Maddey cut in. "Nothing makes an alpha male claim his mate like a little competition."

Chapter Eighteen

G age loved hockey. You had to respect a sport where the guys dropped their gloves and fought it out when necessary.

The suite Jordan's family owned was directly above where the girls had seats down at rink level. They all seemed to be super into the game and he couldn't help but laugh as he watched Rocky's tiny blonde friend bang on the glass, yelling at the players battling it out for the puck in front of them.

Throughout the first period, he noticed a few people with lanyards hanging from their necks who stopped to talk to Jordan and Skye, as well as some of the guys on the Blizzards shout something to them from their bench.

"You know how when we went out last week we told you Rocky was like the mayor of the world?" Vince said when Gage mentioned how much attention the women got.

"Yeah." He also remembered the irrational jealousy that spiked through him as he watched Rocky interact with the college hockey players.

"Well, if she's the mayor—" Vince started.

"Then Jordan's the president," Nick finished.

He found it a very apt description of the tiny blonde.

As Damon passed him a fresh bottle of beer, he realized not once since the girls left had he felt awkward or out of place with the guys. A first for him. Vince ensured he was included in group conversations, Damon had kept him hydrated and lubricated, and talking with Jamie, the frontman of one of his favorite bands, was a damned dream come true.

When the game broke for the first intermission—the Blizzards up by one thanks to a sweet goal from Ryan—he and the guys made their way up from the seats to the main area of the suite to get some food. Jordan and Gemma had even arranged to have meal plan-appropriate selections for Vince to enjoy.

Sean sidled up to their table, hot dog loaded with spray cheese and potato chips in each hand.

"So, little dude. Whatcha going as for Halloween next week?" Vince asked, salivating over Sean's food like a dog would a steak.

"Carlee and I are going as Ducks," Sean responded with a mouth full of junked-up hot dog.

"Like the bird?" Vince sounded as confused as Gage felt. He'd think the kids were a little too old to be trick-or-treating as animals.

"Noooo." Sean dragged out the word as if to say *don't be stupid.* "Like *The Mighty Ducks.*"

"Dude…I loved those movies growing up," Gage declared proudly. "Whose jersey you gonna wear?"

"Charlie Conway. Captain, like my brother."

"Good choice. You going with the old school green jerseys?"

Sean shook his head. "The white ones."

"Yeah, I want to be Julie The Cat." Carlee ran over to join them, stealing one of the hot dogs from Sean.

"Yup. She wants to be the goalie like her brother. And she wasn't a Duck in the first movie," Sean explained.

Gage wondered if all kids were as cool as these two. If not, he hoped he could mold his godchild to be.

His eyes automatically found Rocky as the girls arrived in the suite, a smile growing when she and Maddey chose to join them.

"Hi, Husband," Maddey greeted Sean.

"Hi, Wife." The little charmer winked.

"Hi, Sister-Wife," Maddey said to Carlee with a hug.

"Sister-Wife?" Gage questioned.

"Sean was my little husband before the Donnellys moved next door to the Donovans and he met Carlee here." Maddey pulled the younger Donovan into a side-hug. "So now we share him," she explained while stealing a chicken wing off of Deck's plate.

"You owe me a kiss if you take my food, Madz," Deck said, puckering his lips at her.

Maddey rolled her eyes, placing the now bare bones back onto his plate. "Please, Deck. You couldn't handle me. We all know you could never be with a girl who could beat you in a fight."

Rocky laughed as she did the same to Gage's own plate. He grabbed the back of her chair and pulled her closer as he pushed his plate toward her.

"*Pfff.* You're barely my warm-up weight when I lift, you're so tiny," Deck countered.

"I was referring more to being raised by a guy who could kill you ten different ways with his pinky alone." She held up the finger for emphasis. "You really think Jack McClain didn't make sure his little girl knew how to defend herself?"

"I love your dad," Rocky chimed in around a mouthful of his food.

"Hold on," Gage cut in. "Your dad has the same name as one of the most badass cops in film franchise history?"

"Yup." Maddey nodded. "But to be fair, we spell McClain different and he goes by Jack and not John."

"And he's more Liam Neeson in *Taken*," Rocky added.

"You mean he's more *I have a particular set of skills* and less *Yippie-ki-yay*?" he clarified.

"He's a little bit of both," Maddey said. "He was a SEAL for years before retiring to become a police chief."

"You know, the more I learn about you girls, the more I understand why the guys call you The Coven," he mused.

"Oh, yeah? And why's that?" Rocky challenged him with an arch of one her black brows. Why the action made his pants tighten, he didn't want to delve into.

"You're a bunch of badasses."

"Damn straight," all six of them chorused from around the room, not missing a beat.

Everyone was remaining in the suite for the second period, so he made sure Rocky was close when they settled in to watch the game again.

His hand hung over the armrest, tracing circles on her knee. Her entire focus was on what was happening in the game below, but there was no missing the way she squirmed in her seat. Or the sharp hiss of her breath as he trailed a finger up the toned muscle of her thigh, under the hem of her jersey.

He was working his way toward the v between her legs, toward the heat at her center, when he was startled by shouting.

"Someone take the baby. I *can't* hold her during a Storm power play." Jordan held out the baby.

With the moment broken, he hesitated. But he had probably teased her enough, so he moved his hand to cup her knee and stayed away from the danger zone.

He still hadn't worked out all the details yet, but this cat and mouse game he had been playing was about to come to an end.

Chapter Nineteen

High above the dance floor at Rookies, Rocky braced her elbows on the railing, bottle of beer dangling between her fingers, while she watched people gyrate below and tried to work out the conflicting emotions that always came from a Storm / Blizzards game.

As long as the Storm weren't on their way to another road game right after they played their Jersey rivals, Jase skipped the team bus and stayed with their group for the night. Whenever he did—with the exception of a missing Tucker, who played for the Chicago Fire—it brought back memories of college, and how happy she was to be out as an honorary member of the Titans.

She missed working with puck heads something fierce.

Of course, she loved her job. Mixed martial arts, judo and boxing were as much a part of her as her gray eyes. Working with fighters and knowing she helped keep them in the cage past an age most would think they could fight gave her an immense sense of satisfaction. That wasn't the issue. The problem was the lack of options she'd had in choosing her workplace.

"You know, for a girl whose team won tonight, you sure don't seem like it." Gage's deep voice cut into her thoughts.

Canting her head to the side, she took a moment to soak in the hotness that was Gage James in a tight black t-shirt—it was sinfully unfair what the man did to simple black cotton—as she debated how much she should reveal to him.

"I'm always happy when the Blizzards win." A smile tugged at her lips. "Jordan and I already gave Jase a rash of shit over it."

"You guys are really that close, huh?"

After what happened earlier at the gym, though unnecessary, she was more cognizant of the jealousy he was feeling.

"We are." She paused, knowing she needed to choose her words carefully. "I think Jase and Vince's ridiculous bromance with each other helped more than anything else."

He looked like he was trying not to smirk but eventually lost the good fight.

"I could see that," he said with a nod. "Your brother is quite the character."

She snorted. "That's one way to put it." She looked over her shoulder to where the two guys were yucking it up at the bar. "They are the *worst*. It gets especially bad when Tuck comes home for the summer. The three of them together"—she leaned in as if she were parting with state secrets—"are the ultimate pranksters."

He moved in, playing along. "I'll keep that in mind."

"Good." She shifted back and took a long pull on her beer. Bantering with Gage helped to chase her troubles away.

"So…" He shifted until his arm rested along hers as he mirrored her position on the railing. "Wanna tell me why you seem so down?"

Her sigh was as heavy as his weight class. "It's nothing."

"Rock," he drawled.

"Fine." She rested her chin on her shoulder so she could look at him while she confessed to something very few people knew. "Being here"—she circled a finger to indicate Rookies—"with all the guys, reminds me of how it was with them back in college."

"And you miss it." His eyes remained locked on hers, ignoring everything happening around them.

"Yup."

"What else?"

Damn him for not letting it go.

"And...I guess I'm sadder about not being a part of it than I realized."

"What do you mean?"

She looked away, picking at the label on her beer. "Did you know I was offered a staff position on the Blizzards?"

He nodded. "Yeah, I remember hearing about that. I wondered why you didn't take it. I know those spots are hard to come by."

"They are." Her heart squeezed as the familiar sense of a lost dream hit her. "But it was never part of the *plan*."

"The plan?" A little v formed between his dark brows as he looked at her with way more compassion than she thought she could handle at the moment, forcing her to look away again.

"The Steele Maker is a *family* business."

"Ahh."

Why did him reading between the lines hit her in the feels?

"Don't get me wrong...I love my job and family, but it would have been nice if it was my choice, ya know?"

Gage reached out and squeezed her to his side. She focused on the way the suction cups of the tentacles of his tattoo looked like they were actually grabbing on to the skin in an effort to blink back the tears she felt threatening.

She gave herself a second to enjoy the comfort of his hold. He had an uncanny ability to give her the validation she sought without even trying. He saw behind the mask, beyond the role she played at the gym, to the *core* of her.

He cleared his throat. "I know you feel like you were pushed into your position, but"—he hooked a finger under her chin to turn her face to his—"you were made for it."

She stared at him in surprise.

"You have this way of picking up on things no one else does. Not even your dad or uncle. *Your* eye for detail is the best I've ever seen. There's not a doubt in my mind that your brother will win his upcoming fight and it's because of you."

She scoffed. "Yeah, right. Vince trains his ass off. *That's* why he will win."

"Obviously he couldn't do it if he didn't train. But the critiques you give him and areas you have him focus on are more valuable to how he'll handle himself during his fight than any amount of hours he practices with me."

She blinked as tears pressed against the back of her eyes. He saw her in a way no one else did.

"Thanks Gage." She rested her head in the hallow between his arm and body.

"I got you, Blue."

With his arm around her she believed it to be true.

Having enough of the heavy, she used the excuse of needing a new beer to escape. Gage was able to pick up on all the things she didn't say and she wasn't sure how to feel about it.

She joined her friends at the bar. They all joked as they watched the Lions/Fire game but only parts of their conversation broke through the emotional fog she was in.

The circumstances surrounding her job were complicated enough on their own, adding Gage to the mix—talk about complicated.

"I asked Wade to make sure to hit Tuck a *little* extra hard tonight." Jordan's comment was the first thing to really register with her.

"You did?" Jase asked.

"Of course. He may be my BB3 but you"—she pointed to him—"are my twin. It means I love you most."

"Hey?!" Ryan and Jake cried in unison, offended to hear they weren't her favorite.

"You'll always be my favorite big brother." Jordan patted Ryan on the chest placating him. "And you will always be the love of my life." She raised up onto her toes, throwing her arms around Jake's neck and laying a kiss so hot on him, it was obvious to him, as well as anyone else watching, how much she loved her husband.

Rocky sighed, longing for the kind of love her friend had found with her husband. She dreamed of finding the person who would put her above all else.

Could Gage be that person?

Only time would tell.

WHEN ROCKY WENT to join her friends at the bar, Gage remained at the railing that overlooked the rest of Rookies. He had suspected some of what she had revealed to him, but he doubted many people understood how deep it ran. He was honored she had trusted him with it.

He rejoined the fighters from the gym at the couches they'd claimed and was happy to see the smile had returned to Rocky's beautiful face. He just hated that she was standing next to Jase Donnelly when it happened.

Knowing they had history, *romantic* history, got under his skin like a splinter, festering under the surface until he wanted to cut off the infected area.

The time for games was over. No more teasing or drawing things out between them. He needed to stake his claim and make it known to Rocky and everyone else exactly who she belonged to.

Forcing himself to remain seated and not go all irrational

caveman, he refocused his attention from the group at the bar to the hockey game on the TV. His LA Lions were currently up by a goal on the Chicago Fire.

He must not have looked away fast enough though, because Vince leaned over close enough for only him to hear and said, "There's nothing going on between them besides friendship."

He knew it was true, but he still shot Vince a skeptical look.

"Seriously, bro. Jase is like Becky to my sister. Except with a dick."

It was the dick part he was having trouble accepting.

"What's the deal with all that then?" he asked, pointing to where Rocky leaned her shoulder into Donnelly's side as she said something to Jordan. They looked *cozy*. He fucking hated it.

If he thought about things rationally, he wouldn't be bothered. The guys at the gym stood around with her much the same way, but he wasn't feeling all that rational at the moment.

It didn't help that he still felt like a bit of an outsider when he was with the group. His own doing, but he didn't know how to get out of his own way and connect with them.

"Okay, time for a little story." Vince shifted forward to rest his elbows on his knees, dangling his water bottle from his fingers so it hung between his legs. Before he could start, the catalyst for the conversation joined them as Donnelly dropped into the open seat next to Vince. "Perfect, just in time, bro."

"What's up?" Donnelly asked while greeting everyone else.

"I was just about to give our boy Gage here a history lesson."

That casually inclusive reference of *our* hit him harder than he would have thought.

"*Oooh*, I love story time. Where are you going to start?" Jase rubbed his hands together gleefully.

"I was thinking the beginning."

"You mean where your parents boinked like bunnies and had you and Rock so close together?"

"Bro." Vince reared back in disgust while Donnelly snickered. "Asshole."

Donnelly shrugged as if to say *what are you gonna do?*

"Anyway…"

"Oooh, let me start. Because it's about me and Balboa, right?" The hockey player shifted to mimic Vince's position so now both guys gave him their full attention.

"Am I going to want to hear this?" Gage asked warily.

"Maybe not," Donnelly answered honestly. "But I think if you know the history it might help you *not* look at me like you want to kick my ass, so I'm willing to give it a shot if you are."

He wanted to dislike the guy. He *really* did, but he was making it hard. He nodded for Donnelly to continue.

"So let's see…" Donnelly looked at where the women still stood at the bar. "Okay, I got it." He resumed eye contact with Gage. "I met Rocky my freshman year when she started working with the hockey team and we became friends."

He paused to take a sip of his beer.

"We didn't start dating until junior year when she became close with my sister after we brought her to learn some more advanced self-defense moves after JD's psycho ex went all *if I can't have you, no one else can* on her."

"Well, shit." He blew out a breath.

"I know. Don't worry, he got locked up. Anyway, sometime between graduation and my first training camp things ended. It was like one day we were a couple and the next… we were back to being friends."

"*Really?*" His tone bled with disbelief though he had to give the guy props for not waxing poetic about their relationship. "You were able to go back to being friends like you'd never seen each other naked?"

"Dude." Vince reeled back. "I'm not an idiot. I know my sister is a grown woman, but I do *not* need to think about her having sex."

Leave it to Vince to break the tension.

"To answer your question," Donnelly cut in before Vince could go off on a tangent, "yeah, pretty much."

"How?"

"Honestly, we were trying to force something that was never there in the first place. And I think it's just the way the girls are wired. They love deeply and unconditionally."

He nodded his understanding. That was something he'd witnessed the past few weeks. Everyone was treated like family whether they were related by blood or not. It was one of the things that made the team at The Steele Maker so strong and the main factor convincing him to open himself up to them.

"I think the most important thing for you to know is there are no lingering feelings between Rock and I. We're strictly friends. Some would say best friends, but only friends nonetheless." Again, he looked back at the bar. "Kind of like how Ry and Madz are."

"They're not a couple?" He looked to where Jase's brother stood with the short blonde leaning against his chest, his arms looped around her middle.

"Not anymore."

"Anymore?"

"Yeah. They started dating a few months before me and Rock. I think we all thought they would get married the same way JD and Jake did, but sometime around when Ry proposed, they broke up."

"Shit, Jase," Nick said. "When did you become such a gossip."

"Shut up, it's not gossip. It's vital information. How else

do you expect our boy Gage here to understand the unique dynamics of our squad?"

He was the second person to refer to him as *our boy* during this conversation. Who would have thought being accepted by the ex-boyfriend of the girl he was developing feelings for would be one of the first things to really make him feel officially included.

"You know, you guys really know how to bury the lede." He made it a point to look at each of them.

"How's that?" Vince quirked a brow.

"You guys said your sister dated *some* hockey player."

"Well, yeah. He may be an enforcer but Jase is still a puck head," Ray pointed out.

"Yeah, but he's also Jase Fucking Donnelly." He pointed to Jase. "You guys made it sound like it was just some guy that played for your school, not one of the biggest names in the NHL."

"Aww, stop it. You're gonna make me blush," Donnelly joked.

"To be fair…" Vince pointed at him with his water bottle. "To us, he is *just* Jase. And Rock spends so much time around professional athletes that she kinda doesn't think about the whole famous thing. Now"—he clapped Gage on the back—"even surrounded by some of the biggest names in sports, you, my friend, have always been her celebrity crush."

"What?" There was no way. He was nobody's celebrity crush.

"True," the guys all agreed.

"So the question is"—again, those familiar gray eyes locked on him—"when are you gonna grow a set and finally do something about it?" Vince challenged.

Well, shit.

Looked like it was time for him to step into the cage.

Chapter Twenty

The open-door policy on the twelfth floor worked in Gage's favor when it came to tracking down Rocky. The doors to both apartments down the hall were once again propped open and from the sounds of things, he should find most of them inside the girls' place.

The layouts might be the same but Rocky, Becky and Gemma sure as hell made their home their own with hot pink acrylic barstools and a collection of white, pink, gray and animal print accents scattered throughout.

Like always, his eye went to the wall made up entirely of twinkle lights with pictures hanging from the strands. A few photos including him from the game the night before really drove home that he had found his tribe.

Gage James was officially no longer a loner.

He stood unmoving, staring at the wall while that realization sunk it. *How did this happen?* A lot of it was because of a certain raven-haired beauty.

"You're going down, Madz. Here comes a blue shell," Deck challenged, obviously in the middle of an epic Mario Kart battle.

"Keep dreaming, Deck. Stick to fighting—your Mario Kart game is weak," Maddey clapped back.

Who knew Nintendo could be so serious?

"Boom!" Maddey cheered, raising both hands, including the wheel-shaped controller, overhead in celebration. "Don't mess with the champ, boys."

"I swear you cheat," Deck complained.

"Whatever you say, pretty boy."

"And I swear, you boys will *never* learn," Rocky called out, drawing his gaze to where she stood in the kitchen. She looked adorable as hell in a shirt with "I've got a headache... Voldemort must be close" displayed across the generous swell of her chest.

He grinned when she moved from behind the island and he saw the loose pants with Harry Potter glasses and lightning bolts on them.

"Hey," he said, stepping around the counter.

"Hey," she returned, stretching up to give him a quick kiss on the lips.

He liked that she seemed to get less hesitant with him the more time they were around each other.

"So...I was wondering..." She glanced over her shoulder to the living room full of people. "Wanna go to dinner with me?"

He laughed in surprise as he had walked in the door with the same intention.

He pulled her closer. "When did you have in mind?"

"Tonight?"

"Seriously?"

"Seriously," she said.

He matched her smirk with one of his own. "You don't waste any time, do you?"

She moved in closer, though he doubted the others paid them any attention based on the trash talk going on.

"Well, it's been a week since I almost took a shower with

you. Aside from us breaking the massage table in my treatment room at the gym, all you've done is tease me, and to be
honest, I'm over it."

His smile was just this side of evil. He knew *exactly* what
he'd done to her all week.

"That." She pointed an accusing finger at his face. "That
right there is why I'm not waiting for you to make a move."

"Is that so?" He liked this feisty side.

"Yup."

Her hands came to his chest as he crossed his arms behind
her back, eliminating the last of the space between them. "So
you're saying you only want me for my body," he teased.

"No." She stretched up onto her toes to speak directly into
his ear. "But I figured maybe we should go on a date first,
before we fuck each other."

A shiver ran down his spine. He wasn't sure if it was from
her lips brushing along the shell of his ear or from her direct
words, but both worked for him. He moved in so his mouth
brushed the rim of her ear.

"Sounds like a plan. But just so you know." He paused to
run his nose along the sensitive spot behind her ear, causing
her to endure a shiver of her own. "The night *will* end with
me buried deep inside you. Because I haven't been able to
think of anything else all week."

"Promises, promises," she taunted.

He let out a bark of laughter, drawing attention from the
Mario Karters, but Rocky waved them off and turned back to
him. "Anyway…it's nothing fancy, jeans and a t-shirt are fine.
I'll meet you at your place in a few hours. I'm gonna go
shower."

He let out a growl at the thought of her in the shower.
"Need a hand in there?"

Infuriatingly, she laughed at him. "Relax there, big guy."
She patted his chest. "Dinner first. Then…" She shrugged.

After watching her walk away, he headed for the living

room, exchanging greetings with everyone as he settled into a spot at the end of the couch.

"Wanna play?" Vince held out a controller in his direction.

"Sure. Why not." He accepted the white wheel.

For the next hour, he lost himself in the world of Mario Kart, trading insults, slinging shells and avoiding banana peels with the best of them. No matter how hard they tried, no one could beat Maddey. Nor was he able to get his mind off his first official date in longer than he could remember.

🐙

When Gage opened his door at Rocky's knock, he was momentarily struck speechless by the sight of her standing there in a simple blue and gray dress that touched the floor and leather jacket. She was easily becoming one of his favorite things to look at.

The drive to the restaurant was quick. Hand-in-hand, they followed the hostess through the crowded dining room to their table. He opted to sit to her left instead of across from her. They discussed the menu and what was good to eat, eventually ordering enough food for them to share to feed a small army.

Propping his elbow on the table, he rested his chin on his fist, once again taking in the vision in next of him. Rocky's long, blue-black hair hung straight around her shoulders and tumbled down her back. Her mesmerizing gray eyes had a sprinkling of sparkly eye shadow and her cupid's bow lips were adorned with a pale pink gloss.

"So how'd you get into fighting?" she asked, mirroring his pose. "I don't think I've ever heard you say in an interview."

"My mom." He reached out to stroke the delicate skin on the inside of her wrist while he spoke.

"Really?"

"Yeah." He couldn't help but smile at the memory. "When Wyatt and I were younger, we were...rambunctious."

"You mean you were hella crazy and your moms didn't know what to do with you?" she asked knowingly.

He touched the tip of his nose with his finger. "Exactly."

"Vince and Deck were the same way." Her lips took on a devilish curl. "Though I can't say the girls and I were much better. Beck was always convincing us to do all kinds of crazy things. It's how she earned her text handle."

He'd learned all about the group's crazy text handles last night when Jase and Vince went through his phone updating his contacts. He was still coming to terms with the fact the guy he spent the day being jealous over was inserting himself as a friend, but he was also learning that you didn't have much choice when it came to Rocky and her friends.

"But that's not important here. You get to hear about my crazy every day at the gym. I want to hear about you for a change. So come on, tell me."

"Okay." He dropped an arm around the back of her chair, scooting in closer. "So sometime in middle school, our moms were looking for *anything* that could help burn off some of the excess energy we had."

"What did they find?"

"First, it was karate. Then for me it evolved into Muay Thai and jiu-jitsu. And for Wyatt, it was parkour."

"Parkour?" Her eyes sparkled. "Like Jackie Chan scaling buildings and stuff?"

"Yup." He couldn't help but laugh remembering how often Wyatt got screamed at for demonstrating what he learned in class at home. He was pretty sure his aunt had regretted *ever* enrolling him in the class.

"I have a feeling the class was one of the reasons he became a firefighter."

"That's amazing. But what about you? How'd you hook

up with Tony? You've been with him your whole career, right?"

He nodded, liking how easy it was to talk to her. Thanks to her own background, it made it feel like he was talking to a peer. Her firsthand knowledge of the sport and what the training entailed was a refreshing change from being around girls who either pretended to know what he was talking about or were only able to spout off his stats because they were groupies.

"One of my BJJ instructors saw how promising I was and brought up the whole mixed martial arts thing to my mom. She was hesitant at first—as I would assume most moms would be—but eventually, we met with Tony, and the rest is history."

He had her laughing when he told her about some of his wilder antics with Wyatt growing up. She paused to take a breath, then leaned over for a sip of her mango margarita. When she wrapped her lips around the straw, he imagined what those same lips would look like wrapped around his cock.

If he was lucky, he would get to experience it later tonight.

He really needed to look away as she drank. His mind was firmly in the gutter, because watching her throat work as she swallowed, all he could think of was watching it contract as she swallowed every drop of cum he wanted to give her.

Fuck.

Sucking on that straw, Rocky tilted her head at him when he wasn't able to hold back a groan.

"You okay over there, stud?" A knowing smirk pulled up the corners of her lips.

"Stud?" He laughed as the tension between them broke.

All the little tease did was shrug, causing him to growl in response.

"I'll show you how much of a *stud* I am later."

"Promise?" She bit the corner of her lower lip.

Seeing her teeth sink into the plump flesh snapped the last of his control. With another growl, he placed his hand on the back of her neck and pulled her in to devour her mouth. She didn't hesitate to return the kiss.

The temperature at their table heated as they continued to kiss. He spread his fingers and twisted them between the strands of her hair, giving a slight tug.

Her answering moan was almost enough to make him say screw dinner and drag her out of the restaurant. Luckily, the server arrived with their food before he could give in to his baser urges.

ROCKY JUMPED BACK at the sound of their server behind them, her cheeks heating in embarrassment. She didn't even look up when he asked if they needed anything else after he set down their plates.

They ate in silence for a few moments while they got their hormones under control.

"God, this food is incredible," Gage said around a bite of enchiladas.

"I know. We love it." Jose Tejas was one of her favorite Tex-Mex restaurants. "Vince is going to be so jealous when he hears I brought you here."

"I take it Gem would have his balls if he cheated on his diet right now?"

"You would be correct." She took a sip of her margarita, happy that he was finally starting to be more comfortable with their group's dynamics.

"But I can almost guarantee this is the first place we will come to the day after his fight."

"Well, I'll happily keep him company."

She let out a laugh. "You're not the only one. It'll be like a class field trip—*everyone* will be in for that meal." She paused.

"We'll have to come for lunch to have any hope of not having to wait forever."

"Did you guys all grow up together?"

She explained how each of the guys were connected—Deck a childhood friend, Griff one of Vince's wrestling rivals from a high school a few towns over, and Ray falling in with them after taking a few classes with Vince.

"So your brother is the common denominator?"

She swallowed her bite of shrimp and crawfish quesadilla. "All except Nick and Damon. They played for the Titans and learned about the gym from when I was their trainer."

"And it all comes back to hockey."

Unlike when the subject came up with her father, she didn't hear any judgment in his voice. The biggest fight she'd ever had with her father happened when she tried to leave The Steele Maker to accept the job offer from the Blizzards.

"Are you unhappy at the gym?"

She stilled, unsure how to answer. He was the first person to ask her that.

"No. I grew up there. I just...ya know." What could she say that didn't sound petulant?

"Well..." He continued to hold her hand as he'd been doing all night and a part of her swooned anytime he initiated contact between them. "I guess selfishly I'm glad you didn't take it because now I get to see you all the time." He stroked a finger down the side of her face.

There was something about him that always managed to get her out of her head and away from the negative thoughts she had about her position at the gym. It was like he was the missing puzzle piece to her feeling truly secure in her role.

The server saw their empty plates and came by to see if they wanted anything else. They both declined and asked for the check. When he came back with the tray, Gage reached for it but she was faster.

"I don't think so." She wagged her finger at him.

"Hey! What kind of gentleman would I be if I didn't pay for dinner?" He tried to snag the check again.

But she was too quick and held it out of his reach. "And while I appreciate the sentiment, I was the one who asked you out to eat. So I'm paying, end of story."

He smiled at her, not put off by her sass. "Fine, but I'm paying next time."

"There's going to be a next time?" She raised an eyebrow.

"There's going to be many more next times," he stated with a wink.

Chapter Twenty-One

Gage held Rocky's hand the entire walk from the car, not even letting go when he had to unlock his apartment door, grateful for being a lefty. Before leaving earlier, he'd turned the pendant lights over the kitchen island on, giving them enough light to navigate by.

Once inside, he pressed her to the same wall he had her against the week before. He tilted her chin up with one hand, while using the pressure of his other thumb to open her mouth for his assault. He already knew how amazing it felt to kiss her and didn't waste any time getting reacquainted with it.

She groaned as his tongue painted the inside of her mouth. He loved that she wasn't passive, meeting his passion head on. She tangled her tongue with his as she locked her hands behind his head.

Her height made it easy for him to align their bodies when they were pressed against each other. But she must not have been satisfied, because he felt her rise onto her tiptoes, molding her body against his like cling wrap. He tugged on her long hair as she scratched her fingers through the short hair of his scalp.

Breaking the kiss, he rested his forehead against hers, his lungs heaving as he tried to calm the situation he felt going on in his pants. "I'm never going to be able to look at my door and not get hard."

"That'll make for some interesting greetings. Have fun explaining all that to the guys when they come over," she said with a laugh as she gestured to his pants.

God, he loved her sense of humor. "How about we move this to a more appropriate setting for my boner?"

"Lead the way, hot stuff."

Grabbing her hand, he walked them back to his bedroom, pleased that there was enough ambient light streaming through the windows to be able to see. Her standing in his room felt as right to him as him standing inside the octagon for a fight.

ROCKY COULDN'T BELIEVE she and Gage were finally going to have sex. She felt like they'd been working toward this moment forever. She knew her long-standing crush on him hadn't helped in that regard. Seeing him at the gym every day for weeks also didn't.

Then he went and moved in down the hall from her.

Each day he did or said something that chipped away at the wall she'd built around herself when it came to fighters. Question by question, another brick fell. Comment by comment, he built up a platform to help him scale the wall.

Gage James was a hit combination she had no chance of defending herself against.

Then after her defenses were lowered, there was the hottest kiss of her entire life, plus the almost shower sex that followed it.

"Please tell me you locked your front door behind us," she pleaded.

"I did," he assured her.

"Thank god." She blew out a breath of relief. "Because I swear to god, if one more thing cock blocks us, I might literally explode from sexual frustration."

His answering chuckle was sexy as hell. Too bad she wasn't joking.

Emboldened by his gaze, she slipped off her shoes, then reached for the bottom of her maxi dress and pulled it up and off her body, leaving herself clad in only her black lace demi bra and lacy boy shorts.

She heard a growl from by the door.

That was exactly what she needed. She unclasped her bra and dropped it to the floor. His gaze never wavered. Next, she hooked her thumbs in her panties and drew them down her legs. Standing up, she kicked them away and stood before him in all her naked glory.

Then she quirked an eyebrow at him. "Your move."

"DAMN," GAGE WHISPERED reverently as he got his first look at Rocky naked. "You are a vision."

She was all long, muscular limbs and soft curves. Her blue-black hair curled around full, perky breasts, topped with toffee-colored nipples begging to be sucked. Her waist indented in the perfect hourglass shape and was small enough he was sure his hands could encase it entirely.

He watched the defined muscles of her stomach contract as she took a deep breath and smiled at the jeweled ring decorating her tiny belly button. Her hips flared out, beckoning for him to hold on while he drove himself into her over and over.

The vibrant rainbow colors of a tattoo extended on her left side from the bottom of her left breast to underneath the bump of her hip bone. He was finally going to get the chance to get an up close and personal view of the artwork she chose to decorate her body with.

Down the miles of toned perfection that were her legs, he spotted bright blue nail polish on her toes. Raking his gaze back up her legs, he locked in on the luscious thighs he couldn't wait to bury his face between and sucked in a breath when he saw she was waxed bare.

Christ, he needed to move. His long legs ate up the small space between them and he scooped her into his arms, crushed his mouth against hers.

Her legs wrapping around him was pure heaven.

"One of us is highly overdressed." She pulled at the collar of his t-shirt.

With a chuckle, he finished walking the distance to his California King bed. He laid her down in the middle of it before stepping back and pulling his t-shirt over his head.

She let out a groan as she propped herself up on her elbows to watch the show he put on removing his clothes.

His blood pumped faster at the hungry look in her eyes, so he quickly got to work on his belt while he toed off his sneakers. Popping the snap on his jeans, he slowly pulled down the zipper, careful of his straining erection. Once free, he dragged his jeans and boxer briefs down his legs and kicked them to the side.

When he was just as naked as she was, he approached the bed, but she stopped him with her hand on his chest.

She moved to the edge of the mattress and knelt in front of him. Her hands ran across his chest and down his abdominal muscles. She traced all his bumps and ridges, paying special attention to the deep v cuts on his hips.

"It should be illegal for you to wear clothes. A body like yours should never be covered up," she declared as she continued to trail her hands along his body.

"The feeling is mutual, babe."

Never one to be a spectator, he reached out to toy with her nipples. He brushed his thumbs across the peaks to get them to stand fully at attention. Then he pinched them between his thumb and forefinger, causing her to lean into his touch.

She reached out and mirrored his actions on his nipples. When he squeezed her tits in his hands, she fell against his body and started kissing her way down. Placing little nips here and there, her lips traveled across each bump of his eight pack, and followed his happy trail down to his straining erection.

It was a thing of beauty, if he did say so himself, ten inches of hard steel covered by silky skin. It stood proud off his body and curved up slightly toward his belly. Currently, it was almost purple from arousal, his little fighter as anxious for the feel of something other than his left hand as he was.

As if unable to resist the temptation any longer, Rocky licked along the vein on the underside, from base to tip. She swirled her tongue around the head and licked the leaking pre-cum from the tip, humming as she savored the taste of him, before opening her jaw to take as much of him inside as she could.

As if she had no gag reflex, she slid him down her throat and swallowed.

He groaned as he felt her throat constrict around his length. It felt too good. He had to stop her before things were over before they started. "Rock. Stop." He pulled on her hair slightly.

She released him with a pop. "Why? What's wrong?" Her eyes flashed with concern.

"*Nothing*. Nothing at all. That's just not where I want to finish tonight." He pushed back on her shoulders until she was lying back.

Warmth spread through his body at the sight of her laid out for his pleasure on his bed. Grabbing her ankles, he pulled her ass to the edge and dropped to his knees in front of her. His hands spread her legs wide, opening her up for him.

He ran his tongue up the length of her slit, causing her

back to bow up off the bed. Giving her no chance to prepare, he spread her lips and sucked her clit into his mouth. She tasted like the sweetest honey and he was ready to spend the rest of the night at home between her legs.

She squirmed as the pleasure he gave her wracked her body. He draped her legs over his shoulders and reached a hand up, skimming over her stomach to toy with her nipples.

She let out a scream and he felt her gush on his face as her orgasm burst through her. Not giving her an opportunity to catch her breath, he escalated his oral assault, keeping pressure on her clit as he pressed two fingers inside her.

She dug her heels into his back and squeezed his head with her strong thighs. Reaching down, she ran a hand over his head, grasping for purchase, letting out a growl when there was nothing to hold onto.

He laughed against her pussy at her frustration. "What's wrong, beautiful?" he asked without lifting from his position.

She continued to thrash against him, her second orgasm approaching fast. He redoubled his efforts between her legs, taking her entire pussy into his mouth until she came screaming his name. As she came back down to earth, he placed small kisses and nips against her.

He kissed his way up her body, sucking the steel bar of her belly ring into his mouth, trailing his tongue along her sweet skin, and detoured to suck a nipple.

"You want to tell me what was wrong before?" he murmured against her neck.

She was slow to answer and mumbled when she said, "What's that?"

"I was just wondering why you growled when you touched my head earlier." He kissed along her ear.

She let out a small laugh as she ran her hands over his head again. "I was just frustrated that your hair wasn't long enough for me to hold on to."

He chuckled and gave her a deep kiss. "Should I grow it out for you then?"

"Hell no!" She scratched her nails along his scalp. "I love the buzzed look on you on. Makes you look like a total badass."

He laughed against her lips. There was just something so special about this girl. Even in the middle of getting frisky, she still managed to make him laugh. He wasn't sure how he'd gotten lucky enough to find her, but now that he had, he wasn't letting her go.

She wrapped her legs around his waist. "What's with all the talking? I need you inside me now." Her body ground against him. "Fuck me," she whispered hotly in his ear.

She rubbed herself against his erection, causing him to glide through her lips.

He was reaching for the nightstand when he paused.

"What's wrong?"

He dropped his head to her chest. "I just remembered I don't have any condoms since I only just finished unpacking." He groaned as she continued to slide against his cock.

Her fingers traced patterns on the back of his head. "I'm on the pill and am clean."

"So—am—I," he barely managed to choke the words out. He'd never been inside a woman bare. Honestly, he'd never wanted to—until her. "You know I have regular checkups to fight and I've never been with anyone without a condom before."

"Neither have I. I've never wanted to."

Knowing about her long-term relationship with Jase, the caveman part of him beat a proud tattoo in his chest that he would be the first, and if he had his way, the last person to experience her this way.

"Me either, but the thought of riding you bare makes me want to shoot my load right now."

Her answering groan was music to his ears. "*Oh, god.* Please don't make me wait any longer. Get inside me now."

"Yes, ma'am." His chuckle quickly morphed into a groan as her wet heat surrounded his length.

ROCKY LOST HER breath at the feel of his girth stretching her like nothing ever had before. She was grateful for the moment he gave her to adjust to his size. The fullness was incredible.

Luckily, she was so wet and slick from her earlier orgasms that Gage was able to slide in to the hilt in one thrust. Without the barrier of latex between them, she could feel each vein and ridge of his cock.

He pumped his hips in a smooth rhythm, steadily picking up speed as she clung to his body. Her mouth fell open with each thrust.

"Oh—God—Gage," she moaned.

"You feel so good wrapped around me, babe," he said through gritted teeth.

She wanted to feel him lose control. As she scratched her nails down his back, the fleeting thought that he wouldn't be able to workout shirtless for a few days floated through her mind. If he did, it would broadcast to the entire gym exactly what he did with his free time.

"More, Gage," she breathed in his ear and bit his earlobe. "I *need* more."

"You're so tight." He growled and adjusted the angle of her hips so his body brushed against her clit with each pump.

He set a punishing pace.

In. Out.

In. Out.

In. Out.

Over and over he pounded into her and still it somehow managed to not be enough.

Each time he slammed into her, the prickly hairs of his trimmed groin scratched against her clit, setting off starbursts of pleasure.

"Come on, baby," he growled in her ear. "Let. Go."

At his command she broke apart, his orgasm following right after.

With the neurons of her brain comatose from pleasure, he had to be the one with the presence of mind to shift his weight so it wasn't crushing her. He quickly repositioned them to lay on their sides with her curling against him.

Automatically, she wrapped an arm around his waist, threaded a leg between his, rested her head on his chest and promptly fell asleep.

Chapter Twenty-Two

G age awoke the next morning with Rocky twisted around him as effectively as the octopus tattoo on his arm. Sometime during the night, she'd moved to drape over him and her hair covered part of his face. It smelled like the usual blueberries.

He moved the strands covering his face and tucked them behind her ear. God, she was beautiful. Her long black lashes rested against her cheeks and her lips were still swollen from his kisses.

Snapshots from the night flashed through his mind, causing his morning wood to swell to full mast. With the arm not trapped beneath her, he reached across her body to grab her ass, skimming his hand down her leg to her knee, hitching her leg over his hip, and rolled her beneath him.

He ground his body against hers and gave her the X-rated Sleeping Beauty treatment, kissing her awake while his hand traveled down to find her clit, where she was still slick from their earlier juices.

She stirred as he stroked her, her lashes fluttering open and her lips tipping into a smile. Her legs and arms tightened around his body as he adjusted her beneath him and slid home.

God, she was tight. Even after going at it the night before, her walls gripped him like a vice. He had to pause while the heat of her without a barrier invaded his senses. It was such a heady experience, he didn't think he'd ever get used to it. Once he was sure he wouldn't embarrass himself, he started to move.

He was settling into a groove when Rocky flipped them so she was on top, straddling his hips. He wanted to be surprised by her ability to change their positions, but he'd seen her spar with some of the guys, and he knew the muscles it took to be able to flip a person twice your size.

He was more than willing to let her be in control and have her way with him. When she started to move, he grabbed on to her hips and held on for the ride of his life.

She braced her hands against his chest and swiveled her hips up and down, keeping her movements slow and precise. She moved off him until only the tip of his cock was left inside her body, and then slid down so he was once again buried to the hilt.

She repeated the motion over and over until he was about to lose his damn mind. "Rocky." Lift up. "Babe." Slide down. "If you keep doing that, you're going to make me come too soon."

"Isn't that the whole point?"

His fingers dug into her hips so hard he was sure he would leave bruises, but he was trying to find the resolve to hold back. It wasn't easy—he was barely hanging on by the thinnest of threads. "Yes, but you first."

He placed his thumb on top of her clit and pressed down. Giving her no time to warm up, he quickly set a wild pace to take her over the edge as soon as possible. The flutters of her approaching orgasm gripped his dick and he reached his other hand up and squeezed one of her tits—hard.

Finally, the ministrations of both his hands, along with the grinding of their hips, pushed her over the edge and he felt her gush all over his cock.

She let out a strangled groan and collapsed against his chest. "Oh my god," she breathed against him.

"Just Gage is fine." When she finally let go, he pumped his hips in earnest.

She laughed at his cocky comment as she lay on top of him, catching her breath.

"Gage, you feel so good inside me."

She gasped as he spread his fingers on her ass and took a butt cheek in each hand. Tightening his grip, he moved her hips up and down his length, pumping in and out of her, increasing his pace until their bodies were crashing into each other almost violently.

Her breath hitched. "Oh, god, Gage, you're gonna make me come again."

"Give it to me, baby. Let go." He thrust even harder, his own orgasm boiling up inside.

"Come for me, baby." Her pussy fluttered again. "Now," he growled.

His command was the final push she needed, and she let go with a scream then collapsed on his chest as he shot into her.

She draped across him like a human blanket. He remained inside her, not wanting to break their connection, and enjoyed the final contractions of her body around his. Her breath tickled his neck as she lay unmoving.

"You alright, babe?" he asked while he ran his hands up and down her back.

"I'm dead."

But she breathed against his neck. He chuckled. "You feel pretty alive to me."

"Seriously. I think my brain exploded from that orgasm."

"You aren't the only one, babe."

"You really need to stop touching me."

He immediately stilled against her. "Did I hurt you?" He was afraid he was too rough with her. At his size, he always felt like it was a fine line he had to balance when passion took over.

She must have heard the panic in his voice. "What? No, not at all. I loved *everything* you did to me. Eve-ry-thing." She punctuated the word with kisses. "It's just if you don't stop we might never make it out of this bed."

He laughed as he brought her face around for a kiss. "You say that like it's a bad thing."

She took a moment to kiss him back passionately. "Oh, it's not, but I am hungry."

Her stomach let out an audible rumble and they laughed.

"And I get hangry too," she warned.

"Then I guess it's time to get some food. I don't want it to get around that I don't take care of my girl." He kissed her one last time before rolling out from under her to get off the bed.

After pulling on his boxers, he turned to ask her what she wanted for breakfast and caught her ogling his butt. "Like what you see?" He lifted an eyebrow.

"So much," she responded with a wink.

God, this woman just did it for him. Before he climbed back into bed with her, he turned and headed to the kitchen on the hunt for food. But finding empty refrigerator shelves, he realized he hadn't done much grocery shopping yet.

Well, crap.

He was still in front of the open fridge when he heard her approach. With a sheepish grin, he turned to face her and sucked in a breath. She wore his gray t-shirt from the night before and he sure as hell hoped nothing else.

His gaze traveled from her pretty painted toes, up the long length of her mouthwatering legs, pausing where the hem of his shirt rested at the top of her biteable thighs before he continued up. Her nipples pressed against the front of the shirt, confirming she was braless.

"Damn, that shirt has never looked so good." His long legs ate up the space between them in seconds and he hauled her body against his, kissing her for all his worth. He didn't pull away until his lungs felt like they were going to burst.

"If that's the reaction I'm going to get, I might have to raid the guys' closets for my wardrobe needs," she said with a nip to his lower lip.

"Tease."

"You love it." Her arms threaded around his neck and she scratched the back of his head.

Keeping their bodies anchored together with one arm, he reached back to shut the fridge then pulled her in tighter.

"I have some bad news," he said. She raised an eyebrow in question. "I don't have any food here."

She let out a laugh. "What? How is that even possible?"

"I've been spending most of my time at Wyatt and Beth's, or with you and everybody, so I haven't done a proper trip to the store yet."

"No worries. It's football Sunday anyway. I'm sure Gem is already up making food. Put on some shorts and a t-shirt and meet me at my place in five minutes." She kissed him once more and made her way back to his bedroom.

He followed dutifully to find her pulling her dress over her head. "You could have kept my shirt on, I wouldn't have minded."

She laughed as she adjusted the elastic waist on her dress. "As much as I don't care that everyone knows we are sleeping together, I don't really need to go prancing around in front of my brother of all people in only your t-shirt."

"Good point."

"There is something we need to discuss." She bit her lip like she was nervous.

"Okay," he hedged.

"Our friends *obviously* know about us"—she waved a hand in the direction of the other apartments—"but...we can't act like anything has changed when we're at the gym."

"Your dad?"

"Oh, yeah." A frown tugged at her lips.

"Could you lose your job?" It was his turn to frown, not liking the idea one bit.

She shook her head. "I doubt it since he pretty much pressured me to take it. But...it would be...*bad.*" There was a look in her eyes he'd never seen there before.

She was hurting and he wanted to fix it.

"Should we stop this before it goes any further?" Everything in him rebelled against the idea, but she needed to have the option.

"No," she said quickly, closing the space between them. "I don't want to stop." Her arms looped around his neck. "When we're at the gym, we just have to keep things professional."

"And outside it?"

She pushed up onto her tiptoes and pressed her lips to his. "This. A lot more of this."

Good. Because whether she was aware of it or not, she was now his and he had no intention of letting her go anytime soon.

Chapter Twenty-Three

Rocky let herself into her apartment, happy to see it was only occupied by Becky and Gemma at the moment. For the past week, she had spent more nights sleeping at Gage's place than her own.

Everything about the last seven days had been surreal.

Becky looked up from where she was cutting fruit to take to book club later and gave her a knowing smirk, then nudged Gemma, who was pulling trays of bacon out of the oven.

"Did you have a nice night?" Gemma sing-songed.

"I'd say. Look at her face. I don't think her smile could be any bigger," Becky mocked.

"Shut up." Her cheeks heated, giving her away.

"You do know we are going to need details," Gemma said while arranging the bacon on a platter.

"Yeah, like *right* now, and don't leave anything out." Becky placed the fruit into containers.

Nope, not gonna happen.

"The dirtier, the better."

"Hey, where are you going?" Becky called. "Don't think you are getting out of this. We know where you live."

She walked down the hall to her room, laughing at her friends, knowing they meant every word and this would only be a temporary reprieve.

All week, they'd been pressuring her for details, but she had remained uncharacteristically tight-lipped about the things that happened between Gage's sheets.

And in his shower.

And in his kitchen.

And there might have also been that time in his living room.

She shut the door to her room, heading straight for her bathroom and stripping off her clothes on the way. As she waited for the water to heat up, she took in her reflection in the large mirror. She had beard burn along her neck and across her chest. Her nipples looked bruised from Gage's attention.

Is that a hickey on my boob?

She grinned at the thought of being marked by him. Hooking her thumbs in the sides of her underwear, she pulled them down and noticed a second hickey on the inside of her thigh.

Damn, the man was good.

It was a miracle they hadn't been outed at the gym yet.

With steam billowing out from under the glass door of the shower, she pulled up her *Singing in the Shower* playlist on Spotify, singing along to Inner Circle's "Sweat (A La La La La Long)," and stepped inside. Grabbing her special blue shampoo, she squirted a generous amount on her palm and worked it into her long locks. Watching the blue suds run down her body and down the drain, she smiled, thinking of how amazing it was when she and Gage had finally managed to take the shower they missed a couple of weeks ago. She conditioned her hair then clipped it up. It would be so much nicer to have him washing her body right now rather than using a plain loofah with body wash.

An arm snaked around her middle and she shrieked before melting into the hard chest behind her.

"Sorry. Didn't mean to scare you, babe." Gage dropped a gentle kiss to the sensitive skin on the back of her neck.

Since their first night together, he would casually slip in calling her pet names and she absolutely loved it. It was crazy to think how connected she felt to him after such a short amount of time, but with a best friend as a romance writer, she decided it was probably best to roll with it. The Disney lover in her wasn't about to question a possible happily ever after.

"What are you doing here?" When she tried to turn around to face him, he stopped her, taking the loofah from her hands and running it over her body.

"I missed you."

The puff stroked across her collarbone in a sensual caress.

"I've barely been gone from your place for five minutes." Her voice hitched on the last word as he circled one boob then the other.

"Long enough." More kisses against her neck that sent an electric tingle down her spine. "Plus, I needed to shower too. I figured we could help wash each other's backs."

"How eco-friendly of you," she teased.

"Fuck that. The things I have planned for this shower are the *furthest* thing from conserving water."

His dirty promises sent a flood of wetness between her legs.

Her head canted down so she could watch his thumb brush the suds away from the love bite on her breast.

"I marked you." His voice held a hint of pride.

"There's also one on my inner thigh." She rested back against his shoulder as he slipped the loofah down her stomach and between her legs.

"Gotta make sure you're nice and clean."

The loofah hit the floor of the shower.

He spun her around and dropped to his knees in front of her. Before she could register what was happening, he had his face buried in her pussy and she was halfway to another orgasm.

The clip in her hair lost the battle against the water pressure and her hair tumbled down as she threw her head back, stifling a moan as she came for the third—or fourth, she had no idea, she'd lost count—time for the day.

Her fingers curled uselessly against his head, and she again cursed the lack of length to his hair.

Luckily, he read her well enough to stand from his crouch, lifting her in his arms on the way and pinning her against the shower wall. The tile was cold on her hot skin and she whistled through her teeth but quickly forgot about it as his tongue invaded her mouth while his cock did the same below.

Wall sex had become one of her favorite ways to do it. The ridiculous muscles and strength he had from years of training were certainly put to the test. At five-ten, she'd never really felt all that dainty when she was with a guy, but that was exactly how he made her feel.

She'd had some good sex in her life, great sex even, but nothing in her past compared to the fireworks Gage made her see every single time they were together.

He bit her shoulder as he came with her. He might be a fighter, but she had a feeling he was about to complete his hat trick of hickeys on her body.

🐝

Wrapped in a towel, Gage sat himself on the edge of Rocky's bed, regretting not thinking ahead enough to grab a set of clean clothes before coming over to crash her shower. Normally it wouldn't be a big deal, but he could already hear the chorus of voices on the other side of the closed bedroom door.

"You going to get dressed? Or is this some type of fashion statement?" Rocky joked, lifting the edge of his towel.

She stood before him in one of her bajillion pairs of leggings, these a simple black pair, but there was nothing *simple* about what they managed to do for her legs and ass. Most girls put on slinky dresses to draw a man's eye—and he'd seen her dressed like that as well, he got hard thinking of how she looked in her black dress that night they all went out to The Lounge—but to him, there was nothing sexier than Rocky in athletic wear.

"I forgot to grab something clean to change into."

"A little impatient this morning, were we?" A knowing smile pulled at the corner of her lips.

"Yes. You could say I was *highly* motivated to get here as quickly as possible."

His hands made themselves at home at the dip of her waist, his thumb tracing along the shapes of her tattoo. The artist who did the work was supremely talented—each leaf and petal looked almost three dimensional.

"You know, I don't think I ever asked you if your tattoo meant anything." He continued to trace the shape of the ivy leaves weaved throughout the entire piece.

"I guess it isn't as obvious as yours," she said, running a finger down one of the tentacles of his octopus, the tattoo he got to represent his fighting nickname—The Kraken. He loved when she put her hands on him. There was something about her touch that inspired a raging sense of lust while simultaneously soothing him. He may not understand it, but he accepted it as part of his growing feelings for her.

"Well, I get this one." He took her right hand in his, bringing it to his mouth and dropping a gentle kiss over the tiny witch's hat inked at the top of her wrist.

"Yeah." Her voice was breathy and her pulse fluttered

beneath his lips. "It was this or a brand. And we figured a tattoo was prettier."

He chuckled against her skin.

"Okay...stop having squirrel brain and tell me about this one." He released her hand so it could go back to following the tribal patterns of his ink.

"Hey." Her hand lightly smacked his biceps. "It's *your* fault I have squirrel brain. Don't make fun."

"How do you figure?" He smirked at her trying to blame it on him. Then again, he was a man, he should be used to being blamed for things, regardless if it was warranted or not.

"I'm pretty sure I don't have any functioning brain cells left after what you did to me in your bed, then in my shower this morning. If I had a battery gauge, it would be flashing red right now."

His smirk turned into a full-fledged grin at her words. He was damn proud of how loud he had her screaming his name earlier. The days that he woke up with her in his bed were quickly becoming his favorite of the week. Nothing beat being wrapped up in the limbs of his very own quadrapus.

"Blue, focus." He squeezed her side. "Tattoo."

"Oh. Right." She giggled and looked down at his hand still tracing along her tattoo. "So the aloe plant"—she moved to push down the waist of her leggings so his thumb could rest on the plant inked on top of her hip bone—"represents healing."

That made sense—she was a healer.

"The hyacinths"—she moved his hand so it could span across the pink and purple flower tattooed lower on the other side of her ribcage closest to her back and the orange and the blue one placed higher on her ribs, closer to the top of her stomach—"they stand for playfulness, and games and sports."

Also obvious since she worked in the sports field and was one of the most playful people he'd ever met.

"The honeysuckle and ivy"—she released his hand so it could follow the path of white and yellow flowers weaved with green leaves throughout the entire design—"are woven together because one represents friendship and the other the bonds of love. And for me, I can't have one without the other."

He understood that about her as well. In just his first day at the gym, he saw how close those from The Steele Maker were. They were family, all of them, regardless of blood ties. It took him a while to come to terms with how tight they were, but now that he'd opened himself up to them, he had a hard time imagining how he managed going twenty-seven years without friendships like theirs.

Her tattoo was the perfect representation of how fiercely she loved the people closest to her. And as jealous as he had been at first of her relationship with Jase, he'd learned to accept that was just the type of person she was and he respected her for it.

"It sums you up perfectly." He tugged her closer, into the space between his knees so he could trail a path of kisses around her belly. "Why flowers?"

Her nails—still painted black from Halloween the week before—bit into the skin of his trapezoids as he continued to tease the sensitive skin along her ribcage.

"I've grown up in a tough world—not that I had it rough —I mean fighting is a gritty sport. And with my focus always being on sports in general, I wanted something softer as a showcase."

"I think it's perfect." He grasped her ass and pulled her onto his lap. "Like you." He placed a kiss on her nose.

An obnoxious staccato of knocks pounded against her bedroom door, breaking the moment.

"Yo, lovebirds!" Vince's voice bellowed from his side of the door. "Breakfast."

"Yeah, stop fucking long enough to eat. Gage needs to keep up his caloric intake," Deck added.

"Dude." Gage assumed the sound of flesh hitting flesh was Vince smacking Deck upside the head. "I. *Do. Not.* Want to hear about my sister having sex."

"What?" Deck tried to sound innocent. "You know she's been having sex sin—"

"*Okay, you guys!*" Rocky shouted. "We'll be right out. Now go away." She buried her face in the crook of his neck, muttering something about getting retribution.

To his disappointment, she climbed from his lap—probably for the best so he didn't end up taking her yet again—to finish getting dressed. She pulled on a loose-necked sweater, the same shade of gray as her eyes, adjusting the opening to hang over the shoulder not sporting his latest love bite. The front of the sweater had black letters reading, "Bookmarks are for quitters"—obviously she was dressing for the occasion, as she was dragging him along to his first book club with the group later that evening.

Sitting around in a towel, he was not dressed for any occasion, especially not the trip back to his place. *Screw it.* Making sure the pewter-colored terry cloth was securely knotted on his hips, he strode from the room with his girl.

The guys catcalled and the girls whistled as he made a hasty retreat.

He was really growing fond of the jerks.

Almost as fond as he was of a certain raven-haired beauty with eyes like storm clouds.

Chapter Twenty-Four

age marveled at the gray and tan bricked mansion, with its large white columns bracketing the door and the black shutters. He knew a piece of real estate like this one in New Jersey went for a pretty penny, but instead of the massive structure looking ostentatious, it had an almost homey feel to it.

When Rocky rolled down her window to punch in the code to the gate, it didn't surprise him at all. No, it would have been more shocking if The Coven *didn't* have access to each other's homes. He remained unsurprised when she did the same on the keypad at the front door.

A large black lab greeted them at the front door, barking like crazy at all the new visitors until Rocky gave him a command to sit, and he promptly melted at her feet, rolling to his back for a belly rub.

Obviously as comfortable in the Donovan home as they were back at their condos, everyone tromped through the foyer, down a long hallway, and into a large great room with vaulted ceilings. It looked like furniture had been added and arranged around the room so they all would be able to sit in a circle for their book discussion.

When Rocky first handed him the paperback with the picture of a half-naked guy resting his head against that of a pretty girl and the purple text of the title, he thought she was out of her damn mind.

When he expressed his concerns—who the hell was he kidding, he balked because of some misguided male ego—she laughed, like in his face, bent over guffaws of laughter. After she managed to regain her composure, she explained that everyone—all the athletes from the gym, their hockey playing friends, and Maddey's military brothers—participated in their romance book club. Apparently, the guys first read Maddey's books to support her when she launched her career, but they quickly became converts to the romance genre way.

He had to admit, when he finished reading Maria Luis's *Body Check*, a novel about a hockey team named the Boston Blades, he was hooked and had already started reading the books before it in the series.

"You guys are gonna hurt my tough-guy fighter reputation if it ever gets out that I'm a romance book junkie," he grumbled into Rocky's ear.

"Please." She rolled her eyes at him. "We really need to get you a better social media presence. Because if you paid attention to it at all, you would see all the guys post to support Maddey's books and their top picks. Most of them have posed as cover models for her."

"Yeah, they have," Maddey said with a Cheshire grin as they walked toward her. "I have life-sized cardboard cutouts of them decorating my office where I write at home."

"And we may or may not mess with them and make their antics go viral," Skye said, filling up wine glasses in the kitchen off to the left.

He gave them an incredulous look, but every man in the room was nodding that it was true.

"Well, I guess it's a good thing I hired you two to manage all my stuff for me," he said to Jordan and Skye.

"Oh, don't you worry, we've got you covered," Jordan said, bouncing a baby in her arms. He had no idea which one of the twins it was. "We've already been fielding calls interested in some promotion with you and Vince because of his upcoming fight."

"Later we will have to discuss some things because The Cutter has been posting all sorts of shit trying to get you to rematch," Skye said.

Fucking Cutter. The asshole had been a thorn in his side since the moment he took the belt from him. Even now, his hand unconsciously went to his hip thinking of the pressure he was trying to put on him to fight him again. The UFC was chomping at the bit to get him to agree.

Sure, it would be a pay-per-view gold mine, but he didn't need the money. He was already a multi-millionaire, he could have retired over a year ago and never have to work another day in his life. That wasn't why he continued to fight. No, he did because he genuinely loved what he did, plus it was a pride thing for him.

A rematch with The Cutter though? That would be way more than the typical dog and pony show.

No thank you, not interested. Been there, done that, won the belt.

He told the ladies as much and they let the subject drop.

"Can't wait for your fight, Vin." Ryan exchanged a bro handshake with the older Steele sibling. "We're all coming."

Rocky led him over to a loveseat across the room, lifting her legs to drape across his lap while accepting a glass of wine from Skye.

"All of you?" Vince questioned, taking an armchair near them.

"Yup. We play a home game the night before. Jase and the Storm will arrive home from a stretch of away games that day. And Tuck is playing Philly in an afternoon game and will come up after and fly out to meet the team the next day."

"Good Ol' Cap, knowing everyone's game schedule," Skye teased as she took a seat.

Trays of food were spread out on the coffee table, everyone filling their plates and grabbing drinks as they all took their places.

He tried to focus on the chaos around him, but he couldn't get past the irritation that came from just the mention of The Cutter minutes before.

The door leading to the back deck opened and a muscular guy with brown hair, a beard with a few days of growth to it and green eyes stepped into the room. Gage took him for another hockey teammate based on his build but couldn't recall his face.

"Tink, can you call your mutt? He's too fascinated by something in the yard and is disobeying his commanding officer."

Maddey snorted, so he figured she must be Tink—with her five-foot frame, blonde hair and blue eyes, he could see the resemblance to Peter Pan's favorite pixie. "That's because *I'm*"—she pointed a finger to her chest—"his commanding officer, not you, Justin. Now, sit your ass down so we can get started." She walked over to the open door and gave a whis-tle. "Trident."

Seconds later, a large yellow lab bounded up to the door, sitting obediently at her feet, awaiting his next command. With a hand signal from Maddey, he followed her to her chair and lay down at her feet once she sat.

"Traitor," Justin grumbled to the dog.

"You may be LPO to your team, but I'm the admiral in Trident's life. Deal with it, big brother."

Ryan snorted, and the dog rose from his spot to sit at his feet, resting his head on his leg.

Maddey's brother narrowed his eyes at the oldest Donnelly sibling. "Watch it, Donnelly. You no longer date my sister. You're fair game now."

"*Pfff,*" Ryan was clearly unconcerned. "You know she would retaliate if you did anything to me." He tipped his beer bottle in the guy's direction. "And you know she's been friends with *my* sister for years, so her revenge game has really stepped up. *Careful.*" He sing-songed the last word.

"Fuck you, Donnelly."

"Please, Just. You're like the fourth scariest McClain, I think I'll take my chances."

"*Fourth?*"

"Yup." Ryan made a popping sound with the p. "Your dad, Connor, and Maddey are all ahead of you. Tyler is a puppy dog under his fatigues, and Babs loves me like one of her own. So yeah. Fourth."

"Sonofabitch, you're an asshole."

"Love you too, Just." Ryan blew him a kiss.

"Can you two idiots behave?" Maddey scolded. "Gage, this is my oldest brother, Justin."

He reached to shake the guy's hand.

Before the group was able to come to order, the front door slammed shut and a familiar hot pink and green dyed head entered the room with a flourish. Lyle from the coffee shop and his much more subdued husband, Kyle, entered the room.

"So sorry we're late, lovelies, hope you didn't start without us." He spotted Justin sitting on the couch next to Sammy and Becky. "*Oooooooh,* one of the SEALs is here. I *love* when you guys join us. Now take your shirt off."

Justin ignored him, turning to Sammy on his right instead. "Have I ever thanked you for never objectifying me?"

"Oh, I objectified you. Just not to your face like Lyle," Sammy confessed.

"True. It was one of my *least* favorite subjects," Maddey confirmed.

Sammy was definitely more unassuming when compared to Lyle's loud and proud flamboyance.

"Hey, babe," Jordan called out to her husband. "Can you video call Tuck on the TV stream?"

"Why am I not surprised you had his schedule free for book club?" Jake said as he fiddled with a remote to connect the call.

Jordan shrugged the shoulder the baby rested against. "Someone has to keep you boys in line."

"Yeah, if we left you to your own devices it would be anarchy," Skye added.

There was a chorus of "M-Dubs!" shouted when Tucker Hayes, a winger for the Chicago Fire, filled the screen of the flat screen above the fireplace. Gage saw the guy's eyes widen in shock when he saw him sitting amongst his friends.

"Okay, boys." Becky called the room to order when the conversation turned to discuss the next string of hockey games coming up. "Time to talk about Holly and Jackson and how they give us all the feels."

"Can we talk about how we do too many hockey books, and can we *please* have a good badass SEAL in a story?" Justin complained good-naturedly.

"You don't get a say. I never know when you guys get to actually come for book club, so you get stuck with what we pick." Maddey laid down the law. "Besides, we've done plenty of military romance."

Who knew book club could be so cutthroat?

BOOK CLUB WAS just another excuse for Rocky and her friends to get together.

Did they all read the same book?

Yes.

Did they discuss it at book club?

Again, the answer was yes.

Did they stay on topic?

Hell no. They all had the attention span of goldfish, never able to stay on topic for more than a few seconds.

Was book club a good time?

Abso-fucking-lutely.

"Give me my niece." Jase made a gimme gesture with his hands.

"Umm, I'm *pretty* sure our sister gave birth to a carbon copy of this one, so go get your own," Ryan retorted, shifting his body to hold out an arm like he was posing as the Heisman.

"Yeah, but this one is my godchild. Hand her over and take your own advice and get your own. Lay is mine." Jase feigned lunging for the baby.

"How the hell do you know? It's so hard to tell them apart up close. How are you able to from all the way over there?" Ryan moved so he was on the other side of the couch.

"I'm a twin. We know these things," Jase said confidently.

Ryan let out a bark of laughter so loud he startled the baby on his shoulder and was quick to soothe her before she could cry. "You're a *fraternal* twin, bro. Doesn't count when it comes to telling identicals apart."

"Can you two idiots *please* stop playing keep away with my baby?" Jordan scolded her brothers.

"Besides, Ry, he's right—you're holding Lacey, Rocky has Lu." Jordan pointed to where she sat with her own perfect bundle dressed in a Minnie Mouse onesie and polka dot pants.

"Don't even think about it, Cap." She pointed a finger toward him in warning. "Until your sister pops out another kid and makes me a godmother, I'm getting all my baby loving in with this one."

"I'll fight you for her," Ryan taunted.

"The hell you will," Jordan declared.

"Please." She rolled her eyes so dramatically, it was a

shock they didn't fall out. "There are *so* many reasons why you wouldn't do that."

"Oh, yeah?" Ryan passed Lacey over to her godfather. "Name two."

How did he still underestimate her after all this time?

She held up the hand not cuddling Lucy to tick the reasons off on her fingers. "One, because Jordan would kill you." She pointed at her best friend, looking like the fierce mama bear she was. "Two, your enforcer"—her finger moved to indicate Jase—"is *my* best friend." Her fingers curled to point to herself. "And three, if you try and come after me, my boyfriend—you know the current Heavyweight Champion of the UFC—will kick your ass."

"Oh, I will?" Gage asked with a hint of teasing.

"Yes. You will," she confirmed, never taking her eyes off Ryan.

"Good to know." Out the corner of her eye, she saw a satisfied smirk spread across Gage's ridiculously handsome scruffy face. "Also good to know I'm your boyfriend."

Oh, shit. Did I call him my boyfriend?

Damn, I did.

I mean I think he's my boyfriend. We've spent almost all of our time together lately. We've gone on dates. We're sleeping together almost every day, sometimes multiple times a day. What does it matter that we have to keep it a secret at the gym? It doesn't make it any less real. Right?

Gage chuckled as her thoughts spiraled out of control. "Relax, Blue."

"This is brand new information," Becky cried. Her best friend, the stand-up comedian, ladies and gentlemen.

"Yeah. For someone so smart, Alphabet Soup, you sure are slow," Deck joked and she flipped him off.

"So we're like…official?" Her voice squeaked at the end. Damn if she didn't feel like she was back in high school again.

"How's this for official?" He held out his phone, pulling her against his side, snapping a quick selfie of them.

She watched as he went to his Instagram account, posting the picture and sharing it to all his social media accounts. **@TheKrakenUFC Finally got this pretty girl to tap out and agree to be my girlfriend @RockyToughAsSteele #Couple-Goals #FitCouple #GymBuddy #GymRats #BeautyAnd-TheBeast.**

"You are so corny," she said, but internally she was swooning so hard, if she were wearing underwear they would have fallen through the floor they dropped so hard.

"Oh, you are going to be a *dream* client to manage," Skye said, already clicking away, whispering with Jordan on how to best optimize and promote Gage's post.

She had to agree. Gage really was a dream. She just hoped her alarm didn't go off before she got her happy ending.

Chapter Twenty-Five

Three times a week, Rocky and her father would meet at The Steele Maker about an hour before the athletes would arrive for their training. They would use the time to discuss who was recovering from an injury, who had something she would have to watch, treatment plans, changes to the training curriculum, and anything else either considered it important for the other to know.

Walking into her father's office, black coffee for him in one hand and a pecan pie latte—Lyle's better-than-sex variation on the basic bitch PSL—in the other, she wasn't prepared for his first topic of discussion.

Vic Steele had never been one to play power games. His reputation and stature did the work for him. For that reason, most of his meetings with her and the other members of the staff were conducted sitting in either the armchairs or couch that surrounded a low metal coffee table, as opposed to from behind his desk.

Today he was behind the desk.

As she handed over his coffee, he did the same with an iPad. A quick glance at the screen showed Gage's Instagram post from Saturday.

Welp. Happy Monday morning to me.

She took a giant gulp of her latte, not caring how it scalded her throat. Getting caffeinated as soon as humanly possible was needed—how she wanted an IV drip to speed things along—if she was going to survive "The Talk" with her dad early on a Monday morning.

He didn't say a word, not out loud at least. But his eyes—those were shouting like a fight announcer, looking at her then down at the screen and back again.

"Dad—" she started but he cut her off with the wave of his hand.

"The information itself doesn't surprise me," he stated.

"It doesn't?" She couldn't help but ask.

"No." There was a small curl to the ends of his lips. "I've been married to your mother for over twenty-six years. I know how a man looks at a woman when he's in love."

She was taking another sip of her latte and sputtered into her cup, then a coughing fit ensued as the liquid went down the wrong pipe in her throat.

Love?

It was too soon for Gage to love her. Right?

"That boy has had hearts in his eyes from the day he stepped into the gym. Plus, I've seen the way you've been acting around each other this last week. Again, I'll remind you of your mother."

This was true. Both Steele brothers—her dad and her uncle Mick—treated their wives like queens. The Steele Maker had a strict policy around respect that was a major contributor to developing the woman's self-defense classes. When Vic learned the sordid details of what Jordan went through with Tommy—her dick-weasel of an ex, now thankfully serving a long prison sentence—he'd developed a program so even the smallest woman would be able to defend herself against an attacker.

"However…" The gray eyes she'd inherited were hard as stone as they looked at her. "I can't say I'm not *concerned*."

"Dad—"

"Don't, Raquel." He cut her off again, the use of her legal name making her wince. "I put these rules in place for a reason."

She swallowed thickly. She'd been so caught up in how exciting it was that Gage claimed her as his girlfriend, making her feel like she was the priority for the first time with a fighter, that she completely disregarded the fact that he did it on a public forum.

They had been *so* careful not to reveal anything at the gym —though, based on her father's comments, maybe not as careful as they thought. But the social media posting was a grave error in judgment.

"Gage is new to the gym. He's a title holder. That means his first fight out of our gym will be a title bout. I can't have my fighter distracted because of relationship drama."

And there it was.

It wasn't that Gage was dating his daughter that was the problem, it was that his daughter was dating his *fighter*. Once again, she came in second place.

Will I ever come first?

Choking back her feelings—it wouldn't bode well for her to get emotional—she cleared her throat. "Dad." A deep breath. "Gage and I have been together for over a week and it hasn't affected his training. There's no drama here."

"Oh, no?" Her dad pressed a finger to the picture of the screen. Gage looking all smoldery and too damn hot for his own good in a blue henley a few shades darker than his eyes, only making those baby blues pop more with the contrast, and a few days of scruff on his jaw and her looking all starry-eyed, her messy bun tipping to the side as they mugged it up for the camera.

"Then what do you call this?"

He scrolled down to the comments underneath the post and there in black text was a comment from The Cutter.

@TheCutterUFC: Hey @TheKrackenUFC sleeping with your new coach's daughter won't help you beat me. Stop hiding behind the Princess and fight me like a man. #ScaredToLose #ReallyAPauper #TooScaredToFight #Can't-HandleThePressure #NotUpToTheChallenge.

Taking the iPad, she scrolled, already seeing the post had been shared and reposted *everywhere*. This was bad.

"Cutter has been trying to get Gage to rematch for two years," she said. "This is just his latest attempt."

"Oh, I know." Her father's jaw was clenched tighter than she'd ever seen it. "I've already spoken with Jordan about doing damage control."

"Isn't that a bit dramatic? This will blow over in a day or so."

"*No.*" The word boomed through the room. "I've worked too hard to establish the Steele name throughout the UFC. I'm not going to let this asshole use you to ruin our reputation."

Her heart felt like it went the five full rounds inside the cage. She knew her father loved her, she *never* questioned that. But when it came to The Steele Maker, it was like Vic Steele wore blinders to everything except the success of his legacy, including his daughter.

"This is why we have the rule about dating inside the gym."

She braced a hand on the chair in front of her. He couldn't possibly mean…

"You—you want me to break up with Gage?" She kept her face impassive while everything inside her railed against the idea.

"Yes."

Her heart stopped beating as she waited for him to elaborate, to say more on the subject, but nothing else came. No, she was just expected to do as he said, no questions asked.

"No."

"Raquel, this isn't up for debate. Besides…it's against the terms of your employment."

What? Was he out of his mind?

"You mean the job you practically *forced* me to take? Is *that* the job you're referring to?" She was seething, so fucking angry she could breathe fire. How dare he throw her job in her face. She didn't even want it. She *wanted* to work for the Blizzards but like the dutiful daughter she was, she gave in to familial obligations.

"Don't be melodramatic, Raquel. This gym is your legacy."

It took everything in her power not to roll her eyes or stomp her foot. She didn't want a legacy, she wanted love. She wanted to be seen for who she was. To be put first for once.

"One last thing."

Now what?

"Your mother already called demanding a family dinner. It seems someone at the hospital saw the post and was asking all about her daughter's new boyfriend. "

Family Dinner AKA The Inquisition.

"We expect *all* you kids over for dinner at the house tonight." There was no getting out of it.

"You will come to dinner. You will bring Gage. Let your mother have her moment to celebrate. But make no mistake." He leveled her with another hard look. "You *will* end this relationship with *my* fighter before you step foot inside my gym tomorrow."

What the fuck am I going to do?

❦

ALPHABET SOUP: So Papa Steele just laid down the law this morning. Family dinner tonight. Clear your schedules Gem and Beck

PROTEIN PRINCESS: Way to over dramatize. Family dinner rocks

YOU KNOW YOU WANNA: Yeah. Especially if Gem's mom is the one doing the cooking

YOU KNOW YOU WANNA: *GIF of Fat Bastard saying "Get in my belly!*

ALPHABET SOUP: Normally I would agree. But for this dinner, he told me I have to bring Gage

PROTEIN PRINCESS: Oh shit *shocked face emoji*

YOU KNOW YOU WANNA: *GIF of man cocking a shotgun*

MOTHER OF DRAGONS: OMG!! If I get my parents to watch the girls can I come?

MAKES BOYS CRY: Me too. There's no way in hell I want to miss this

· · ·

MAKES BOYS CRY: *GIF of movie watcher wearing 3-D glasses eating popcorn*

MAKES BOYS CRY: If you didn't understand why I chose this one. It's me rocking some sweet 3-D glasses so I DON'T MISS a thing.

QUEEN OF SMUT: Hold up. I'm writing out of EP today. DO NOT

QUEEN OF SMUT: I repeat DO NOT say anything to the guys until I get there. I'm sure this will make for an epic scene in one of my books.

QUEEN OF SMUT: *GIF of kid with head bent over frantically writing in a notebook*

ALPHABET SOUP: YOU GUYS ARE SO NOT HELPING RIGHT NOW. THIS IS A BIG DEAL.

ALPHABET SOUP: HUGE

ALPHABET SOUP: EPIC

ALPHABET SOUP: SIT GAGE IN A CHAIR, SHINE A SPOT-LIGHT ON HIM AND QUESTION WHEN HE'S GOING TO PROPOSE AND GIVE MY MOM GRANDBABIES

. . .

ALPHABET SOUP: WE JUST STARTED DATING. HE'S GOING TO RUN SCREAMING FROM THE ROOM

MAKES BOYS CRY: Ooooo. Shouty Capitals. She means business girls

ALPHABET SOUP Can we cut the *Fifty Shades* references and get serious please

MOTHER OF DRAGONS: Ok we'll behave. Tell us what's got your panties in a bunch

YOU KNOW YOU WANNA: I DID NOT agree to behave

MAKES BOYS CRY: Me either

PROTEIN PRINCESS: Plus you know she doesn't wear underwear at work. She never does underneath her leggings

MOTHER OF DRAGONS: Me either. Thank god for kegels otherwise I'd have a serious problem after pushing the twins out my hoohah

ALPHABET SOUP: *screaming face emoji* *facepalm emoji* Gah. I need new friends

. . .

QUEEN OF SMUT: Chillax. I'll bring you one of Lyle's banana nut muffins when I come over

ALPHABET SOUP: I'll keep you. The rest of you bitches, I'm on the fence

MOTHER OF DRAGONS: Hey! I take offense to that. But seriously what's the problem? Gage sees your dad and uncle everyday training at the gym. I'm missing what the big deal is

MOTHER OF DRAGONS: And if it's obvious I blame it on Mommy Brain

ALPHABET SOUP: The BIG DEAL is Gage and I officially became a couple like two seconds ago. Now he has to have dinner with my whole family.

ALPHABET SOUP: Did you guys not read what I sent earlier? That boy is going to run screaming for the hills

PROTEIN PRINCESS: We may have missed it while you were ranting.

YOU KNOW YOU WANNA: Please. You may have only just put a title on it but that boy has wanted you from the jump.

. . .

YOU KNOW YOU WANNA: You guys should have seen the way he looked at her that first night at The Ring.

YOU KNOW YOU WANNA: *GIF of a girl fanning herself with her hand.*

MOTHER OF DRAGONS: Hold on, there's someone else we need to loop in for this. This is serious

THE BIG HAMMER (Jase): Holy Shit. I really get to be included in a group chat with The Coven??

THE BIG HAMMER: Is this real life

MOTHER OF DRAGONS: Behave Jase or I'll kick your punk ass out

MOTHER OF DRAGONS: Now make yourself useful and help your bestie out

THE BIG HAMMER: What's the sitch?

MAKES BOYS CRY: Omg! Did you really just quote *Kim Possible*???

. . .

THE BIG HAMMER: *GIF of Kim Possible saying "What's the sitch?"*

ALPHABET SOUP: *facepalm emoji*

ALPHABET SOUP: *GIF of girl banging her head against the wall*

YOU KNOW YOU WANNA: Gem is driving so I'm responding for her.

YOU KNOW YOU WANNA: And she said we should probably focus before we break Rock *squirrel emoji* *Dory fish emoji*

THE BIG HAMMER: As honored as I am to be invited into the situation room for your plots on world domination and all... I do have to leave for morning skate in a few

MOTHER OF DRAGONS: Rock has to bring Gage to dinner with her family tonight and she's a tiny bit nervous it might scare him off

THE BIG HAMMER: Are you kidding me Balboa?

THE BIG HAMMER: I swore he was going to release The Kraken on me when I came to visit you at the gym

• • •

THE BIG HAMMER: Guy's got it bad for you

YOU KNOW YOU WANNA: Told you so

THE BIG HAMMER: Wait a second?? If you have to bring Gage to family dinner that means your dad knows you're dating? Isn't that against the rules? Weren't you keeping it a secret?

ALPHABET SOUP: Kinda hard to keep it a secret when it's splashed all over The Gram

QUEEN OF SMUT: Truth. But you gotta admit that post was totally swoon worthy

Rocky shook her head as she slipped her phone back into the pocket of her Flash leggings, staring down at the yellow lightning bolts decorating the red material, trying to corral her scattered thoughts and emotions into some sort of order.

She knew the *real* problem had *nothing* to do with how her mom would inadvertently bring up wanting grandbabies, but if she didn't use her friends to make her laugh, she would cry. She needed them to be her happy place if she was going to make it through the next six hours at the gym without turning into a basket case—that was the *only* reason she didn't say anything about the breakup edict.

As if her father's declaration wasn't bad enough, she then had to sit there for almost an hour while they discussed the last few weeks of Vince's training camp like he didn't just ask her to dump her boyfriend for no other reason than "Because

I said so." She had never been so grateful to retreat to her own office for some alone time.

Pulling the sleeves to her black shirt so her thumbs could pop through the thumb holes, she tightened her ponytail and left the sanctuary of her office.

Maddey pushed through the doors of The Steele Maker, handing over the promised muffin, and, as if knowing caffeine was essential to process everything, she followed it up with another heavenly latte.

"I freaking love the crap out of you," she said, cradling the paper cup to her chest.

"I know," Maddey retorted, hopping up to sit on the reception counter.

A minute later the doors pushed open again, this time Beck and the guys entering.

"Did you tell them?" she asked Becky.

"What? And do your dirty work for you? No way." Becky wore an evil smile as she leaned back on her elbows against the reception desk next to Maddey. "You think I wanted to miss the show?"

Sometimes she really questioned her ability at picking best friends. It was probably time to start accepting applications for new ones.

When she caught sight of her boyfriend—the boyfriend she was supposed to be breaking up with—the butterflies swarming in her stomach were for a completely different reason than the *Survivor* challenge masked as a family dinner later tonight.

Swaggering to the counter where she stood—yes, swaggered, the man oozed it from his pores like he did sweat during his workouts—he cast a quick glance around the gym and with the coast clear, hooked an arm around her waist, bringing her body flush against his, dropping a kiss that was more a brand than a kiss hello to her lips.

"*Mmm*, you taste good, babe," he said loud enough for

those around them to hear, before bringing his mouth down to her ear, whispering only for her, "Not that that's something I haven't said to you before."

Hot damn.

The guy should come with a warning—*will ruin your panties*. Or in her case, she was double screwed since her friends were correct in that she wasn't wearing any.

"It-It's Lyle's pecan pie latte." Her words came out all breathy, as lust flooded her body. "It's my favorite seasonal flavor."

"Yup. It's the best," Becky agreed. "I think it's described as better than sex."

She watched Gage's eyes flare at the words. Holy smolder, Batman. Things were creeping toward DEFCON 1 levels of needing a change of clothes.

"Challenge accepted." His even tone promised more than the dirtiest words ever could.

How the hell do I give this up?

ON THE DAYS Rocky went into the gym early, Gage carpooled with the rest of the guys. For someone who grew up hanging out with mostly his cousin, assimilating into such a large squad was coming surprisingly naturally. He was sure it had a lot to do with a certain long-legged beauty with an ass that wouldn't quit.

He was disappointed she didn't wake him up when she left his place that morning, but seeing her smiling face when he entered The Steele Maker more than made up for it.

The first thing he did when he set eyes on his girl—after making sure the patriarch of the Steele clan wasn't around— was claim the kiss he was deprived of earlier. As his tongue licked across the seam of her lips, he relished the taste of her. She always tasted delicious—a fact he could testify to because he'd spent almost as much time with his mouth on her body in the past week than not—but there was a lingering flavor of something sweeter.

Oh, shit.

The realization of what he did over the weekend hit him like an uppercut to the jaw. They were supposed to be keeping their relationship quiet. He shouldn't even be kissing her at the gym, but he couldn't help himself. But posting on his Instagram *definitely* wasn't the smartest decision.

After coming to his senses and breaking the kiss, he noticed his girl didn't look as blissed out as she normally did.

Hooking a finger under her chin, he tilted her face back up so he could see her silvery eyes.

"What's up, Blue?" He loved the reminder of the dark hue in her hair.

Her bottom lip disappeared inside her mouth, her teeth sinking into the plump flesh, turning the edges white. He'd never seen her like this before and it was making him nervous.

"Well…I hope you didn't have dinner plans tonight because we're being summoned to a dinner at the Steele house this evening."

Vince bent over in guffaws of laughter.

Rocky whipped her head around to lock onto her brother. "Oh, no. You too, jackass. It's a *family dinner.*"

The way Vince's face instantly sobered caused a niggling sense of nervousness in Gage's body, but he'd met each member of the Steele family in the six weeks he'd been a member of The Steele Maker team. How bad could dinner really be?

Chapter Twenty-Six

At the front door of her parents' house, Rocky stopped short from opening the door, causing Gage, Vince, Gemma and Becky to bump into her from behind at her abrupt action. With a fighter's reflexes, Gage prevented her from taking a header into the door by wrapping an arm around her middle.

Shit, she was nervous. She couldn't even bring herself to open the door.

"Blue?" His deep voice rumbled from behind her.

God, she loved that he called her that. It made her supremely grateful for the special blue shampoo she washed her hair with, giving her blue-black locks that little extra something to enhance the color.

"I want to apologize in advance for anything that might happen once I open that door." Not to mention what she was supposed to do after, but she wasn't going to mention that part.

"It'll be fine. I'm around most of your family every day. I promise I won't run screaming from the room."

No. But what would you do if you knew what my dad wanted me to do?

"Yeah, besides…" Vince's words trailed off as he swallowed thickly. "It'll be worse for me than you two. Now that you're bringing a boy home, the moms are really going to put the screws to me. Asking *me* when I'm going to settle down with a *nice* girl of my own."

Oh, Vin, if you only knew.

"Come on," Gage prodded. "Open the door, Blue. They're *your* family. They won't bite."

"I wouldn't be so sure about that. You haven't met my mom yet," Becky jokingly warned, *so* not helping the situation.

She pulled up her big girl panties and opened the door to the house she grew up in.

"We're here," she called out while they all hung their coats in the closet by the door.

"Perfect timing. The roast just came out of the oven," her mom answered from the dining room tucked in the back of the house.

Reassured by Gage's hand holding her own, she followed her brother and cousin down the hallway leading to the dining room. The television in the living room was turned on to a Blizzards game, the team playing in Dallas. She was too damn anxious to even check out how her friends were faring.

"Smells good, Mom," Vince said, walking over to drop a kiss on their mom's cheek.

"Thank you, honey. But I can't take the credit. This was all your aunt's doing." Vicki Steele waved a hand over the spread laid out on the table large enough to seat twelve.

Becky, god bless her soul, took care of making introductions between Gage and her mother, Tracy.

The ten of them took their places at the table. Rocky sitting to Gage's right so his dominant hand was free and not trapped between them. The feel of his right hand holding her thigh under the table grounded her.

She prayed Gage would still want to date her by the time the night was over.

Then again, if he didn't, it would solve *one* of her dilemmas.

The meal was over and everyone was settling in with after-dinner drinks and coffees, and Gage still hadn't been able to pinpoint what Rocky had been so nervous about.

Getting to witness his hard-ass trainers in their natural habitat at home was an experience in and of itself. Watching two people known to make grown men cry in the gym become utter softies when it came to their wives was more fun than he would have thought. He'd make a joke about them being whipped, but one, he wasn't an idiot and liked his head firmly attached to his neck where it belonged, and two, he was coming to understand the effect the love of a good woman could have on a man.

He gave Rocky's thigh a squeeze under the table, and when she tilted her head to look at him, he dropped a gentle kiss on her temple. Something was up. She had been off all evening and it was more than just being nervous over a meal with her family.

"You know, I just don't understand why you didn't tell us Gage was your boyfriend, Raquel. Having to learn about your daughter's relationship status on social media, well now," Vicki scolded.

He felt Rocky wince at the use of her full name.

"To be fair...I wasn't aware of the status until the post either."

A smile bloomed at the major side-eye she shot his way.

"She's right, Mrs. Steele. I guess I never did actually ask her."

"Oh, Gage. How many times do I have to tell you to call me Vicki or Mama Steele?"

He chuckled. "I still can't believe your names are really Victor and Victoria."

"Oh, god. Don't remind them." Vic rested his head on his upturned hand. "Do you have any idea how many times I was subjected to that movie because of it?"

"*Victor Victoria* is a classic." Hope Steele, Gemma's mom, said.

"Yeah, don't knock it," Tracy Reese warned.

Over the course of dinner, he had quickly learned where Becky got her take-charge personality from. The older female Reese worked at the hospital and raised her daughter as a single mom. There wasn't room for bullshit with the woman.

"What did your family say when you told them you were dating your new coach's daughter?" Tracy asked the hard-hitting question.

Rocky stiffened beneath his hand. The tension he had felt earlier now radiated from her body.

"Well...when they called me when they found out, they were more interested in the fact I *had* a girlfriend than who she was," he admitted.

"You mean you didn't tell your parents either?" Vicki asked.

"Excuse me," Rocky said, pushing back from the table.

He frowned as he watched her practically flee the room. Vince wore a similar expression when he caught him eyeing the doorway.

"No, ma'am." He hoped his manners would earn him a few points as he tuned back into the conversation. "My cousin, Wyatt, informed them, after calling me and giving me sh—, I mean wringing me out for not telling him either."

"You have family nearby?" Vicki asked.

"Yes. Wyatt moved out here with his high school sweet-heart Beth after she was accepted to the U of J. They're married now and expecting their first baby in a couple of weeks. We're close like these guys." He indicated the Steeles still at the table, wondering how long Rocky would be gone.

"High school sweethearts," Hope said, looking at Mick adoringly. Both Steele brothers had met or started dating their wives in high school.

"He's your age?" Tracy questioned while slowly stirring honey into her tea.

"We're only a month apart."

The look Vicki sent her son across the table made him incredibly grateful to not be the recipient of it.

"When are *you* going to settle down and meet a nice girl?"

"*Geez*, Mom." Vince sent his mother a *what the hell* look from across the table. "I'm only twenty-five, give me a break. It's not like I'm the last of the Mohicans or anything."

She waved him off, as if he was being ridiculous. "Still... you're getting up there."

"And that's my cue. Excuse me," Vince said, dropping his eyes to Rocky's empty seat before pushing away from the table.

Gage spent the next few minutes talking about his cousin's upcoming baby. The conversation continued to flow easily until Vince shouted, "HE SAID WHAT?"

ROCKY RAN TO the bathroom, slamming and locking the door before collapsing back against it, hand to her chest to keep her heart from beating out of it.

She couldn't do it. It was too much.

Against all odds, she was falling in love with Gage. How the *hell* was she supposed to break up with him? She had asked herself that exact question a million times already and was no closer to an answer than she was that morning.

A soft knock on the door preceded her brother's voice. "Rock, it's me. Open up."

Vince slipped inside as soon as she did. One look at her and he pulled her into his arms, wrapping her in one of those hugs that always told her he had her back. And he did.

He was the first person to encourage her to take the job with the Blizzards when the offer came and then didn't judge her for not taking it even when he knew it was her dream. He made it a point to illustrate the positives of her being with him at the gym instead.

"What's wrong? You've been weird all day. And don't try to tell me it was because of family dinner." He was quick to cut her off before she could utter the lie.

She *needed* to talk to someone and he'd just volunteered himself as tribute.

"Dad said I have to break up with Gage."

"HE SAID WHAT?" Vince roared, his voice echoing in the room and she cringed, knowing their family had to have heard it. Not that it mattered, since he yanked the door open and stormed out of the room.

She hurried to catch up, not knowing what she would do when she did, but it didn't matter. He was already in the dining room, hands on his hips, glaring at their father.

"Please. *Please,* tell me you *did not* tell Rocky to break up with Gage today?" he demanded of their father.

A shocked gasp came from the matriarchs of the family while Gage turned around in his seat to look at her, disbelief shining in his eyes.

"Victor, this *better* not be true." Her mom looked aghast at the suggestion.

"Sweetheart—" he started but her mom cut him off.

"Don't you *dare* sweetheart me right now, Victor Steele." She folded her arms across her chest. "What on earth would possess you to say such a thing to your daughter? Your *grown* daughter, I might add."

God love her mom.

"We have rules in place for a reason. A relationship between the two will only mess with Gage's concentration."

"Bullshit," Vicki spat. "You and I were *married* when you won your gold medal, so don't even try to give me that."

While her parents argued, Gage got up from the table and came to her, pulling her into his arms and holding her tight. She had no idea what he could be thinking at the moment but chose to focus on how good it felt to be held by him instead.

"Now, you listen to me. Unless you want to be bunking at your brother's house for the foreseeable future, you will forget all about this *asinine* idea and let your daughter be happy with the very nice man she is dating."

Rocky held her breath as she waited for her dad to relent.

Vic Steele maintained his silence with his arms folded across his chest.

"Victor Steele, so help me god, if you don't get your head out of your ass, I *will* do it for you."

The silence in the room was deafening while they waited for what would happen.

After what felt like hours, her father gave the barest of nods.

"Good. Rocky, Gage, please come sit back down."

They did as her mother asked, tension settling around the table like a thundercloud.

"Okay, then." Her mom clapped her hands in front of her. "Now that your sister has a boyfriend and is well on her way to giving me grandbabies, let's work on you, Vince."

"What the hell, Mom?" She buried her flaming cheeks in her hands. How they went from being on the verge of her having to *end* her relationship to having babies, she had no idea. "We've only officially been a couple for forty-eight hours. Can we wait until our relationship has a longer life-span than a mayfly before you start renting out my womb?"

"Technically, mayflies only live up to twenty-four hours, so…" Becky let her comment hang in the air.

"Not. Helping," she growled at her best friend and shot Gage a look that said *if you ever want to see me naked again, you'll stop laughing.*

"Sorry," Becky said, then turned her attention to put Vince firmly back in the hot seat. The definition of *chicks before dicks.* "So, yeah, Vinny boy. When are you going to find yourself a *nice* girl and make me an aunt? Please…I'm *dying* to know."

"Hate you." Vince spoke out the side of his mouth, not loud enough for the moms across the table to hear, but she and Becky certainly did.

Becky pursed her lips at him, making kissing sounds as she did.

"You act like our entire squad is married." He buried his face in his hands.

The moms continued to badger her brother with questions about his dating life, her dad wouldn't look her in the eye, and she just wanted to know what Gage was thinking.

Would the drama still cost her their relationship?

Chapter Twenty-Seven

G age was *way* too quiet on the drive back from her parents.

What is he thinking?

Oh my god. Is he going to break up with me?

Shit, maybe I am too much drama like Dad said.

Thank god for the moms. First her own laid down the law, having her back in a way that still left her reeling. Then they went and turned the conversation back around on Vince in an attempt to break the tension. Needless to say, dinner didn't last much longer after the bombshell was dropped.

Wordlessly, walking hand-in-hand, she followed Gage into his apartment as he headed to his living room. The designer he hired to decorate the place did a really good job of balancing the masculine elements with homey ones, thus preventing it from feeling like a bachelor pad the way the guys' place down the hall did.

She focused on his championship belt hung above his flat-screen TV instead of how her stomach was trying to eat itself from nerves. Just as every other time she saw it, her breath caught in her chest. Like her father's Olympic medal, it was a symbol of great achievement. She may not have known Gage when he won it, but the fact that he did win it, and then defended it, made her immensely proud.

He looped his arms around her waist, slipping his hands inside the back pockets of her skinny jeans to squeeze her ass. Her own hands went to his rock-hard stomach, trailing up the expanse of his chest to fiddle with the buttons of the royal blue Oxford he was wearing.

Used to seeing him in gym clothes or jeans and a t-shirt, this was a nice treat. The only other time she'd gotten to experience him dressed up was the first night he came out with their squad to The Lounge. The things his forearms did to the rolled-up sleeves of the button up should be censored—legit arm porn, NSFW.

Her chin rested on his chest as she looked into his eyes. She loved when he wore blue. Anytime he did, it was like his irises soaked up the pigments, brightening the already vibrant color.

"Congratulations on surviving your *first* Steele family dinner."

His eyes crinkled in the corners briefly before turning serious. "Why didn't you tell me?"

She was too ashamed to look at him and dropped her gaze to the floor.

"Blue."

She said nothing.

"Blue, look at me." The plea in his voice had her head snapping up, her eyes reconnecting with his.

It was too much—the hurt she saw there.

"Why didn't you tell me your dad wanted you to break up with me?"

She sighed.

His hands left her pockets to cup her face.

"Blue, baby." He stroked her cheeks. "When I first met you, I may have been reluctant to start something with you for some of the same things your dad was concerned about.

But...there's *one* thing you need to understand when it comes to me." She watched his throat move as he swallowed.

"When I made the decision to date you, I was in, *all* in." His hold on her tightened. "We are a *team*. You and me work as a unit. Your pain is my pain. Your problems are my problems."

Holy shit. He was putting her first.

He.

Was.

Picking.

Her.

"We have to trust each other, baby, and tell each other these things, or this won't work."

Oh, my heart.

She loved him.

She, Raquel Anne Steele, who swore she would never fall for a fighter because they would never put her first, had done just that.

"I know. And I'm sorry. So, *so* sorry." She tried to look away again but he wouldn't let her.

One of his hands glided down her back to slip under the hem of her shirt, stroking across the sensitive skin of her lower back. All evening, he'd maintained some form of physical contact, every brush of his body, caress of his hand, or reassuring squeeze adding up to her being turned on in a way that was highly inappropriate while having dinner with her parents.

But now.

Now they were alone.

She had enough of the heavy for the evening. She may not be brave enough to admit her feelings out loud, but she could show him.

Flattening her palms against his chest, she shoved him, catching him off guard enough for him to drop onto the leather couch behind him.

He was quick to catch on to what she had in mind, spreading his knees wide, while leaning back. But when he reached out a hand to pull her onto his lap, she ignored the gesture and sank to her knees in front of him.

Her gaze remained locked on his as her hands skimmed from his knees, up the tree trunks he called thighs, until she came to the buckle of his belt. Guided by touch, she slipped the leather from the metal buckle, popped the button, and slowly, so slowly she could hear each individual click of teeth, released the zipper.

His eyes darkened to the color of the night sky outside while her hand slipped inside the band of his boxer briefs, pulling him from the confines of cotton. Then she looked down.

He was hard as a rock, his erection standing proudly at attention, the tip shiny with pre-cum.

Gripping him at the base, her fingers barely managed to touch around his girth. Her eyes flicked back up to his as she opened her mouth and took him deep, her lips only stopping when they touched the hand keeping him in position.

He let out a rough, masculine moan as she swallowed around him.

"*Fuck,* Blue. Don't fucking stop."

She had zero intentions of stopping.

AS A PROFESSIONAL fighter, it wasn't often someone was able to knock Gage off balance with a simple shove. When Rocky did just that, it was a true testament to how absorbed he was in her to render his most innate instincts useless.

If he was shocked by how easily she managed to knock him on his ass—literally—it had nothing on the jolt he felt watching her sink to her knees in front of him. Splayed out on the couch like a king on a throne, he watched as his raven-haired beauty boldly took his cock in hand, opened her mouth and took him balls deep.

Holy hell, her mouth felt like heaven.

"Fuck." He hissed as her throat contracted around him when she swallowed.

She sucked him like a damn Hoover, and if he wasn't careful, he would be coming down her throat in an embarrassingly short amount of time.

Like point two seconds amount of time.

Tugging on her hair, he pulled her up until she released his dick with an audible pop.

"Take your top off. I want to see your tits."

Her eyes had darkened to the color of charcoal, telling him she was as turned on by the blowjob as he was.

Diligently, she pulled her top from her body, carelessly tossing it to the side.

"Bra too."

As much as he liked the way the pale blue lace contrasted against her tan skin, he wanted to see her pretty nipples more.

His hands reached out to cover the pebble-tipped globes as soon as they were bared. She leaned into his touch as he cupped and squeezed.

Leaving him to play with her breasts, she bowed her head to take him back inside.

She worked him over good. Mouth sliding up and down in even strokes.

"*Jesus*, babe."

Down to the root.

Up to the tip.

A swirl of her tongue around the sensitive cap of his tip, rolling it along the underside of his cock before repeating the process all over again.

Down.

Up.

Down.

Up.

Little *mmm*s of pleasure escaping her mouth as she worked him.

When he was balancing on the knife's edge of pleasure, she took the plump curves of her breasts in hand and wrapped them around his raging erection.

"*Fuck.* Fuck. Fuck." He chanted the curse as pleasure consumed him.

He'd fantasized about titty-fucking her more times than he could count. The way her sports bras pressed them together, creating the perfect channel of cleavage, it was only natural for him to envision what his dick would look like filling the space.

But to have her be the one to initiate the move. Fucking wet dream come to life.

"Shit, Blue. Do you have any idea how many times I thought about fucking your tits?"

His grip on her hair tightened.

"That's it, babe."

Another tug.

"Oh, yeah."

Her braid was completely destroyed at that point and he used a hand to brush the now loose strands from her face.

"Just like that." A hitch of breath. "I'm gonna come, babe," he warned but she only pressed deeper, swallowing every drop he had to give.

Ropes and ropes of his cum painted the back of her throat. He had never come so hard in his life.

His body melted into the leather around him. He was going to need a second, or a million, to recover from the intensity of his orgasm.

With slitted eyes, he watched as her tongue laved his cock, catching the last drops of his release, and fuck if he wasn't ready to go again that instant.

"Good?" His girlfriend—yeah, *his* girlfriend—asked,

tilting her head back to maintain eye contact with him as she settled back onto her heels. The way one of her black brows arched, and the knowing smirk that played across her lips alerted him that he didn't need to actually answer—she knew.

Without a word, he scooped her in his arms and reversed their positions.

He was going to be dragging ass at training the next day, but it sure as shit was going to be worth it.

Chapter Twenty-Eight

Normally when Rocky had a naked slumber party with Gage, she woke up with her body tangled around him like she was trying to imitate his tattoo.

When a feathering of kisses trailed a path across the skin of her upper back—an area with a direct line to her clit—it took a few moments for the veil of sleep to lift enough for her to realize Gage had shifted them at some point in their sleep to be the big spoon to her little.

She knew they needed to discuss some of the things her father had brought up the day before, but she wanted to live in their bubble just a little longer. The drama with The Cutter, signing off on his next opponent, and figuring out where he wanted to take his career next would all still be there, later. The true question was—where did all this leave her?

Sure, things were hunky dory now, but all that could change once he booked a fight and entered training camp. She had firsthand knowledge of how intense those six to twelve weeks leading up to a fight were. Already she was dreading being pushed to the back burner like she had her whole life.

Luckily, Gage's kisses were enough to shove all those

thoughts away. His lips were petal soft, a direct contrast to the morning scruff on his chiseled jaw scratching in their wake. Every graze sent a bolt of electricity down her spine, settling itself into what was swiftly becoming a pounding bass in her lady taco.

His impressive morning wood rode the cleft of her ass as her back arched in response to each wave of tingles washing over her.

"Morning, Blue." His voice, still rough from sleep, rumbled through her as he spoke against her skin.

"*Mmm.*" Her eyes shut, relishing the sensation of his teasing touches. "Can we just stay in bed all day?" A yawn broke free as the lack of sleep, resulting from hours of doing the horizontal mambo, caught up with her.

Totally worth it.

She wondered if it was possible to orgasm to death. She wasn't sure, but Gage sure as hell attempted the feat the night before.

"I'd be fully on board with that plan, but..." His words trailed off as he kissed up the curve of her neck to the place behind her ear that made her lose reason.

"B-But what?" The words stuttered out of her as her eyelids fluttered shut. How he was able to command her body with the barest of touches?

"But we work with your dad. And I would prefer he *didn't* kick my ass. Because I'm pretty sure he could take me."

A bark of laughter rushed out of her. He might be right. Her father may have royally pissed her off the day before, but both he and her uncle kept themselves in fighting shape.

"You make a go—" Her words cut off at the sound of a door slamming followed by her brother calling, "Yo, Octoman."

She let out a screech and tossed the covers over her head to hide.

The force of Gage's laughter had her rocking back and forth, so she threw an elbow into his gut and smiled when he let out an *oof* from the contact.

Served him right.

Who wanted their brother walking into the room when they were naked in bed with their boyfriend? Not this girl.

Holy mother of all things awkward, this was going to result in one hell of a story.

"Dude, are you ri—" Vince's words abruptly cut off the closer his voice sounded. "*Shit.*" The curse sounded pained. "Fuck, man. Is my *sister* in there with you?" he asked in the same tone he'd use to ask if Gage had killed a litter of puppies.

"She *is* my girlfriend, Vin," Gage said confidently, like he wasn't caught naked in bed by the brother of the same girl he was pushing his *still* hard dick against.

How the hell is he still turned on right now? Oh, god, kill me now.

"Vin, what are you doing here?" she whined from her safety beneath the covers.

"I was checking to see if Gage was riding with us or you."

"Don't you knock?" Her grip on the blankets tightened when she felt Gage tug on them.

"The door was unlocked. Figured if you were sleeping here it'd be locked."

Her groan was pained and she shot back another elbow.

"Blue," Gage cautioned, but the move cost her and he was able to pull the covers down enough to expose her face. Her brother stood in the doorway with his hand dramatically covering his eyes.

Maybe he was wishing for bleach.

She sure was, or a lobotomy maybe to erase this entire encounter from her memory.

Thank god they hadn't gotten to the sex before he barged in. Talk about *awkward*.

"Why the hell are you still here?" She thrust a finger at the open door behind him. "Get. Out."

Vince guffawed as he made his way out of the room. "Oh, man. Hope your phone's charged, sis. You know those Coven conversations are hell on the battery."

The jerk knew them too well.

🐙

Rocky let the door slam behind her as she stormed into her apartment cursing her brother under her breath.

"What did Vince do now?" Gemma's voice alerted her to the fact that maybe she wasn't promising to get retribution as quietly as she thought.

Her cousin was pouring a protein shake into a to-go cup at the counter when she stumbled to a stop to fill her in on her rude ass wake-up call.

Gem's laughter followed her down the hall to her room.

Her phone pinged as she was pulling on her green Hulk t-shirt because she was feeling very *Hulk Smash* at the moment.

She expected it to be the girls, but when she looked at the screen, it wasn't one of them.

THE BIG HAMMER: I guess I should be grateful Vince never walked in on us in bed?

THE BIG HAMMER: *GIF of Mike Tyson cracking up*

ALPHABET SOUP: We are NO LONGER best friends

THE BIG HAMMER: Oh don't be like that Balboa

· · ·

ALPHABET SOUP: It's not funny!!! *Angry face emoji*

ALPHABET SOUP: How would you like it if Jordan walked in on you with your flavor of the month??

ALPHABET SOUP: And TECHNICALLY we were in bed, but we weren't *doing* anything when he came in like a wrecking ball

ALPHABET SOUP: *GIF of Miley Cyrus swinging on a wrecking ball*

THE BIG HAMMER: 1st off. Gross *puking face emoji*

THE BIG HAMMER: 2nd, I don't have a flavor of the month

ALPHABET SOUP: Suuuuuuurrrrrreeeeee

THE BIG HAMMER: You know I was texting to see if you were ok. But if you're gonna be like that…

ALPHABET SOUP: What a gentleman

THE BIG HAMMER: *GIF of a cowboy tipping his hat*

From The Coven's Group Message Thread

ALPHABET SOUP: JD I need a good way to get back at Vince

MOTHER OF DRAGONS: Oooooo. You NEVER call me JD. This MUST be serious. What happened?

YOU KNOW YOU WANNA: *GIF of Jake blocking a shootout shot and the ref signaling no goal*

MOTHER OF DRAGONS: It's early and the twins are teething. So can you clue me in on what my husband has to do with Vince?

PROTEIN PRINCESS: Vince went all sexual Soup Nazi on Rock and Gage this morning. Busting into the room on them and essentially declaring "No sex for you!"

MOTHER OF DRAGONS: Well shit

MAKES BOYS CRY: Did you at least do it after he left?

QUEEN OF SMUT: Oh man, brothers are the WORST

MOTHER OF DRAGONS: Amen *praise hands emoji*

• • •

ALPHABET SOUP: Of course we DIDN'T get to finish. My bun went without its hotdog this morning.

MAKES BOYS CRY: I thought you said he was more like a sausage

YOU KNOW YOU WANNA: Or bratwurst

ALPHABET SOUP: NOT THE POINT!!!

QUEEN OF SMUT: Uh oh. Watch it she's channeling her inner Christian Grey

MAKES BOYS CRY: Ooo DETAILS NOW

ALPHABET SOUP: *string of squirrel emojis* *string of Dory emojis*

ALPHABET SOUP: Stay on topic

ALPHABET SOUP: Anyway… the important part is my V went without any P this morning and I'm feeling especially vindictive. So I'm reaching out to the expert

MOTHER OF DRAGONS: *GIF of girl twiddling her fingers in an evil plan*

· · ·

MOTHER OF DRAGONS: I got you

Chapter Twenty-Nine

Being interrupted by his girlfriend's brother was not something Gage had much experience with—okay, he had none—but he found it entertaining. That probably said something about him, but as he continued to grow more comfortable with the overbearing, no-boundary-having group, he basked in the feeling of finally finding his tribe.

Rocky, however, not so amused. At least if the daggers she hurled Vince's way with her eyes before climbing into Becky's car were anything to go by.

The oldest Steele didn't seem bothered in the least by his sister's ire. Or maybe he had no sense of self-preservation given the moment the cars were parked at The Steele Maker he instantly threw an arm around her shoulders and practically held her in a headlock for the walk inside.

Needing a moment to compose himself as the events from last night hit him, he hung back, feigning looking in his gym bag for something, while he got his emotions in check.

He still had no idea how to deal with Vic Steele, knowing he tried to have a hand in ending the first real relationship Gage had had in twenty-seven years. Professionally, he had the utmost respect for the man, but personally he kind of wanted to punch the guy in the face.

Rocky wasn't some high school girl trying to run away with a drop-out. She was twenty-four, a college graduate, had a job she did better than anyone else he had ever met and he was a disciplined and financially-responsible man.

As his coach, he could respect Vic's main concern that his training could be affected, but as a father, he was falling down on the job. Gage could admit he had some similar concerns when he first contemplated starting a relationship with Rocky, a woman that was so closely tied to his career, but they remained professional during training hours.

Working with her actually had him training *harder* every day, his macho, competitive side pushing to the forefront to prove himself to his woman.

He spotted Rocky wrapping Vince's hands as he made his way inside the gym and toward the locker rooms in the back. He stripped off his hoodie, stowed his bag and brought his own blue wraps—in honor of her—with him to the floor.

"Man, we gotta get you some new wraps," Vince said, holding up his own hands covered in Superman symbols.

"I like blue," he said, handing off the wraps to Rocky and sharing a secret smile with her.

"Eww. Don't be going all mushy in front of me." Vince mimed gagging while Rocky let the material unroll to the matted floor.

"Well, we wouldn't *have* to be mushy with each other if *someone* didn't barge in on our sexy time," she tossed out.

"La, la, la, la, la." Vince plugged his ears with his fingers. "No. Nope. Nah-uh. I don't want to hear it. *Gross.*"

"I swear, Sean is more mature than you some days," she said as she finished wrapping one hand and started on the other.

"Don't be a hater, sis."

They were still laughing when Vic Steele strode up to them, cutting off any further conversation.

"Okay, enough chitchat. You two"—he pointed a finger at Gage and Vince—"go warm up with the speed bags. And you"—he narrowed his eyes at Rocky, and Gage's hackles rose at his tone—"go work with Nick and Damon."

"What?" she asked. He was never that specific on who she worked with or when during the day.

"Did I stutter, Raquel?"

Vic's harsh words even had Vince sucking in a breath beside him. Gage's hands clenched in to fists at the compulsion to defend his woman.

"No." He could feel the effort Rocky made to keep her own tone civil. "I'm just confused why you want me to work with Nick and Damon. I've been almost exclusively working with Vin and Gage for the last week."

"Not anymore."

"Why not?" She folded her arms over her chest, mirroring her father's stance.

"Unless Gage is injured, you are officially off his training plan."

"Excuse me?" Her voice rose a few octaves.

"I've had enough of your attitude, young lady."

"Attitude?" Hurt started to bleed into her words.

Vic Steele was currently trying to overtake The Cutter as his least favorite person.

"I may not have been able to put a stop to this"—Vic's fingers bounced between Gage and Rocky—"but you are strictly forbidden from working together, unless there is an injury to treat."

"Forbidden?"

"Stop with the dramatics, Raquel."

She was seething and he wanted nothing more than to reach out, wrap his arms around her and hold her until she felt better. Given the current conversation, he knew that would never fly and kept his arms down by his sides.

"The subject is not up for debate. Now get to work, *all* of you."

Decree made, Vic Steele turned on his heel, walking away and leaving three stupefied people in his wake.

🦑

Not even Rocky's Boston boys were able to expel the driving need to hit something from her. Hours later, she was still angry about her father treating her like a child, blatantly disrespecting her role as a member of The Steele Maker staff.

She couldn't even *look* at him right now.

All her life, she had been daddy's little girl. The only time they had ever really argued was when she wanted to leave the gym to work for the Blizzards. For days, they went back and forth until she finally gave in, turning down her dream job and stepping into the role she currently had full-time.

But this? Everything else paled in comparison to the rage she felt bubbling under her skin.

No matter what her father said, her eyes tracked for the millionth time to where Vince and Gage were sparring, analyzing the way each man moved as they did. At least it looked like her brother had finally kicked the last of his tells.

Gage had his hands hooked behind Vince's neck, holding him in place while he drove his knee up and into Vince's side.

She frowned the longer she watched. Gage's gait was off. It was minute, barely perceptible, but it *was* there. She may have been strictly forbidden from working with him, but it was her *job* to keep the fighters, *all* of them, healthy and something was up.

"What's with the face, Rock?" Nick asked as he and Damon relaxed out of their fighting stance, noticing her distraction.

She hesitated, not wanting to seem *stupid* given the current situation.

"Spit it out, Alphabet Soup. You're giving yourself wrinkles." Damon, always the charmer. It wasn't true, but it was enough to break her from her haze.

"I'm not sure." She paused, eyeing the pair across the gym again. "I feel like there's something wonky going on with Gage. He's off."

Shaking it off, she blew out a breath and turned back to the pair she was *supposed* to be focusing on.

Nick's expression turned serious in a way it so rarely did. "If you think something's up then it probably is."

"This is true." Damon agreed with a nod. "No one spots injuries better than you, Rock."

"Fact. There have been times I swear you caught them *before* they happened."

Intellectually, she knew the guys respected her position at the gym and had most likely made similar comments before, but it was like she was *hearing* them for the first time.

What changed?

Gage. Gage James happened. He entered her life, knocking down more than just the walls surrounding her heart.

Emboldened by what the guys said, knowing it wasn't going to go over well but not giving a fuck, she headed in their direction. No matter what her father thought, she wasn't the type to let her personal relationships prevent her from doing the best job possible.

"Raquel." The use of her legal name said more about her father's current feelings than the gravelly way he spoke it did.

She spoke through gritted teeth as she choked down her feelings. "Something is off with Gage."

The sigh her father let out was worthy of a soap opera. "Raquel." Again with the legal name. "This is why you can't work with him. Taking hits is all a part MMA. You're too close to this."

"Dad." Her tone turned frosty. "I don't need you to explain how MMA works. I grew up on the sport. And that's not what I am talking about here."

She waved her hand at the duo circling each other. "He's moving different. Something's up."

If her father was the type to roll his eyes, they'd be back in his brain if the scoff he let out was any indication.

"Gage," he barked, bringing a stop to the sparring session. "Are you hurt?"

"What?" A v formed between his brows as he ran one of his wrapped hands over his buzzed hair.

"Your *girlfriend* is concerned you're injured."

He said the word girlfriend the same way most people spoke about Nazis.

You cannot hit him. He is your father. He may be acting like an ass right now, but you cannot *hit him.*

GAGE REMINDED HIMSELF it would be bad for his career if he throat-punched his coach, but the struggle was real. Listening to Vic essentially talk down to Rocky in front of him did not sit well at all.

Neither did the fact that he was about to be forced into lying.

It came as no surprise Rocky once again picked up on him favoring his hip. He'd tweaked it earlier and with each passing minute, the pain only increased. He was usually better at compartmentalizing it, but he was already on overload trying to navigate the family drama happening inside the gym.

The ironic thing was Vic was the catalyst to everything he accused Rocky of potentially being.

Personal reasons aside, the last thing the situation needed

was his injury becoming public knowledge. And yet he didn't want to give weight to Vic's obvious attempt at a brush-off.

He was stuck between a rock and a hard place—no pun intended.

"I came down a little funny earlier, but it already feels back to normal."

There, that was perfect. An admittance to validate Rocky's concerns, while downplaying the severity of the actual injury.

"See, Raquel. I told you that you were overreacting."

Okay, he didn't like *that* response.

"I wouldn't go that far," he cut in while steam practically poured from Rocky's ears. "On my first day, you yourself told me not to try and hide an injury from Rocky. It may not be an injury, per se, but she did still pick up on something being off. I think it just goes to show how right you were about her skills."

The tension lines around Rocky's stormy eyes eased at his words. She mouthed *thank you* to him and when Vic wasn't looking, he sent her a wink.

This situation was not ideal, but he would find a way to fix it. He had a feeling he would have to help bridge the gap between father and daughter for that to be possible.

He was up to the challenge. He would do anything for his Blue.

Chapter Thirty

I t wasn't until the end of the week—one of the worst
weeks on record—that their schedules finally lined up
for them to have dinner with Wyatt and Beth. Rocky
knew Gage's cousin in passing, as he and a few other firemen
worked out at The Steele Maker, but not on a personal level.

She followed Gage as he let himself inside the cute ranch-
style home, obviously as close with his cousin as she was with
her own friends. She couldn't help but notice how much
different she felt about dinner with his family versus hers. It
probably helped no one inside the house had demanded they
break up, but tomato tomahto.

A woman she assumed was Beth, as she looked about
ready to pop, came around the corner with a beaming smile
on her face. "Dumbass," she said, pulling Gage into as close
of a hug as her belly would allow.

"Pita," he returned affectionately.

Beth released Gage, belly bumping against Rocky as they
hugged also. "And you must be the girlfriend."

"I am," she answered with a smile of her own. "It's really
nice to meet you."

"You too." Beth stepped back, looking her up and down

before treating her to a knowing grin. "I always knew whatever girl with the magic vagina who could make this knucklehead"—she punched Gage in the arm—"want to date would have to be gorgeous, and I was right. You're a babe."

She snickered, unsure how to respond to someone talking about her lady parts within a minute of meeting her.

"You'll have to forgive my wife." Wyatt stepped into the room, pulling Beth to his side and greeting his cousin with some sort of complicated bro handshake. "The pregnancy brain has basically removed her verbal filter."

"*Pff.* From what I can remember, she never *had* a filter."

"It's not nice to pick on a pregnant woman, Gage Elliot," Beth scolded as she led them out to a three-season porch where there was an impressive spread of chicken kabobs, grilled vegetables, and roasted potatoes set out.

"Middle-named, huh?" Rocky giggled. "You *must* be in trouble."

"Both these two suck, not having whole first names," Beth complained, making a v with her index and middle fingers to indicate both James men. "If I'm pissed or annoyed at them, what am I am supposed to say? Wyatt-athon and Gage-topher?" She shook her head. "I think not."

Rocky buried her face behind her hand as she tried to get her peals of laughter under control. This chick would fit in perfectly with the girls. She would have to keep her in mind the next time they all got together.

"You're a real riot, Pita. You know that?" Gage cupped a hand over her knee as they sat, a bolt of heat shooting up her leg at his touch. She kept waiting for the time when his touch wouldn't cause an instant reaction, but so far it had only intensified instead of waning.

"Pita?" One of her brows lifted with the question.

"Yup. *Elizabeth*"—Gage dragged out the syllables to prove a point—"has been a pain in my ass since these two started sniffing around each other our freshman year."

"I was *not* a pain in the ass. You were just too much of an idiot to appreciate my charms, Dumbass."

Again, she tried to hide her reaction behind her hand without much success.

"What's so funny, Blue?" Gage pulsed his hand against her ribcage, tickling her side. She squirmed in her seat to get away.

"Oh, nothing," she hedged.

His tickling picked up speed, not believing her for a second.

"Okay, okay." She tapped on the corded muscles of his forearm. "I'm tapping out." Her breaths heaved as she tried to get herself back under control thanks to the unexpected attack. "I was thinking about how much fun Beth would have with *The Coven.*" She whispered it as if they were some sort of secret society.

Gage's blue eyes sparkled with mischief as he considered the implications.

"No. Way," Wyatt said. "I've heard the guys talking about your little group of friends around the gym. I'd rather sit back and enjoy my cousin being with a member than be married to one."

"You run into burning buildings for a living. Yet you're scared of a group of girls?" Rocky taunted.

Gage snorted beside her.

"*You* still chose to date me," she said.

"Ahh." He stroked a finger along the underside of her jaw, her head moving to follow the movement. "But I'm more of a man than my cousin."

"Fuck you, cuz." Wyatt flipped Gage off with a smile.

She enjoyed hearing embarrassing stories of Gage growing up. It seemed only fair since he heard something about her on an almost daily basis. One downside to working with your family.

"How do you handle working with your brother every

day?" Beth asked, rubbing her belly. "I think it would drive me *insane*."

"It's actually fun." She loved her brother, maybe not so much when he was serving as a cock block, but since then, she made sure Gage *always* locked his door. Especially now that they needed to make the most of their private time since they were restricted from spending any time together while working. A fact she still hadn't forgiven her father for.

"I couldn't do it." Beth shook her head vehemently. "Going through high school with these two was bad enough."

"Yeah, because you were *such* a walk in the park."

She liked this new playful side of Gage.

"*Please.*" Beth rolled her eyes. "Should I tell your girlfriend how you both wanted to go to prom dressed in tuxes straight out of *Dumb and Dumber*?"

"They did not?" She slapped a hand over her mouth to cover her shock, having a hard time picturing Gage in a powder blue tuxedo with a ruffled shirt. The picture just didn't compute.

"They *did*," Beth confirmed. "Thank god I went with them when they went to rent their tuxes."

"What?" Gage shrugged. "It would have made my eyes pop."

When they finished consuming an impressive amount of food, they settled back to digest instead of automatically getting up to clean up.

"I still can't believe you never said anything about Gage being your cousin," she told Wyatt. "You work out at a fighting gym, for Christ's sake."

Gage absentmindedly twirled a section of her hair. He was always finding ways to touch her throughout the day, even with their new restrictions.

"I didn't want to seem like a name-dropper," Wyatt said with a shrug.

"It wouldn't be name dropping. He's your family. You

don't consider it name dropping when I talk about my friends and they're professional athletes too." Her eyes bounced between the cousins. "Though now that I know. I can't believe I didn't put it together earlier. You guys look *a lot* alike."

They both had the same crayon-bright eyes, and while Gage kept his short, Wyatt's longer hair was the same chocolatey brown shade.

Being a firefighter was a physically demanding job and Wyatt's body was a finely tuned instrument, but it had nothing on the defined bulk of muscle earned from years of training as an MMA fighter.

Gage wasn't overly bulky like muscle-head gym rats. His dense physique reminded her of Henry Cavill in *Superman*, with the exception of his buzzed hair. He was sinewy around each bulge and ridge of muscle and she loved to run her hands, and tongue, over every inch.

He was so much more than his panty-ruining good looks. All week he'd been her rock, her anchor during the emotional storm she had been put through by her father. Anytime she came close to breaking, he was there holding her together, reminding her it was a temporary setback in the grand scheme of things. The conviction with which he spoke made her believe the ban inside the gym wouldn't last forever.

Wanting a break from her once again spiraling thoughts, she offered to help Beth clean up when she waved off Wyatt's attempt to do so.

She was happy Gage had people who loved him to help him adjust to all recent changes he'd made for his career.

She was putting the last of the dishes in the dishwasher when she heard Beth let out a gasp. Her head snapped up, locking onto Beth's wide brown eyes.

"What's wrong?"

"Ummm. I'm pretty sure my water just broke."

Having been with Jordan when she went into labor with

the twins, she managed to tamp down any feelings of panic and took charge of the situation.

"I'll get the guys."

With hurried steps, she retraced the path to the back porch, pausing inside the doorway and clearing her throat.

"Looks like we're going to have to take this party on the road, boys." Two sets perplexed eyes met hers. "It's baby time."

BETWEEN SETTLING IN to his life in New Jersey, aiding in Vince's training for his upcoming fight, starting things up with Rocky and the drama surrounding it, Wyatt's work schedule and Beth's pregnancy, Gage hadn't spent as much time with his cousin as he would have liked.

While Wyatt had been wifed up since his freshman year in high school, Gage had never brought a girl home to meet his family. Bringing Rocky to have dinner with them tonight was technically meeting his family, but it wasn't anything like the pressure he had to face at the Steeles' earlier that week.

Being personally connected to all six members of The Coven, he could understand Wyatt's balking at his wife joining the fold, but it didn't make it any less comical.

Jake had told him once that he was sure if the girls put their minds to it, they could take over the world and have the people thanking them for it. Gage didn't think he was far off with the assessment.

"I saw you were trending this week," Wyatt said, uncapping a bottle of beer for each of them.

He thought back to the pictures he saw posted on his social media thanks to his new PR firm. It was after hours since that was the only time he could be with Rocky in the gym, and he was messing around training with her. One of the guys—he assumed Vince—snapped the pics of him doing pull-ups wearing Rocky. In both shots, she was wrapped around him like a monkey. In the first picture, he was hanging from the bar with his arms fully extended while she looked at him with a devil may care smile on her beautiful face. In the second one, his body was crunched up, his legs creating almost a table for her to sit on, as the two of them shared a kiss above the pull-up bar he lifted himself over.

Thanks to her father's treatment, his girl had not been herself anytime they stepped inside the gym. The night the pictures were taken, he'd made a conscious effort to bring the joy back to the place she spent the majority of her time.

He had no idea anyone took a photo of them until it blew up on the internet. Since his post announcing he was officially off the market, the public had been *real* interested in learning more about the girl who was able to capture The Kraken.

It didn't help that The Cutter commented on every one of his posts and even tried to get at him through Rocky's accounts. It had gotten so bad she made her accounts private.

He didn't bother trying to understand the guy's motives. Cutler already had his next fight lined up so it wasn't like he *needed* Gage for his career. It was ego more than anything else.

He couldn't give a shit. All that mattered was that the asshole stay far away from his girl.

He did agree the pictures were hot, and they may or may not have been the new background on his phone. Don't judge.

"You know," Wyatt said, regaining his attention. "I'd never thought I'd see the day."

"What's that?"

"The day you fell ass over head for a chick." His cousin had such an elegant way of putting things. "Being in love suits you."

He froze.

Love?

Is that what this is?

Could he really have fallen for Rocky that fast?

Holy shit. I love her.

The realization hit him like a knockout punch.

"I'm happy for you, bro." Wyatt's smile was knowing, probably because the fucker could read his mind.

He may have been in the middle of a lightbulb moment, but he didn't get any more time to obsess over the discovery because Rocky was clearing her throat from the doorway.

"Looks like we're going to have to take this party on the road, boys."

Wyatt was as clueless as he was.

"It's baby time," Rocky explained.

They both froze.

Then, like someone hitting the play button on a remote, they jumped from their seats, rushing around the room like two chickens with their heads cut off.

"Will you two chill?" she advised—the woman he had just figured out he was in love with—and if that wasn't enough of a banner moment, now it looked like his goddaughter wanted to make her entrance into the world a week early.

Chapter Thirty-One

The day of a fight was a long one for all those involved. The fights listed on the main card didn't start until nine o'clock, and Vince was the head-lining fight, which meant he wouldn't step into the cage until closer to midnight. With weigh-ins done the day before—Vince coming in at exactly two hundred and five pounds—they had spent the time rehydrating him and helping him put back on some of the weight he'd cut.

For the most part, Vic tried to keep his fighters close to their natural weight, giving them the advantage of not losing strength from severe weight cut practices. Some fighters were known to cut upwards of fifty pounds to make a weight class —which was both unhealthy and could affect a fighter's ability to fight.

The team from The Steele Maker took over the entire upper floor of a hotel across the street from Madison Square Garden. The Presidential Suite had a full-sized kitchen—one Gemma was currently using to cook Vince's next meal now that he could eat again—while he took one of many naps throughout the day.

Most of their friends had already arrived—each of them

also getting rooms in the hotel a few floors lower—and now they were all gathered inside the Steeles' suite. Rocky sat with her back resting against Gage's side, his arm looped over her shoulder and resting down her chest, while Jordan, Skye, and Vic discussed the possibility of him defending his title for the third time.

Vic scowled every time he looked at how they sat together, but they weren't at the gym so Gage would do whatever the hell he damned pleased. He didn't miss the way Rocky flinched anytime her dad let out a passive aggressive comment and he hated it.

He wasn't sure if it was the continued distance with her father or not, but she had been even more distant, almost even closed off, as they got closer and closer to Vince's fight. He hadn't broached the subject with her, not wanting to pile on to what she had to already be feeling.

It looked like it was finally time for him to take it to his tribe to see if they could help him help his girl.

As the others continued to discuss his career, he knew there was no way to put it off any longer. It had already been more than six months since his last fight.

"Our office, and your agent, have been fielding countless calls on when you're going to announce your next fight," Jordan explained as she pulled up something on her iPad.

"The biggest question they've been asking is *who* your next contender will be. We know there have been musings that Cutler has been looking for a rematch, but you have been unwaveringly against it."

Since the day he took the belt from The Cutter, the guy had been trying everything in his power—even now goading him through Rocky—to get him to accept. As the current title holder, he had final say on his opponent. It wasn't that he was scared to lose—he worked hard at being at the top of his game, hip pain notwithstanding—it was that a rematch with The Cutter would be more of a grudge match than a title fight, and he had no desire to give in to the juvenile taunts.

"I know I need to arrange my next fight. This has been one of my longest breaks between fights, but when I pick an opponent, it *won't* be Cutler," he said vehemently.

"Doesn't matter either way to us," Jordan said. "We just want you to be prepared to field questions on the topic. Between announcing your switch to The Steele Maker, the promotion for Vince's fight, and all the pictures of the two of you"—she pointed at them—"your media presence—both social and news-wise—has grown considerably."

He could attest to the accuracy of the statement. Since signing with ATS, he'd landed himself two more endorsement deals, a rarity when not coming off a fight, but these two women sure knew what they were doing. He understood why the Donovan/Donnelly boys were financially set so early in their careers.

"We can help run interference tonight. Skye and I always have passes to be in the backrooms before fights with Vince, so if anyone gets too aggressive, send them our way."

He eyed the five-two dynamo in front of him. Most people would take one look at her and laugh at the thought of her protecting his six-seven self from hordes of reporters, but he'd witnessed firsthand how much of a pit bull she was. Her husband was famous for blocking shots in the net, but Jordan was a true goalie of life.

A door clicked open and a bleary-eyed Vince entered the room, collapsing into the open chair in the room with them.

"Have a nice nap, princess?" Jake teased.

"Bite me, puck head," Vince retorted with a smile.

"Sorry, bro. I'm a one-woman kind of man. I save all the biting for my wife." He leaned down to nibble on his wife's earlobe. The two might have married young and had two babies already, but the sexual tension still radiated off them constantly.

"Eat this." Gemma came into the room, a plate loaded with food for Vince. "And drink this." A liter of water was placed on the floor beside his chair.

"How very *Alice in Wonderland* of you, Gem," Vince stated, already digging in.

"Yeah, well, if you don't listen, I'll go all Mad Hatter on you, smartass. So be a good boy and do as you're told." She patted him on the head like a child.

"Damn Coven," Vince mumbled with a full mouth.

He held back his own laughter, already knowing this was a look behind the curtain to what he could expect the day of his own fight, once it was booked.

"You'd think you'd be used to it by now," Jase said from where he lay on the floor playing with his nieces. "You *do* live across the hall from three of them."

"Oh, yeah? Then what's your excuse when you complain about them? One of them might be my sister, but one of them is your *twin*."

"Ahh. But she's their faithful leader, so it's like ten times worse."

Vince flipped him off.

"No fair. Mom doesn't let me give anyone the bird," Sean pouted, entering the room with plates of food for him and Carlee. Anytime Gage saw one, the other wasn't far behind.

"That's because you're eight, dude," Ryan supplied.

"Not fair."

"Life's not fair, kid."

"You're gonna kick this guy's ass tonight, right, Vince?" Sean asked.

"Language, little man." Maddey ruffled his hair. "Your mom doesn't want you to flip someone off, do you think she'll want you cursing?"

"Yeah, careful or she might not let you hang with us anymore," Deck added.

The youngest member of the Donnelly clan was a trip. There was no way he had been that cool in elementary school.

Since Vince wasn't fighting for a title, he had no obligations until his fight later that night, so they spent their time relaxing. They tuned in to watch the Fire take on the Liberty for the afternoon game and at some point between eating and napping, Vince and Jake disappeared.

Being at a fight that wasn't his own was a new experience for Gage, but he couldn't complain. There was good food, ridiculous conversation with friends, and the girl he loved by his side. Now if only he could work up the courage to admit his feelings.

⚓

Fighters had their routines and traditions before a fight, but they had nothing on how superstitious hockey players were.

But one of the things Vince always did before a fight was have Rocky wrap his hands. For some of his fights, she would be a corner person for him also, but even on the fights she watched in the audience instead of cage-side, she *always* wrapped his hands.

With an official from the UFC and the chief second of Vince's opponent watching to sign off, she went through the process of wrapping her brother's hands. She'd done it so many times she didn't even need to speak to get him to do what she needed.

Looping the soft gauze around his thumb, she wrapped it down his wrist three times, before wrapping it twice more up toward the hand. She carefully wrapped around the thumb, then over the bottom set of knuckles while he kept his fingers spread to make sure she didn't cut off his circulation. As she worked between his fingers, it was almost a choreographed dance of him spreading wide then forming a fist.

Once she finished another wrap around the wrist and that

layer was signed by the official, she repeated the entire process with surgical tape, ending with another signature in bold black Sharpie.

Aside from the occasional cloud of tension radiating from her father when he watched her with Gage, the atmosphere in the room was mostly jovial and relaxed. Vince preferred to stay mellow and hang with friends before a fight instead of isolating himself—the chaos of people centered him better.

Some of their squad was already sitting in their cage-side seats with Jordan, Skye because she was avoiding Tucker, Deck, Ray, Jase, and Gage staying behind until they got closer to Vince's fight.

"Sure you don't need any last minute fight tips? I really showed O'Doul not to drop the gloves with me last night in Nashville. I could teach you a thing or two." Jase leaned against the padded table Vince still sat on, their bromance on full display.

As the rest of the room carried on, she ignored the millionth look from her father and rested her head against Gage's shoulder, her head tipping to nestle inside the curve of his neck. They slipped into their own private bubble now that her job was done for the moment.

"Those two seem to have quite a bromance." He gestured with his chin to Vince and Jase.

She let out a snort. "Oh, yeah." Her fingers traced along the tentacles decorating the corded muscles of his forearm. "The two of them are actually the ones who gave The Coven its name."

"You know Wyatt is losing his shit over you guys adding Beth into your little group."

She couldn't help but smile thinking of how easily Gage's cousin-in-law molded into their original six. Then again, she shouldn't have been surprised—Beth did refer to an MMA badass as a dumbass on a regular basis. There were no damsels in The Coven.

"She's a perfect fit."

"Okay, so tell me how you guys got your nickname," he whispered in her ear.

The feel of his scruff along her neck distracted her from the question.

"Blue."

"Oh, right." She paused to think, trying to remember how it happened. "Jor," she called, "when did the guys name us The Coven."

"Umm...I think the first time they called us that was... Ry's last Frozen Four, maybe?"

"Oh, yeah." She snapped her fingers. "Wasn't it some bull-shit about how we weave a spell to get them to do what we want?"

"It's not bullshit," Jase defended.

"It's fact," Vince agreed with his partner in crime.

"You have been referred to as magical," Gage whispered hotly in her ear. Sure, it might sound like he was agreeing with the two idiots in the room, but she knew he was refer-ring to Beth's magical vagina comment from the night they had dinner. The memory of the things he said while going down on her that night were hot enough to have her cheeks heating even now.

Finally, it was time to start getting ready for Vince's fight. As her brother shadow-boxed to stay loose, she walked the rest of their friends out, before coming back to be one of Vince's corner people with their father.

Jase had gotten waylaid by someone from the Storm's front office attending the fight so Gage hung back to wait for him. She was happy to see her boyfriend had gotten over the jealousy he was feeling all those weeks ago. Then again, Jase was an easy guy to like.

"All good?" she asked Jase when he was done.

"Yeah. He just wanted me to pass a message to my sister

about one of the upcoming Garden of Dreams events coming up."

Both Jordan and Skye had worked with the charity organization since their freshman year of college. Now that they had graduated, they were members of the board, each playing an integral role in planning some of the events the foundation put on to raise funds.

"Well, well, well. If it isn't the *illustrious* Gage James," a taunting voice interrupted.

She recognized the brown-haired, brown-eyed man with the crooked nose immediately. Curtis "The Cutter" Cutler, looked at the three of them with a disgusted sneer on his been-punched-too-many-times-in-the-face face.

She instinctively put herself between Gage and the guy she knew he detested.

"This *is* surprising." Cutler carried on like he wasn't the *last* person any of them wanted to see. "You know, if you're into sharing, James, you and I could have some fun with your little chippy," he taunted when Jase shifted so part of his body blocked hers the same way she had done to Gage.

"Fuck off, Cutler," Gage spat.

"What?" Cutler held up his hands, feigning innocence. "I know all about who your little girlfriend is."

Little? I'm five-ten, asshole.

"I also know she used to date this guy a few years back." He waved a hand at Jase. "But since he's still around, I'm only going to assume there's still something going on there. And I'm sure I'd be a better second than the hockey boy."

A shudder ran through her at the implication. She also couldn't stop the eye roll at him calling Jase a *hockey boy*, like he wasn't the top defender in the league.

"If you want to make it out of here without your nose being broken *again*, I suggest you turn around and get the fuck out." She felt Gage's body coil with tension and she reached an arm behind her to put a comforting hand on his.

"What, James? Scared I'd give her the dick better than you can?"

"Mother. Fucker," Gage growled, surging forward. Thank god Jase was still with them and stopped Gage from attacking.

"Yeah, that's got to be it. Is she still tight?" Cutler continued as though he wasn't seconds away from being pummeled into the ground. "I could fix that for you. Give her to me for a night and I'll stretch her right out."

When she spotted the Garden's security walking toward them, she had never been more grateful for event security than she was in that moment. Both her boyfriend and best friend were about to murder this guy and that was the *last* thing they needed. It was bad enough Cutler's vile words made her feel dirty and in desperate need of a shower.

The tunnel under the Garden reeked with testosterone as the two alpha men beside her seethed in anger. She placed a hand on Jase's chest and implored him to find his seat after security escorted Cutler away—she was going to need a moment alone with Gage.

Those issues taken care of, now it was time to focus on the other.

She ran her hands up Gage's heaving chest, looping her arms around his neck, hooking her hands at the wrist and scratching across the buzzed hair on the back of his head the way she knew he liked.

"Hey," she called to get his attention, since he was still staring at the space where security hauled away The Cutter. When his blue eyes finally met hers, they were more the color of a stormy sea than the bright, crayon-like color she'd grown to love. "You okay?"

His hands came up to cup her face. His touch so gentle and at odds with what she was sure he was feeling. The way he looked at her was almost reverent in its intensity. It was a touch and a look she'd only seen when he was holding his brand-new goddaughter.

"I feel like I should be asking you that." His words were hushed compared to the guttural response earlier.

"I'm fine. Really." She added when he scoffed. "It takes more than a few dickish comments to get to me." Not exactly the truth but there was no way she was admitting that when he still looked homicidal.

"The fucker had no right to talk about you like that."

"Forget about it, babe. He's inconsequential."

Gage moved until he had her pressed against the cinderblock wall of the tunnel, resting his forehead on hers. "He may be, but you aren't." He placed a soft kiss in the middle of her forehead. "You are the thing that matters *most* to me. I fucking love you, Blue."

Her heart soared at his words. For weeks, she'd felt the same but was too afraid to admit her feelings out loud. She didn't know if it was the adrenaline from what had just transpired or if it was hearing him say those three magical words first, but she wasn't afraid anymore.

Her hands tightened around his neck as she rose onto tiptoe to seal her mouth over his. She squeezed her eyes shut and she poured every ounce of love she felt into him.

When they were both breathing heavy, this time not because of a douchecanoe, she released his mouth.

Against his lips, she confessed, "I love you too."

Chapter Thirty-Two

J ase was waiting for Gage when he finally made it to his seat. Some of the raw rage he had felt abated slightly learning Rocky loved him back, but it was still there simmering under the surface.

"You good?" Jase's tone lacked his usual jovial air. He had wondered if anything was able to ruffle the guy's feathers. Looked like he'd found that something.

"Yeah." His answer was clipped as he took his seat in front of the black octagon. From the look on the rest of his new friends' faces, they were already filled in on what happened backstage.

"You know, Blondie, I think you and The Coven really do practice some type of voodoo magic," said the guy sitting next to Jake that he recognized as Tucker Hayes.

"Oh, yeah?" Jordan leaned across her husband to look at his best friend. "And what makes you say that?"

"Well, I mean ATS was building a good enough reputation branching into fighting with your boys at The Steele Maker, but look at you guys managing to land yourselves a ringer locking this guy down." Tucker hooked a finger in his direction.

"Oh, BB3. Ye of little faith."

"Careful, Tuck," Ryan cautioned. "Don't mess with their leader."

"Yeah, man," Jase agreed.

"You guys are just jealous she loves me most. We all know who her favorite brother is, blood relation or not," Tucker declared.

"Yeah, me." Ryan, Jase, and Sean stated simultaneously.

Jordan only laughed, not acknowledging their claims. As an only child, he always wondered what it would be like having siblings. Now that he had been welcomed into this group, he knew. It was freaking crazy.

"Haven't you learned not to poke the bear, Tuck," Jake said to his friend. "She'll have you signed on to endorse jock itch cream if you're not careful." He pressed a tender kiss to his wife's temple.

"Oh, can we sign him up for a jock itch endorsement?" Skye said with an evil gleam in her eye.

Tuck waved off the threat. "Yeah. And I'll be laughing all the way to the bank."

"So will I, bro, since I share a bank account with my wife who will enjoy profiting off your torture."

As entertaining as the conversation around him was, he knew this was his chance to try and glean insight into his girl's headspace.

"I need to ask you something," he said to Jase. The guy had the experience of being both Rocky's friend and boyfriend—though he was loath to remember that fact—and Gage hoped he would be able to see both sides of the coin. He always seemed directly involved with the drama at the gym like the girls.

"Sure, man. What's up?"

"Has—" He hated having to go to someone else about Rocky, but at the moment it seemed like his only option. "Has

Rock said anything to you about what's been going on with her dad?"

Jase frowned. "Yeah. And I have to say, I'm surprised Vic is still holding on to that ridiculous idea. There's *no way* it's not tearing him up as much as her."

"I agree." He ran a hand over the scruff on his jaw. "To be honest, I would have thought they would have made up by now. But I swear, as we got closer to today, Rocky has gotten worse. Not that I thought that was even possible."

Jase was quiet for a minute, staring at the octagon where the officials were resetting for Vince's upcoming fight. "That might have more to do with the two of you than what's going on with Papa Steele."

That was not the answer he expected at all.

"What do you mean?"

Jase rolled his lips between his teeth while he thought. "Did you know that before you she didn't date fighters? Like it was her own personal rule, one that had nothing to do with Vic's reaction now?"

"Yeah, I heard her mention it once."

"Do you know why?"

He mentally scrolled through their past conversations but couldn't recall a time she ever said why. He had assumed it was because of her job, but from what Jase was saying, that wasn't the case. He shook his head.

"She might kill me for telling you." He paused, letting out a long exhale. "But with everything that's going on with her dad, I highly doubt she'll be willing to open up those scars, and you need to know if you're gonna have any hope of breaking through her walls."

He braced himself for what he was about to hear.

"All her life, she's felt like The Steele Maker and Vic's fighters came before her. It was one of the main reasons she wanted to work outside the gym."

"I knew about the job stuff. I try to reiterate how essential she is to the staff as much as I can, but this crap with her being banned from working with me does not help."

"No, it doesn't," Jase agreed. "But you have given her a sense of...accomplishment she hadn't had before. Ever since you started training at the gym, the narrative has changed whenever she speaks about work. That's *all* you."

It felt good hearing that his efforts to make her see she was valued in her role at The Steele Maker were hitting home.

"Unfortunately," Jase continued, popping that bubble of warmth, "even if she and Vic make up, things are probably going to get worse before they get better once you book a fight."

"Why?"

"Right now, it's like she's waiting for the other shoe to drop. The shoe being you pushing her to the back burner in favor of your career. It's not something she would *fault* you for, it's just what she's been conditioned to expect."

A remixed version of the Superman theme song blared throughout the Garden as Vince and his team made their entrance down the corridor leading to the cage, cutting off any further conversation.

His eyes automatically tracked to where Rocky stood with Vic. His girl was a total badass. She wasn't intimated in the least by the macho posturing that oozed from an event like this. There was no chance of anyone telling her she didn't belong, and if they tried to get fresh with her, she would put them in their place.

He'd witnessed it in person and hell if it wasn't one of the things that attracted him most to her. No one fucked with his Blue, not unless they wanted to end up black and blue.

IN A PERFECT world, Rocky and Gage would be back in their hotel room, using their bodies to express those three special words they shared.

He loved her.

Gage James loved her.

The declaration played on repeat through her mind. Not even the chaos of following Vince down the tunnel and out into the arena filled with cheering fans was able to dull the glow.

It wasn't until the cut man was doing his final inspection of Vince, prepping his face with Vaseline, that her focus snapped back into place. Now wasn't the time to moon over Gage James loving her, that would come later. No, now she needed to help her brother kick Nunez's ass, putting him that much closer to his chance to compete for the Light Heavyweight title.

She and her father stood off to the side, standing shoulder-to-shoulder, arms crossed as they listened to the cage announcer give his spiel, followed by the referee. The two fighters tapped gloves and the first round got underway.

Like Gage, Vince was a grappling specialist, his years on the wrestling team evident in his dominance on the mat. But unlike her boyfriend, her brother had a solid boxing technique thanks to growing up with their Uncle Mick.

For five minutes, she watched as Vince and Nunez traded blows.

"He's not going to beat him on his feet," she observed, speaking her thoughts out loud to her father. Things were still strained between them, but here at a fight, they were a united front. She could only hope it wouldn't get worse when Gage booked a fight.

"I agree." Her father kept his eyes locked on the fighters in the cage. "He's got to take him to the mat."

Hockey was the sport she focused on while at school, but fighting was where she was raised. Her dad may call her his Pumpkin, but he also liked to refer to her as his secret weapon. Knowing how easily her studies came to her, she retained an almost encyclopedic knowledge of fighters from all the hours she logged watching footage of them.

The first round ended and they entered the cage to evaluate Vince and his injuries. He was in decent shape, luckily able to duck or block more hits than he took. Still, she didn't want to be him come morning.

Her father took her brother's face between his bear paw-sized hands, leaning in to rest his forehead against Vince's sweaty one. "Take this fucker to the mat. He can't compete once you knock him off his feet."

Vince nodded.

"You've taken Gage down enough in training. This guy doesn't stand a chance when you've been practicing taking down The Kraken," Vic said.

She gave her brother a sly smile and a nod, letting him know she agreed.

"Can you try and finish this round? I'm hungry and want some pizza." Their dad took the coaching role—she went with the annoying sister approach.

Vince's gloved knuckles bumped hers twice, the steely determination flaring in his eyes telling her everything she needed to know.

There wasn't going to be a third round.

GAGE WATCHED AS Rocky and Vic entered the cage at the end of the first round, Vince looking no worse for wear after a physical first round. But Vince wasn't going to get anywhere if he didn't get Nunez onto the mat.

The Steele siblings shared a knuckle bump. He could only imagine what smartass remark she was making at the moment. The smile on her face was the only tell he needed to know Vince had the fight in the bag.

Sure enough, ten seconds into the second round Vince dropped Nunez flat on his back in a double leg takedown. He scrabbled around, wrapping his legs and arms around Nunez from behind, locking him into a rear naked choke until Nunez was tapping out.

Vince jumped to his feet, the referee holding his arm up and declaring him the winner while the rest of his team flooded into the cage, Rocky jumping into his arms in celebration.

If this was how his girl reacted when her brother won a regular fight, he couldn't wait to see what she did when he successfully defended his Heavyweight title.

Over Jase's head, Gage's eyes met Jordan's.

"Start working your PR magic. It's time to teach The Cutter some respect."

Chapter Thirty-Three

Two days after Vince's fight, instead of the brief respite The Steele Maker was used to, it was a hubbub of activity. Gage's decision to give The Cutter the rematch he so longed for had been one of the biggest stories to come out of the UFC in years.

Granted, Gage could admit he probably could have handled making the announcement better. Unfortunately, with his adrenaline still running high from his earlier confrontation with the douchemonkey, a comment or two had slipped out in front of some of the reporters doing their post-fight interviews with Vince.

He sat on the edge of the boxing ring, upper body draped over the middle rope, arms crossed, Rocky resting her head on his shoulder, while they listened to the plan their war room of people had come up with.

"Are you sure you want to do this?" Vic stood with his arms crossed at the head of the group in the middle of the matted floor looking as formidable as Bruce Willis in an action movie.

"Without a doubt," he confirmed.

Vic and Mick shared a look he couldn't read before facing

him once again.

"Since The Cutter is already committed to a fight with the UFC, the date can't be changed," Mick said.

"So if you do this, your training camp wouldn't even be a full six weeks," Vic cautioned.

He was right to do so. Most training camps leading up to a fight were anywhere from six to twelve weeks, with six being the bare minimum. To consider taking on a fight—a title bout —with less than that could potentially be setting himself up for failure, but he was determined to have his shot at teaching The Cutter a lesson about respecting women.

Especially when that woman was his.

A quick glance at Rocky revealed a peculiar expression on her beautiful face. It wasn't doubt in his ability to defend his title, but concern was definitely evident.

He lifted an arm from the ropes, looped it behind her back, and rested a possessive hand on her hip, tucking her more firmly against him.

Vic's lips were twisted down in a frown, though he wasn't sure if it was from the thought of him taking on his first fight for the guy with a shortened camp or if it was because he was acting couple-ly inside the gym. Either way, he didn't care. He was taking the fight and there wasn't a chance in hell he wouldn't offer comfort to the woman he loved when he was distinctly picking up unsure vibes from her.

"It's true," he conceded. "It would be the shortest camp I've ever had. But to be fair, it's not like I'm coming in cold. The last seven weeks have almost been like a mini-training camp being Vince's main sparring partner."

"He's got a point, Dad," Vince said, leaning back in a wheeled leather chair, his body decorated in an array of Kinesio tape and ice packs to help promote healing, courtesy of his sister the physical therapist. There was also a goofy smile on his face, but he had a feeling it had more to do with whatever pain killers and anti-inflammatories Rocky had dosed him with for the day.

"Why don't you take a day before you decide. You might feel different after being home," Vic hedged. "Today's a wash for training anyway."

He could appreciate how his coach was looking out for him. It was obvious he had his best interests at heart. Deep down, he knew he wasn't going to change his mind, but if it helped give those who cared for him a little piece of mind, he could wait twenty-four hours before signing any contracts.

From the tension he could feel radiating off Rocky's body, maybe a quiet night spent together would assuage her worries. Plus, they hadn't really had much alone time since they'd declared their feelings for each other. A night filled with multiple orgasms probably wouldn't hurt.

He placed a kiss on the crown of her head, inhaling the fresh scent of blueberries. "I'm good with that. But since everyone is here now, let's get all the details and logistics figured out so if I do end up signing, we don't have to lose another day of training."

Vic and Mick agreed, turning over control to Jordan and Skye. The fact that both women were there proved what a big event this fight had the potential to be. Both owners of ATS rarely consulted on the same client.

"Are you sure you don't want to have this discussion in a more private setting?" Skye said, looking around the gym that was empty save for their team of full-time fighters and trainers.

"No, it's fine." He shook his head. "Most of it will be public knowledge anyway."

He was no stranger to people knowing how much money he made—hell, you could Google his net worth. Along with Conor McGregor, he was one of the highest grossing fighters to ever come out of the UFC.

"Okay, then." Skye looked to Jordan to take over.

"So just from signing your name on the dotted line, you're guaranteed a flat four million."

"The early stats we've seen come in since the sound clip leaked of you saying you would fight the twat waffle are some of the highest we've ever seen."

"Twat waffle?" he cut in to ask.

"If the shoe fits." How Skye was able to say it with a straight face, he had no idea, but the rest of the room fell into guffaws of laughter. "Anyway…like I was saying." The broad smile revealed she was amused at the interruption. "The early numbers are showing you earning upwards of another seventy-five mil based on pay-per-view projections."

"Right now, those numbers are showing over three million viewers," Jordan added.

A breath whistled through his teeth as he let the information sink in. It wasn't like he *needed* the money. He already had more money than he would be able to spend in a lifetime. But those numbers, even if only projections, were the highest he'd ever seen in his career.

"Honestly," Jordan continued after a minute, "the biggest concern I have is the amount of promotion the UFC is going to require. With an already shortened training camp, you don't want the time you do have cut more from that."

"It's a necessary evil though," he stated.

"It is." She agreed with a nod. "We can, however, make sure they come to you and adhere to any scheduling parameters we set for them."

"They want this matchup even more than you do," Skye added.

Doubtful.

Sure the UFC was a business, and the money potential was enough to make a grown man cream in his pants, but since hearing the asshat talk about fucking Rocky, there was no one, *no one*, who wanted to see Curtis Cutler get his ass beat more than Gage did. He was just the lucky SOB who would get a chance to do it in a sanctioned event.

"We've already told them everything has to be coordinated through ATS, and one of us will be here at all times during any filming or press." Jordan waved a hand between her and Skye.

"We'll both also fly out with you when you head to Vegas the week leading up to the fight. You'll have an entire team of people to handle any extraneous details so your focus can remain on your training."

He listened as the two listed out how the next month and a half would flow. It had been barely twenty-four hours since the sound bite leaked that started the ball rolling and already these two had all the details worked out.

The Coven was real people.

⚜

Rocky followed Gage into his condo. It was barely dinner time and already she was ready to call it a night. The last forty-eight hours were catching up with her. Vince's fight, the nasty run-in with The Cutter, celebrating Vince's win, Gage unintentionally declaring he would give The Cutter his rematch, followed closely by *when* the UFC wanted the fight to be, all combined into a ball of stress and she was officially done.

He may have said he was taking the night to think about the potential pitfalls of a shortened training camp, but she knew him well enough to recognize his mind was made up. As soon as Cutler added her into the equation, it was a done deal.

She'd witnessed her man get jealous and possessive—in the hottest alpha-romance-hero way, not in the creepy jerkwad way—over non-threats. There was no way he would let a direct insult be forgiven. Especially if the one slinging the barb was already on his shit list.

Wordlessly, he led her into the bedroom, pulling her into the circle of his arms, cupping the side of her face in one hand, love shining in his eyes clearly as he looked down at her. She had been in love before, twice actually, but neither of those times evoked the all-consuming adherence she felt for him.

His mouth sealed itself over hers, only breaking away long enough to lift their shirts and her bra from their bodies. His long arms pushed down her leggings halfway, then he stripped out of his joggers while she finished stepping out her leggings.

Not a word was spoken as he hooked an arm under the curve of her ass, lifting her in his arms so her legs wrapped around his narrow waist, and crawled into the center of the bed.

His mouth traced a hot path along her jaw, down her neck, across her collarbone, down her cleavage before pulling one of her sensitive nipples inside. The suction combined with the swirling laves of his tongue had her back arching off the bed and her nails raking across his buzzed head.

"God, you taste so good, Blue." He spoke against her skin as he continued down her body until he was settled between her spread thighs, hovering over where she needed him most.

"Gage." Her voice broke as he treated her clit to the same treatment her nipple received.

"If I could live off the taste of you I would." His words vibrated through her core.

Slowly, he licked from the top of her clit down to her entrance and back. No matter how much she urged, he maintained his languid pace.

She clutched the duvet under her as the first orgasm washed over her. His name released as a broken plea from her lips.

Instead of getting to the main event, he lifted her legs so they fell over his shoulders, and keeping with the same frustratingly unhurried pace, slipped two fingers inside her center.

"More, Gage. More," she begged.

His fingers hooked to hit that spot in the front of her vagina and she saw stars.

He released her legs, leaving her to lay like a starfish on the bed, as he kissed a path back up her body. From the pressure of some of them, there would be at least two new love bites left in their wake. Since the first night they spent together, she had consistently sported at least one somewhere on her body.

He clearly had a thing for marking her as his own.

Bracing himself on his elbows, his hands cradled her head, tilting it up for his kiss.

"God, I love you, Blue."

He kissed her again at the same time as he slid his hard length inside her inch by slow, glorious inch.

She gasped into his mouth.

"Oh…Gage."

She linked her ankles behind his back, bringing her pelvis flush against his as they rocked together.

"*Oh.*"

The trimmed hair of his groin brushed her clit.

"Gage."

A swivel of his hip.

"Oh, god."

Slow.

In.

Out.

In.

Out.

"Oh, god, Gage. I love you." Her neck bowed back as they tipped over the precipice together.

Without pulling out of her, he shifted so they lay on their sides, her partially on top of him to maintain their connection.

"I'm going to ask you something and I want you to be honest with me." His fingers lazily combed through her hair as he spoke.

"Okay." She shifted so she could see his eyes.

"Do you not want me to fight Cutler?"

She suspected he sensed her reservations, so she wasn't completely caught off guard by the question, but the way he was studying her, waiting for her answer, caused a tightness in her chest. It was so earnest, she had a feeling if she told him she didn't want him to fight, he wouldn't.

"It's not that." She struggled to find the right words. "I love going to fights and being able to see one of yours in person is like a dream come true."

"But…" He could tell there was more she wasn't saying.

"But I'm concerned you're letting what happened at the Garden goad you into making a rash decision. Cutting your camp…" *Or getting so lost in training because it's shortened that you forget about me.* But she didn't dare say that out loud.

"I'll be fine, babe." His thumb brushed along her bottom lip.

"I'm not worried about you losing. But can you honestly say you would be taking this risk if he didn't use me to get to you?"

She appreciated how he took the time to consider her words instead of pacifying her with what she wanted to hear.

"Yes, that's a part of it. There's always been a bit of bad blood between Cutler and me. The guy is a grade-A prick. The things he said about you were only the tip of the iceberg."

"I get it. But I don't want you rushing into something because you feel like you need to defend my honor or something. I'm a big girl. I can handle myself."

His hand drifted down to cup her ass. "Oh, babe, I know. I've seen you in action, remember."

She smiled at the memory of the night they met.

"But I meant what I said earlier. Helping Vin train was like a mini-camp for me. I'm not going into this cold like I normally would. Plus, I fight in my natural weight class, so I doubt I'll even have to worry about cutting weight and…you know as well as I do, that's half the battle during camp."

He was right. Without having to balance cutting weight, he would be able to train harder than most people preparing for a fight. Not having to cut calories or limit his water intake, he would be able to push himself to the max every day.

Just because she was scared training camp—an accelerated one, at that—would have him pushing her to the background like everyone else had throughout her life when it came to The Steele Maker, she couldn't use it as an excuse to keep him from doing something that could be major for his career. It was her baggage—she needed to learn how to carry it without weighing him down.

"Okay." She resolved to be the supportive girlfriend and not the insecure person she felt like.

His eyes widened in shock. "Okay?"

"Yeah. Okay."

A smile bloomed across his too handsome for his own good face.

"You gotta promise me one thing though."

"What's that, Blue?"

"Kick his ass."

"Like that was even a question."

Chapter Thirty-Four

I ncessant knocking sounded on Gage's front door. Since the morning-that-shall-not-be-talked-about when Vince served as a human alarm clock and general cock block, he had made sure to always lock his door when Rocky spent the night. They didn't need any more surprise visitors during sexy times.

Knock. Knock.

Knock-knock-knock.

Knock. Knock.

As the knocking persisted, Rocky stepped out from their bedroom—he hadn't considered it his since their first night together—dressed only in one of his t-shirts. Not that he made a habit of it in the past, but on the occasion he did have a girl spend the night and they wore one of his shirts around the house, he was used to it hitting closer to the girl's knees thanks to his tall frame.

Not Rocky. With her model height, the hem of his shirt hit her somewhere above mid-thigh, allowing him to see most of her spectacular stems.

As he watched her run a hand through her bed-mussed— okay, fine, it was totally sex hair—he wondered if she had on panties or if she was completely bare underneath. His fingers itched to find out.

Knock. Knock.

Knock-knock-knock.

Knock. Knock.

The familiar pattern tapped again, this time drawing a smile from Rocky as she looked at the front door.

"Expecting someone, Blue?" he asked over the rim of his coffee cup.

"Me? No. You." The look she gave him over her shoulder, gave him his first glimpse of why she was also a feared member of The Coven. "Yup." The playful way she popped the p did nothing to ease the nervousness he suddenly felt.

"You're earlier than I expected," Rocky said as she stepped aside to let Gemma into his apartment.

"Blizzards are in Canada for the week on a stretch of away games," she explained. "Jase is the only one I have to prepare meals for." She paused as if mentally running through the list of clients she meal prepped for. "Well, and Jordan, but she doesn't count. I figured I'd get a jump start on this guy." She hooked a thumb in his direction.

"I already have your nutrition guide, Gem," he said, passing Rocky her own mug of coffee.

"True. But during training camp, you don't put anything in your mouth I haven't approved."

His eyes met Rocky's mischief-filled ones over Gemma's brown ponytail. His half smirk telling her *exactly* what things he wanted in his mouth—her. Specifically, the nipples currently straining against the black cotton of his shirt she wore.

"*Eww.*" Gemma smacked him, the sound ringing out as her hand hit the bare skin of his chest. "Can you guys wait until I'm *gone* before you eye fuck the shit out of each other. *Some* of us aren't currently getting laid on the reg." She dropped a clear scale at the base of his feet. "Now step."

"Why?" He was still biting back laughter from her chastising him for his dirty thoughts.

"I need to see where your weight is now, so I know how to plan out what you need to balance meeting your weigh-in requirements while maintaining the muscle mass to kick The Cutter's ass."

"How'd you know I decided to do the fight?"

"Please." She rolled her eyes, giving him a look that screamed *do I look stupid?* "You boys are all alike."

He raised a brow in question.

"When one of the women in your life"—she sent a pointed finger at her cousin behind her—"is threatened or disrespected, all those macho alpha man tendencies bubble up inside you demanding retribution."

Rocky snorted, trying and failing to cover up her laugh at Gemma's pretty spot on description.

"Honestly." Gemma popped a hand onto her hip. "It's a miracle Vince's fight didn't turn in to Wrestle Mania, with both you and Jase bearing witness to what that scrotum wrinkle said."

He was unfortunate enough to be taking a sip of his coffee as Gemma launched her insult. He sputtered into his cup as he tried to clear the java from his throat.

"Scrotum wrinkle? Where the hell do you guys come up with this stuff?"

"One of our besties is a writer. She's creative," Rocky answered with a shrug.

I can't even.

He really needed to step up his insult game if he was going to be able to hang.

"Now, enough stalling. Get your fine ass on the scale. I got things to do. I'm hoping to get done with Thor's meal prep early enough to go to his game. He's got some cute teammates I'm hoping to be introduced to."

He did what he was told but asked, "Thor?"

"She means Jase." Another amused smirk bloomed on Rocky's face.

"Yeah, he looks like he could be the long lost Hemsworth brother." Gemma looked down at the scale. "Wow, two-sixty, right in range. Good job." She patted him on the shoulder like you would a dog. "Plus, we're very superhero-centric in our group."

"Aren't girls obsessed with the Hemsworths?" he asked.

"Oh, we are," Gemma deadpanned and he cast a look at Rocky. With his close-cropped, dark hair, he was the furthest thing from the God of Thunder.

"To be fair, I've always had more of a thing for Superman," Rocky mentioned.

Gemma made a gagging sound. "That's your *brother's* nickname."

Rocky waved her off. "He may have the crest tattooed on his shoulder, but he's way more Theo James than the actual Man of Steel."

Gemma appraised him closely. It made him feel like a bug under a microscope. He'd faced down opponents who literally were out for his blood, but hell if they had anything on the Covenettes.

"Well…he *is* very Henry Cavill," Gemma concluded.

"Yup. Even down to the chin dimple."

"Wonder what he would look like in all that spandex."

Rocky gave a one-shoulder shrug.

"Think we could get him to put on a cape?"

Another shrug from his girlfriend.

His gaze ping-ponged between the two women as they discussed him like he wasn't standing right next to them.

"While this has been"—he searched for the appropriate word—"*informative*, yeah, let's go with that. Now that we've established that I do fall within my weight class, I'm going to go shower so we can head to the gym."

They unabashedly laughed as he strode from the room, their laughter following him until he shut the bathroom door.

His life since switching coasts was never boring. As entertaining as the morning was, there was one thing that needed to be handled before his training got in full swing.

❦

As was routine when they arrived at The Steele Maker, Gage went to the locker room while Rocky went to her office. The difference today was instead of heading out to the main training once he was ready, he leaned against the wall in the hallway, waiting for Rocky to make her reappearance.

His conversation with Jase hadn't been far from his mind the last few days. It was time to take a stand and get his favorite trainer back.

"Gage." Her hand flew to her chest, his presence clearly catching her off guard.

"Blue." He pushed off the wall, closing the short distance between them.

"What are you doing?" Her head swirled around checking to see if the coast was clear.

"Fixing something that should have been handled weeks ago." Without another word, he linked his fingers with hers and pulled her with him down the hall to her father's office.

Without knocking, he pushed open the door, interrupting whatever conversation the two Steele brothers were having.

"Gage?" Vic asked.

"I wanted to tell you I'm taking the fight."

"Figured as much. Mick and I were just discussing your training schedule." His eyes fell to where Gage's hand was clasped around Rocky's. "What's this?"

"There's a few things I'd like to discuss before we move forward." He gave a gentle tug, his arm wrapping around Rocky's back and tucking her against his side. They were a team and needed to show a united front. "Rocky is back to working with me, effective immediately."

"That's not your call to make," Vic countered.

"But it is. I'm the fighter. It's my training."

"And *I'm* your coach."

He nodded. Vic wasn't wrong, but Rocky was a member of the training team.

"You are. And you just might be the best one I've ever had, *but*"—he held up a finger to stop any further comment—"Rocky is the best trainer you have. No one knows the ins and outs of individual fighters better than she does."

He smiled at the shocked breath he heard her suck in at his words.

"I'm not doing this without her."

He refused to blink as he stared down her father.

"I understand your reservations, but they are unfounded. We are *all* adults and professionals. This mandate of yours has gone on long enough. Now I'm going to go out there and warm up while you two"—he bounced a finger between Vic and Rocky—"figure out a way to come to terms with this."

He dropped a kiss on the top of Rocky's blueberry-scented head and strode from the room.

ROCKY'S JAW WAS somewhere on the floor as she watched the door swing closed behind Gage. There were no words to describe how his words made her feel.

She was still battling her insecurities over what could happen over the next month and a half, but there he went showing her how much she meant to him. She wanted to pirouette around the room like a teenager who'd just been asked to prom by her crush.

She would have to save that for later though, because right now her father was looking like he swallowed a bug.

Her uncle rose from his seat, clapped her dad on the

shoulder, and turned to leave, shooting her an encouraging smile as he exited the room to give the two of them privacy for this long overdue conversation.

Her father's bulk seemed to shrink as he blew out a heavy sigh. "Please sit down, Rocky."

Oh, good. I'm back to being Rocky.

She did as he asked, opting for one of the chairs opposite the couch.

There was so much she wanted to say but she held her tongue.

"He's right," he said after a long minute of silence.

"I know."

His eyes widened at her words. It was the first time she'd ever taken ownership of her role at the gym. Gage had helped give her the confidence to do this. It was his unwavering support that encouraged her to see her own value and she was going to embrace it instead of running from it.

"You pushed me to take this job."

"I did. This gym is part of your legacy."

It was her turn to sigh. "And for the longest time that was the *only* reason I thought you pushed as hard as you did."

Her father's entire expression fell at her words. "I'm sorry, Pumpkin, that was *never* my intention."

"I know." She reached out to place a hand over his scarred one. "It took me a long time to be able to see it, but I do now."

"Because of Gage?"

"Because of Gage," she answered with a nod.

They didn't say anything else for several minutes, letting the silence help soothe the wounds left over the last several weeks.

"Okay, enough of the mushy. Let's get out there and make sure your boyfriend is ready to kick some ass."

Chapter Thirty-Five

G age did his best to ignore the small camera crew filming around The Steele Maker. For the most part, he was successful. It helped that Jordan was like a pit bull, making sure they kept their distance unless he was specifically being interviewed.

As far as training camps went, this one had to be one of the best he'd *ever* had, the time constraints not even an issue. When he was asked what he thought was the biggest difference, he credited having teammates supporting him on his journey, which was true, but he knew deep down it was Rocky.

Aside from keeping him healthy and his body in top shape, she made the mundane fun. He actually enjoyed watching footage of both his own and The Cutter's past fights, picking apart strengths and weaknesses, looking for things he could use inside the octagon. He wanted to say it was because she was seriously knowledgeable about the sport and had a keen eye—and she did—but he was man enough to admit it probably had more to do with having breasts pressed against his back and long legs wrapped around his waist while he sat in front of her watching film that did it.

Even during the strenuous hours of training, she made sure he stayed out of his head. Challenged him in ways that kept him from being too serious.

That was who she was though.

His Blue was fun.

Like right now, for example. Not giving a fuck what her dad had to say—things had been better since their talk, but they were pushing boundaries—she lay on his back while he did pushups, ignoring him completely in favor for reading whatever it was Maddey had just finished writing.

"Holy shitballs, Madz. That's flipping hot as hell." He grunted as she shifted to see her friend.

He pushed so his arms were fully extended then lowered himself until his nose brushed the gray and black mats beneath him.

Up.

Down.

Inhale.

Exhale.

"Seriously. You can't have me read a scene like this when Jake's completing an arc of away games. Our phone sex game might be fierce, but it's not the same as the real thing." Jordan's reprimand caused him to laugh hard enough to jostle his lounging girlfriend.

"You know it's not appropriate to have porn in the work-place, right?" Out the corner of his eye, he saw Nick drop an arm around Jordan's shoulders.

"Pff. You're just jelly she doesn't let you beta for her."

"Damn straight I am."

Nick's vehement response caused another bark of laughter to escape him, once again causing Rocky to have to resettle herself on his back.

"You doing alright down there, Champ? Or am I getting to be too much for you to handle?" Smartass. He knocked out three more pushups in quick succession to prove a point.

"Please, we all know how well I *handle* you." Up. Down. "Or do *you* need a reminder?"

"I want to say yes to see what you would do, but no sex at work." The way she said the last part promised all sorts of naughty things once they were home later.

"Yeah, not unless you want to share," Nick said, followed by an *oof* when Jordan elbowed him in the gut.

"Don't be a jackass," she scolded. "Shit like that wouldn't fly back in college, what makes you think it would now?"

"Damn, JD."

"Don't you JD me, Nicholas," she said using her mom voice. "He may not *technically* be your captain any longer, but I'll tell Ry you're talking out your ass when it comes to a Coven member."

"Savage."

"Don't you forget it."

Jordan and Nick had a long history together from his days playing for the BTU Titans.

"Mother of dragons," Damon bellowed from across the gym. He was another former Titan puck head.

"Can't take them anywhere," Jordan said with a shake of her head.

"Not without risking embarrassment," Rocky agreed. "Come on, Champ. Head down. You owe me a hundred more," she said helpfully when he paused in the plank position.

"Demanding woman," he retorted but continued his reps.

"It's okay. I'll let you boss me around later."

And now he was hard.

He wouldn't recommend trying to do pushups with a boner.

Sonofabitch.

He tried to think of something, anything, to will the blood away from his aching dick. He didn't want to worry about bruising it against the floor while he did his pushups.

The smell of his gym bag, blue cheese, clowns—he fucking *hated* clowns.

"I thought you weren't supposed to be taking it easy until you got to Vegas," Wyatt heckled him as he, Beth, and his godchild made their way into the gym.

The girls gushed over the baby while his cousin stepped close enough for his feet to enter his field of vision. His family had been coming by the gym a few times a week so they could see each other, even just for a few minutes, while he was in the grind of camp.

He had arranged for his parents as well as Wyatt's to come to the fight. It made it easier for Wyatt and Beth to come without worrying about who would watch the baby during the fight.

"For years, I stayed safe from the infamous Coven, then you move out here and"—he snapped his fingers—"Beth's a member."

"First off." Up. "You've been following Beth around like a puppy since ninth grade." Down. "So I doubt much has changed." Inhale. "And second." Exhale. "I'm doing pushups with a grown-ass woman on my back, this isn't exactly *taking it easy.*"

He swore he could hear Wyatt roll his eyes.

"I'd be more impressed if it was the other Steele on your back."

He bet he would. He also knew Vince was just enough of a goofball to do it, so there wasn't a chance in hell he would mention it, even jokingly. There was only one member of the Steele family he wanted pressed against him and she was currently fulfilling the role.

As if reading his mind, she rolled from his back only to climb back on, this time with her front pressed to his back, her face peeking over his shoulder and ponytail brushing the floor as he finished off his set of two hundred pushups.

"I hope you're not too burned out from this set." Her lips

grazed the shell of his ear as she spoke. "Because I think you should do more later."

"Oh, yeah?"

"Yup. But this time with me beneath you and both of us naked."

And he was hard again.

🐙

"You know," Vince said, once training was done for the day, "camp is almost over, and Gage has never had to face you in the ring." His sweaty arm dropped around Rocky's shoulders.

She looked around the gym, trying to spot their father to see if he heard. He must not have because both he and her uncle were walking back to their offices.

"Oh, yes, please." Nick clapped his hands together. "Please, please, *please* let us watch you put someone else in their place for a change."

"You guys realize I only ever spar with you. I could never take any of you in an actual fight."

"Debatable," Damon said with a shrug.

She rolled her eyes. These guys were ridiculous. Sparring with them was one thing—fighting them was something else entirely.

"Are you really going to try and stand there and say you haven't picked up on any of Octoman's tells after watching *hours* of film?" Why did her brother have to know her so well?

"I'm game if you are, Blue," Gage said when she glanced at him.

"You just want a reason to put your hands on me."

"Yeah, because he needs to use *that* as an excuse." Becky snorted.

"Come on, Rock," the rest of her friends encouraged.

Giving in to peer pressure, she grabbed a pair of pink hand wraps.

She was already pushing her luck by doing this without her father's supervision so she made sure to slip on the padded sparring helmet. Attractive it was not, but at least she was protected. Though she doubted very much that Gage would come at her with any *real* punches.

Like a gentleman, he held open the door to the octagon, following once she stepped inside.

"Sure you want to do this?" she asked, slipping a mouth guard in place.

"Do your worst, Blue." The playful smirk on Gage's face only made her want to prove herself more. Sure, he was the professional fighter, but there was a thing or two she'd picked up on studying his past fights.

It was time to use them to her advantage.

Shaking her arms out by her sides, she bounced on the balls of her feet as they circled each other, neither one making a move.

Eventually, Gage threw a cross at her, the punch so lack-luster she ducked easily and hit him in the middle of the chest with a jab, a chorus of *ooohs* echoing from outside the cage.

She didn't want to box with him. And she knew the guys wanted to see if she could manage to put him down. As one of the instructors for the self-defense classes, she was well-versed in ways to take down an opponent larger than herself. Combining that with her own education through the years, she had a good idea what move would work best.

She kept a close watch on Gage's arms, waiting for her opening. An arm drag into a kouchi gake was going to be her best bet.

She bided her time until she was able to grab his right arm with her left, pulling it straight across her body, while looping her right one underneath to hook a hand around his tricep, tugging the arm into her and causing his body to step forward. With their legs scissor split together, she let go instead of latching onto his arm, dropping to the mat and hooking her right leg around his left.

Her knee and foot lay flat to the mat, protecting her toes and ankle, while trapping Gage's ankle in the bend of her knee. Hooking an arm behind the knee of his trapped leg, she used her shoulder to drive into his middle and pushed him back to the floor.

The move was successful in taking him down, but she wasn't able to escape, Gage's muscular arms wrapping around her and rolling her beneath him.

She bit back a moan as he ground his hips against her, her legs wrapping around his waist to leverage herself but she only managed to continue their almost dry humping.

She tried to slip under his arm and swing around his body but he had her pinned to the mat.

She heard Becky ask, "Does anyone else feel like we're watching their foreplay?" and her brother gagged in response.

Gage reached out to undo the Velcro strap underneath her chin and removed the padded helmet from her head then spit his own mouth guard out so it landed next to her ear.

He bent close, his nose skimming along the tendon of her neck, breathing in deep.

"Can we go home now?" His tongue followed the path of his nose. "I very much want to do this with you without any clothes...or an audience."

All of her hormones stood up and shouted *yes please* as she shuddered in his arms, giving him a nod of consent.

Show over.

Chapter Thirty-Six

The weeks ticked by as The Steele Maker focused on the training for Gage's upcoming fight to defend his title. Rocky still felt a lingering sense of trepidation when she thought of what was essentially an upcoming grudge match, but she had to admit, the more she watched him spar, the more obvious it became he was in peak fighting form.

He slipped out of Vince's triangle choke, reversing their positions into an arm bar, his graceful movements at odds with his size.

Her sexy AF man was currently sporting a pair of basketball shorts—only a pair of basketball shorts—as he popped up from the ground like a ninja.

"You and your boyfriend are totally doing a cover for me soon," Maddey said from her spot on the oversized beanbag chair they kept at the gym specifically for her. She had angled down the screen of the MacBook Pro perched on her lap to watch the action taking place in front of them.

She had to agree. Gage, like the other men they surrounded themselves with, was totally bookgasm, romance hero material. The way the sweat from his workout glistened, highlighting the contours of muscle on his body, made her want to lick him from head to toe. The black wraps on his hands only added to his tatted-up, bad boy appeal.

"Not that I'm sitting here lusting after your boyfriend or anything, but any similarities in my next hero are purely coincidental."

"Please, Madz." Becky dropped down next to the beanbag to enjoy the floor show as well. "We all know one of your first best sellers was a fictionalized version of how Jordan and Jake got together. I could pick out each one of us in your books."

"Well, somebody's got to be my inspiration since I'm currently not getting any," Maddey grumbled.

"Well, you're the one that broke up with Cap," Becky said offhandedly.

Oh, shit.

She watched her friend's face turn red like the pixie her brothers had nicknamed her after. The way Becky's face went lax with shock proved even she couldn't believe that slipped from her mouth.

They had known just how much their friend agonized over ending the years-long relationship. The fact that the two had remained as close post-breakup as she and Jase had, if not closer, was a testament to how truly special the Donnelly brothers were.

"You guys broke up like a year ago." She couldn't keep the shock from her voice.

"Fourteen months." Maddey's lips tipped down in a frown.

She shared a wide-eyed look with Becky, neither one saying a word, the silence between them growing heavy.

"Ogle away." She finally offered, waving a hand to where Gage was once again grappling with her brother.

The three of them lapsed back into silence as they watched the guys do their thing. She forcibly switched her brain from lustful girlfriend to physical therapist and trainer, watching with a critical eye for anything that could affect Gage during his fight.

Back and forth, two of her favorite men battled it out on the mat. As she watched Gage slip out of the arm bar Vince tried to pin him with, there was something...different.

She narrowed her eyes, trying to pinpoint what it was she was picking up on.

She ignored the slap of the mat, barely blinking as she continued her inspection.

Her dad called for them to move on to practicing hip throws, one of the moves he himself had mastered as a judo champion. It was when Gage swung Vince around his hip and dropped him to the mat that she knew, *knew* he had been hiding an injury from her. From everything she had observed, it was old, but it was there.

He lied.

THE GRUELING SCHEDULE of a shortened training camp was finally starting to take its toll on Gage's body. For the first time in months, the pain in his hip was an active thing, instead of lingering around with the occasional twinge or tightness.

It was bad enough as he scrambled around the mat, digging in his toes to get enough traction to flip Vince over. Now practicing hip throws, a move that had him taking *all* of Vince's body weight and swinging it over the injured area, he was no longer able to mask it.

An arrow of pain shot down his leg as he dropped Vince to the mat in his first throw. Son of a bitch, that hurt.

"Stop." Rocky's voice called out in a tone he'd never heard her use before. All eyes in the gym—well, the training area— went to her.

"Gage." The cold look in her mercurial eyes hurt more than his throbbing hip, and that was saying something.

She knows.

"Vin…go…do…something." She struggled to get the directive out. "You"—she pointed at him now—"are done. Come with me." Then without waiting for a response, she spun on her heel, high ponytail swinging around, and stalked toward her treatment room.

I'm fucked.

He'd been warned, from day one, not to try to hide an injury from her. But that's exactly what he'd done —repeatedly.

He shut the door behind him as he stepped inside the room, Rocky leaning against the treatment table, arms crossed over her chest as she waited for him. He didn't think he'd ever seen her look so pissed.

"You're hurt." She cut right to the chase.

He nodded, knowing lying would only make things worse.

"You're hurt and you didn't tell me."

Again, he nodded, thinking it might be safest for him to keep quiet.

"You're hurt. You didn't tell me. *And*…you *lied* to me about it." This time she ticked off each of his crimes on her fingers.

Fuck.

"Blue—"

"*Don't.*" She cut him off. "Don't you *dare* Blue me right now." Jordan's text handle may be mother of dragons, but it was Rocky who looked like she was ready to breathe fire.

"I don't get it." She threw her hands up in frustration. "Why would you lie to me? There's no way this is a new injury, not with the way you're moving. I can tell *that* much now that I'm looking for it."

He had no idea how to answer without digging himself in deeper.

Defeat sagged her shoulders as the fight left her. "I knew something like this would happen."

"That what would happen?" he asked as her eyes got suspiciously wet. There was more than him lying about his injury going on here, he just wasn't sure what.

"I can't really blame you. It's your career. I just—" Her voice broke. "I just thought you were different."

Panic seized him. *Why the hell does this sound like a breakup?*

"Rocky. What *exactly* are you saying right now? Because it's starting to sound suspiciously like you're about to break up with me."

She wouldn't even look at him and he was across the room in two long strides, the ache in his hip be damned. Taking her face in his hands, he cradled it between his still wrapped palms, his thumbs pressing under her chin to lift it so he could see her eyes.

"Talk to me, Blue." Fuck if he wasn't using his name for her. "I *need* to know what's going on it that beautiful head of yours because, not gonna lie, you're scaring me right now."

A sob broke free and a tear streaked down his tough girl's cheek. This wasn't the Rocky he knew at all.

"Blue. Baby." His grip on her tightened.

"You *lied*," she whispered.

"I know. And I'm sorry." His thumbs moved to wipe her tears. "I didn't want to risk *anyone* knowing."

"I'm not *just* anyone, Gage. I'm your girlfriend."

"I know."

"I'm your *fucking* physical therapist, for Christ's sake." The volume of her voice started to rise.

"I know that too."

"It is"—a poke to his chest—"*literally*"—another poke—"my job"—this time a smack—"to know."

Never having been in a serious relationship before, he didn't know how to handle the situation. He wished real life was like *Who Wants to be a Millionaire?* and he could phone a friend and call Wyatt for advice.

"It's my fault." Her sudden change of heart made him nervous. "I should have *known*. I don't know why I expected you to be any different. You're just like the rest of them."

It was his turn to get pissed. What the hell did that mean?

"Care to explain who you're trying to lump me in with?" It took all his self-control not to sound as angry as he felt.

"You. Them." She waved a hand toward the gym beyond the walls. "I even bet my dad was all, 'Oh, Rocky doesn't need to know. She's only going to want you to sit out this fight if she knew.' Am I right? Don't want to risk your girlfriend putting the kibosh on things. Career first, after all."

Ahhh. Now things were starting to make sense. This wasn't about him. Okay, maybe a little bit of it was about him seeing as he *was* the one to keep the information from her, but this was more about her needs or opinions being pushed aside for the sake of the gym. Hell, her dad wanted her to dump him when he first found out about them.

He thought they'd worked through these issues weeks ago when he laid down the law and got her back as one of his trainers, but it looked like some of them were only lying dormant until now.

"Listen. To. Me." He didn't even blink while he spoke. What he had to say was too important to break contact for the millisecond it would take to do so. "No. One. Knew. Not even Tony."

The mention of his old coach seemed to be the thing to pierce the haze of her anger enough for her to hear him.

"I'm sorry I was too scared to tell you. I should have." He let out a humorless laugh. "Hell...I'm sure if I did, I wouldn't be in the pain I am now. If anyone can fix me, it's you, Blue."

"Don't suck up," she scolded.

"But I'm so good at sucking." He bent to gently suck on the spot where her neck met her shoulder. "Not as good as you, but good enough." He spoke against her skin and her body started to melt at his touch. "Do you forgive me?"

He held his breath as he waited for her answer.

"How long?" she said instead of answering. "How long have you had this?" He hissed as she punched his hip.

"About a year," he reluctantly admitted.

"*A year?*" A full rim of white surrounded her gray eyes as they widened in disbelief. "For a whole year, you've been training with an injury without doing anything about it?"

He felt like a scolded child. "Yes?"

"Oh, Gage." She massaged the ridge of her brow. "You stupid boy."

Though the last part was an insult, hope bloomed as his feisty girl started to reappear. Unable to help it any longer, he claimed her mouth in the kiss he craved, not stopping until she pushed him away.

"Now, get on the table." She reversed their positions. "Let's see if I can fix whatever could-have-been-avoided-if-you-told-me-damage you ended up doing."

He did as she asked, all while wondering if she really did believe and forgive him.

As she got to work on the best way to treat him, he worked on figuring out how to prove to her once and for all she was number one in his world and always would be.

Chapter Thirty-Seven

Between the executives of the UFC and The Coven, their group had been booked into luxury suites at the MGM Grand and all travel arrangements were made. Rocky could tell Gage was surprised by how many people were going to be there to support him for his fight. For as comfortable as he had grown with them, it still took most people time to understand exactly how close their group was, and even then, witnessing it firsthand was something else.

He had a small taste of it when Vince had his own fight, but Madison Square Garden was essentially local—Las Vegas, not so much.

The look on his face when Skye came by with the itinerary for their trip and all the information about the plane they chartered to fly them all out there was priceless. When he questioned if a plane was really necessary, Skye simply ticked off all the people they had to transport from the NY-NJ metro area.

She didn't mention that Sammy and Jamie would be flying out the day of weigh-ins on Jamie's private jet and would also be bringing out Wyatt, Beth and the baby, and Sean and Carlee with their parents.

To say the last two were stoked about being able to go to Vegas for the fight would be like calling Mickey just a mouse. She had a feeling managing the two of them would be akin to wrangling raccoons after they raided the dumpster at a candy factory.

Gage had originally booked his cousin to fly out, but Wyatt told him he wasn't sure if he would be able to get the shift off. She knew he was disappointed and couldn't wait to see his reaction when they showed up.

Things had been strained with Gage since she discovered he was trying to train through an injury, keeping it a secret instead of telling her. It also didn't help that the day before they flew out to Vegas, she caught him and her father having a closed-door meeting. She cleared him to fight, so she couldn't imagine what it could have been about. Not asking about it was one of the hardest things she ever had to do, but she had refused to be the distraction her father worried she'd be.

She shook off the negative thoughts the memories brought and focused on watching Gage's reaction to their surprise arrivals in the hotel suite.

"What are you guys doing here?" he finally asked after standing still for a solid minute, then exchanging hugs with his cousin and Beth, before liberating the baby from her mom.

She loved to describe him as panty-melting, but when he cradled his infant niece, her tiny body barely bigger than his forearm, she swore she could literally *feel* her ovaries exploding like a bottle of Diet Coke with Mentos shoved in it.

Sure, she'd seen him interact with the Donovan twins, but they were fast approaching toddlerdom, turning into little people. It was different than watching him with an itty-bitty baby.

"*Really?*" Wyatt feigned like his heart hurt. "You're asking that?"

"Come on, Dumbass. Have we ever missed a title fight for

you?" Beth shook her head and patted him on the chest as she made her way into the room, plopping down on the couch next to Rocky.

"No," Gage conceded. "But Wyatt said he couldn't get off and you did just have a baby, so I wouldn't have held it against you for missing this one."

"I didn't *just* have a baby." Beth rolled her eyes. "She's old enough to have had her shots and, as you can see, babies are portable." She pointed to her daughter currently snuggled in the crook of his neck.

"And I switched shifts," Wyatt explained. "There wasn't a chance I was missing *this* fight."

While Gage and his cousin caught up, the rest of the room went back to watching the Storm take on San Jose. Jase would be catching a flight to Vegas after the game when the rest of his team took the team plane back to the east coast.

Sammy and Jordan worked out the details of the suite they would be watching the Blizzards game from later that evening. Since it was an away game for their boys, they would watch them play the Vegas team from one of the luxury boxes instead of ice-level seats. Plus, Jamie was a major celebrity and it was better for them if he had a way to escape the general public. At least the night of the fight he would be surrounded by a bunch of professional hockey players as well as his built husband.

With Jake and Ryan playing the home team, it made the logistics of them attending the fight a cakewalk.

"So, Gage," Jamie called out to get his attention. "Spins and I have a *very* important question for you."

She didn't miss the way he still got the tiniest bit starstruck when faced with the singer. "Sure."

"*Just* how superstitious are you?"

"How so?"

Jamie looked at Sammy to pick up the train of thought. "Well...our hockey boys can be very *particular* about their pregame rituals, and we weren't sure if you were like that before a fight, or if you were open to try something new."

She smiled at how true that statement was and just how weird some athletes could be with their *rituals*. Any of the Titans who had gone pro continued to tape up their uniform socks with rainbow-colored tape dubbed *Sammycorn Tape*, since the Titans went on a fifteen-game winning streak going into their second Frozen Four win after a lost bet to Sammy somehow led to Ryan wearing the colorful adhesive. Cap had scored a hat trick that first game and so the tradition began.

Nick and Damon even carried on the tradition when they fought, adding a piece of the tape to the inside of their fight shorts.

Tucker had a pair of laces from when his high school team won State that he tied onto one of his skates and Jase always wore one of Jordan's hair ties on his wrist. Then there was how Jake always had to kiss Jordan through the plexiglass before a game.

Aside from Nick and Damon carrying on the Sammycorn thing, the fighters were nowhere near as bad. Vince's only tradition was having her wrap and tape his hands.

Now, as she waited for Gage's answer, she was a little disappointed she hadn't thought to ask him herself.

"Umm." She could see him mentally scrolling through his pre-fight traditions. "I always wear the same pair of beat up sneakers. But other than that, I guess not."

Sammy and Jamie shared a look she couldn't read. "So you wouldn't be opposed to say…changing your entrance music?"

Confusion crossed Gage's face. "What? You don't like that I use a Birds of Prey song?" That would certainly be awkward at this late stage and coming from the band's front man.

"Fu—" Jamie's eyes tracked over to Sean and Carlee as he cut off the curse. "I mean, hell no. That shit's awesome."

Guess a rock star could only change their vocabulary so much. "But now you're friends with Spins."

Before Sammy became the sought-after music producer he was today, he'd started off his career as a popular DJ, occasionally still headlining clubs when the mood struck. Rocky started to smile, assuming that he had remixed Gage's entrance music.

Sammy pulled out his phone instead of explaining, hitting a button so the Birds of Prey song Gage had always walked out to started playing. Remixed into the song was the theme song to *The Pirates of the Caribbean*. The way the two pieces came together, swelling into a climax of notes, added a whole new dimension to the original rock hit.

"Shit, that's pretty fucking awesome," Gage marveled as he listened to the song played a second time.

"Yeah, my boy has skills," Jamie said proudly, causing Sammy to blush.

"I figured you needed something to go along with your moniker, and pirates and Krakens have always gone together."

The sudden shouts of Sean and Carlee cut off any further conversation.

"Oh, yeah. Drop the gloves, drop the gloves." Sean looked downright gleeful as he watched to see if Jase would follow instructions.

"Do the sweater thing. Do the sweater thing," Carlee added, bouncing on the balls of her feet.

Though they had the game on, not everyone had been paying attention. But they sure were now, spurred on by a pair of bloodthirsty second-graders.

Jase circled around with one of the defenders from San Jose, the guy more goon than enforcer. Almost simultaneously, the two tossed their gloves, sending them bouncing haphazardly across the ice. The San Jose goon swung out wide, Jase easily ducking under the arm and coming up with a jab of his own. With one hand gripping the front of the guy's jersey, Jase got in a quick series of punches, and to Carlee's utter delight, pulled the jersey partway over the guy's head before they were separated by the referees and sent to the sin bin.

"You guys are a bit bloodthirsty, aren't ya?" Gage said on a laugh.

"You have no idea."

Chapter Thirty-Eight

UFC weigh-ins were filmed and televised. There wasn't a lot of pomp and circumstance around the procedure, but there were promotional requirements for the fighters, such as the traditional stare-down between the two contenders after they made weight.

Gage waited in the backstage area with his team until his name was called. He would be the last fighter to walk to the stage since they went in weight class order and he was the reigning champion.

Weigh-ins could be a stressful part of the process for most fighters, but it never really was for him. He settled back in his seat, arm around Rocky, letting Vince and Deck make stupid snaps on their Snapchat accounts.

"What's going on, Las Vegas?"

The event emcee's voice boomed through the sound system at the MGM Grand.

"Welcome to the weigh-ins for UFC 235."

The announcements continued for the undercard then main card fights as fighters took their turns on stage.

Unlike his past fights, where he would spend the time blocking out the world around him with a *Harry Potter* book playing through a pair of noise-canceling headphones, he now had his teammates to pass the time with.

"And now for the main event, James versus Cutler. The two battle it out for the championship belt for the Heavyweight title."

There was a pause while the crowd cheered.

"We have Curtis 'The Cutter' Cutler versus our current champion Gage 'The Kraken' James. First up to the scale, please welcome Curtis Cutler."

For the first time all night, he looked toward the projection screen at the front of the backstage area to watch what was happening.

With a scowl on his face, The Cutter made his way on stage for his weigh-in. Once at the scale, he slipped out of his slides, dropped his sweatpants and tossed his shirt to the ground, getting onto the scale clad only in a pair of dark gray boxer briefs.

"Two sixty-five," the official called out.

"Two sixty-five, the official weight for our contender Curtis 'The Cutter' Cutler. Now his opponent, the UFC's Heavyweight Champion of the World, Gage 'The Kraken' James."

Gage stepped forward, followed closely by his small entourage of Vic, Vince, Gemma and Rocky. He repeated the same process of shedding his layers before taking the scale in his black boxer briefs. He had specifically worn black since the champion always wore black during a fight. He had no plans of relinquishing his title anytime soon, and he was making sure it was known from the start. Head games were part of the fight.

"Two sixty-three." The official in front of him read the display, confirming he made weight.

"Two sixty-three for your champ," the emcee announced.

He sent a wink to Rocky and Gemma, standing off to the side of the stage. Not once during his training camp had he come in over the weight limit and he took pride in officially staying under the line by two pounds. Those girls had worried too much. He was hoping to put on five or ten pounds once he rehydrated.

He made his way to shake the UFC's president's hand. He also had to get close enough to Cutler for the photographers to get the obligatory stare-down photo. Not something he was particularly looking forward to. No, all he wanted to do was take a page out of Jase's playbook and metaphorically drop the gloves.

He had perfected his badass, fierce fight face years ago. With it in place, he pushed all thoughts of Rocky telling him it was so hot her panties dented the floor because they dropped so hard, and stood inches from the guy he couldn't wait to pound into the ground the following day.

Thanks to his considerable height, he was able to look down on the dickwad and Cutler was forced to look up.

A smarmy smirk formed across Cutler's face as he leaned in to whisper, "Don't worry. After I take my title back, I'll throw your girl a bone and show her what it's like to fuck a *real* man."

His vision went black—not white, not red—black with anger. Without thought, he charged forward so sharply that the force of bumping him with his chest caused Cutler to stumble back a few steps. Deep within, he found the where-withal to not throw the punch that burned for release in his arms and shoulders.

The president's arms separated them even as he felt Vince instantly at his back, while Cutler's people did the same for him.

After a few charged seconds, the emcee's voice broke through the melee. *"The title is on the line. Gage James and Curtis Cutler."*

Chapter Thirty-Nine

Fight day.

Grudge match.

A clash of titans.

A battle for the ages.

A chance for redemption.

An alpha defending his mate.

The rematch the world had been waiting for.

All these and more had been tossed around while the day bloomed with a bright sunrise the way only the desert could. Thanks to the room's heavy blackout shades, Rocky and Gage were able to sleep in until their bodies naturally rose.

She woke before Gage, content to lay wrapped around his hot-as-sin body even with her bladder screaming at her to pee. Though he would nap on and off throughout the day, she didn't want to be the cause of him missing out on a second of sleep that morning.

After the drama the night before, she was taking care of him like it was her job. *Technically,* it was her job as his physical therapist and trainer, but the way she'd been acting fell more along the lines of girlfriend than professional. She was shocked her dad hadn't commented on it.

The only surefire way she knew to calm Gage down was sex, and that had been expressly forbidden before the fight by his coach. As she was in the room when her father dropped that edict, it had been awkward as hell.

Thank god for Jase.

He had seen the weigh-in clip trending while waiting for his flight out of San Jose. Once he did, he changed his plans and came directly to the hotel as opposed to the hockey game originally on his agenda.

She never thought she'd see the day where her bestie of an ex-boyfriend would be the one her boyfriend sought out for comfort. But that was exactly what happened. The two had formed some sort of weird alpha male bond over all the shit going on with The Cutter, and the enforcer served as the MMA fighter's emotional support animal.

Gage stirred beneath her and she felt his lips brush across the top of her head. "Morning, baby." His sleep-roughened voice did delicious things to her body and she cursed the fact it would still be *hours* before she could do anything about it.

"Morning, Champ." She placed a kiss over the eye of the octopus tattooed on his chest.

His impressive morning wood was pressing against the inner thigh stretched across his body. It really was a shame it was going to go to waste.

Stupid rules.

At least she'd been able to veto the suggestion she sleep in a different room. That was *so* not happening.

"Come on, time to get up." She reached for her phone on the nightstand to do a time check. "I'm surprised Gem hasn't busted in here already with your first round of food, so let's not give her the chance."

Once she'd taken care of business and pulled on a pair of leggings and a baggy Steele Maker t-shirt, they made their way out of the room and found most of their friends already spread out around the main floor of the suite. Sure enough, as soon as they stepped off the final stair, Gem was handing Gage a protein shake with strict instructions to drink up.

On her way back from the kitchen, fresh mug of coffee in hand, Skye stormed into the room and tossed a phone at Jordan with a sound of frustration. "You need to talk to your BB3 before I *murder* him." The *murder* came out with a slight growl.

She and Jordan shared a look. *Well, I guess things aren't better there yet.*

As Jordan lifted the phone, Rocky was able to see Tucker on the screen, the FaceTime call already in process.

"Yo, Blondie." Tuck's voice called out clearly. "Can you tell your bestie to chill with the *Blair Witch* photography. Damn, she about made me seasick."

"*Uggggh.*" Skye ran both hands through her hair in frustration, collapsing on the couch next to her. "Seriously, Jake, you might need to start accepting applications for a new best friend, because you're this close"—she held her thumb and forefinger a breath apart—"to your current one no longer being an option."

"It's fine. I have Ry and Jase too. I'm covered." Jake and Jase shared a knuckle bump.

Rocky put her arm around her friend in a show of support. The dynamic between Skye and Tucker had always been strained at best, but lately, things had been worse than ever. The two of them were the only past pairing in their group that hadn't settled into an easy friendship after they stopped hooking up. She wondered if it was because they had never been an official couple and stayed in the FWB area.

"Tuck," Jordan started, "I already have two kids of my own. I don't need another one right now, thank you very much. Why do you insist on being a shit starter so early in the morning?"

"Dude," Vince said, bending over the couch so his face was next to Jordan's and he could see their friend on the screen. "Don't mess with The Coven when you aren't here to suffer the consequences."

"I second that," Jake said, pulling his wife so she was settled between his legs, leaning back against his chest. "It's like a violation of the bro code."

Tucker let out a hard snort. "You and your damn *How I Met Your Mother* references. But whatever. Now speaking of kids, show me my girls."

Jordan's face visibly softened as she shifted around so Tucker could see the twins, both girls giggling and trying to take the phone when they saw their uncle on the screen.

"You guys are a little bit crazy, you know that?" Gage said, taking the remaining spot next to Rocky, protein shake in hand.

"Not crazy. Codependent," Becky clarified. Rocky shot her finger guns. *Nailed it.*

"Aren't you glad you decided to date me?" She placed a kiss on the underside of his jaw.

"Every. Single. Day."

She didn't know what made her want to jump his bones more, the way his bright blue eyes locked onto her as he spoke or the words themselves. What she *did* know, was that after his fight, it was on like Donkey Kong.

GAGE HAD FOUGHT in over two dozen fights throughout his career with the UFC. This was his fourth title bout—once to win it, plus two defenses—but never had he had a day of a fight be quite like this one.

First, he woke up with a girl in his bed and that had never happened before. His focus had always been on the fight first, his dick second. An anomaly amongst the male sex, he knew, he didn't need to be told. Then again, he was considered one of the best pound-for-pound fighters in the UFC so he must have been doing something right.

It was also strange, but good, to be surrounded by people who supported him in ways that had nothing to do with being his coach or trainer.

Sure, Gemma was there to make sure he was taking in the calories and hydration he needed to be in optimal shape for his late-night fight. Vic and Mick were also in the suite and there was talk of the fight, but he spent more of his not-napping time bullshitting with his new friends than anything else.

Wyatt liked to give him shit for his wife's recent membership into The Coven, but he had a feeling it would have happened regardless of him dating Rocky because he spent so much time with the rest of the guys in their world. As he sat there with his goddaughter snuggled on his chest, it was clear both his family members blended into the group perfectly.

He startled slightly as Jake tapped him on the shoulder. "Come on." Jake tilted his head back. "Pass the baby off, we got work to do."

He looked at the goalie, confused.

"You need to stay loose today and we have the perfect solution. The guys all use it when they have a fight. You're just lucky enough to have me as your partner." Jake clapped him on the shoulder one more time and stood to lead the way. "Beck, take the baby so I can school this guy in some pong and still have enough time to take advantage of my wife in our hotel bathroom before the fight."

"Bro." Ryan conveyed both his disgust and a reprimand with the single word. "How many times do I have to tell you I *don't* want to hear about you doing my sister?"

"Sorry to break it to you, man, but that baby you're playing with"—Jake circled his finger around, indicating one of his daughters—"*isn't* a product of immaculate conception."

"TMI, bro. T. M. I."

"Oh, don't be such a prude, Ry," Maddey said, snickering with Jordan somewhere else in the room.

Gage had never been more grateful to not have a sister as he was in that moment. Beth was the closest thing to it, but he had only ever known her as Wyatt's girlfriend so he never had the gross out factor come into play if the subject of sex ever came up.

After making sure his godchild was fine with Becky—soft snores could already be heard—he let Jake lead him to where he was unfolding a ping-pong table.

He reflexively caught the paddle Jake tossed his way once the table was set up. A few of the others migrated over to watch, including Rocky and Jordan. Vince moved one of the dining room chairs to the opposite side of the table, sitting backward in it and declaring himself a line judge for the game.

"Sweet," Vince said, crossing his arms over the top of his chair. "It'll be nice to see someone else lose to Brick for a change."

"Brick?" he asked.

"Yeah, Mr. Brick Wall over here." Vince fluttered a hand in Jake's direction, causing Gage to laugh at the apt description of the Blizzards goalie.

"I take it that's his text handle?" He made a mental note to ask Rocky about his own text handle next time they were alone.

"Yup, in everyone's phone except JD's," Skye said with a sly smile.

"Yeah, in her phone he's—"

"Please, for the *love* of god, don't finish that sentence." Jase broke in quickly, cutting off the rest of what Becky was trying to say.

"Seconded," Ryan chimed in.

"Third."

"And fourth," Nick and Damon tacked on.

"You guys are such hypocrites. Do you have *any* idea how much I had to hear about your sexcapades with the bunnies during college? You should be *happy* for your boy for getting laid on the reg." Jordan gestured with her hand like she was done with them all.

He bounced a ping-pong ball on the table as he listened to the ludicrous conversation volleyed around the room. "You guys are like goldfish the way you change topics."

"Eh. You get used to the squirrel mentality after a while," Jamie called out from where he was battling it out in a game of Mario Kart with Maddey, Sean and Carlee.

The singer was one of the few outside people who merged into the group, so he probably was speaking from personal experience.

"Come on, serve." Jake gave him a nod and the game got underway. He knew the goalie was a righty, so he was surprised to see him playing with his left hand.

"Why ping-pong?" he asked after they volleyed back and forth a dozen times or so.

"For you, your girl will tell you it's a good way to stay loose while focusing on your hand-eye coordination and keeping you light on your feet." Jake sent the white ball whizzing past him for the first point of the game. "And for me, my darling wife taught me it was a good way to hone my glove-saving skills." He gave Jordan a wink that made her blush.

"Ahhh." He was able to put a nice backspin on the ball to earn himself his first point. "Now it makes sense why you're playing lefty."

The ping-pong game originally meant to be an easygoing way to stay loose, steadily increased in intensity as they traded points back and forth. Rocky scolded him a few times that he was supposed to be taking it easy.

He put on a good show but eventually he was trounced by the hockey player.

🦑

Rocky got ready in one of the other rooms of the suite to avoid disturbing Gage while he took his final pre-fight nap. She dressed in a pair of stone-washed skinny jeans and a tight, black v-neck t-shirt. To show her support, her shirt had a gray screen-printed octopus on the right side, whose tentacles stretched across the front and back.

Her makeup for the night was on point—a subtle smoky eye and sharply winged liner made her gray eyes pop and a fierce blood red lip stain completed the look. Now to deal with what felt like a Rapunzel amount of hair.

Grabbing her blow dryer and paddle brush, she flipped her head over and set to work blowing out her long locks. Her nerves were finally starting to set in as the clock ticked closer to the actual fight. For weeks, she had been shoving them down, assuring herself Gage had it under control.

"So this is where you're hiding." Gage's amused voice startled her, causing her to jump and whip her head up to face him.

"Jesus." Her hand flew to cover her erratically beating heart while he watched her with a smirk. She switched off the blow dryer, silencing it so she wouldn't have to shout over the sound.

"You okay there, Blue?"

Gah! Why does he have to be so damn sexy?

He had his shoulder propped against the doorjamb, arms and ankles crossed, blue eyes sparkling like he knew *exactly* what sort of effect he had on her.

"Peachy," she deadpanned. She ran her hand through her hair, smoothing it around her face.

"Fuck, you look hot, babe." He pushed off the door, staring her down as he walked toward her. His hands came around to cup her face, his long fingers tangling in her hair. One of his thumbs stretched out to rub along her bottom lip and her eyes closed at the touch. "Do you have any idea what it does to me when you wear red lipstick?" His voice turned husky and his eyes darkened as he stared at her mouth.

Her tongue slipped out to moisten her lips as she got lost in the spell of his words, and she swore he let out a growl when it touched the pad of his finger.

"Well…" She had to clear her own lust from her voice before she could continue. "Seeing as I'm best friends with a romance author, I think I have a general idea. But maybe after successfully defending your belt, you can tell me all your fantasies"—she pushed onto her toes so her mouth was at his ear—"in *explicit* detail."

"*Fuck.*" The curse was strained as he crushed his lips to hers, her nipples straining toward his chest and his dick erect against her belly.

"And maybe I'll see about making a few of them come true," she finished when he finally released her mouth. Thank god for long-wear lip stain, otherwise the two of them would look like they could be related to The Joker.

"You're such a damn tease," he said on a laugh.

"It's only a tease if I don't follow through." She paused to meet his eyes. "And I damn well plan on it."

His husky laughter followed her out of the room as she pulled on her stiletto-heeled, knee-high leather boots.

"Shit, Rock, you're breaking the rules," Jordan said as she entered the suite while Rocky finished zipping up the second boot.

Her eyes tracked over the flat soles of her friend's riding boots. It was an unwritten rule in their group that taller members—meaning herself and Skye—were only able to wear heels if the short ones did. It was one of the longest running jokes between them. Maddey almost always wore heels, so they were generally safe when going out with her.

"There's always time to change before we need to be there," she offered since they didn't need to be at the arena for the last of the promotional shots for another hour.

Because of the beating most fighters took in the octagon, they took photos of the fighters holding the championship belt before the actual fight. As long as the night went as planned, it would be Cutler's only opportunity to get a picture with the belt.

Around the room, people prepared for the fight. Rocky made sure she had everything packed to wrap Gage's hands and her dad checked for fight and injury equipment. Since she was dating Gage and had unwittingly been the catalyst that led to the rematch, she thought it best not to be one of his cornermen for the fight. Instead, she would watch from the seats with the rest of their friends.

The other guys from the gym would be there to cheer him on ringside, including her brother and Jase.

By the time Gage stepped into the room in a pair of black joggers and a black t-shirt with a replica of his tattoo on the front and "Release The Kraken" stamped across the back, everyone else was ready.

Time to get this show on the road.

Chapter Forty

With the dog and pony show of pre-fight activity over and the traditional good luck exchange with his parents done, Gage sat on a padded table, his hot AF girlfriend standing between his spread thighs, though not in the way he longed for, while he attempted to marshal his thoughts and get his head in the game. He needed to focus on the beatdown he planned to dish out to The Cutter and not how much he wanted to peel the curve-hugging cotton from Rocky's body and bury his face in the mounds of her chest.

He was totally thinking about the best strategy for beating The Cutter a second time and not how ball-tinglingly good it felt when those ruby lips were stretched around the girth of his cock.

And without a doubt, he was mentally replaying his first fight with The Cutter when he took the belt for the first time and not plotting the fastest way to get her pants peeled from her body, have her lifted into his arms, and fuck her against a wall. He was so primed he doubted they would make it to a bed for their first time.

But *seriously*, he needed to start doing all that and ignore the sweet scent of blueberries wafting from her hair as it fell in front of her face while she wrapped his hands. If he didn't, he was going to have a very *obvious* situation going on—way more than what the officials were there to witness.

Once his hands were signed, he slouched back against the wall behind the table, hooking a finger through one of her belt loops and tugging her with him. Curling a finger under her chin, he angled it up so he could claim those tempting berry lips.

"Fuck, woman." He spoke against her lips so only she could hear. "You are *pure* temptation."

He felt her mouth stretch into a smile against his before she pulled away. There was still a lingering sense of unease between them, but he hoped his plans for after the fight would dispel them once and for all.

"Okay, then." Her hands curved over each of his bent knees. "My job here is done. I'm going out to watch a few of the other fights. I'll see you after you raise this above your head again." She patted the gold plated and leather championship belt on the table beside him.

Part of him was worried about her heading out through the tunnels, but Nick and Damon were waiting to walk back with her.

"Come on." Papa Steele clapped him on the shoulder. "Go do some shadowboxing. Get loose and out of your head."

He'd made the right choice in picking Vic Steele as his new coach. The guy didn't miss a beat, able to read what was going on in his head—at least when it came to fighting, and thankfully not about his daughter—knowing exactly what to say to pull him back into the headspace he needed to bring home another victory.

There was no way he was losing his belt tonight.

⚓

This was the first time Rocky had traveled with the team from The Steele Maker and not watched as a cornerman. Sure, her seat in the block where her friends sat was in the front row and practically on top of the cornermen and support team, but it wasn't the same as being a part of the action as it was happening.

It was her suggestion that she wasn't cornering for Gage, not wanting to be a distraction or add to the animosity already surrounding the fight. But she didn't like it.

She wanted to focus on the Welterweight fight currently taking place in the cage, but it wasn't doing anything to distract her from the butterflies swirling in her stomach.

"He's going to be fine," Becky said, pulling free the section of hair she had been worrying around her fingers.

"I know," she said, blowing out a breath.

Her friend looked at her like she didn't believe her. "Yeah, right. Real convincing."

She tried to maintain eye contact but failed miserably.

"What's bugging you?"

"I don't know, Beck. I just feel like this is all new for me. But it shouldn't be. I watch Vince fight all the time. It's not like I'm not used to watching someone I care about take a few punches."

Becky studied her for a long moment before speaking. "That may be true...but this is the first time you were *in* love with the person taking a beating."

Her friend might be on to something.

"How'd you get to be so smart?"

Becky put an arm around her in support, her head bobbing as her friend shrugged. "What can I say? It's a gift."

The fight in front of them concluded and the octagon mat was cleared of as much blood as possible as things got set for the main event. The atmosphere inside the arena grew charged with anticipation.

The Jumbotron above the octagon started to play the hype

reel the UFC had put together to promote the fight on the pay-per-view televised broadcast. Rocky was surprised to see shots of herself in the footage. She cast a knowing look back at Jordan when she saw footage of Gage doing pull-ups and pushups with her weighting him down.

The reel included clips from Gage and Cutler's first fight, cut between voiceovers of commentators boasting how this was the fight the world had been waiting for.

The video ended with the heated showdown from weigh-ins the day before and the crowd lost its collective mind with excitement.

As the challenger, The Cutter was first to make his grand entrance into the arena, cheers and boos greeting him as he did.

From across the cage, she watched as he preened for the crowd like a complete douche and finished his prep for the fight.

Once that was complete, the first notes of Gage's new entrance music blared through the arena. Sammy's remix sounded even more intense played at concert volume than it did playing from his phone.

Where the crowd was a mix of emotions for The Cutter, it was clear The Kraken was who they were pulling for, the cheers in the arena exponentially louder.

Even standing over six feet in her heels, she was unable to see him through the crush of people forming a human barricade around him. Luckily, the giant screens around the arena allowed her to see her man, looking like a total badass with his buzzed hair, bulging muscles straining against his t-shirt, and scowling fight face.

Vince carried the championship belt over his shoulder as the group from The Steele Maker made their way out with Gage toward the octagon.

Like Cutler had done, he stripped down to his black fighting shorts, waited for the cut man to apply Vaseline to his face, and submitted himself for a final inspection before stepping into the cage.

Unlike her brother, Gage was never known to posture for the crowd. When he entered the cage, he did raise both hands above his hand to acknowledge his fans but quickly switched to moving around to stay loose. The cheers for The Champ reached deafening levels as he did so.

"Ladies and gentlemen."

The fight announcer's voice cut through the noise of the crowd.

"This is the main event of the evening."

He ran down the list of judges and other pertinent UFC information, introducing the referee and ending with the fight sponsors.

"Aaaaand now. This is the moment you have truly been waiting for. The rematch two years in the making. Live from the sold-out T-Mobile Arena in Las Vegas, we have a fight to decide who will take home the UFC Heavyweight Championship belt."

The sold-out crowd let out an ear-splitting roar.

"Introducing first, fighting out of the Blue Corner. Standing at six foot five inches, coming in at two hundred and sixty-five pounds, fighting out of Brooklyn, New York, coming to reclaim his title as the Heavyweight Champ of the world. The challenger, Curtis 'The Cutter' Cutler."

This time the boos drowned out any cheers.

"Now fighting out of the Red Corner with an impressive unde-feated record. Standing at six foot seven inches, coming in at two hundred and sixty-three pounds, now fighting out of The Steele Maker in New Jersey. I present to you your current, reigning, undisputed UFC Heavyweight Champion of the World, here to defend once again the title he took over two years ago from The Cutter himself, Gage 'The Kraken' James."

She screamed herself hoarse cheering on her man.

The referee inside the ring reiterated the rules with the fighters. When he asked if they wanted to tap gloves, Gage kept his arms resolutely at his sides. The Cutter said something as he stepped back into place, and though she couldn't hear the words, she didn't miss the way Gage's body visibly tensed.

The ref made the call.

It was time to fight.

Ding-ding.

Chapter Forty-One

The roar of the crowd.

The bumping bass of the music.

The changing and fading lights.

The booming cadence of the announcer's voice, all came together to paint the stage for the gladiator match about to take place inside a seven hundred and fifty square foot octagon.

The crowd cheered and fans reached out trying to touch him, but that all barely registered as Gage walked with Papa Steele and his team. Instead, every cell in his body was locked on a single-minded focus of how he was minutes away from finally, *finally*, being able to give The Cutter the beatdown he deserved.

This wasn't going to be anything like their last fight. He was so keyed up, the only reason he wouldn't lay the guy out the second he stepped inside the cage was because he had a lesson to teach. Then he would put the guy down.

He went down the line, sharing knuckle bumps and bro handshakes with Deck, Ray, Griff, and Jase, saving Vince for last.

"You remind this fucker *why* you were able to take the belt from him in the first place," Vince said to him before bumping him with his knuckles twice, like he had seen him do with Rocky before his own fight.

"Don't hold back," Jase said with a nod to the cage behind him. "You teach this pussy a thing or two about why we don't disrespect women."

"Already planning on it," he said with a smile that promised a world of hurt.

"And if you wanted to get in an extra hit or two for me, I wouldn't complain."

"Didn't spend enough time in the sin bin after your own fight yesterday?" He quirked a brow.

"You're the only one allowed to drop the gloves—metaphorically speaking—with the asshat, so sue me for wanting to live vicariously."

Playtime over, he stood for the UFC's cut man's inspection, and stepped inside the cage, more than ready to drive home proper morals.

It wasn't a requirement for fighters to touch gloves at the start of a fight, so when the referee gave the opening to do so, there wasn't a chance in hell he would be giving The Cutter the respect of doing it. If there was ever any doubt he didn't deserve it, it was reconfirmed when the scumbag leaned in for one last parting shot before the bell. "After I knock you out, I'll celebrate by fucking your girl."

Dead.

The man was dead.

Ding-ding.

Bouncing on the balls of his feet, he circled the cage, waiting for Cutler to make the first move. In their last matchup, they went almost the full five rounds before he won with a submission tap out. Not tonight. He was about to *own* The Cutter.

Cutler's eyes betrayed his surprise when Gage didn't rush him. It was obvious Cutler thought his taunts and slurs were enough to goad him into reacting out of anger. Instead, he chose to let it fuel him for when he did make his move and fought smart. He had a reputation for getting hit in the face less often than other fighters, and he planned to maintain that tonight so he could keep his post-fight plans with Rocky.

He gave a *come on* motion with his hand. As if on cue, Cutler charged him, arm cocked back too early, allowing him to block it with ease and land an uppercut to his jaw.

Cutler stumbled back a few steps and Gage let him go, falling back to bounce on the balls of his feet again. Still, he didn't make a move, letting Cutler come at him again for another easy deflection, this one ending with Cutler taking a roundhouse kick to the ribs.

Minutes passed with them performing their little dance. The Cutter was able to land a few rare body shots, but Gage blocked or stepped out of everything else. Cutler's frustration visibly increased with each second that ticked away in the first round.

Done with this game, he made the decision to end it before the round was over. On The Cutter's next charge, he angled his body, putting his shoulder into the guy's armpit and hooking his arm up around his neck. Dipping his own shoulder, he turned his back and took two steps into Cutler's body, getting into position for a hip throw takedown—the judo move he'd trained to perfection under Vic Steele's tutelage.

Cocking his hip out, arms locked tight around Cutler's body, he used his own momentum against him, swinging him around his hip and dropping him onto his back on the mat. There wasn't even the barest twinge in the joint, thanks to Rocky giving it the proper treatment he'd neglected with his silence.

The mat was where he shined. Not giving Cutler a chance to react, he stepped one foot out around his head, dropped his other knee across his chest, and rolled to his back, pulling Cutler's arm up through his legs into an arm bar.

He locked Cutler's body in place with his legs and pulled his arm back, centimeters away from dislocating the elbow. Not that the asshole would know, but he thought it was fitting for him to win using the move that first brought Rocky to his attention.

He eased the pressure for a second, giving The Cutter a chance to tap out. When he didn't, he increased the pressure again until he felt the satisfying pop of the joint, finally followed by the tap on his arm with Cutler's submission.

ROCKY WAS ON her feet, unable to remain seated for the fight, her body so flooded with adrenaline it was a miracle she wasn't vibrating off the ground.

She'd expected Gage to attack first—considering how apoplectic he was over the entire situation—but that's not what he did.

"He's toying with him."

"Gotta admire his restraint to do so." Nick's voice was the first clue she'd spoken her thoughts out loud.

She didn't dare take her eyes off the fighters in the cage, settling for shifting closer to her friend instead. "I wouldn't have expected this of him. He's been so *pissed.*"

"Ahh, come on, Rock." Nick put an arm around her, tucking her against his side. "You know better than any of us how brilliant this strategy is. Cutler's been trying to get under his skin for weeks, yet by sitting back, waiting for him to make the first move, it's the *ultimate* mind fuck."

As she watched Gage continue to deflect most of the hits Cutler took, she did have to agree it seemed to be working. There was a part of her that assumed Gage would lead more with a boxing mentality, throwing punches to beat on Cutler the way he deserved, but she should have known better. Boxing wasn't his strength and her guy was a skilled enough fighter to keep his emotions in check to fight smart.

Gage rarely had a fight that made it past the first round—it had only happened twice in his career—and as the clock wound down, she wondered if this fight would.

Then as if someone flipped a switch, Gage charged, executed a textbook perfect hip throw, then seamlessly transitioned it into a killer arm bar—her personal favorite.

Her squad lost their collective shit as Gage strutted around the octagon in celebration, her father and brother making their way inside the cage for the presentation of the championship belt.

The referee stood between the fighters, raising Gage's tattooed arm up as the announcer made the presentation of the champion while the UFC's president wrapped the belt around his waist.

She was smiling so hard as she watched the spectacle that she was afraid her face might crack.

The rest of the guys from The Steele Maker made their way inside, joining the celebration until Gage was pulled aside for his post-fight interview.

"Rocky, baby. Get your fine ass in here," Gage said as soon as the microphone was put in front of his face, ignoring the interviewer's question entirely.

She was stunned immobile. Surely she wasn't the first thing he would ask for. It wasn't until she was shoved in the back that she snapped to attention.

"Well…" Becky said when she turned to face her. "You heard your man. Get up there."

Not needing to be told a third time, she pushed her way through the crush of people surrounding the outside of the octagon and climbed the stairs into the cage.

Gage buried his hands in her hair, the edges of his fingerless gloves catching amongst the strands. She breathed in the smell of blood, sweat, and the underlying scent that was pure Gage as he devoured her mouth in an all-consuming kiss.

Everything around them faded away as she got lost in the

stroke of his tongue on hers, the bite of his teeth on her lips, and his hard muscles pressed against her soft curves.

It wasn't until the slimy voice of The Cutter spoke from behind her that they pulled apart.

"You know I'm the one who lost. Shouldn't you be on your knees kissing my boo-boos away?"

Gage let out a feral growl.

Having had enough of this guy's derogatory comments, she stilled Gage by placing her hands on his sweat-slicked pecs, holding him in place with gentle pressure.

"I've had *enough* of your shit." She whipped around to face the scum of the universe. "Maybe if you weren't such a *tool,* you wouldn't have any issues getting a girl without harassing them."

"Oh, come on, baby." Cutler reached out to stroke a finger down her arm.

"*Don't.* Touch. Me." She jerked her arm away from his touch. "And I am *so* not your baby."

"Don't be like that." His tone was oily.

When he ignored her warning and reached to touch her again, she snapped. Quick as a whip, her arm struck out, landing a solid jab to his crooked nose. The satisfying crunch of cartilage under her knuckles told her he was the recipient of a broken nose—courtesy of the girlfriend of the first guy to break it.

"Damn, Blue," Gage said on a laugh as he picked her up to spin her in his arms. "*Fuck,* I love you." His eyes sparkled like sapphires as he looked down at her.

She buried her face in the crook of his neck as the interviewers tried to get a comment on what just happened.

Gage kept her close with an arm around her neck, while stretching a hand out and calling to Vince. She heard something hit his hand as if her brother tossed him something.

He pinched her chin between her fingers, pulling her away far enough to see her face.

"I may have won the belt tonight, babe. But I can't consider myself a real champion until"—he dropped to a knee in front of her, the crowd gasping in shock along with her—"you're wearing my ring"—he flipped open the lid of the velvet box—"on your finger."

She stood frozen, unable to process his words.

He took her hand in his, running a finger over the swelling knuckles. "Well"—he looked down at the bruised skin—"that is, if it fits after your killer jab."

She loved how since the night they'd met he was never intimated by her ability to handle herself in dicey situations. If she were being honest, she was *pretty* sure it turned him on.

"What do you say, Blue? Wanna marry me and have a bunch of kickass babies with me?"

"Dude, wait for her to say yes before you try and knock her up." A quick glance at her brother showed him cracking up with Jase.

"Should I be worried you took one too many hits to the head? This is crazy—we haven't even been together for six months," she said, looking down to where he was still kneeling in front of her.

"Never gave him the chance to touch me." He ran a hand along his jaw. "When you know, you know. So what do you say, Rock? Marry me?"

She looked deep into his eyes, clouds meeting sky. It might be fast, and slightly unconventional, but starting that first night when he let her handle a drunk instead of stepping in himself, she knew he was her perfect match.

"Of course I'll marry you, Champ." She mimed ringing a bell. "Ding-ding."

Epilogue

C haos.

Complete and utter chaos.

That's what happens when the winner of a UFC Championship fight proposes to his girlfriend in front of a crowd of twenty thousand people while being broadcasted to millions watching on television.

Rocky and Gage snuck out of the arena and back to the MGM Grand like they were auditioning for the next *Mission Impossible* movie. Tom Cruise would seriously be proud of how well they were able to evade the press looking for interviews and statements. And she thought she did it one better than Mr. Cruise because she did it in three-inch heels.

By the time all their friends and family converged on their hotel suite, Jordan and Skye needed to turn their phones off thanks to the barrage of phone calls and messages they were receiving as Gage's PR firm.

Champagne was popped. ESPN showed fight highlights on the flat-screen. People celebrated the victory.

While all that happened, Rocky sat tucked tightly against Gage's side, hand held out in front of her, admiring the way the large cushion-cut diamond caught the light. She wiggled her fingers, watching the rainbow prism of light dance.

She was engaged.

She was engaged to Gage-Flipping-James.

Is this real life?

"I did good?" he asked in her ear as they cuddled in their own private bubble.

She dropped her head back against his biceps so she could see the stupidly handsome face of her fiancé. Her. Fiancé. *Eeeek.*

"So good," she answered with a smile so big the International Space Station could probably see it.

"You know…" He took her left hand in his right, stroking a finger along the diamonds inlaid in the platinum band. "When I originally planned all this, I didn't quite factor in what it would do to our own after-fight celebration."

The way his eyes burned like the hottest part of a flame spoke of all the dirty things they had promised to do to each other.

"You mean the type of celebration where we're the only two people on the guest list?" She ran her nose along the underside of his jaw, reveling in his swift intake of breath.

"Yup." His hand skimmed along her thigh, dipping down around the curve of her ass. "I didn't even think we'd make it to a bed before I needed to be buried inside you."

Now it was her turn for her breath to hitch.

"Go to the bedroom. I'll meet you there in a minute." He nudged her to get off the couch.

Rocky was a smart girl and did as she was told, pausing halfway up the staircase to see Gage pull Jordan aside to tell her something in private. She was too turned on to worry what all that was about.

She was about to cross the threshold of their bedroom when he came up behind her and scooped her into his arms bridal style.

"Gage," she screeched in surprise.

"What?" He feigned innocence.

"You're supposed to do this *after* we're married."

"I'm practicing." He kicked the door closed with his heel, locking it before letting her body slide along his as he lowered her to the floor.

Her feet had barely touched the ground before he had her shirt pulled over her head and her bra joining it on the carpet.

"*Fuck,* you're beautiful." He crushed their lips together, cradling the back of her head in one hand to protect it from banging off the wall as their bodies crashed into each other, his dominant arm hooking around one of her legs, lifting her again with ease.

Her legs automatically wrapped around his waist, grinding against him as she felt his erection pressing against her center, the seam of her jeans providing a delicious friction.

Using his hips and legs to anchor her to the wall, he deftly released both the button and zipper of her jeans. If she wasn't wet already, the way he was able to strip the denim from her body without ever putting her down would have done it.

Once her legs were back in position on his hips, he pushed down the waistband of his joggers enough to free his dick and slid himself home in one gloriously hard drive inside her.

Her head thunked against the wood of the door behind her as she stretched around him. The feeling of fullness was overwhelming.

"Oh, yeah." His hips pumped in and out. "*This* is what I needed."

One hand gripped the back of her neck possessively as the other did the same to one of her ass cheeks while he continued to pump inside her in steady strokes.

In.

Out.

In.

Out.

"Fuck, Blue. I love feeling you wrapped around me in *every* way."

Her hands scrambled for purchase on the cotton of his shirt, ripping it over his head as fast as humanly possible, *needing* him bare like her, hands and nails scouring down his chest once he was.

"Fuck, babe. I don't think I can go slow right now."

"Fuck slow. Give it to me hard and fast." Her teeth bit into his shoulder as he followed directions, increasing the speed and force of his thrust.

"God, you're perfect for me."

Their mouths fused together again, mimicking with their tongues what their lower bodies did to each other.

The pace was fast.

The thrusts were hard.

It was the best kind of down and dirty quickie, their orgasms crashing over them one after the other domino-style.

He kept her pinned to the wall as they came down from their highs, heaving breaths returning to normal.

"I love you, Gage," she whispered against the side of his sweat-slicked neck.

"Fuck, I love you too, Rock."

WHEN HE WAS sure his legs were no longer shaky from coming harder in his life than he could ever remember, and he wasn't at risk of dropping his fiancée—damn straight, she said yes—he walked them into the lavish bathroom for the shower they both desperately needed.

For weeks, he'd agonized over if his plan to propose after the fight was the right decision, the ring box taunting him from his drawer every night she slept in his bed.

He couldn't recall a time he was more nervous than he was the day he asked Vic Steele for permission to marry his daughter. He was prepared for him to argue, tell him it was too soon, Rocky was too young, but he did none of that. Instead, he stood in front of him, leaning on his desk with his arms crossed, and stared at him for a solid two minutes, eyes assessing. Right when Gage was *sure* he was going to say no, he uttered one word—okay.

And so the plans were put in place to make sure anyone important in Rocky's life was in Vegas to witness him put his heart on the line.

He reached inside the shower to start the water then sat her on the counter next to the sink while they waited for the water to heat.

"I do have a very important question to ask you," he said as she ran her hand over the buzzed hair on his head the way he loved.

"I'm pretty sure I've already answered it for you." She held up her left hand, wiggling the finger sporting his ring, his heart swelling with pride at the sight.

"Smartass." He dropped a kiss on her forehead, gathering his courage for the second time that evening. "How do you feel about eloping?" he asked cautiously.

"Like with an Elvis impersonator and all that jazz?" Her tone was amused, so he decided it was safe to proceed.

"If that's what floats your boat." Another kiss, this one to the tip of her nose. "I meant more as a generality."

Her silvery eyes shined like the band of her engagement ring as she watched him, the room quickly filling with steam.

"Well, I'm not opposed to it."

"So if I was to say to you... *Well, we are in Vegas.* What would be your response?"

Her eyes widened in shock.

"You mean you want to marry me *before* we fly home in two days?"

"No." The way her expression fell gave him the resolve to make his craziest suggestion to date. "I mean in like an hour from now."

Her jaw nearly hit the floor.

"Wh-what?" she sputtered. "How would we even manage that? Every member of the press on the strip is trying to get an interview with you since you won the belt and popped the question."

"Jordan's working out all the details. All you have to do is say yes and I'll get to wake up with you as my wife."

Wife. He liked the way that sounded.

"You're serious?"

"As a fucking heart attack, baby."

She blinked slowly as she digested his words.

"Okay."

"Okay?" He needed to make sure he heard her correctly.

"Everyone we love is here, so yeah, why not."

His *whoop* of delight echoed around the room as he lifted her and spun her around.

"I fucking love you, Mrs. James."

"Not yet," she teased.

"Tonight," he confirmed.

"Tonight."

And as she pressed her lips to his, he marveled at how the submission specialist inside the cage happily tapped out and submitted his heart to love.

🐙

Want to see how Rocky and Gage manage to elope? *Click here for your invite.*

Can't get enough of the BTU Alumni Squad? *They are back* SWEET VICTORY.

· · ·

Reviews are the life blood of an indie author. So if you're one of the cool kids who writes them here are the links to Amazon, Goodreads, and BookBub. Smothering toddler hugs and sloppy puppy kisses!!!

Alley

Thank you!

Thank you so much for taking the time to read *Tap Out*. It means everything to me that you took the time to read it. It's because of people like you that make it possible for me to do this author-ing thing.

If you liked my words and want to hear more about the crazy crew from BTU, I have many more stories coming your way.

Tap Out will release on September 9th, but if you would like to leave an early review on Goodreads, you can do so by tapping here.

Smothering toddler hugs and sloppy puppy kisses!!!
Alley

Playlist

---

*

Fugees: "Killing Me Softly With His Song"
Alexandra Stan: "Mr. Saxobeat"
Lonestar: "Amazed"
*NSYNC: "I Want You Back"
*NSYNC: "Bye Bye Bye"
Jess Glynne: "One Touch"
Inner Circle: "Sweat (A La La La La Long)"
One Direction: "They Don't Know About Us"
Lukas Graham: "Love Someone"
John Legend: "All of Me"
Klaus Tadelt: "The Black Pearl"

Randomness For My Readers

Hello new friends!

I hope you enjoyed hanging out with Gage and Rocky and meeting the new members of the BTU Alumni Squad.

If everyone was new to you, you can see where the group began is *Power Play* (Jake and Jordan's story)

Did you know... when I first starting writing *Tap Out* it was supposed to be a book in any entirely different series.

So, how did Rocky and her peeps join up with Jordan and hers to form The Coven? Well... when I was in the process of editing *Power Play* back in the day, inspiration hit and I was like, "OMG, Rocky just has to be friends with Jordan." And so I went back and reworked the first 30k words of *Tap Out* so it was in the BTU Alumni family.

So now for a little bullet style fun facts:

* I love yoga and even my mini royals like to "practice" it as well.

* The GIFs The Coven use in their group chats are ones used all the time in my own group chats.

* My main squad is huge like the BTU crew and most of us have been friends since high school or sooner.

* *Friends* is obviously one of my favorite TV shows.

* I spent many nights getting no sleep watching some of the bigger UFC fights in my day. I was a huge Rousey and McGregor fan.

* I'm a major and proud Potterhead and wish Espresso Patronum was real

* Gage's inspiration all started with a tattoo. You can see a pic of it on *Tap Out*'s Pinterest board.

* My own playlist is just as random as The Steele Maker's

* The restaurant Gage and Rocky go on their date to is real. Jose Tejas it is amazing

* Though my hero is an MMA fighter, I of course had to give a shoutout to one of my hockey series with book club reading *Body Check* by my girl Maria Luis.

* No I do not have The Coven tattoo yet BUT I will be getting it.

If my rambling hasn't turned you off and you are like "This chick is my kind of crazy," feel free to reach out!

Lots of Love,

Alley

For A Good Time Call

Did you have fun meeting The Coven? Do you want to stay up-to-date on releases, be the first to see cover reveals, excerpts from upcoming books, deleted scenes, sales, freebies, and all sorts of insider information you can't get anywhere else?

If you're like "Duh! Come on Alley." Make sure you sign up for my newsletter here.

Ask yourself this:
* Are you a Romance Junkie?
* Do you like book boyfriends and book besties? (yes this is a thing)
* Is your GIF game strong?
* Want to get inside the crazy world of Alley Ciz?

If any of your answers are yes, maybe you should join my Facebook reader group, Romance Junkie's Coven

Join The Coven

Stalk Alley
Join The Coven
Get the Newsletter

Like Alley on Facebook
Follow Alley on Instagram
Hang with Alley on Goodreads
Follow Alley on Amazon
Follow Alley on BookBub
Subscribe on YouTube for Book Trailers
Follow Alley's inspiration boards on Pinterest
All the Swag
All Things Alley

Sneak Peek at Sweet Victory

Prologue

Shit!

   Shit!

   Shit!

Holly Vanderbuilt cursed herself as she scrambled to toss yet another drawer full of clothes into the suitcase open on the four-poster bed.

A plan. She really needed to have a plan.

Bras.

Why didn't I make a plan?

Underwear followed by socks went next.

How the hell did I let this go so far?

She stepped inside the walk-in closet, ignoring the fancy gowns and proper clothes hanging on the racks, instead grabbing the comfortable tunics and other "common" pieces from where they had been relegated to the back.

Seriously, Hol, you're too smart for this.

She never should have let things get this bad, she thought as she sat on top of her Tumi luggage to get the zipper to close.

A quick glance at her rose-gold Rolex made her curse. She needed to be out of there in less than ten minutes if she was going to manage to do so without being caught.

One more cursory look around the room, double-checking she had everything of importance, and she was wheeling her two large suitcases from the room.

By the time she had her Mercedes-Benz AMG S 63 loaded she peeled out the driveway and through the wrought-iron gates of the estate with only a minute to spare.

She prayed her call wouldn't go unanswered.

Acknowledgments

This is the where I get to say thank you, hopefully I don't miss anyone. If I do I'm sorry and I still love you, just you know, mommy brain.

I'll start with the Hubs—who even though *this* book also isn't dedicated to him he's still the real MVP—he has to deal with my lack of sleep, putting off laundry *because... laundry* and helping to hold the fort down with our three crazy mini royals. You truly are my best friend. Also, I'm sure he would want me to make sure I say thanks for all the hero inspiration, but it is true (even if he has no ink *winking emoji*)

To my Beta Bitches, my OG Coven: Gemma, Jenny, Megan, Caitie, Sarah, Nova, Andi, and Dana. Our real life Coven Conversations give me life.

To Jenny (again) my PA, without her I wouldn't be organized enough for any of my releases to happen. Thank you for being the other half of my brain and video chatting all hours, damn our timezones.

For Jess my editor for pushing me to take Gage and Rocky's story to the next level.

To Gemma (again) for going from my proofreader to

fangirl and being so invested in my characters stories to threaten my life *lovingly of course*

To Dawn for giving *Tap Out* it's final spit shine.

To my real life squad for giving me the memories and constant source of inspiration needed to throw a fictional twist on.

To my street team for being the best pimps ever.

To every blogger and bookstagrammer that took a chance and read my words and wrote about them.

Thank you to all the authors in the indie community for your support and answering ALL of the questions I had and will continue to have. Without you all this wouldn't have happened.

To my fellow Covenettes for making my reader group one of my happy places.

And, of course, to you my fabulous reader, for picking up my book and giving me a chance. Without you I wouldn't be able to live my dream of bringing to life the stories the voices in my head tell me.

Lots of Love,

Alley

Also by Alley Ciz

BTU Alumni Series

Power Play (Jake and Jordan)

Musical Mayhem (Sammy and Jamie) BTU Novella

Tap Out (Gage and Rocky)

Sweet Victory (Vince and Holly)

Puck Performance (Jase and Melody)

Writing Dirty (Maddey and Dex)

Scoring Beauty- BTU6 Preorder, Releasing September 2021

#UofJ Series

Cut Above The Rest (Prequel)- Freebie

Looking To Score

Game Changer

Playing For Keeps

Off The Bench- #UofJ4 Preorder, Releasing December 2021

The Royalty Crew (A #UofJ Spin-Off)

Savage Queen- Preorder, Releasing April 2021

Ruthless Noble- Preorder, Releasing June 2021

About the Author

Alley Ciz is an internationally bestselling indie author of sassy heroines and the alpha men that fall on their knees for them. She is a romance junkie whose love for books turned into her telling the stories of the crazies who live in her head…even if they don't know how to stay in their lane.

This Potterhead can typically be found in the wild wearing a funny T-shirt, connected to an IV drip of coffee, stuffing her face with pizza and tacos, chasing behind her 3 minis, all while her 95lb yellow lab—the best behaved child—watches on in amusement.

facebook.com/AlleyCizAuthor

instagram.com/alley.ciz

pinterest.com/alleyciz

goodreads.com/alleyciz

bookbub.com/profile/alley-ciz

amazon.com/author/alleyciz